ANOTHER TIMELINE

He took my silence as an opening, and leaned closer again, touching my shoulder. "I can tell you don't quite understand, but you're intrigued. My friends and I are here to help if you need us." He gestured to a few other men, all wearing black armbands around their biceps, handing out zines to other women in the crowd. Despite the distraction of Grape Ape onstage, they'd managed to get quite a few people to take one. Fear filled my guts with ice. This guy and his buddies were planting ideas, playing a long game. Trying to eliminate choices for these women in the future. It was a textbook example of a forbidden traveler's art: editing the timeline.

By Annalee Newitz

Autonomous
The Future of Another Timeline

THE
FUTURE OF
ANOTHER TIMELINE

ANNALEE NEWITZ

www.orbitbooks.net

ORBIT

First published in Great Britain in 2019 by Orbit

1 3 5 7 9 10 8 6 4 2

A CIP catalogue record for this book
is available from the British Library.

ISBN 978-0-356-51123-8

Printed and bound in Great Britain by Clays Ltd, Elcograf S.p.A.

Papers used by Orbit are from well-managed forests
and other responsible sources.

MIX
Paper from
responsible sources
FSC® C104740

Orbit
An imprint of
Little, Brown Book Group
Carmelite House
50 Victoria Embankment
London EC4Y 0DZ

An Hachette UK Company
www.hachette.co.uk

www.orbitbooks.net

For Charlie Jane—rebel girl,
I know I want to take you home

Up to this point, travelers have merely observed history.
The point is to change it.

—SEN. HARRIET TUBMAN (R-MS) (1883)

He never saw the streets of Cairo
On the Midway he was never glad
He never saw the hoochie coochie
Poor little country lad

—LADY ASENATH (1893)

I like to see the tall girls
I like to see the short girls
I like to see the fat girls
I like to see the thin girls
I like to see the trans girls
I like to see the cis girls
I like to see the brown girls
I like to see the blondies
I like to see the sweet girls
I like to see the bitches
the bitches the bitches I like to see the bitches

—GRAPE APE (1992)

ONE

TESS

Drums beat in the distance like an amplified pulse. People streamed over the dirt road, leather boots laced to their knees, eyes ringed in kohl, ears and lips studded with precious metals. Some gathered in an open square below the steep path to the amphitheater, making a bonfire out of objects stolen from their enemies. The smoke reeked of something ancient and horrific; materials far older than humanity were burning. A rusty sunset painted everyone in blood, and shrieks around the flames mixed with faraway chanting.

It could have been Rome under Nero. It could have been Samarkand when the Sogdians fled. It could have been Ataturk's new Istanbul, or a feast day in Chaco Canyon. The technologies were industrial, Neolithic, and medieval. The screams were geochronologically neutral.

I paused, smelling the toxins, watching a woman with jet-black lips and blue hair pretend to eat a spider. One of her companions laughed. "Michelle, you are so gross! This isn't an Ozzy concert!" They paused at the ticket booths to flip off the Vice Fighters, a gang of conservative protesters waving signs covered in Bible quotes. Some

of them were burning CDs in a garbage can, and the stench of melting plastic formed a noxious bubble around their demonstration.

The Machine had not delivered me to an ancient war, nor to an
anti-imperialist celebration. I was at Irvine Meadows Amphitheater
in 1992, deep in the heart of Orange County, Alta California. Soon
I'd be seeing one of the greatest punk bands of the decade. But I
wasn't here for history tourism. Somewhere in this rowdy concert
crowd, a dangerous conspiracy was unfolding. I needed to find out
who was behind it. If these bastards succeeded, they would destroy
time travel, locking us into one version of history forever.

I bought a lawn seat and raced up the winding pedestrian walkway to
the seating area, lurid with stadium lights. The theater was relatively
small and open to the sky, with a steep grade of loge seats above
the prized orchestra section next to the stage. The lawn formed a
green semicircle above it all, pocked with mud puddles and beer
cans. Still, even up here, the air vibrated with anticipation for the
headliner. Spotlights sent a cluster of beams racing around the stage.

Grape Ape's lead singer Glorious Garcia strutted out alone, se-
quins on her tattered skirt shimmering in the glare. She let out a
furious howl. "HOLA, BITCHES! IF ANYONE CALLED YOU
A SLUT TODAY, SAY IT WITH ME! SLUT SLUT SLUT!" All
around me, women joined the chant. They wore battered combat
boots, shredded jeans, and wrecked dresses. They had tattoos and
black nail polish and looked like warrior queens from another
planet. Tangled hair flashed in every possible artificial color. "YOU
SLUTS ARE BEAUTIFUL!" Glorious fisted the air and aimed her
mic at the crowd, still chanting, "SLUT SLUT SLUT!" Back when I
went to this concert for the first time, I was an angry sixteen-year-old
with too many piercings for suburbia, wearing a military jacket over
a 1950s dress.

Now I was forty-seven on the books, fifty-five with travel time.

My eyes flicked to the things I never would have seen back then. Everyone looked so scrubbed and affluent. Our rebel fashions were cobbled together from the expensive stuff we'd seen in some *New York Times* story about grunge. But what really jolted me was the way people occupied themselves as they waited for the music to start. Nobody was texting or taking selfies. And without phones, people didn't know what to do with their eyes. I didn't either. I watched a guy in a Dead Kennedys shirt urging a hip flask on a woman who was already so drunk she could barely stand in her platform creepers. She stumbled against him, swigging, and he gave a thumbs-up sign to his pal. The punk scene, once my inspiration, now looked like a bunch of future bankers and tech executives learning how to harass women.

The rest of the band charged on stage, Maricela Hernandez's guitar squealing over the clatter of drums and bass fuzz. Cigarette smoke and sound merged into a throbbing haze around us. From my distant perch, Glorious was a tiny figure with the biggest voice in the world.

"THIS IS A SONG ABOUT THE GIRLS FROM MEXICO WHO ARE PICKING FRUIT IN YOUR IRVINE COMPANY FARMS! LET'S RIP DOWN THE FUCKING BORDER NET AND STOP THE KILLING!"

That took me back. In 1991, a huge group of refugees fleeing Mexico had drowned in the Gulf of California, just as they'd almost reached the safety of U.S. soil in Baja. They'd gotten tangled in offshore nets the border patrol set up to stop illegal immigrants.

The music tore through me until it merged with muscle and bone. I had a job to do, but I couldn't move. Grape Ape was the only thing here that hadn't been warped by my disillusionment. They still had the power to replace my cynicism with a feeling that careened between hope and outrage. Strobe lights churned the darkness, and the audience frenzy reached beyond fandom, struggling toward something else. Something revolutionary.

Then I felt a broad hand on my upper arm, squeezing a little too hard, and a large male body pressed against my back. I tried to elbow him and wriggle away, but the still-invisible stranger held me in place. He leaned down to whisper-yell in my ear, blotting out the music. "I know you must have many daughters at your age, and you are worried about their future." His voice was smooth, and his warm breath smelled like lavender and mint. With his free hand, he started massaging my neck as he continued to grip my arm. "That's why you come to places like this. To find a better way for women. We want that too. Maybe you'll look past your prejudice against men and read our zine."

At last he released me and I whirled to face him. He pulled his zine from a rumpled Kinko's bag. Grainy Xeroxed images of women in chains adorned the cover, and letters torn from magazines spelled out the title: COLLEGE IS A LIE. Flipping through the pages of ten-point Courier font and smeary cartoons, I scanned a few typical punk rants against suburban brainwashing: college teaches conformity, turns you into a corporate drone, destroys true art, blah blah blah. But there was a weird strand of gender politics in it. Over and over, the anonymous authors preached that college "destroys feminine freedoms inherited from our ancestors on the plains of Africa" and "is anti-uterus." I scanned a paragraph:

> Women are naturally empathic, and college tortures
> them with artificial rationality. Millions of years of evo-
> lution have led men to thrive in the toolmaking worlds
> of science and politics, and women to become queens
> of emotional expression and the nurturing arts. Col-
> lege denies this biological reality, which is why so many
> women feel bad about themselves. But it doesn't have to
> be that way! Fuck college! It's time for liberation!

The entire zine was about why women should drop out of college. I looked sharply at the man, a nasty retort on my tongue, but his face stole my words. It couldn't be. I would never forget those features, so perfectly formed it was as if he'd been grown in a vat full of men's magazines. I'd last seen him in 1880, at a lecture on suppressing vice in New York City. He was one of the young men clustered around Anthony Comstock, lapping up the famous moral crusader's invective about the evils of birth control and abortion. Later, at the protest, he'd given me a beautiful smile before punching me in the chest. Gasping for air, I'd dismissed him as one of the many YMCA boys under Comstock's spell. Now it appeared he was something more—a traveler. I feigned interest in the zine and shot another glance at him. The man might be a few years younger than he'd been in 1880, so maybe this was his first time meeting me. His blond hair was currently spiked in an embarrassing imitation of Billy Idol.

He took my silence as an opening, and leaned closer again, touching my shoulder. "I can tell you don't quite understand, but you're intrigued. My friends and I are here to help if you need us." He gestured to a few other men, all wearing black armbands around their biceps, handing out zines to other women in the crowd. Despite the distraction of Grape Ape onstage, they'd managed to get quite a few people to take one. Fear filled my guts with ice. This guy and his buddies were planting ideas, playing a long game. Trying to eliminate choices for these women in the future. It was a textbook example of a forbidden traveler's art: editing the timeline.

I was looking for anti-travel activists, people who wanted to shut down the Machines. It was hardly the kind of political stance a traveler would take. But everything about this guy was off. So I followed at a safe distance, watching him whisper in women's ears, pointing them away from one of their few pathways to power. Eventually, at the very edge of the loge section, the black armband men came together. I stood nearby and bummed a cigarette from an old crusty punk, catching snatches of the traveler's conversation.

"I think we converted a few today. Good work." That was the Billy Idol guy, the one I'd seen over a century ago in Comstock's orbit.

"Do you think we'll be able to make the edit before time stops?" another man asked.

"We may need to go back a century."

"How long until we have our rights back? This is taking too long. I think we should hit the Machines now."

The crowd began to roar, burying their voices.

A terrifying hypothesis coalesced in my mind. There's only one reason why a traveler might want to lock the timeline, and that's if he planned to make a final, lasting edit that could not be undone. I looked at the zine again. It was exactly the kind of propaganda that Comstockers would use to revert the secret edits made by people like me and my colleagues in the Daughters of Harriet.

The Daughters often debated whether we were working directly against another group. Even when it seemed like we made significant progress in the past, the present remained stubbornly unchanged. But we had no evidence of oppositional reverts, other than our constant frustration. It was like we were fighting with ghosts.

Now the ghosts had become men.

The Comstocker was delivering a final rallying speech. He gestured at the loge section. "This is what happens when men become victims. But once we take control of the Machine, nobody will remember this world."

At that moment he looked over and saw me listening. His face went ugly and asymmetrical: he'd recognized me, and realized I wasn't a temporal local.

"Get her! She's one of them!" He pointed. Suddenly, four men with black armbands and pale skin had eyes on me.

I took off running, edging my way past the security guards, aiming for the mosh pit. Grape Ape roared through a song I couldn't hear over the thump of blood in my ears. My momentum was swallowed by a swell of bodies, diverting our chase into a chaotic circle of flailing limbs. Women who smelled like cloves and disintegrating nylon rammed into us. The Billy Idol guy was so close that I could see the acid-wash streaks in his jeans when he grabbed me by the collar. "Get your hands off me!" I shouted. "I have friends at the Chronology Academy, and I guarantee they won't like the way you're trying to change the timeline with your shitty Comstocker zine. They'll send you back to your home time and you'll never travel again." Onstage, Maricela shredded a solo. I glared and hoped he believed me, because there was no guarantee the Chronology Academy would agree that he'd violated regulations. Or that they wouldn't catch me doing the same thing. But the threat worked. He released me with a sneer.

"You misandrist bitch!" He was close enough that I could smell his strangely sweet breath again. "You and your sisters are a genetic dead end. Next time I see you downstream, I'll make sure you're punished for spreading lewdness and vice." Then he shoved me into a young woman who bounced away and smashed back into him with a maniacal cackle. Screeching and spinning with her arms out, she battered the Comstocker over and over until he fought his way out of the mosh pit and disappeared into the crowd. Good riddance—at least for now. I moved with the circle, bumped and bruised and safe inside its performative violence. Bursts of light from the stage illuminated the Comstocker rounding up his black armband pals and heading for the exit. Hopefully I'd scared them a little, though it had been stupid to reveal myself like that.

At least I'd confirmed Berenice's report at the last Daughters of Harriet meeting. She'd traveled to early 1992 in Los Angeles, gathering data at ground zero for the anti-travel movement. One of her sources said he'd met some extremists hanging around in the alternative music scene. I suggested this concert would be a good place to look for them. This particular Grape Ape show had been famously controversial, called out by the Vice Fighters as a gateway to hell and by *Rolling Stone* as the most anticipated show of spring. Everyone would be here, especially if they considered themselves radicals.

Of course, I neglected to tell the Daughters that my younger self had been at the concert too. They never would have agreed to send me if I'd mentioned that little detail. Nobody knew what happened to travelers who met their younger selves; it was both illegal and so morally offensive that most scholars avoided the topic. The only detailed description came from a medieval manuscript about the life of an old, impoverished traveler who took the Machine back thirty years to advise himself to save money. When he returned to his present, the traveler found that his house had become a beautiful mansion. But then his bones began to break themselves, and he was plagued by attacks from a cloud of tiny demons that flew around his head unceasingly.

I wasn't worried about demonic fantasies. They were a staple of medieval manuscripts, along with women giving birth to monsters. I was thinking about evidence-based threats to the timeline, our only timeline, whose natural stability emerged from perpetual revision.

The woman who'd harried the Comstocker earlier was spinning back toward me, and my stomach dropped. I'd been too rattled to recognize her before. Now I could clearly recognize Heather, one of my friends from high school. She barked her crazy laugh again, and I could see the Wonder Woman Returns T-shirt clearly under the lacy bodice of her dress. We'd all been obsessed with the Tim Burton Wonder Woman movies in high school, with their badass heroine in fishnets and leather.

I looked around in a panic. Was I here too? I thought I'd been in the loge section during the concert, which was why I'd avoided that area. But my recollections of tonight were murky. Maybe that was the problem. My younger self seemed so distant that I'd figured— stupidly—it would be easy to avoid her. I kept searching for my lost self until the spotlights poured illumination across the steeply angled seats and I caught a brief glimpse of her—me—with my two best friends at the time. Soojin was on my right, frowning with concentration as she studied Maricela's fingering technique. And there, on my left, was the person who had been my best friend since we were little kids. The two of us were scream-singing along with Glorious Garcia, fists in the air. Seeing us from a distance, I realized how our closeness had even manifested in dressing like each other. We wore the same trashed vintage dresses and combat boots. People were always mistaking us for sisters back then, which wasn't far from the truth. We were angry riot grrl clones, except for the hair.

A pasty white boy grabbed Heather roughly and she stumbled toward him, a red lipstick smile bright in her brown face. The boy's right ear was crusted with safety pins and dried blood. Piercing injury. Very punk rock.

What was his name? A jagged shard of imagery was lodged in my mind, painful and opaque. Oh fuck. The slurry of psychological muck that usually buried my high school memories was gone, leaving behind a crisp picture of what that kid's face would look like in three hours, when it was covered in blood. I stared at him as he twitched to the music, angry and alive. I had to intervene. If I didn't, something horrific was going to happen. Many horrific things. And they would all lead, in the end, to a broken and beloved body, robbed of the consciousness that hurled it off a bridge.

Now that I was here, maybe I could undo that whole narrative and make everything right. I muscled my way out of the orchestra section, away from Heather's laugh and my own age-reversed face, back down the path to the parking lot. Passing the merch table, I felt a painful twist of nostalgia as I read Grape Ape's once-familiar slogans: MAKE BAJA MEXICAN AGAIN! SUCK MY PLASTIC DICK! SLUTS OF THE WORLD UNITE! At last I reached my rental car. I'd made it out before the encore, which should give me enough time to make an edit. As I turned the key in the ignition, recklessness oozed into me. Had I really come back because of Berenice's report, or had I been hoping subconsciously for something like this to happen? Some excuse to intervene in my own past?

I wished I could remember my favorite shortcut from thirty-eight years ago, through Irvine's palimpsest of malls, churches, and walled subdivisions. I'd have to brave traffic. Merging on the 405 freeway, I slowed down and considered what the hell I was doing. The Daughters of Harriet were waiting for me back in 2022, and I needed to tell them about the Comstockers. I should be headed back to the Machine. But this was an emergency. I had to save that boy's life.

T W O

BETH

I love the pause right before an encore. We could pretend that Grape Ape wasn't coming back unless we broke the world with our noise. The whole crowd stood up and screamed and I kicked the folded-up seat of my chair until it felt like Irvine Meadows was the epicenter of a shallow quake, its high-frequency vibrations booming through the Earth's crust. For a few rare seconds, we were a number on the Richter scale. I looked up at the sky, scattered with ancient blobs of exploding gas, and wanted the anticipation to last forever.

"Where's Heather?" Lizzy leaned in close, and I could feel the prickly tips of her soap-stiffened mohawk on my cheek. People used to say we looked like sisters until she went bleach blond and pierced her lower lip.

I pointed at the mosh pit. "She went down there with Scott!"

Glorious returned to the stage, trailed by Maricela on guitar, and they tore into the title track from their first EP, *Our Time Was Stolen*. I still had the poster for it on my bedroom wall at home, with its lush drawing of what the Machines looked like hundreds of millions of years ago, before their interfaces eroded away to nothing. It was an aerial view, showing two red, crescent-shaped rocks curving around a circular pearlescent canopy that covered the entrance to the wormhole. From that angle it looked like a beautiful, stylized vulva and clitoris. But it was also an ancient rock formation. I loved it instantly, and loved everything Grape Ape had done since.

When the last chord died, everything sounded faraway and dull.

"I hope we can find Heather," Lizzy grumbled. "She has my fucking cigarettes."

Shrugging, I tried to hold on to the pre-encore rush but felt myself returning to a baseline of sadness. Maybe the concert had been pretty good, but I still hated everything. Grape Ape didn't play that one new song I really loved. My tights were scratchy. Pretty soon I'd have to go home and deal with my parents. Music was nothing like life. When Glorious stopped singing, I missed her magnificent sound, with its power to merge my soul with the crowd and obliterate loneliness. I was stuck in a body. I had to communicate using the pathetic phonemes of language. Suddenly my throat hurt and my eyes were burning and I had to swallow hard to keep myself from breaking down right there in front of every punk rocker in Irvine. This was always happening to me—something random would make me want to cry. But it had gotten a lot worse lately. It was harder to stop the tears before they fell.

"There they are!" Lizzy pointed at Heather and Scott, waving to us from the bottom of the suddenly floodlit arena. Roadies were grabbing things off the stage and we joined the slow river of people draining into the parking lot.

Soojin had watched the show in rapt silence next to us, but now she wanted to discuss Maricela's new guitar pedal in great detail. "I think she had that thing engineered just for her." She readjusted a plastic barrette in her bobbed hair with thoughtful intensity. "I haven't seen anything like it in the catalogues."

Heather bounced up with the cigarettes and Scott played with the blood-caked safety pins in his ear as we made it out the front gate.

Everybody started talking about the show, and Scott disagreed with Soojin's opinions about guitar pedals while Heather made faces behind his back. It was the same pointless debate they always had. With each passing word and sentence, I felt like I was lagging further behind the conversation. Their voices were nothing but a distant whine now. Maybe I was sliding downstream in time, doomed to vacillate endlessly between weeping and numbness. While my friends barreled into the future, I was back here in the past, unable to move on.

But when Lizzy spoke, I snapped back into the present. "You guys, let's not go home yet," she said. "We can drive up to Turtle Rock and look at the lights."

Heather rubbed her hands together with a high-pitched giggle. "Let's do it!"

Soojin gave a thumbs-up sign.

I still had an hour before curfew and my urge to cry had evaporated. "Okay. As long as I'm home by midnight."

Lizzy's car was one of those infinitely long station wagons with two rows of generous seats and a long, carpeted cargo area that ended in a rear door designed to drop down and become a tailgate picnic table. It was designed for parties of another era. In the front seat, we were blasting The Bags, rehashing the best moments of the show, and smoking weed out of a perforated Coke can.

From the top of Turtle Rock, we could see a fringe of lights from the subdivisions around UC Irvine. Dark puddles of undeveloped land spread outward from our parking spot at the edge of the road. Lizzy started imitating the way our hippie social studies teacher always made air quotes around the phrase "Western belief system." Soojin and I could not stop cracking up.

In the cargo area, Scott and Heather were making out.

"Let's get some air." Lizzy shook the pack of cigarettes and raised an eyebrow.

I nodded and spoke in a loud, stagey voice. "Yes, let's stretch our legs."

"We're going to stay here where it's warm!" Heather called from the back.

"No shit," I mumbled.

We scrambled out of the car and walked up an unlit dirt path, sharing a cigarette and trying to find a spot with a better view.

When the car was out of sight, Soojin snorted a laugh. "It was getting a little awkward in there."

"How long should we give them, do you think?" I picked up a rock and threw it down the hill.

Lizzy let out a long stream of smoke. "I dunno. Ten minutes? Fifteen? How long do you think it takes to give that dumbass a blow-job?"

We burst into giggles.

"Okay, I'm definitely going to need another cigarette then."

Lizzy handed over the pack and I slid out the matchbook she'd tucked into the cellophane.

That's when we heard a noise almost like a wolf howl. "What the hell was that?" We stood silently for a minute and it came again. It almost sounded human.

Lizzy's eyes widened and she stamped out her cigarette. "That's Heather." She took off running faster than I'd ever seen her, spiked hair wobbling as she scrambled past us and half skidded on the sandy path.

Soojin and I raced after. Within seconds we could see the car and it was obvious that Heather was screaming, "NO NO NO!" and Scott was laughing in a way that was the opposite of laughing and somebody's bare foot was sticking out the back window at a weird angle.

Lizzy reached the car first and pulled open the tailgate door, launching herself inside the station wagon. "GET YOUR HANDS

OFF HER, YOU FUCKER!" She wasn't yelling. It was more like a war cry.

It was so dark that at first all I could see was the dim slope of Lizzy's back. She was perpendicular to Scott, and had settled the weight of her left side against his throat while she looped her arms under his back, pinning him down uncomfortably. Every time he kicked the roof or tried to wriggle away, she followed his body with her own, levering herself against him with a bent leg. He groaned. "Can't you take a joke? It was a joke, okay?"

Heather scrambled into the back seat, gasping and crying and holding her hand to a red bruise wrapped around the side of her neck. Her long black hair was tangled and eyeliner was smeared in wet streaks around her dark eyes. Soojin came in through the passenger door and scrunched next to her, gently touching the mark. "What did he do to you?"

"He was strangling me!"

"What the fuck are you talking about? We were playing around!"

"No, Scott! Don't fucking lie! You said you wanted to kill me!" Heather's voice shook.

"I was joking, *obviously*!" Scott struggled again, trying to escape from Lizzy's grip, but she twisted around to crush his right arm beneath her shin while she kept his chest pinned. He was practically immobilized.

"That hurts! My arm is going numb!"

"It should hurt." Lizzy was growling. "I'm going to let you up, and you're going to get out of the car and walk home. Do you understand?" He didn't answer and Lizzy shifted her weight, pushing harder.

"Yes! Yes! I understand!"

Slowly she crab-walked backward, dragging him with her out the back door, yanking him onto the asphalt outside. It was only then that I realized he was naked from the waist down. Scott looked dazed for a minute, and Heather threw his underwear and jeans at him. "What the fuck is wrong with you, rapist!"

He stood up and lunged so fast it was like he was on angel dust. Hell, maybe he was. Before any of us could react, he was back in the car, reaching into the seat where Heather was cowering, smacking her face, head, shoulders—any part he could hit from that angle. Then he grabbed Heather's breasts in clawed hands like he wanted to rip them off her chest.

Heather was screaming and Soojin was pulling at his fingers and then Lizzy was on Scott's back, reaching around to put him in a chokehold.

Except it wasn't a chokehold. A knife flashed in her hand—one of those Swiss Army deals that they always tell you to bring to Girl Scout camp.

"Lizzy, stop! What the fuck are you doing!" It felt like I was screaming underwater. I crawled into the back of the station wagon and reached out, connecting with her shoulder blade. It spasmed under my hand. Lizzy was stabbing the knife in the direction of her own body to penetrate his neck and face. Eventually she was going to miss and impale herself.

"LIZZY! STOP IT NOW!" I grabbed her arm in mid-puncture and she finally went still, her breath the loudest sound in the car. Scott slumped over the back of the seat between Heather and Soojin. His neck was wet and shredded. The knife was buried in what remained of his mouth.

Blood was everywhere. It was running in the seams of the faux leather blue upholstery. It was splattered on the steamy windows. It was dripping onto the floor. It was soaking Heather's lacy dress. Soojin's knees made indentations in the seat that quickly turned to bloody pools. It was like a burst watermelon, I thought in a surreal haze of incomprehension. Because this couldn't be happening. My life hadn't turned into a gore movie.

Heather was holding herself and hyperventilating. The bruise on her neck had darkened to purple. I crawled around Lizzy and Scott to hug her, the seat back an uncomfortable lump between us. She buried her wet face in my shoulder, whimpering words I couldn't hear.

"It's okay it's okay it's okay," I said to her, to us, to myself.

Lizzy was more practical. She poked her head out of the rear door and checked whether anyone was watching us. Through the windshield, I could see the streets were empty except for a distant figure, a woman in a bulky jacket who kicked the front tire of her car before driving away. There was no way she could have seen anything.

"Coast is clear. Right now, nobody knows what happened here." Lizzy climbed outside and wiped a bloody hand on Scott's jeans, wrinkled on the ground along with his underwear. Glancing at his body next to me, I realized that he really had been getting off on this. From the waist down, it looked like he was raring to go. I crawled back through the cargo area, past his bare feet, and threw up. Down the hill I could see that woman's car, headlights tracking the twisted streets that led back to reality. Lizzy yanked up the back door, slamming it hard. She led me around to the driver's side and all four of us crowded into the front seat, away from the blood.

Heather talked between panicked hiccups. "What you did was right, Lizzy. That was self-defense." A hiccup. "He said . . . he said . . . he was going to rape me to death. And then he started strangling me. He put his hand over my mouth. I thought he was going to . . ."

"We're all witnesses. We saw it." Soojin nodded vigorously as she talked, and the tiny plastic barrettes in her hair began to lose their hold.

"We should drive to the police station right now, and tell them what happened. He strangled Heather. He was raping her. You saved her, Lizzy. It wasn't just a lucky edit. You saved her." I was babbling.

I still couldn't believe he tried to do that with us right there, a few yards from the car. But Scott had always been a dick—he thought

rape was totally punk rock, in an ironic, GG Allin kind of way. We
tolerated him because of Heather. But my guess was that all of us,
including Heather, had fantasized about knifing him in the face at
some point. Plus, fuck GG Allin. His music sucked, and so did his
politics.

Everyone in the car was silent, and Scott's body started to smell
really bad, like diarrhea mixed with something worse. I returned to
my earlier point. "Lizzy, he went full psycho and attacked Heather.
We need to go to the police *now*."

Lizzy was shaking her head slowly back and forth. "We've got to
get rid of the body. And clean the car."

For some reason Heather thought this was a great idea. "Yeah, we
can't go to the cops."

"What. Why." I had a terrible feeling it was already decided.
Lizzy was always the decider.

Soojin looked at me, then back at Lizzy, waiting for an explanation. I rested my fingers on the door handle, wondering if I should
get out right then. I hadn't done anything wrong. Not yet.

"Beth, we can't go to the cops. They'll tell our parents. We're not
even supposed to be here." Heather was right about that. We were
supposed to be seeing a movie at one of the theaters near the South
Coast Plaza megamall. "Plus my mom says that the police always
take the easy way out. They won't believe us. We have no proof."

I thought about the time a cop stopped us on the street to ask
Heather if she was "legal," and demanded to see her driver's license.
When he saw her Iranian last name, Sassani, he asked where she
was from. She lied and said the name was Italian. He apologized
profusely, muttering something about how he should have known
that her "olive skin" was Mediterranean, not Mexican. We laughed
about all the intricate layers of racist bullshit at the time, but it wasn't
funny now.

Lizzy turned on the overhead light. "What's our proof? A
bruise?" Heather's makeup was smeared, and despite her shaking

hands, she'd managed to pull a giant, furry sweater over her stained dress. "Look at her. Does she look like she's been attacked? I mean, anybody can have a bruise like that. Maybe it's a really giant hickey. Can you imagine the cops believing her against him?" She gestured at Scott's white body, its fluids slowly leaking away.

I was being ripped into two versions of myself. One knew Lizzy was wrong. One knew she was right. And one of those versions had to die.

"Okay, so where do you think we'll get rid of him?" Soojin sounded dubious.

"Woodbridge Lake. We can drive right up to that spot where there are no houses."

There was a secluded place where we went to get stoned by the artificial lake at the heart of the Woodbridge subdivision, hidden from the street by a small rise in the carefully manufactured grassy hills.

"The water's so shallow, though. Wouldn't he stick out?" The words popped out of my mouth before my brain caught up. I guess I was doing this.

Lizzy thought we should make it look like a sloppy murder, something that Scott's friends would do in a drug-fueled haze. Dump the body in the lake, no frills. Somebody would find him in the morning. If anyone asked, we'd say we had no idea what Scott had been up to. We'd been watching *Lethal Weapon 3*, and then we went to Bob's Big Boy for fries. Lizzy outlined our lie while driving down the freeway. Nobody talked as she took the exit and followed narrow, townhouse-encrusted streets to the lake. Scott's body made a farting noise and the smell got worse.

Heather stayed in the car while we dragged Scott to the water's edge. She'd read in a true crime book that shoe prints are like fingerprints, so we went barefoot in the cool dew of the grass. We wrapped concert T-shirts around our hands to cover our prints. Lizzy tugged the body out into the water, hiking up her skirt to wade through the muck that softened the lake's cement bottom. Scott was a lump of pale pink in the middle of an oily, spreading stain. When she emerged, a piece of algae clung to the place where she'd repaired her fishnet stockings with the thin wire from a twisty tie.

"Some poor jogger is going to find him tomorrow." My voice sounded weird and my mouth throbbed like it did when the orthodontist tightened my braces.

"Yeah. Gross." Lizzy shrugged.

Soojin started to shiver with more than cold. "C'mon, you guys, let's go home."

Back in the car, we cleaned most of the blood off ourselves with a pile of prepackaged wipes that Lizzy's mom had left in the glove compartment for emergencies. Heather's sweater covered the splatters on her dress, which she vowed to burn. Soojin took off her bloody stockings and wadded them into a baggie. Somehow, I'd managed to stay pretty clean. That left the horrific mess in the back seat.

"Don't worry about that. I can deal with it." Lizzy sounded utterly certain, and completely calm. It was why she was our decider. She always seemed to know what to do, even in the worst situations.

"Really? Are you sure? Can I help?" I knew I should offer, even though I wanted desperately for her to say no.

"It's going to be fine. In the immortal words of Lynn Margulis, 'We are the great meteorite!'" Lizzy glanced at me, smirked, and started the car. I cracked a smile for the first time in what felt like a thousand years. Lizzy and I were obsessed with that PBS series *Microcosmos* in middle school, watching it over and over. We loved when the famous evolutionary biologist Lynn Margulis got all philosophical about how humans transform global ecosystems, her voice lowering to a portentous whisper: *We are the great meteorite.*

Thinking about *Microcosmos* made everything feel normal again. When we got to the curb next to my house, I opened the front door quietly and crept upstairs to take a shower. It's exactly what I would have done if I'd been coming back from the movies.

Looking at my fluffy yellow towel through the tropical flowers on my shower curtain, I tried to convince myself that the whole night had been a hallucination. The hot water was washing everything away: blood, mud, smells, weapons, words. Everything except Glorious Garcia, singing. Maybe if I thought about Grape Ape hard enough, the sound of her voice would replace the images encoded by every memory-clogged cell in my brain.

My parents remained asleep down the hall, and I tingled with relief. Setting down my damp toothbrush, I stared at my face in the steamy mirror. An unremarkable white girl looked back: hazel eyes, skin heat-blotched red from the shower, shoulder-length brown hair that my mother called "dirty blond." Did I look like a murderer? I peered more closely, relaxing the muscles of my jaw and lips. I knew from years of practice how to look innocent when I was guilty. Shrugging at my serene expression, I combed my hair and thought about those stupid, frantic seconds when I demanded that we go to the police. High on weed and horror, I'd almost forgotten that there was something more awful than being arrested for murder. It was what my father would do if he found out I'd broken the rules.

THREE

TESS

Flin Flon, Manitoba-Saskatchewan border (1992 C.E.) . . .
Los Angeles, Alta California (2022 C.E.)

I stood inside a vast hangar, ceiling so high that it sometimes generated its own puffs of cloud and misty rain. The floor was pure Canadian shield bedrock, a piebald of red and gray veined with white, covered in a few patches of hardscrabble lichen. Here, the Earth's crust had endured virtually unchanged for over 3 billion years, studded with metal deposits and ambiguous Cambrian fossils. The five known Machines had all been found in places like this, their control interfaces embedded in rock that originated before life evolved on land.

Facing me was a row of refrigerator-sized server racks connected by fat wires to bulky CRT monitors on desks, cameras on metal stalks, and something that looked like the severed head of a traffic light whose color signals had been replaced with atmospheric sensors. Travelers in the process of leaving or arriving lined up outside the processing booth on the opposite side of the hangar, their voices nearly indistinguishable from the nearby hum of the servers. A professor wandered past the equipment, trailed by a clot of excited students and postdocs. They had come to watch the Machine startup sequence.

A couple of techs typed on rugged keyboards, booting up the six tappers arranged in a circle around me. Half a billion years ago, these Machines had a sophisticated command interface made from what geoscientists called the ring and the canopy, but now all that was left was the rocky floor. The tappers, invented in the nineteenth century and refined in decades since, were crude, limited versions of what those old interfaces must have been. They looked like low steel tables punctuated by dozens of pistons, now moving up and down in a test pattern. Essentially the tapper was a reconfigurable set of padded hammers—much like those inside a piano—that would bang out a pattern on the rock. That pattern programmed the interface, and the interface would open a stable wormhole between the present and the traveler's chosen destination in the past. With these humble devices, we manipulated the fabric of the cosmos.

Geoscientists barely understood the Machines better than the first humans to describe them in writing thousands of years ago. Sure, we could control the exit date more precisely than our Bronze Age ancestors. Our tappers could produce complex rhythms that were accurate to the microsecond. So that was progress. We knew each Machine consisted of an interface within the rock, though so far our instruments could not detect anything *in* the rock other than the expected elements. Then there was a wormhole that came from . . . somewhere. Sadly, our biggest breakthrough was probably that we understood the Machines' behavior in the context of geology, rather than magic. Even after thousands of years of using them, we still didn't know much about how they worked, let alone why.

"Ready when you are." The tech with red hair and flushed cheeks looked up at me and made a shooing gesture.

I made sure I was at the exact center of the tapper circle, knelt, and put my fists against the rock. There was the thrum of the hammers, their rhythms vibrating my whole body until I couldn't tell where my skin ended and the Earth began. That's when the rock softened to liquid. A wet-but-not-wet fluid rose past my hands, then waist, blurring the warehouse walls as it crept past my eyes, enveloping me in a shimmering cylindrical column. It took me a second to adjust to the familiar, uncanny sensation of breathing in water.

Then I sank into the wormhole.

Textbooks say it's like submerging yourself in a warm bath, but that's only one sensation. There are many textures as you slide between nanoseconds: fine dust, cool gas, feathery ash. They're probably all illusions created by the brain in the absence of perception. Or maybe they're real, for some value of "reality." There's a lot of ambiguity in the geosciences. Sometimes people enter the wormhole and never return. We're left to speculate about whether they stayed deep in the past or were erased in transit. Floating toward my possible death, I always got slightly superstitious. So I had a ritual. I tried to focus on the molecular composition of my thoughts. As long as that skein of sugars, tissues, and electrons functioned, I was still myself. Chemicals pulsed through my brain and I waited.

After minutes or millennia, there was a hazy light ahead, like fire through warped glass. Then solid ground knit itself together beneath me, the liquid drained away, and I could breathe air again. I was in the same position, kneeling, dry except for the place where my knuckles and knees met the salty puddle left by a mostly incomprehensible doorway into spacetime.

The techs in 2022 didn't look much different from the ones I'd left behind in 1992. Same fieldwork chic: heavy boots, easy-wash pants, and padded canvas jackets with the colorful Flin Flon Time Travel Facility logo embroidered over the right breast. Everyone wore toques. It could get chilly up here, even in summer.

The far end of the hangar was occupied by the same processing office full of battered metal furniture. Inside, a Canadian government official was eating bannock and reading a paperback with swords on the cover. Outside was a line of about fifteen people, waiting for her to check them in or out of the present. I tried to figure out if any of them had come down from the future. Nobody stuck out as particularly anachronistic, and I decided we were all probably in our own present. So far, geologists had only figured out how to make the Machines send us to the past, and it always seemed like most of the traffic here consisted of people going back into history or returning from it.

Once the union-mandated lunch break ended, our queue moved pretty fast. The official looked up when I opened the door. "Identification?"

I raised my shirt to show the identity tattoo, a unique design created by algorithm and drawn partly with fluorescent ink as a half-hearted security measure. The university paid to have it needled into the skin of my left side before I traveled for the first time. Beneath a maze of tangled lines and dots was my date of birth: 1974 C.E. Most people looked exclusively at the date, especially in times before the 1930s. Sure, magistrates and monks in the 400s had heard about our computer-generated codes, but they didn't have a way to read them. Until somebody figured out how to transport objects through time, or persuaded the masses of another era to build anachronisms at great expense, people were pretty much stuck with the tech of their age.

She swiped a bulky handheld reader over my tattoo, and peered at her monitor. "What was your business in 1992?"

"I'm a geoscientist from UCLA, doing some fieldwork for the Applied Cultural Geology Lab. I was at a concert."

"What kind of concert?"

"A rock concert, in California. Do you know the band Grape Ape?"

The fan on her computer whined as she typed. "Nope. Was that one of those grunge bands?"

I flashed back to what "grunge" had meant to me when I lived through 1992 for the first time. "No. They're something different."

She didn't bother to ask anything else. I'd been using this Machine for most of my academic career, and there was a long digital record of my comings and goings. No need for further investigation.

Outside the damp hangar, I took a walk through the sprawling Flin Flon Time Travel campus. The air smelled faintly of mown grass, and people were out having lunch at picnic tables dotting the open plazas between buildings that hugged the northern edge of Ross Lake. The campus was deceptively peaceful. All those buildings were teeming with bureaucrats, operatives from vaguely menacing state agencies, travel reps for every possible industry, and quite a few scientific labs.

I caught a shuttle to the airport, rolling past strip malls, housing tracts, and a cavernous Canadian Tire. The city had changed a lot since the late nineteenth century, where I did most of my observation. Back then, Flin Flon was nothing more than a few cuts in the ground surrounded by tents and shacks, a podunk mining town named after an interdimensional traveler from a pulp novel. When prospectors discovered the world's fifth known Machine, all that changed. Flin Flon was hardly a megacity, but now it was a thriving urban hub on the border between northern Manitoba and Saskatchewan, supporting a steady stream of visitors whose jobs touched the timeline.

Many of those visitors were a captive audience, waiting out their 1,669 days to qualify for travel. All five Machines had limitations, but the hardest to surmount was what travelers called the Long Four Years. Wormholes only opened for people who remained within twenty kilometers of a Machine for at least 1,680 days. The number seemed arbitrary until geologists realized that it was roughly the length of four years during the Cambrian period, half a billion years ago, when the Earth was spinning faster. Cambrian days were roughly three hours shorter than ours, meaning the years were about 417 days long. Any device designed to measure years using a set number of day-night cycles, rather than revolutions around the sun, would wind up with longer and longer "years" as the eons passed.

I spent the Long Four Years working in a small Flin Flon lab surrounded by trees, returning home each night to a nougat-colored block of subsidized student housing on the Saskatchewan side of town. Through my dirty double-paned windows, I could see a golf course and condo complex for rich people with time to squander on a chance at temporal tourism. But that was rare. Most people in Flin Flon were there for work or professional training. All of us doing the Four Long Years were hoping it would pay off in a travel certification from the Chronology Academy.

After the revisionist assassinations during World War I, the five nations with Machines—India, Jordan, Australia, Canada, and Mali—founded the Chronology Academy, which imposed international law on all five travel complexes. Other member nations created additional rules to govern travelers, but Canada and the U.S. went strictly by Chronology Academy regulations. Which made things easy for me, but sticky for travelers from places that had stricter laws—or looser ones.

We rolled up to the airport terminal, a long brick building with four gates that mostly serviced puddle jumpers to Winnipeg and Saskatoon. I had a couple hours to kill before a tiring series of flights and layovers, so I poked idly through my e-mail and news alerts. A story was bubbling up from the conspiracy networks about how a traveler from the 2020s had caused climate change by going back in time and teaching people to use fossil fuels. I rolled my eyes. If only it were that simple.

As travelers, we could observe, maybe spy, and sometimes save a life. But centuries of scientific inquiry suggested that it was extremely difficult for one person to alter the timeline in all but the most superficial ways. You couldn't cause the world to industrialize before the eighteenth century, nor could you change the fate of nations by assassinating a famous leader. After killing the nineteenth-century tyrant Emmanuel, travelers were frustrated to find that Napoleon laid waste to Europe instead. It was the same discovery that travelers from the Tang Dynasty had made centuries before. There was no way to stop the Sogdian warlord An Lushan's rebellion. Slaying one Sogdian warlord simply spawned another who rose against the emperor. An Lushan was the third one to rise; his sack of the legendary city of Chang'an could not be edited from the timeline.

Geoscientists of the early twenty-first century eventually settled on the theory that small things change but big things don't. Trying to cause a significant divergence in the timeline was simply bad science, a honeypot for fools and failing tyrants. It was also against Chronology Academy regulations.

The Daughters of Harriet had a different theory. Call it a hypothesis if you must. Geologists agreed that the timeline was constantly in flux. Travelers exposed to edits returned with memories of lost histories, previous versions of the timeline they had witnessed. Agents and corporate operatives occasionally alluded to covert missions to shift the balance of power. Ancient scrolls contained references to travelers offering magical revelations that changed people's fates. It seemed obvious to the Daughters that we lived in a heavily edited timeline, and that small changes could add up to something bigger.

One did not admit that at academic conferences, however, so we had a cover story. The Daughters of Harriet had an official name, the Applied Cultural Geology Group, with the mandate to observe major social transformations as they happened in the past. We'd been recognized as a legitimate scholarly organization by the American Geophysical Union, which made it easier to apply for grants and schedule trips on the Machines. Every month we had a research meeting at my best friend Anita's house in Brentwood, close to the UCLA campus where we worked. There, we did a lot more than share discoveries and scotch. We made plans to edit history.

Los Angeles glowed with smoky orange light as we touched down. Fire season had come early this year, and it was yet another reminder that I was back home in 2022, when industrialization meant dystopia rather than progress. I caught a rideshare to Anita's place and felt the familiar dislocation of homecoming as we rolled past bungalows with high-performance windows and fake lawns. After years spent in the past, it was hard to feel like the present was anything more than ephemeral. Everywhere I looked, I saw previous versions of the city: these streets were once ruled by horse-drawn wagons, then cable cars, then finned Chevy convertibles full of kids in zoot suits inching past giant movie theater marquees. Today we drove through merely one version of Los Angeles, balanced in a precarious moment, and always on the brink of disappearing.

When I arrived, Anita was putting out cheese and crackers, her flip-flops smacking the tile floor as she wandered between kitchen and living room. Snowy dreads fell in an elegant cascade around her dark, angular face. Hugging her, I felt something solid for the first time since returning to my present.

"How was your trip?"

I dumped my backpack on the sofa and flopped next to it. "Tiring. Weird."

Anita raised an eyebrow and put out a bottle of Balvenie. After the living room had filled with a dozen people, snacking and chatting, Anita called the meeting to order.

We always started by going around the circle, describing lost histories we remembered. There were many events that existed only in our memories because we'd been present for the edits. We recited these stories partly as a ritual, and partly to update each other on current research projects.

Enid got us started. "I remember the Family Tax Reform Bill of 1988, which gave tax breaks to any family where the women could prove they had quit their jobs to become homemakers." That was a new one for me. Enid, a Chinese American woman with salty hair cut into a dapper fade, had recently gotten back from the late eighties.

There were murmurs of thanks from the group for deleting that particular gem out of our current version.

"I remember this café chain called Farrell's that used to have outlets all over L.A." Shweta reported her memory with a puzzled face. "Now it's gone. It seems like there are more Starbucks, too, but it's hard to tell."

"Wait—why would a café chain disappear? Did you travel to the period when it first opened, or do something to the people who worked there?" C.L. always asked questions like that, usually while picking delicately at the sparkly designs in their latest nail art. They'd only been traveling for a few months, after working on a Ph.D. in shield rock formation. Their work focused on the physical mechanism of time travel, so they were still getting used to applied history.

Shweta gave C.L. a tired look. Her brown eyes were sharp, but the skin around them was far more weathered than it had been last month. I realized she might have been away for years. "I was in Bermuda observing the slave trade," she said at last. "And it was 1723 when I left."

"But there must be *some* connection." C.L. sounded almost desperate. They wrapped a lock of hair around their fingers, and I noticed that they'd glued tiny red rhinestones to each nail.

"There probably is, but we can't always figure it out. That's why we call them orthogonal deletions," I said, shrugging. "We often see small, random changes like that and the causality is so complex that it's impossible to say why they happened."

Anita looked up from the tablet where she kept our change log and spoke. "Let's continue the circle." She paused. "I remember abortion being legal in the United States."

There were a couple murmurs of "me too." It was unusual for multiple people to remember a deleted event. Anita thought this meant the change to abortion's legal status was the product of multiple edits and reversions, its effects felt by many travelers exposed to various edits as they took. I wasn't one of them. Like nearly everyone on the planet, I had no memories of legal abortion in the United States.

Back when I was training at Flin Flon, I'd promised myself I was going to revert that edit if I got my credentials. That's what pulled me back to the nineteenth century again and again, to haunt the edges of Comstock's influence, seeking cracks where an edit might take. It was an intriguing historical problem, but my interest wasn't purely academic. I had other reasons, their roots tangled up in old feelings. Until I saw Grape Ape again, I thought I'd managed to replace those messy personal desires with clean political aspirations. Now I had to admit it was impossible for me to tell them apart. And maybe, with the right strategy, I didn't have to.

"I think I've found hard evidence that we're in an edit war with anti-travel activists." My announcement got everybody's attention. "I was in 1992, at a Grape Ape show." I filled them in about the Comstocker. "Seems like he and his buddies are trying to make some final edits before trying to shut down the Machines. The question is—"

Anita cut me off. "Wait, why were you in 1992? Your period is the nineteenth century."

I was confused. "Berenice told me to go. She had evidence that anti-travel activists were hanging around the indie rock scene. Grape Ape caused a huge controversy around this time—the Vice Fighters kept going on TV calling them obscene feminazis, so they became punk heroes. This concert would have been catnip for Comstockers trying to target young women with one last reversion."

I remembered the conversation clearly, at our last meeting. Berenice wanted to go herself, but she'd burned out of most of the 1990s. One of the hazards of studying a specific period was that the Machine would not open its wormhole for people tapping back to a time they'd visited before. We called those times "burned"; it was annoying, but it also prevented people from returning to the same moment over and over, destructively reliving or reediting a targeted stretch.

"Berenice?" C.L. was playing nervously with their phone. "Who's that? Does she study the 1990s?"

"What do you mean? Berenice! Our friend? She published a huge book about the origins of trans activism in the 1990s. UC Press made it one of their featured titles in the fall catalogue."

"No . . . I don't know her . . ." Shweta, one of the most tough-minded scientists I knew, was at a loss for words.

"Does anyone remember Berenice?" Fear was crawling along my spine.

Everyone was shaking their heads. C.L. poked their phone again. "What was Berenice's last name?"

"Ciccone. She was . . . shit . . . she's been coming to these meet-ings for years." I spluttered to a stop as the reality sank in. Berenice had been edited. And then I looked at Enid and realized something horrifying. "Enid, you and Berenice were partners . . . you were about to move in together . . ."

Enid drew in a sharp breath. "What? That can't be. I can't have lost . . ." She trailed off, her eyes searching our faces. But there was nothing we could do. How do you help someone mourn a lover they don't remember?

Shweta spoke gently. "Tess. You said she was researching trans activism?"

"Yes."

She held out her phone, its screen illuminated by a 1992 AP ar-ticle dredged from the Nexis database. It was about a person police described as "a man in a dress," murdered outside a gay bar in Ra-leigh. There was a grainy picture of Berenice, unmistakable mop of curls forming a crazy halo around her much younger face. My throat constricted. "They've misgendered and deadnamed her, but that's definitely Berenice."

Nothing like this had ever happened before. At least, not that we knew of. I looked around the room. Was it possible that more of us had been edited out of the timeline, and we didn't remember? I spoke without thinking. "We have to go back there and revert that edit."

Enid shook her head slowly, eyes reddening. "We need to do a lot more than that."

Foreboding settled over the room.

"Who would make edits like this? By literally killing travelers?" This time, C.L.'s question didn't seem naïve. We were all wondering the same thing.

"Do you think this has anything to do with the man from the concert, the Comstocker?" Anita mused. "Berenice sent you to look for him, right?"

"Yeah. It's possible these guys saw Berenice as a threat to their cause. Especially if they knew she was onto them. So they murdered her younger self."

C.L. blinked in shock, and accidentally popped a rhinestone off their thumbnail. For once, they had no questions.

Anita coped with the stress by going into analysis mode. "So let's assume there's a group of travelers working with Comstock, who are reverting some of our edits. And some of us." Her voice cracked. "If this is part of a larger plan to lock us into a timeline that can't be changed, what is their goal with these edits? Is it something about Comstock?"

"I don't think it's Comstock himself." I fought to stay focused, despite my rising panic. Who else had those men erased from our memories? "Their zine was all about why women shouldn't go to college. And the guy who talked to me—he sounded like some mashup of a Comstock speech and the Celibate4Life forums we see today. They could be infiltrating different movements over centuries. Comstock's Society for the Suppression of Vice successfully eliminated abortion and access to birth control, so it would appeal to anyone who wanted a timeline where women's rights are restricted. I think they must be coordinating a much bigger edit across several time periods."

"What else do we know?" Anita was typing on her tablet.

Enid cleared her throat. "If you're wondering why they were in 1992, there was a huge backlash against feminism at that time. It probably started with obscenity law reforms—specifically, reforms of the Comstock Laws."

"So could they be C4L types from our present, going back to key periods for women's rights?" C.L. asked.

I had a more urgent question. "What if they're from the future?"

Anita gave me a sharp look. "What difference would that make?"

"It could mean that they know something we don't. They might be responding to a future feminist revolution."

"Future feminist revolution. Give me a break." Shweta snorted. "That's not how history works. Every so-called revolution is simply a long, drawn-out series of profound compromises and co-optations."

"There *are* revolutions. Maybe they take time, but there are huge changes." I felt my cheeks getting hot. "Sometimes we don't compromise. Sometimes we do things like abolish slavery and declare universal suffrage."

"And then spend the next century and a half trying to make brown people into slaves again."

"We're derailing here." Anita was always the voice of reason. "The fact is that we don't have enough data to know when these dudes are from, and we can't go to the future. Still, we know they're out there now. It's possible that they're working directly against the Daughters of Harriet, or maybe against women's rights more generally. Either way, it's probably related to why our memories are so divided on reproductive rights."

"So what should we do about it?" Shweta folded her arms.

"I'm going to 1992 to stop those fuckers from murdering Berenice." Enid was shaking with a determination that wavered between sadness and fury.

Shweta was nodding. "You're pretty familiar with the time period from traveling to the eighties, so that's not a bad plan." Then she touched Enid's arm, and spoke without any of her usual impatience. "But be careful."

As I pondered Enid jumping from the eighties to the nineties, I suddenly had an idea. "I've been researching Comstock in the 1880s, but maybe I should skip forward. He scored a major political victory for his cause in 1893, at the World's Fair in Chicago. My guess is our Comstockers had something to do with it. I think if I could edit that moment it might turn the tide." I didn't mention that there was another advantage to being in the nineteenth century. Record-keeping at the Flin Flon Machine was terrible until the 1920s. It would be easy to sneak from 1893 up to 1992 again, where I had already left a paper trail proving I was observing the music of temporal locals. With a little subterfuge, I still had a chance to prevent the next murder. Or maybe the next after that.

Anita nodded and made a note. "Our current grant will cover several more trips back to the late nineteenth, so that's a good idea. Anyone else?"

"I'm researching Ordovician ocean sediments and the origin of the Machine at Raqmu," C.L. piped up. "Can this grant cover my expenses in Jordan? Raqmu is right by the airport there."

I was dubious until C.L. explained a few odd properties of the Machine at Raqmu. It was the first described in recorded history, found by ancient Nabataeans in a city they carved into the sandstone walls of a valley in Jordan. C.L. had read some papers about new evidence showing the Raqmu Machine could affect the other Machines' behavior. If a group of crazy extremists wanted to lock the timeline, they would probably focus their sabotage efforts on Raqmu.

"All right, C.L., why don't you work up a protocol that will allow us to check for people tinkering with the Machine." Anita made another note.

The meeting wound down after that, and we all promised to report back when we had new information.

I gave Enid a long hug before she left. "I'm so sorry."

"I miss her, even though I don't know her." Her face reminded me of shattered safety glass, utterly broken but still somehow holding its shape.

"You're going to fix this. I know you will."

Enid cocked her head, and ran a hand over the freshly shaved hairs on the back of her neck. "I know you will too. Safe travels." That simple pleasantry suddenly felt like a powerful talisman.

"Safe travels," I replied.

My anxiety hardened into a new sense of purpose. After years of work in the 1880s, I'd changed nothing. But now, at last, I had hope.

FOUR

BETH

Irvine, Alta California (1992 C.E.)

For over a week, we'd been referring to it as "the thing that happened." We acted normal, following our usual routine, taking advantage of open campus at lunch. Kids could leave school grounds at noon, as long as they came back for fifth period. But it was Friday, so fuck fifth period. Lizzy, Heather, Soojin, and I went to the mall down the street from Irvine High, stopping in at the pizza place, not even bothering to pretend we weren't ditching class.

"Wanna go to Peer Records?" Soojin didn't need to ask. We always went there after pizza, following an unblemished sidewalk that divided the parking lot from a monumental Ralph's supermarket. A nondescript storefront in a jumbled row of shops, Peer Records was our gateway to the world beyond aerobics studios and lawn furniture. Long and narrow, its walls were plastered with posters, T-shirts, and bumper stickers. Rows of record bins turned the tiny space into a maze. When I bent down to check out the overflow boxes on the floor, hunting first for an Alley Cats album, then X-Ray Spex, I blocked the entire aisle.

Heather kicked me lightly with her taped-up boot. "Get out of
the way, girlie. I want to check out what they have by The Selecter."

"I love their song 'Murder.'" I bit my tongue way too late. Now
Soojin and Lizzy were giving me the bug eye. I hadn't meant it that
way. But maybe I had.

"Have you guys heard anything about . . ." Heather trailed off
awkwardly.

"Nope."

"No."

"Maybe we should take a walk." Lizzy tilted her head at the door.

We wandered in silence until we found one of those ornamental
lozenges of grass between housing tracts that the Irvine Company
called "greenbelt." We were sitting next to a large intersection, but
nobody glanced at us. Just a group of invisible girls on a Friday afternoon.

Lizzy broke the silence. "Do you think anybody found him yet?"

"They must have." Heather's cheeks flushed a deep red, her eyes
full of outrage and tears.

"Did your parents ask you anything?" I was talking to the group,
but looked at Lizzy.

"They thought it was very nice that I volunteered to clean the
whole car after somebody, uh, barfed in the back. Luckily all that
shit hosed right off."

None of us really understood Lizzy's relationship with her parents. They were almost never around, and her brother was already
off at college. When I went to her place for sleepovers, her parents
would say hi then go back to work on whatever it was they did. Something to do with engineering. They seemed benignly neglectful,
which was definitely better than my parents, who demanded to know
everything I did in minute detail. Heather's parents were similarly
watchful. Soojin had three loud sisters, so she was able to evade parental surveillance most of the time. None of our parents had said
anything about what we did that night. At least, not yet.

"I guess we'll see something on the news when they find him, right?" Heather sounded almost hopeful.

"Maybe," Soojin cautioned. "But the police might want to keep it secret if they're looking for suspects."

"People will notice that he's not at school. They'll have to say *something*." As I spoke, I realized how wrong I was. Last year, a guy in eleventh grade had killed himself and the school administration never said anything official about it at all. We only knew about it through rumors from other kids.

Soojin added another barrette to her hair, which did nothing to hold it in place. "I dunno, Beth. We might never know what happened to Scott."

"I know what happened to him." Lizzy narrowed her eyes. "He was a fucking asshole who tried to kill Heather and we fucking killed him first."

We all sat frozen, shocked. Was that really what had happened? The more I thought about it, the more I realized Lizzy was right. It made me feel dizzy and powerful, like a superhero that nobody had a name for yet.

"Yeah, fuck that guy." Heather ripped a hunk of grass out of the ground, its roots still clotted with soil. Then she threw it as hard as she could into the street. It landed with a sound that nobody heard.

The news finally got out a month later. There was a short blurb in *The Orange County Register* about a high school boy murdered by "transients, probably from the Los Angeles area." And then some group of parents, or maybe teachers, decided to turn Scott's death into a lesson. There was a school assembly in the gym. A cop came to show us a movie about the horrors of "weed and speed." The school counselor waved around some tattered *Just Say No to Drugs* paraphernalia left over from the eighties. Then the principal talked about the great tragedy of a promising young man's life cut short, and how drug use is a cry for help, and we should all report our friends if they were using drugs. Lizzy nudged me and rolled her eyes.

I could see some of Scott's friends off in the corner of the bleachers. They were uncharacteristically silent, their backs stiff. I only knew one of them by name—Mark—because a few months ago he tried to carve the word "PUNK" into his narrow, pimply chest with a razor blade during open lunch. We'd driven to the park to feed some ducks, but somehow the trip turned into the boys impressing each other. Mark's stunt was a sad imitation of something he'd seen in a movie about Sid Vicious, but Scott thought it was awesome. He kept talking about the dirtiness of the razor, and the amazingness of Mark's stalwart efforts, until Lizzy told him to shut up or she wouldn't give either of them a ride back to school.

Flashes of that long-ago conversation kept interrupting today's anti-drug lecture. As we filed out of the gym and back to third period, I thought about the principal praising Scott's ability to absorb dozens of knife blows in the spirit of punk rock. It made way more sense than what the principal had actually said, about how Scott had been such a promising boy. Our teachers really thought we'd believe that the cruel authors of Scott's tragedy—anonymous except for those male pronouns—had forced him into some kind of drug orgy, then killed him when he tried to resist.

Lizzy and I walked home from school along the railroad tracks that cut between two mirror-image housing tracts sealed behind cinderblock sound barriers. When we were kids, we used to leave pennies on these same tracks and wait for the train, expecting the coins to shoot upward in an arc of fire, or be flattened beyond all recognition. Maybe the cars would be derailed. No matter how many times we did it, we never found the pennies again. The train continued dragging its freight, oblivious to our violent intentions.

"Want a cigarette?" Lizzy pulled a Marlboro hard pack out of her battered denim jacket. Our friend worked at the local gas station, and sold us cigarettes sometimes when he felt generous. We sat on the tracks and shared one, passing it back and forth until the nicotine made me dizzy.

"Do you feel weird? Different? Like we're evil now or something?" I looked over at Lizzy.

She cocked her head, the mesh of her earrings catching the light. Her platinum hair was like a crushed dandelion today, soaped and dried into stiff, crazy angles. "No. I feel exactly the same. I mean, maybe *that's* weird."

"I don't know." I could see the roofs of my housing tract peeking over the wall fifty yards from us. Each one was exactly the same, their shingles kept in perfect order by the Irvine Company. "Everything is fucking weird." I rested my head on my knees and thought about how there was only one more year until I'd be in college.

"Let's do something tonight. Want to go to the movies?"

Of course I did. It was our default plan every Friday. "Let's go to my house and we can call Heather and Soojin."

Lizzy nodded and crushed the cigarette butt under a rock. We scrambled over the wall, wedging our boots into the crumbling mortar between bricks, and landed on some greenbelt next to the community pool. A few kids were splashing around with their mothers, who gave us dirty looks. Punk girls being disobedient. At least they noticed.

My house formed one end of a rectangular block of condominiums built with shared walls, like the suburban architectural equivalent of conjoined quintuplets. Each facade faced the quiet street with the same lopsided face, three windows and a door, painted in matching shades of 1970s tan. But the corner houses, like mine, had one extra window on the side wall that faced the street. My father called it "the deluxe model," but he didn't seem to enjoy it much. We had a strict rule in the house that the curtains always had to be drawn, unless it was raining, in which case they had to be open to let in extra light.

Actually, we had a lot of complicated rules, and they changed depending on my father's mood. It kept me vigilant. Coming home, I always felt like I was donning futuristic sensor gear for detecting minute shifts in ground elevation. My lasers swept the area, bouncing off every surface, light receptors primed to detect any change. I unlocked the front door. Had any temblors perturbed the landscape? No. My parents weren't home.

We went upstairs to my room and I popped a tape into the boom box. I had already memorized most of the new Million Eyes EP, though it still felt kind of new in my head. Lizzy dialed Heather and Soojin to make movie plans while the band yowled: "REBEL GIRL YOU ARE THE QUEEN OF MY WORLD!"

I cranked it up, but not loud enough that I wouldn't hear the garage door opener announcing my father's arrival in his classic VW with the fancy engine upgrade. Sometimes he picked my mom up after she taught her last class, but sometimes he headed straight home from the auto repair shop he'd inherited from my grandfather. When I heard a grinding squeal coming from outside, I turned the volume down and shut my bedroom door. I could feel my father's rage seeping through the floor from downstairs. It usually took him a few hours to simmer down after work, especially at the end of the week.

Outside the sun was drowning in a Technicolor bruise of pollution, but inside we ate spaghetti and my mom made small talk.

"How are your parents, Lizzy?" She was using her high school teacher voice on us, which meant she was paying attention. Usually at dinner she read the paper and ignored whatever lecture my father was delivering.

"They're good, Ms. Cohen. They just got back from a long trip."

"Oh, how nice! Where did they go?"

Lizzy twirled her spaghetti deliberately. "Someplace in Jordan? It's for work."

My father was completely silent until Lizzy got up to use the bathroom.

"Why are you wearing shoes in the house?" He was whisper-raging. A couple of months ago, he'd gotten really focused on shoes. I'd come out of my bedroom with bare feet, and he'd ordered me never to set foot inside the house without shoes. Since then, I'd never taken them off unless I was getting in the shower or bed. Apparently, there'd been a reversal. I braced myself, sensors on alert.

"We got the carpets cleaned last week. Why would you *ever* think that you should wear shoes *in the house*?" His voice had a poisonous edge that meant he was working his way toward a total meltdown. I stared at the ground, took my shoes off, and carried them to the foyer. Instant obedience and no questions were the best way to calm him down. I could intercept Lizzy on her way out of the bathroom and tell her to take hers off too. One of the many reasons I loved Lizzy was that she never cared when I asked her to do odd things, like suddenly take her shoes off in the middle of dinner. She accepted that we were taking our shoes off now, and then there would be more spaghetti.

"What are you two doing tonight?" My mother continued the small talk when we returned in our socks.

"We're seeing a movie at the Balboa Theater with Heather and Soojin."

"There won't be any boys with you, will there?"

My father made a disgusted noise and nudged my mother's elbow. "Delia, you do realize that if she were your son, you wouldn't worry about girls being around. This is the 1990s. Everybody should be treated equally. So Beth is allowed to go out with boys."

I couldn't help but smile at my father, and he smiled back. It was one of those days when his rule-changing mania flipped back around to reward me. Sometimes he decided that we were allies. I wished I knew why, but in my seventeen years on Earth I had yet to discover a predictable pattern.

FIVE

TESS

Chicago, Illinois (1893 C.E.)

In fall, I headed back to the late nineteenth century. Once the official paperwork was filed, all I had to do was grab an overnight bag and get to Flin Flon. We couldn't send more than the clothes on our backs through the Machine with us, so it didn't make sense for me to bring anything more. C.L. was fond of saying that theoretically we should be able to send anything through a wormhole. The only thing stopping us was an interface setting that geoscientists hadn't figured out how to control with our tappers.

I texted goodbye to the Daughters, and left myself a few notes in my office about some outstanding questions from students that I wanted to answer in my next lecture. Even if I traveled for a few years, I'd be back at work next week.

One of the many things that drives me nuts about *The Geologists*, that BBC show about time travelers, is how the characters are always obsessing about period costumes. It seems like half the plots revolve around getting the right style of straw bonnet, or freaking out because somebody is wearing stockings that are made of non-period nylon. First of all, nobody pays that much attention to the small details of your underwear. And second, there are many ways to dress in every era. If I were to look like a proper nineteenth century lady from *The Geologists*, I'd blow my mission. I wasn't trying to mingle with ladies. I needed New Women, those outrageous revolutionaries, college students, and artists who smoked cigarettes, read *The Alarm*, and supported Senator Tubman. To meet them, I wore a bicycling look of knickerbockers, thick knee socks, and a high-necked cotton blouse. A warm jacket fit snugly over the top, and I completed the outfit by tucking my long brown hair into a wool maritime cap. It was basically riot grrl style for the Gilded Age. And you'd be hard-pressed to find it in most history books, let alone a TV series.

When I arrived in early April 1893, I had ice cold mud in my leather shoes. There was no bank of networked computers. An engineer was feeding coal to a single, steam-powered tapper connected to a massive turbine that dominated the mining camp's wood plank warehouse. The room smelled like smoke and machine oil.

I stood up unsteadily, taking in the rough walls, patched here and there with epoxy. Miners had stumbled on the Flin Flon Time Machine only fifteen years before, making it the most recently discovered of the five known Machines. That meant travelers who used Flin Flon to go back further than 1878 found themselves alone on a rocky outcropping next to a beautiful lake. No shack, no tappers, nothing. With training, a person could use stones to pound the Machine interface and return to their present. But I'd learned on tappers, so I generally used the Flin Flon machine only to explore the nineteenth and twentieth centuries. To go further, I took the Machines at Raqmu and Attirampakkam, discovered thousands of years ago. Using those, you could go back pretty far and find bureaucrats from long-dead regimes to greet you—along with people trained in the art of tapping by hand. I'd never used the other two Machines, at the Super Pit in Kalgoorlie, Australia, and Timbuktu in Mali. Unless there was a compelling reason to be in those places, grants typically covered booking in only the closest Machines.

Light came in from the doorway, and I could see my greeting committee now. A white man with an elaborately waxed moustache and dusty overcoat doffed his hat as he entered. He spoke with a faint Quebecois accent.

"When are you coming from?"

I showed him my tattoo. "A few decades upstream: 2022."

"Welcome. How was the day up there?"

"I came in fall, so it was pretty chilly."

He grinned and rubbed his chapped hands together. "Bet you're glad to be here in the heat of spring! What's your business?"

"I'm a geoscientist from California, and I'm here to see the Columbian Exposition in Chicago." That got him talking about the wonders that awaited me. Everybody in this period knew about the first American World's Fair, known in the 1890s as the Columbian Exposition because it fell on the four hundredth anniversary of Columbus arriving in the Americas. We sat on a log outside, where it felt barely warmer than the month I'd left, and I tried vainly to scoop all the mud out of my shoes. I'd never come through wet before—the water vanished with the wormhole. I thought about the Comstockers' plan to sabotage the Machines and hoped this wasn't a sign that they were succeeding.

Wax Moustache interrupted my thoughts. "So you'll be needing a canoe down to Winnipeg to catch the train, I expect."

"Do you know anyone going down?"

"Old Seacake is heading out pretty soon. He's been trapping all the way up and I think he's full up on beaver and mink. Good man. Mushkego tribe. He'll get you there in a couple weeks, as long as you keep him away from whisky—you know how his kind like the fire water." He winked, like he expected me to laugh at his racist joke. I frowned and pulled my shoes back on.

"Do you know where Seacake is?" I knew a very limited amount of Cree, but I thought maybe the name "Seacake" was an extreme mispronunciation of a Cree word for skunk. Then again, maybe it was slang for hardtack, the long-lasting sailors' crackers that white settlers brought to the bush.

Seacake turned out to be a middle-aged guy with two thick braids and battered Levi's jeans that would have been the envy of millennial hipsters up in '22. He was packing his campsite into tidy canvas sacks.

"Hey, Seacake, I got a traveler who needs to get to Winnipeg."

Seacake ignored Wax Moustache and looked at my knickerbockers. "You an anarchist?"

I laughed. "No. I'm a geoscientist. And I like rational clothes."

He pondered for a minute and then nodded. "Okay. I'll give you a ride if you strike camp and do the cooking."

That seemed like a good bargain, so we shook on it. Luckily, Seacake was heading out soon, and I was able to avoid Wax Moustache for the rest of my stay at camp.

Most of the trip, Seacake rowed in silence. I burrowed into the furs and thought about my plan for an edit that would thwart the Comstockers. Ice clotted thickly at the edges of the water, and the canoe seemed to nose its way through sheets of melting sugar. It had been three days of dried meat and hardtack, and I watched the water hungrily.

"You're a traveler, huh?" Seacake cocked his head at me.

"Yeah."

"From the future?"

"I couldn't be from the past. We can only travel backward from our present, not forward."

Seacake snorted. "Really? That's what you think? White people really don't know anything about time travel."

I sat up straighter. We knew the Cree used the Flin Flon Machine before white settlers claimed it, but very little information about their work survived. "Do you know people who can go forward in time?"

"I'm not going to tell you." Seacake's tone was halfway between playful and annoyed. Was he messing with me?

"Well, nobody in my time thinks it can be done. It's one of the Machine's hard limits."

Seacake shrugged. "Maybe the problem is that you think it's a machine, and not an animal made of rock and water."

Despite the completely deadpan tone, I was pretty sure he was being sarcastic. I sighed. "So you're really not going to tell me whether you can go to the future."

"Figure it out yourself."

"I'm sure somebody already has, somewhere in the timeline."

"Exactly." Seacake finally cracked a grin. "Are there any good songs when you're from?"

I nodded, thinking about Grape Ape.

"Can you sing one?"

I was on a fur trapper's canoe somewhere in northern Manitoba, hundreds of kilometers and decades from the world I knew. It seemed like the right time to sing a Grape Ape classic: "Racist Cops Suck My Plastic Dick." For the next two minutes, the trees shivered with Glorious Garcia's words, delivered in my off-key shriek.

Seacake seemed to like it.

When we finally got to Winnipeg, he gave me a couple of beaver pelts to sell for train tickets and a room with access to a bath. I thanked him profusely and he shrugged. "You can pay me back when you come through again."

The CP Line cut through tiny towns and thawing prairie farms, the varnished wood of its seats transducing our bumpy passage over the tracks into repeated jolts that I felt as one long ache in my lower back. In St. Paul, I spent a nickel on some cheese and hard candy before transferring to a U.S. line that would take me to Chicago via New York City.

Traveling through time is easy, but getting to and from the damn Machine will kill you. Sometimes literally, if you meet a microbe our inoculations don't cover. Thankfully I arrived at Union Station in downtown Chicago merely broke and hungry. The cold air brought gusts off Lake Michigan that smelled like rotting flesh and sewage. It wasn't like I smelled much better. I'd been living on train station food for days, sleeping in a cramped berth, and my neck was a burning knot of pain. But I'd arrived at last, and the prospect of starting work had me excited. Straightening my jacket, I walked south along the putrid water to reach the geology department at the University of Chicago. Most big-city universities had a small fund set aside for traveler loans, and I needed a few dollars to tide me over until I had a job.

Before I begged for university funds, though, I'd be passing through the Columbian Exposition. Opening day was months away, but the Expo was already packed with venues looking to hire. Ideally, I'd pick up a job before I ever got to the geology department. Travelers were trained to be participant observers, so I was supposed to earn a livelihood when I went downstream. At least the nineteenth century had an economic system I understood.

I knew I was getting close when I saw domes and spires in the distance. I'd studied faded photographs of the Expo, but still got the familiar traveler's rush when I saw it in person, rickety and real. Construction crews had spent the past year converting a swampy lakeside mess called Jackson Park into a maze of sprawling European-style buildings, artificial lagoons, and angel-encrusted facades. Today, in its half-finished state, the place looked like an insane fairy tale. Tourist brochures would call this area the White City, both for its color and for the way it embodied a spotless, shining Victorian futurism. I paused for a minute, marveling at the sheer size of the display halls, swarming with workers. Delivery wagons clattered past, piled with everything from live ostriches to bonsai trees. But this wasn't where I wanted to land a job. I was looking for the Midway Plaisance, the long, dirty tongue of parkland that stuck out of the White City's prettied-up face and deep into the city of Chicago itself. The Expo attractions there would inspire carnival sideshows for at least a century to come.

I took a right turn and there it was: the Midway, its landscape rough and scarred by carriage wheels. I avoided puddles of liquefied manure and passed between exhibits that looked like villages jumbled together from various locations around the world: Java, Germany, the Ottoman Empire, Japan, Austria, Samoa, Egypt. Many of the concessions were still skeletal. Ahead of me loomed the monumental "Cairo Street" exhibit, a walled-in world of restaurants, shops, theaters, and bazaars that merged to form a colonial hallucination of various cities in the Maghreb. Men with hammers climbed all over Cairo Street's hulking "Luksor Temple." Others were erecting two plinths covered in hieroglyphs for full pseudo-authenticity.

This segment of the Midway was almost entirely blocked to traffic by a pile of enormous steel spokes, arranged like lumber in the mud-clogged street. They would eventually converge to form the world's first Ferris wheel, a modern mega-machine designed to dwarf the minarets of North African architecture below. Dozens of workers were ripping up ground to lay the steam pipes that would power the thing. Across from Cairo Street were the Moorish Palace and Persian Theater, both little more than wooden foundations with a few rickety beams hinting at the large crowds they would hold in a few weeks. I couldn't believe this place would soon become an American obsession.

I poked my head around the corner from the Luksor and found a side street with one building whose slightly faded awnings gave it a lived-in appearance. Topped by gilded domes and covered in rows of bright tiles, it had a plain marquee that read "ALGERIAN THEATER." In curly script below, the place promised to deliver "Moorish Kabils—Algerian Negre & Oulades Nai'le Dances." Another sign helpfully elucidated: "Performance Every Hour! Dancing Girls!" A fountain stood outside, beautifully painted, full of murky rainwater. It sounded like people were drumming inside, but I couldn't be sure.

I was turning to leave when two women materialized in the shadows of the entrance. One was tall and pale, rolling a cigarette with tobacco she'd pulled from a tiny pouch hidden in her skirts. The other was short, her jet-black hair wound into braids around her brown face. She wore a man's wool overcoat to cover her costume, visible only as a few metallic tassels against her thick black stockings.

The tall one called out to me. "You here for the audition?"

"No, I was just passing by." I tried to sound casual. Like somebody who wasn't desperate for a job.

The one in the wool coat gave me an appraising look and grinned. "I like your knickerbockers. Want a smoke?"

I did.

"I'm Aseel, and this is Sophronia."

"Everybody calls me Soph."

"I'm Tess. You guys dancers?"

"I'm a dancer. My stage name is Lady Asenath. But I'm also a translator. And pretty much everything else, including manager for the fellow who brought this troupe over from Africa." Aseel made a grand gesture, like she was showing off a palace full of treasures.

Soph handed me a tightly rolled cigarette. "I'm a journalist," she said. "Did you know this is the first time these traditional dances have been seen in America? It's incredible. I'm working on a story about it."

I took a drag and tried not to choke. Nineteenth-century tobacco is intense. "What else do you write about?"

"Mostly I write pamphlets about how I'm fucking an angel."

I've heard a lot of weird things in my twenty-five years of travel, so it was easy to keep my tone conversational. "What kind of angel?"

"I don't mean a real angel. The goddess wouldn't take physical form like that. But I teach women about family health and the marriage bed, and it helps if they can tell their husbands that they're reading spiritualist tracts."

Aseel broke in. "I ordered one of her newsletters when I was having woman problems back in Arizona. When I came to Chicago, the first thing I did was call on her." The two women looked at each other and giggled.

"You look like a New Woman." Soph raised her eyebrows. "What do you do?"

"Actually, I'm looking for work."

"But you don't dance?" Aseel was dubious. "Can you do mending? We are desperate for a seamstress."

"Sure I can."

Soph did a little pirouette. "Wonderful! Delightful! It's as if the goddess herself brought you to us!"

I grinned and nodded. This was an incredible stroke of luck. I'd landed a job in the exact place where Comstock would try to crush women's rights in a few months.

Aseel reminded me of every female boss I've ever had, no matter where I traveled. She wasn't technically in charge—that honor went to Sol Bloom, a young event promoter from San Francisco who managed the entire Midway Plaisance. But everyone knew Aseel was the person with all the answers. Though she had no job title, she did everything at the Algerian Theater, from accounting and hiring to project management and choreography. And of course, she was paid less than the guys following her directions on how to build the stage.

Also like every female boss I've ever had, this situation annoyed the shit out of her. My second day on the job, I arrived to find Aseel chewing out the cast and crew. "What are you oafs doing? We open on May 1! The sets aren't finished, the roof is leaking, and you're all dancing like donkeys!" Then she yelled at everybody in Arabic for a while before whirling on me. "And how about the costumes? Salina's jacket is in tatters!" I hung my head along with the rest of the team. We couldn't all be as competent as the great Lady Asenath, the star of our show and scourge of lazy proto-carnies.

Still, I passed the afternoon pleasantly enough, adding modest chemises to the traditional, midriff-baring vests that some of the dancers wore with their skirts and tassels. These additions had to be transparent enough to show the women's stomach muscles, but opaque enough to prevent nice midwestern white people from freaking out. Next there were endless tiny beads and sparkly coins to replace on jackets, pantaloons, scarves, and shoes. As I licked another piece of thread and poked it through the needle's eye, Aseel sat down next to me and groaned.

"Long day. And we have a performance in a couple of hours."

I was surprised. "I thought the show started in May."

"Why do you think the costumes are already so ripped up and broken? I've been putting on a preview show for the past few weeks. Two bits a head. We've made plenty of dough and the Midway isn't even open yet." There was a note of pride in her voice.

I started attaching coins to a bodice, carefully placing them so they overlapped like kissing buttons. "How long have you been dancing with this troupe?"

She sorted through the dish of coins and handed me a few of the right size. "Oh, I didn't come over with them. I joined up last year, when Sol put a notice in the paper for a manager who spoke Arabic."

"He hired you as the manager?"

"Well, technically he hired me as a dancer. But then he figured out that I can speak English and Arabic, and that I know how to run a show. My parents are from Egypt, and they owned a saloon back in Arizona. I learned African dances to entertain the guests, but my dad taught me how to run the business too." She looked down, suddenly sad. "He was a good man. Always treated the girls as well as the boys."

"Why did you come to Chicago?"

"After he died, my mother remarried and . . . well, perhaps you can guess. Not all men are equally good."

"No, they aren't." I carefully placed another coin and thought about my past, waiting like an unpopped blister in the future. "Leaving is probably better than the alternative."

"The alternative . . . I considered that." Aseel gave me an appraising look, and I wondered if we were both talking about murder. Then she winked and smiled. "But now I'm here, with my own show."

Sol poked his head into the dressing room, a fat cigar in his mouth. "I think you mean *my* show. It's almost preview time, Aseel."

She stood, face smoothed into professionalism again. "We're ready."

He clapped her on the shoulder with a grin. "Of course you are. Of course." Then he slipped her an extra two dollars. That was, as I learned, a typical Sol move—he took credit for the show, but he also made sure we knew that he appreciated the real force behind its success. His small gestures made a big difference. Nobody in the show ever questioned that Aseel was their boss.

I was making $1.50 per day, which was actually pretty good for a seamstress in this period. The political gains from suffrage were helping a new generation of ladies move out of their fathers' houses and into a few limited areas of work: garment-making, nursing, teaching, landscaping, and the arts. Newly founded colleges like UC Berkeley and the University of Chicago opened their doors to a fully coed student body.

Like many other unmarried women of the day, I rented a room in a boardinghouse—a three-story brick building on Dearborn Street that Soph recommended. Her consulting parlors were right down the hall, and that meant a steady trickle of visitors came past my door seeking spiritual guidance.

That night, I lay back on the hard cot in my room, read the *Tribune*, and eavesdropped on two well-dressed ladies gossiping about how Soph could cure anyone's broken heart with a prayer. An hour later, three women arrived from jobs in the garment district, their faces drawn and fingers raw. One was crying. "God have mercy on me, but I cannot have this child," she whispered, voice quavering. "He is not a good man. After what he did to me—" Her sobs came again, a seizure of melancholy. Another shushed her. "Soph can help. We will pray. She knows the secrets of angels." The third snorted. "You mean she knows a certain midwife."

As the afternoons blurred together, each one warmer than the last, I witnessed a nearly forgotten facet of feminine culture in the Gilded Age. These were Spiritualists, devotees of a mystical blend of paganism, occult beliefs, and Christianity that was embraced mostly by American women. Soph was one of Chicago's best-known practitioners.

Watching women demur to men in public and suffer the consequences of their abuse in private, it was hard to believe we were at a transition point in history when women's growing power could unsettle a long-established social order. But change is never linear or obvious. Often progress only becomes detectable when it inspires a desperate backlash. Which is why I was almost certain to find the Comstockers here and now, laying the groundwork for their malicious edit.

S I X

B E T H

Lizzy had the biggest car, so she always drove when we did things as a group. Which was good, because it turned out Heather had invited her cousin Hamid, and Soojin had brought that poseur Mark. As we drove to the movies, I wondered whether Mark still had scars from his unimpressive experiments with chest carving. And then I remembered with a nauseated jolt that we'd left Mark's best friend floating in Woodbridge Lake a couple months ago. Maybe I'd try to be nice to the guy for once.

The double bill at the Balboa Theater that night included *Total Recall*. As we piled into the stained pseudo-velvet seats in the balcony, I wound up between Lizzy and Hamid. I was a little annoyed at first, but it turned out that Hamid had seen *RoboCop* on video, and could actually string together a few sentences about it.

"I really liked how *RoboCop* had those advertisements and news propaganda bits." He turned to me and offered some of his popcorn. Hamid and Heather hung out sometimes, so we'd met before, but all I knew was that he was a senior who had gotten into UCLA.

"Yeah. I love movies that are violent and funny at the same time. The ads made it seem like *Total Recall* will be that way too. Plus it's the same director."

"Exactly! Paul Verhoeven is rad."

I'd rarely met anyone who cared that movies had directors, let alone that those directors might have something to do with the tone of the film. I hadn't really thought about it before, but Hamid was pretty cute. It wasn't his looks, which were perfectly fine but not particularly noteworthy—he had short black hair and one of those perfect golden-brown California tans that all of us wanted. The main thing was that I liked talking to him. We discussed our favorite directors until the lights went down, at which point I was definitely developing a crush.

We started holding hands around the point where Arnold Schwarzenegger's eyeballs pop out in the thin Martian atmosphere. It was one of those surreptitious moments in the dark, eyes carefully averted, that I'd experienced half a dozen times with other boys. Usually all that came of it was extra popcorn butter on my fingers and a few awkward glances once we'd returned to the light.

Not this time. During our post-movie excursion to the donut shop, Hamid managed to jam a folded napkin into my hand. Much later in the evening, alone in my room with headphones blasting Million Eyes, I peeked. There was a phone number. Below it, he'd written: "Get your ass to Mars. Or call me. Or both." Of course I called.

The following weekend, Hamid picked me up in a beat-up old sedan that was clearly a family hand-me-down. School was finally out for the summer and I'd spent the day listening to my mom on the phone signing me up for SAT prep classes. It was a relief to sit on the cracked seats with someone who had opinions about things other than my academic future.

"Air conditioning's broken. Sorry about that."

I didn't mind. Hot air blew in the open windows and the horizon was smeared with a dirty orange sunset. He'd installed a decent stereo, so I fiddled with the cassette player. A tape popped out with no label.

"What's this?"

"A mixtape Heather made for me. You'd probably like it."

He was right. Trouble for Nora filled the car with sound and we drove toward the beach.

"So what are you going to major in at UCLA?" I asked.

"I have no idea, honestly. I'm undeclared and I plan to keep it that way for as long as possible."

I was taken aback. Lizzy and I both planned to study geoscience, and spent a lot of time talking about how we'd organize our careers. Everything started with escaping from Irvine, of course, but usually ended in some remote Arctic region where we'd discover the secret of how life evolved.

"Isn't there something that you want to study? You could major in film."

He laughed bitterly. "My parents are paying for college. I'm not allowed to major in film."

"What do they want you to major in?"

"Pretty much either pre-med or business."

"That sucks."

He turned to me briefly with a lopsided smile, and for a moment he was so gorgeous that I lost the thread of my dark premonition that one day he'd be a depressed middle manager posting about cult movies on Usenet.

"What do you want to major in?"

"I'm going to be a geoscientist."

"Oh yeah? You going to travel through time?"

I rolled my eyes. "That's cultural geology. They only call it that because the Machines are found in rocks. I'm going to study actual geology. You know, like how the Earth was formed."

He laughed and sped off the freeway toward Balboa Beach. "I like you, Beth Cohen. I think you might be the coolest girl I've ever met."

Everything we did that evening was an excuse to have a long conversation. We talked about the artificiality of high school as we ate pizza; we talked about the movie *Wings of Desire* as we took off our shoes to feel the sand where it met water. Around us were the amplified noises of the Fun Zone—a mix of videogame zoinks, music from half a dozen speakers, and kids getting off on sugar and booze—but all of it was muffled by the retaining wall of our voices. Eventually we were silent again, holding hands in the dark and soaking up what remained of the day's heat as it radiated from the sand.

"Sometimes I think going to college is kind of like dying. You're this one kind of person, with all different interests, but then you have to cut those off and become somebody totally different." Hamid looked down as he spoke, digging a hole in the sand. I felt joined to him by mournfulness, plus the tragedy of how we were only now getting to know each other. He was about to disappear into a future neither of us could imagine.

Impulsively I ran my fingers through his hair, and it felt soft but also sad and profound and terrifying. And then, suddenly, it was scalding hot and urgent. Hamid turned to me and we were kissing, and also touching each other in a way that made my muscles tighten involuntarily. I was filled with an ache I'd only seen described in cheesy erotica they stocked in the "sexuality" section at Brentano's bookstore.

We paused and I whispered in his ear. "You are so beautiful." I had always wanted to say that to someone and mean it.

He looked into my eyes, his face serious. "So are you."

We stood up, arms wrapped around each other, bodies pressed together as closely as possible.

"We should probably go home."

"Yeah, we should."

As we kissed again, I wondered if what was happening between us meant anything. Maybe we would never do this again, or maybe we'd have some kind of John Hughes–style summer romance. Maybe we'd fall in love. We trudged back to the parking lot, which was mostly empty. Then we spent a while listening to music in the car and saying we should leave but instead figuring out how to configure the seats so that we could lie next to each other.

I wanted to kiss every part of him that I'd read was a good place to kiss: his neck, his eyelids, his chest, his stomach. Everything. Each time he returned my kisses, place by place, and I could feel the softness of his lips even in the parts of my body he wasn't touching. At a certain point it seemed like the most obvious thing to do was cover ourselves in a musty blanket from the back and take off all our clothes. I had never been naked with anyone like this before, for the sole purpose of exploration. It was like science.

As we fumbled toward what I'd been told would give us pleasure, I kept wondering what my body was supposed to be feeling. Intermittently I went numb. Images popped into my head whose origins I didn't want to remember. Angry hands between my legs. A voice that turned my name into a curse. Concentrating intensely, I reoriented to the sound of Hamid sighing and ran my hands down the shallow ravine of his spine. But I'd lost the thread of what we were doing. It was like watching a movie where you didn't get a bunch of the key references. Good—maybe very good—but also confusing.

Afterward we held each other, shaky and sweating and engrossed by conversation again.

"I guess I thought that would hurt more." I spoke into the curve of his neck, and could feel the cords of his muscles move before he shifted onto his elbow to look at me.

"Wait, why?"

"Well, because . . . you know, it usually hurts the first time for girls."

Hamid was startled. "You were a virgin? I thought . . . well, you don't act like one."

"What does a virgin act like?"

"I mean, you're one of Heather's punk friends. I thought you guys were all worldly." He laughed, and managed to look both adorable and embarrassed. "I guess that sounds stupid."

"I mean, I think I'm flattered?"

"I was a virgin too." He looked uncomfortable, then put on a mock pedagogical expression. "So, I guess that's welcome to adulthood, kids. I hope you're ready for the important responsibilities."

"I'm ready." I hugged him hard.

For the next several weeks, I divided my time between the crucial hours spent with Hamid and the irrelevant ones devoted to everything else.

Hamid and I became regulars at a restaurant in Woodbridge Mall called Knowlwood. It was elaborately decorated like an idealized 1950s house, complete with white picket fences, World War II paraphernalia, and flowery wallpaper. There were antique portraits of a white family on the walls, their cheeks and lips airbrushed into various shades of rosy pink. Every time we visited, I wondered who those people were.

I watched Hamid eat a pile of fries covered in melted cheese and bacon bits, debating whether to ask him what he was doing tomorrow. Would that seem weird? He hadn't called for a couple of days and I didn't want to seem needy. But then, before I could ask, he told me everything I wanted to know.

"So my entire family is going to Florida for a month." Hamid sighed and shook his head. "They are obsessed with Disney World. There's some new thing called Pleasure Island that my aunts and uncles say is the greatest resort ever built."

Reflexively, I put on my best movie preview voice. "It was a simple family vacation. They thought it would be paradise . . . but they wound up in HELL."

"Don't even get me started." Hamid shrugged in disgust. "It's going to be so boring. There will be nothing to do but play with my five-year-old cousins in the pool. Maybe Heather and I can go see some Disney movies if we're lucky."

I couldn't think of a good reply. There was a stopper made of doubt in my throat. I wanted to feel like none of this mattered, but I was starting to suspect it did.

Hamid called me that night. We talked for a while about the stupidity of Disney World, and how it was like wanting to take a vacation inside a plastic replica of a vacation. Then I tried to defend Disney on the basis of *Who Framed Roger Rabbit?* and *Tron*, and we wound up in a half-serious, half-giggling debate that reminded me of talking to Lizzy. It was nice to have a conversation with a guy who wasn't trying to impress me or snub me or worse. Then I thought about all the evenings we'd spent in his car with the reclining seats, and remembered how Hamid wasn't like Lizzy at all.

"I've had a lot of fun these past couple weeks." My heart pounded as I said it.

"Me too."

"We should hang out when you get back."

I could hear him moving around and maybe shutting a door. "Yeah, I want to. We'll be back in July."

He was infuriatingly casual about it. We'd lost our virginity to each other! It seemed like we should be saying something more profound, or romantic, or explicitly dirty. But I couldn't think of a way to get us there, without an extremely awkward detour. So I resorted to irony.

"Awesome. I'll be awaiting our rendezvous with excitement."

It turned out to be the right move. "Totally." He laughed, and then it was almost like I could hear him accumulating seriousness in the low hum of our phone connection. "I'm going to miss you."

Something was squirming in my chest like an alien. It felt good, but I also wanted it to stop. Part of me was glad I wouldn't have to see him again for a while.

"I'll miss you too. Send me the worst Disney postcards you can find."

"Challenge accepted."

I hung up with a smile on my face.

S E V E N

T E S S

'd been working at the Algerian Theater for two weeks when Aseel announced that we'd have a rare night off. She told the men they could take advantage of an offer from the Expo bosses, who promised bonus pay to laborers willing to work through the night on construction. The women filtered out to Cairo Street, where dozens of Egyptian entertainers were cooking up real dinners in their fake homes.

I was on my way to the brand-new industrial wonder known as the L train when Aseel caught up to me. "What are you doing tonight?"

"I'm going home to get some supper."

"Soph and I are going to see Lucy Parsons speak. Do you want to come?"

I was torn. Like anyone who studied this period, I knew the anarchist Lucy Parsons. In just over a decade, she would found the Industrial Workers of the World, known to cowering bosses and idealistic unionists as the IWW or Wobblies. Seeing her in person would be a thrill. But it would also, inevitably, be a disappointment. I'd learned that the hard way, after meeting some of my heroes among the anarchists of New York a decade before. I really hoped Aseel and Soph weren't entangled in the sectarian garbage fire of this decade's socialist politics.

"Are you interested in joining Parsons's movement?" I asked.

Aseel shrugged. "I like women who can make an auditorium full of men listen to them. I'll attend to what she has to say before deciding."

I laughed. "That's a good reason to see Lucy Parsons." I agreed to come along, and we linked arms as we strolled. If nothing else, I could use this lecture as a chance to gather legit academic data about the founder of the IWW. We had to maintain the facade of the Applied Cultural Geology Group, and I couldn't exactly return to 2022 and report to our funders that all I'd done was wage an edit war.

The lecture hall was packed with Chicago's finest rabble-rousers and intellectuals. Lucy Parsons was one of the most famous anarchists in the country, and her speeches were legendary. Her writing burned up the pages of *The Alarm*, and she'd founded a new anarchist publication here in Chicago called simply *Freedom*. She was always getting arrested for her articles, especially after publishing a simple recipe for TNT because she believed everyone should know how to make bombs. A few years earlier, the state had executed her husband for his role as a supposed bomb-thrower during the Haymarket Riot. Parsons suffered for the cause, and radicals loved her for it. Besides, anarchy was having a moment. Banks were closing around the world, unemployment was spiking, and the Chicago steelworkers had led a successful strike. Parsons and her comrades seemed to have the right medicine for an ailing nation.

Soph met me and Aseel in the back of the hall, where we added our cigarette smoke to the general haze overhead. When Parsons strode onto the stage, plain black dress buttoned to her throat, her charisma was palpable. She didn't wait for an introduction, and she gave no preamble. Even without a microphone, we could hear her voice booming: "I AM AN ANARCHIST!" She pushed a lock of tight curls behind her ear and continued, her tan face luminous with determination. "Today we are celebrating a victory for labor in this city. Boss Burnham has agreed to a minimum wage for Expo workers, and is granting overtime pay on nights and Sundays. We forced him to agree to overtime on Labor Day!"

Cheers erupted, and I looked around at the room. Workers still reeking of the stockyards rubbed elbows with tweedy professors. New Women passed flasks of gin to governesses. A lady in a fancy French dress took rapid shorthand notes in her stenographer's notebook.

"I am an anarchist, but that does not mean I carry bombs. I carry something the capitalists and politicians know is far more dangerous. A vision of freedom from their rule! Freedom from life on the street, from starvation, and from work that is meaner than slavery!" Parsons passed her level gaze over the whole room, taking our measure, absorbing the cries of her fans. "We cannot stop with this one victory. The city of Chicago murders anarchists! We need to fight for justice now more than ever!"

Watching her reminded me of what I felt when I was at that Grape Ape show. Cheers and chants erupted all over the hall, and I could feel a new sense of purpose flooding through all of us—including the cynics like me. Maybe I'd been wrong to say that Parsons wasn't helping to build a better world. She wasn't perfect, as I knew well from working with the anarchist movement. But without her call for direct action, my present day might have looked very different. When the politicians ignored us, and the capitalists strangled us, we could always link arms like the IWW and refuse to comply.

After the lecture, Soph fanned herself. "Well! I need a drink after that."

"Let's go to your parlors!" Aseel jumped up and down. I almost did too. I hadn't been inside Soph's rooms yet, and I was dying to see her Spiritualist headquarters. It was like that high school feeling of heading to a friend's house when her parents were gone, so we could drink their bad liqueur and listen to music. Then I remembered my last look at high school life, blood dribbling from that old car, and was consumed with regret.

We passed the door to my room like all the other Spiritualists did, and entered Soph's place through a parlor with some wooden chairs and a coat rack. Double pocket doors opened into a high-ceilinged living room—though temporal locals would probably call it a sitting room. I was surprised to discover it wasn't jammed with Ouija boards and crystal balls atop velvet draperies. Instead there were overstuffed pillows, fainting couches, chairs, sofas, and an archipelago of coffee tables stretching across a thick fur rug. Streetlamps outside provided dim illumination through two ample window seats, also piled with fur and pillows.

"Let me light the lamps and get some glasses." Soph put a match beneath a couple of glass fixtures on the wall and slowly the rest of the room came into view. There were several display nooks, clearly designed for knickknacks, which Soph had crammed with books and pamphlets. Two carved wooden vanities were shoved together against one wall; one was repurposed as a writing desk, and the other held dozens of tiny glass bottles, pocket mirrors, and small boxes inlaid with ivory. Pulling a key ring from a pocket in her skirts, Soph knelt to unlock a cabinet in the latter, from which she withdrew three glasses and a bottle of gin. A lock of blond hair slid from her updo, and it briefly curled into the shape of a question mark before settling on her shoulder.

"Please don't tell me you want sherry." Soph gave me a sideways glance.

"Fuck no. I love gin."

"Thank the goddess for that!" Soph laughed as she poured generous slugs and raised her glass in a toast. "Here's to freedom." We clinked and drank. I thought of the fancy gin bar in my neighborhood back home, where all the Silver Lake hipsters went to sample the spirits made with locally sourced juniper. On weekend afternoons, I sometimes met Anita there to talk about research, politics, and everything else in our lives. As I tasted Soph's gin, I had a vivid recollection of Anita's "no more fucks to give" face as we dissected the motives of that douchebag on the geoscience department hiring committee, whining about how diversity had gone too far. What I loved most about Anita was the stubborn way she refused to describe setbacks as failures. Several years ago, Berenice was denied tenure because, according to the committee, they couldn't count her postdoctoral work because it had been written under her deadname. We'd gone out drinking to commiserate with her. "Every edit is an invitation to edit again," Anita said. "The shitballs will never win as long as history can be revisited." We'd been talking about the timeline, but it gave Berenice an idea. She sued the tenure committee for discrimination, and now she was the first tenured trans woman in our department. At least, she had been. Fuck. I thought of Enid, who had sworn at our last meeting to save Berenice. Had she succeeded? Was Anita drinking with her and Berenice upstream? Suddenly, I missed my friends so much that my chest ached.

I gulped the rest of my drink and set the glass down more forcefully than I intended. I needed to find out where my new friends stood. Were we merely drinking buddies, or were we going to get serious and do some edits? "So what do you ladies think about Lucy Parsons? I thought she gave a damn good show."

"I admire her. But I think there are a lot of struggles that she ignores." Soph gestured around her parlors. "We need liberation from the government in our homes, too."

Aseel nodded and poured us another round. "Back in Arizona, I heard about Lucy Parsons from some folks who knew her in Texas. They said she used to be a slave. But she won't admit it! If anyone asks, she says she has 'a touch of Spanish blood.' She's passing as white. I don't understand how she can say she wants freedom for all when she won't even admit what her real background is. I mean, a lot of people would benefit from seeing a colored lady telling white men what to do."

"Are you talking about Sol?" Soph laughed.

"No!" Aseel frowned. "I mean, yes, but also all of them. All the men."

"It's not exclusively men who are the problem, though," Soph replied. "There was a letter in the *Tribune* from the Lady Managers Association about how it was a mistake to give former slaves the vote along with white women. I guess their candidate is running on some kind of de-abolitionist platform."

"Why doesn't Lucy Parsons talk about that white suffragette crap?" Aseel took another drink and looked like she was going to smash something. "Thank goodness for Senator Tubman."

I raised my glass. "Cheers to Senator Harriet Tubman!" We all drank another shot, and I was suffused with drunken love for these two women, fighting alongside the Daughters of Harriet without realizing it. But I wasn't here to revel in intersectional sisterhood across the centuries. I was too old to spend years in the past, tentatively building a network of sympathetic allies. I needed to find out right now whether Aseel and Soph were on my side. And the only way to find out was to gossip.

"You know who is absolutely the worst? Emma Goldman. I worked with her in New York a few years ago, and she was . . ." I searched for the right words but was too tipsy for nuance. "She was an asshole. Love her writing, she's a big inspiration to me, but what a mess. She's obsessed with using violence to change history. Remember that whole thing where she sent her boyfriend to kill Henry Frick? I mean, first of all, that was a terrible idea. The press was already destroying Frick for sending Pinkertons to kill strikers. We were winning! And *then* she decides it's time to send her completely useless boyfriend to kill him? On top of everything *else* that's awful about that idea, she couldn't do it herself?"

"I read about that in the paper." Aseel made a face. "Didn't he shoot Frick twice, and then stab him? And he still couldn't kill the guy? What was his name again? Emma's boyfriend?"

"Sasha Berkman." I smacked my forehead as I thought about him again. A hot intellectual bad boy—though definitely erring on the side of hotness rather than intellect. "A couple of strikers actually saved Frick from Sasha. That's how bad it was. Our *own people* protected a murdering boss from being murdered."

Soph nodded sympathetically. "I like her ideas about free love, but violence is always the wrong way forward."

That gave me a pang of relief. I couldn't team up with people who liked to watch things burn. Unless those things happened to be cigarettes. Soph extracted some tobacco and papers unsteadily from a drawer and returned to flop on a pillow. We smoked silently for a minute, looking up at the wriggling rings of light cast on the ceiling from the lamps' glass globes.

"Nobody hates Emma Goldman more than Lucy Parsons. And vice versa." Aseel's tone hung between annoyed and amused. "Their war is endlessly nauseating." It seemed like she'd been following this particular political train wreck closely, but didn't like the infighting. That was a good sign too.

"Regale us with all the sordid details, my dear." Soph rolled over on her back, buoyed by pillows, and looked at us upside-down.

Aseel swirled her gin and batted her eyelids theatrically. "Well. So, a few years ago, Emma started publishing articles about how women should be permitted to enjoy sex the same way men do. You know all about that, darling." She winked at Soph and I felt a twinge of jealousy. Travel is always a lonely business, and I wanted to be a part of their easy rapport. I wanted to trust them. But what would they say if they knew who I really was?

Aseel continued her story. "After a while, that Puritanical dingus Anthony Comstock got Emma arrested on indecency charges. So Emma demanded that Lucy write a testimonial supporting her as a fellow anarchist. But *instead* Lucy published an article about how sex shouldn't be part of the revolution, and that free love is a distraction from the fight for workers' rights. Of course Emma had to write her *own* article about how Lucy has lost sight of the true nature of liberty. I couldn't be bothered to read the awful thing Lucy wrote in reply, and what Emma wrote after that."

That sounded like Emma. After years of working with her, I knew she was always surrounded by a blast radius of toxic drama. She was doing good work. But she also loved to pit her friends and followers against each other, demanding unreasonable loyalty, or seducing people then going cold. She played so many power games in her personal life that it was hard for me to believe she truly wanted to abolish power structures.

Soph leaned on her elbows and flicked ash onto a dainty shell plate. "Maybe Lucy enjoys the publicity because she wants more fame. She's probably never had to struggle for anything in her life."

"I tell you, she *was a slave*!" Aseel banged a hand on the table, dark eyes narrowed. "She's struggled!"

"It's well documented that she was a slave," I said. Both women stared at me. That's when I realized my mistake. The evidence had only come to light a few years ago, in my present.

"What do you mean, well documented?" Aseel had a knife in her voice. "Documented by whom?"

"Well, I . . . I guess . . . scholars?"

"How do you know that?" Soph was wary. "What did you do after working with the anarchists?"

I thought about our conversation up to this point. Both women were clearly open to radical ideas, but they had a healthy skepticism, too. They were against violence and sectarian drama. So I decided to take the risk. "I'm going to level with you. I'm a traveler. In my present, scholars have discovered strong evidence that Lucy Parsons was African American. A former slave."

"African . . . American?" Aseel tried out the unfamiliar term.

"People study women in your time?" Soph's face lit up.

"Yeah. In fact . . . I'm on a mission for a group of people who research women's history." I really hoped that I wasn't making a giant mistake. But if I wanted their help, they needed to know.

Soph sat up, smoothed her collar, and poured another round. "Okay. Tell us everything."

I cleared my throat and felt a nervous tingle. "I'm a geoscientist, and I'm trying to make an edit in the timeline." Aseel and Soph gaped at me. What I'd admitted was taboo, even among subversives. The Chronology Academy hadn't been founded yet, but deliberately editing history could still get you banned from the Machines.

I continued. "I can't tell you much, but I've witnessed men—travelers—trying to revert women's rights to education. Trying to control our bodies, sometimes lethally. I'm trying to stop them." I thought of Berenice again, and quelled a rush of terror. "I came here because they seem to be taking inspiration from Anthony Comstock. I don't think he's their leader, but he's some kind of . . . historical beacon."

They glanced at each other. Soph toyed with her glass but didn't drink. "Comstock arrested my friend Penny in New York. He . . . he dragged her to the police station when she was in the middle of an abortion, along with her patient. They let the poor woman die, bleeding on the floor of the police station. Penny committed suicide rather than go to prison."

I was shocked. "I heard him give a speech in New York where he bragged about how many abortionists he'd driven to suicide. But I thought he was saying it for effect."

Soph shook her head and I realized she was on the brink of tears. "I'm so sorry," I said gently. "That's why I want to make this edit and stop the men who follow him."

Aseel looked grim. "That's a tall order. Comstock is a special agent for the post office. He can snoop on anyone's mail and have them arrested if he thinks it's obscene or indecent."

I nodded. "He's looking for newsletters exactly like the ones you write, Soph. He's gotten some courts to agree that information about birth control is obscene."

"I know." Soph walked to the window, looking mournfully into the empty street. "I've worked very hard to stay out of his way."

"How do you plan to make this edit?" Aseel demanded.

I desperately wanted to spill the whole plan, but I'd already broken too many rules. Revealing the future was against the law in most time periods. It was also a form of cruelty, a theft of people's agency. Of course some travelers did it, but I wasn't going to stoop that low. I needed a way to explain myself without causing harm.

"Comstock is making laws now that will last generations. But we can't stop him directly. I've already tried that, with the anarchists. We have to taint his ideas somehow, make them seem repugnant to the general public."

Aseel cleared her throat in the same way she did at the theater when she was running out of patience. "Very well, but as I asked before, how are you going to do that *specifically*?"

"Comstock is trying to branch out beyond New York and go national with his crusade. That much he's already announced in various places. It's a matter of public record. You can see why the theaters of the Midway are something he'd be very, very interested in." That was as much as I could tell them, without veering into dangerous territory.

"He's already shut down some theaters in New York, right?" Aseel asked.

"He has. And some bars. But the Midway could turn the tide back against him. If I can interfere with his work there, I think I can make the edit. But I can't do it alone."

Soph's face had gone from somber to mischievous. "I'm in."

"You are?" Aseel was dubious. "I mean, I like you, Tess. But I barely know you."

"I understand that. We don't have to do anything yet. All I ask is that you keep your eyes open and watch for any hints that Comstock or his YMCA boys might be coming."

Aseel raised her glass. "Okay. I'll drink to that."

We all drank, but a mood of sobriety had overtaken us and it wasn't long before we retired to bed.

EIGHT

BETH

A couple of postcards came, but Hamid didn't write much on them. One featured a bizarre 1930s incarnation of Mickey and Minnie, and another was a 1970s "family photo" of Donald Duck's more obscure relatives. I grabbed them out of the mail before my parents did, tucking them into my SAT study guide between the sections on multiple choice guessing and algebra review. The only people who knew about me and Hamid were my friends, and I planned to keep it that way.

I got Hamid's final postcard on a scalding day when the air conditioner filled our house with an otherworldly whistling noise. In a supposedly happy scene from Disney World, people dressed as the Seven Dwarfs ogled Snow White in an especially creepy way. I flipped it over to read his note: "See you after July 15 I hope." That was a week away. I immediately ran to the bathroom and threw up. The alien was back in my chest, and I had to get it out.

Or maybe something else was going on. The next morning, I threw up again. On the third day of hurling, I started to panic. My period was late and I was barfing for no reason. I kept thinking about a movie we'd watched in seventh-grade health class about a girl who died from a coat hanger abortion. The teacher gave us one of those unconvincing "I'm your buddy" speeches about how abstinence was the only way to prevent pregnancy. I could still hear his voice in my mind as he dispensed this wisdom. "There's one simple rule: Wait. Until. You. Are. Married." He punctuated each word by smacking a fist into his open hand. "That's why sex education is so simple. Because there's only one rule. See how easy that is?" He grinned right at me and winked. I think it was supposed to be fatherly, but it made me nauseous.

Which brought me back to the present, where I was hanging on the edge of the toilet, gagging and gasping and telling myself that I couldn't be pregnant. What was I supposed to do? I could hear my mom talking on the phone downstairs—she spent her entire summer vacation on the phone—and my dad was at the shop. I needed to talk to Lizzy right now.

Dropping my bike in Lizzy's front yard was already making me feel better. This was normal. I was going to my friend's house. I was not about to die.

But when I rang the doorbell, I realized my hands were shaking, and I wasn't sure I'd be able to talk. Luckily I didn't have to say anything when Lizzy opened the door.

"Holy shit, Beth. What the fuck is wrong?"

I must have looked pretty terrible, and suddenly I was crying so hard I could barely stand. Lizzy's eyes widened and she reached out to grab me in a hug. "Come up to my room."

I caught a brief glimpse of her mother down the hall, reading something at the kitchen table, then we were mounting the stairs with their mashed-down shag carpet. This pathway was as familiar to me as the one to my own room. Lizzy shut the door and we sat on the floor, our backs against the fluffy bulk of her bed. She put on

the Grape Ape EP *Terrorist State* while my hiccups subsided. Their
words rained down on my head like missiles:

> IT'S TIME TO TAKE CONTROL
> ONLY WE CAN STOP THE PAIN
> THIS WAR IS KILLING EVERYONE
> IT'S TIME TO MAKE A CHANGE

Lizzy put her arm around me and I thought about how this room
had been our laboratory when we were ten. We spent that whole
summer pretending to be geoscientists, keeping notebooks full of ob-
servations about the rocks we found in the neighborhood.

"Do you still have those boxes of rocks we collected when we
were kids?" My voice sounded shaky and strange.

"Maybe? I'm pretty sure my mom kept them for a little while."
She gave my shoulder a squeeze. "Are you going to tell me what's
wrong?"

"I think I might be pregnant."

"Oh shit. Shit, Beth. What the fuck. Didn't you use a condom?"

"I mean, mostly. But then there was one time . . . but he pulled
out before . . ." I put my face in my hands.

Lizzy didn't say anything for a long time and I stared into the
darkness of my eyelids as Glorious Garcia yelled about melting every
gun in the world.

"You know that's bullshit, right? Pulling out is not . . . it
doesn't . . . I mean, you are my best friend in the universe, but this is
not an unlucky edit. That was really stupid, Beth."

"I know." I mashed fingers into my eyes until I saw red spots. "I
know, I know!"

"Does Hamid know?"

"No! I don't want to tell him. I don't even know if I want to see
him again." As I spoke, I finally looked at Lizzy and realized it was

true. My so-called relationship with Hamid could hardly sustain a month of one-sentence postcards, let alone something like this.

"Well, it's partly his fault."

"I guess so. But I barely know him. I don't know what he would do, anyway. It's not like he's some kind of magical abortionist." I started crying again. "He's just some . . . idiotic guy."

"He's definitely an idiot." Lizzy shook her head. Then she said the very last thing I would have expected. "We should talk to my mom."

I'd grown up with Lizzy, but I'd never thought of her mom as somebody we could talk to about anything more serious than what we wanted for dessert. She was one of those vaguely liberal parents who'd told me to call her Jenny instead of Mrs. Berman, her job involved a lot of travel, and that was roughly all I knew about her. When we found her downstairs, still reading, I noticed that she seemed older than when I'd last seen her a couple of weeks ago. Maybe she was tired.

"Mom, we need to talk to you about something private."

She looked up, her faint smile fading into concern. "What's going on?"

We sat down on the other side of the table and I looked helplessly at Lizzy. I had no idea what to say.

"Beth thinks she might be pregnant."

My cheeks burned and I stared at my hands. I couldn't believe Lizzy was saying it out loud like it was no big deal. But her mom— Jenny—seemed totally unfazed. She put a hand on my arm comfortingly.

"Okay, let's think. Beth, are you sure? Have you done a pregnancy test?"

I shook my head and felt more tears blobbing up in my eyes.

One trip to the pharmacy and two hours later, it was official. The blue stripe meant I was definitely pregnant. My mother would have been spiraling into total meltdown, hurling accusations, but Jenny gave my arm another pat and looked sympathetic.

"I told Lizzy that she should come to me if something like this happened because I know a doctor who can help. Do you understand what I'm talking about?"

I stared at her, shredded by panic and hope. "Do you mean . . . abortion? What kind of doctor does that?"

"I met him through a friend, when I needed help." Jenny and Lizzy glanced at each other, and for a second I could see the same lines in their faces. "He's a regular family doctor who has a little business on the side. It's all done in his office after hours."

Lizzy put her hand on my other arm. "Do you want us to help you?"

I thought of all the times my father had told me I was doing the wrong thing. I thought about how he flipped rules around arbitrarily and invented new ways for me to disobey him. And then I thought, dizzily, that I was not in my father's house.

"Yes. I want an abortion."

"Okay. Let me make some calls. The sooner you do it, the easier it will be." Jenny headed for the phone. For the first time, it occurred to me that Lizzy hadn't been born a decider. She'd learned it from her mother.

NINE

TESS

The morning after I came out to Aseel and Soph as a traveler, I navigated between a headache, yet another carriage full of ostriches, and monumental chunks of Ferris wheel to reach the Algerian Theater. Sol was addressing the whole troupe when I arrived, while Aseel translated into Arabic. With opening day right around the corner, he'd arranged for a special preview show at the local press club for that afternoon. Several of the dancers would perform, with Aseel's Lady Asenath routine as the main attraction.

"What? This afternoon?" Aseel whirled on Sol, glowering. A few of the dancers cracked smiles. They were always amused when Aseel fought with Sol.

To his credit, he looked sheepish. "That's the only time they would give us. But a lot of press are coming! We should get lots of notices."

There was nothing to be done but to make the best of it. Aseel swung into action. "Salina, Amina, and Bertha, come with me. We'll figure out something. And you too, Tess. We need our costumes to look perfect."

I followed them to the dressing room. As I sewed furiously, Aseel went over their set. Each dancer would do her number while the others watched, and of course Lady Asenath would be the climactic act. She also dispensed some advice. "Remember to bring a veil to rip off your face at some point. Those white gentlemen love it."

Salina looked dubious. "A veil? How does that fit into my dance?"

"I trust you can make it work."

Salina shrugged and looked at me. "You got a veil?"

"I can make one for you right now." I looked over at Aseel. "You want something to cover her nose and mouth? Or her whole head?"

"Nose and mouth is fine."

"Nothing on my head with it? Who wears a veil over her nose and mouth without a head covering?" Salina threw up her arms.

Aseel rolled her eyes. "Look, I know. But trust me. They will eat it up."

Sol brought us in a carriage to the press club, where we found Soph pacing back and forth outside. She was fuming. "They won't let me in, despite my press credentials!"

"Come with us, and I'll get you in." Aseel crooked her finger for Soph to follow.

When we reached the entrance, the doorman scowled. "This is a men's club. She can't come in."

"I'm press, sir! It is a *press* club." Soph's pale cheeks had gone red and her hair was coming undone.

Aseel stepped forward. "She's with us. We're the reason why everyone is here." And with that, she swung the dark wool coat off her shoulders to reveal her *danse du ventre* costume, with its nearly transparent chemise and ropes of beads shimmering over the generous curve of her belly.

"What . . . what . . . are you . . . Lady Asenath?"

"I am. And we're going inside for our press conference."

The man gaped.

I wondered what made him gaze at her like that. She was beautiful, but not in this era's conventional sense—she fit no Gilded Age ideal with her brown skin and thick waist. Was he rocked by moral indignation? Titillated by the idea of a live-action French postcard? Whatever it was, she forced him to look beyond the phantasm his desire conjured. She radiated authority. Despite all evidence to the contrary, Aseel took it for granted that men would do what she said. And it worked. In the face of her supreme certainty, the doorman stood aside.

"Why, thank you, sir." Aseel gave a curtsy that made her look even more regal. "I do hope you'll come visit us on the Midway."

Soph sailed in after us, the row over her credentials completely forgotten.

The setup was not ideal. Some of the younger press men had cleared a space along one wall of the smoky room, arranging over-stuffed chairs and heavy tables in a haphazard imitation of cabaret seating. We had no dressing room, so the dancers retreated to a sofa in the corner to shed their coats and fix their veils in place. All of them wore beaded belts and tassels over the puff of their long skirts, cinched beneath the swell of their stomach muscles. Their little vests were basically push-up bras adorned with all the gold thread and coins I could muster. Though the effect was diminished somewhat by their modesty camisoles, which covered them from neck to el-bows, we all knew it was racy enough to inspire headlines. That's why we were here.

Sol gave a brief preamble, explaining to the assembled men that in his humble opinion, as director of the Midway, the dancers of the Algerian Theater were going to be the most impressive and aston-ishing attraction anyone had ever seen. He talked about how these dances originated with the Berbers of the Maghreb, and would ed-ucate Americans about the enchantments of other cultures. As he spoke, I could see Soph writing swiftly in shorthand, nodding as Sol thanked each of the dancers by name. She'd found a seat next to an elderly man with hamster-sized muttonchops, who kept glancing at her as if she were a radish come inexplicably and irritatingly to life. I did some final adjustments on Amina's skirts and then withdrew further into the corner, where I could watch everyone's reactions to the show.

Bertha went first, walking daintily to the center of the room, practically tiptoeing in her incongruous, Western-style slippers. She flitted through a pantomime routine, waving handkerchiefs as she pretended to be a lady fretting over her toilette. Then came Amina and Salina, who did a short version of the *danse du ventre*, then tore their veils off with comical enthusiasm. It wasn't part of the traditional dance at all, but Aseel was right. When the women's round cheeks and rouged lips were revealed, some of the men gasped audibly and there was a general shuffling of notepads. Meanwhile, Aseel was whispering furiously to Sol, pointing at a dusty pianoforte in the corner. I knew immediately what she was getting at. They needed music. Desperately.

"For the act you've been waiting for . . . Lady Asenath . . . I'll be providing some music." Sol sounded uncertain, but the press men moved chairs out of his way so he could sit at the instrument. Aseel made a "go go" gesture with her hands and Sol looked pensive for a moment, then began to pluck out a simple tune.

Was I going crazy, or was he playing a Ke$ha song? I bobbed my head and tried to recall the lyrics to "Take It Off," until they blurred in my mind with the lyrics to a song we sang as children: "There's a place in France where the women wear no pants . . ." I couldn't believe it. Had Sol Bloom invented a tune that would last for generations, and become synonymous with both strippers and shitty Orientalist tropes? I pondered. More likely, he was playing a variation on a tune that some anonymous keyboard-tickler had written. Still, he was transplanting it into a new context. I was actually here for the origin of a meme. This was the kind of thing that got you published in *Nature*.

But as soon as Aseel stepped into the middle of the room, my thoughts of academic fame evaporated. She stood completely still, head down, slowly lifting her arms to wield the clashing finger cymbals on her hands. As she raised her bare face—no veils for Lady Asenath—her shoulders started to move with the music. She shivered and stopped, shivered and stopped, her tassels flashing in and out of her skirts like fish in sunlit water. Soph stopped writing and watched in open admiration, her lips parted. Many of the men wore the same expression.

When Aseel began to undulate, her necklaces ringing, she made the room hers. Her body pulsed like an artery. She barely moved her feet, and yet she embodied a motion more fluid and frenetic than anything a ballerina could evoke with whirls and kicks. As the music reached a crescendo, so too did the rolling waves of her muscles, rippling down her midriff into the trembling layers of her skirts. There was something sexual about it, but not in the kittenish, saucy-ironic style these men had seen in burlesque shows. This was a body that would resist them if they dared to approach it. She swayed and flexed and showed her strength.

From the back of the room there was a loud bang and the sound of a scuffle. Three men were overturning chairs, while others were trying to restrain them. As Aseel delivered a final clash of her cymbals, one of the agitated men stood up on a table and began to yell.

"This is evil, Satanic filth! These foul sluts are nothing more than savage beasts! Send them back to the dark country that spawned them!"

Then his buddy jumped up next to him, and my heart almost exploded. It was the shitbag from the Grape Ape concert—the Comstocker, older now, his face partly obscured by a beard shot with gray. "You are upstanding men! Do you want this vile obscenity to sicken the minds and bodies of every innocent who visits the Midway?"

There were shouts as the press men scrambled to pull the Comstockers off their perch. But they wouldn't shut up. "We will put a stop to this! Mark my words!"

The third man, young with slicked-back hair, waved a rope that he'd coiled into a noose. "Will you let a Jew and his black bitches *lead you to hell*?" Then he ran at Salina, dumping a can of machine oil over her head before we could stop him. She screamed as the reeking black fluid ran down her face and stained her chemise. Sol raced to drape her in his jacket and I grabbed some spare fabric to clean her up.

The room degenerated into chaos, and cries of "Stand down, man!" mingled with further ranting from the Comstockers, as they were dragged to the door. As I helped Salina into another chemise in the corner, I heard Soph's unmistakable soprano above the baritone din. "The Devil take you!" she screamed. "There is no goodness left in your putrid souls!"

A group of press men shoved the Comstockers into the street and Aseel appeared at my side. She was utterly calm, and said something quietly to Salina that made the weeping woman break into a shaky smile. Then Aseel turned to me, her lips thinned with rage. With a fierce yank on my shoulder, she pulled me close enough to hear her jagged whisper. "What you talked about last night? I'm in. We are going to bring those men low."

Before I could reply, Sol took to the center of the room and waved his hands to quiet everyone down. "Chicago is a great city! A city of progress and industry! We don't need yesterday's moralists to tell us what's right and wrong. We can see for ourselves, and judge for ourselves. I hope you gentlemen learned something from the show." Then he winked. "And maybe you had a little fun too, before that ruckus. Remember, the Algerian Theater is right next to Cairo Street, below the great Ferris wheel! You can see more of this beautiful, secret tradition for only two bits! Show opens on May first!"

And with that, he hustled us back to the carriage waiting outside. I had never seen Sol upset before, so I couldn't be certain that's what I was witnessing now. He kept up the jolly patter as we rode back to the Midway, complimenting the women on their performances, and giving each of us an extra dollar for our trouble. Still, I thought I saw him wince a few times. When we got out of the carriage, he told the driver to take him straight to his favorite club for a drink.

Aseel looked thoughtful as he drove away. "You know he makes the same salary as the president? But they still call him 'Jew' instead of Sol Bloom. Kind of makes me feel bad for him."

"Yeah."

I thought of my father reading the Haggadah at Passover, letting me ask the Four Questions for the first time. I stumbled over the unfamiliar word "reclining," and my grandfather gently corrected me. As a kid in the liberal 1970s, I had no way to understand how much anti-Semitic shit they'd eaten in their lives. Of course, there were things about me that they would never understand either.

T E N

B E T H

It had been a week since I took the home pregnancy test, and three days since Hamid said he'd be home. He hadn't called yet, which was a bitter kind of relief. I didn't want to tell him anything about my plans with Lizzy and her mom Jenny, but maybe if he'd called I'd have changed my mind.

I told my parents I was sleeping over at Lizzy's house, so they suspected nothing when Jenny and Lizzy picked me up. It wasn't a complete lie, of course: I would be staying with the Bermans that night. I left out the part where we'd be driving to Garden Grove for an off-the-books doctor's appointment, paid for with a year's worth of my saved allowance.

I kept having panic flashes as Jenny drove. I was going to die. My parents would find out. A fucked-up larva covered in teeth and eyes would squirm its way out of my womb and eat the world.

The doctor was a kinetic, pale man with matted hair on every part of his body except his head. It was weird to see him sitting in the receptionist's chair when we walked in. "You can call me Bob, because we don't stand on ceremony after hours." He reached out to shake my hand, then grabbed my fingers and turned the gesture into a little bow. "Milady. Welcome to my humble chamber." I could see bright lights in the office behind him, and a vinyl-covered exam table with metal stirrups attached.

Jenny hugged me. "We'll be right out here, honey." She and Lizzy sat in the waiting room while I followed Bob to the back.

He kept up the mock chivalry routine, twirling his hand in the air as he gestured for me to sit on the table. "You're quite a young one. How old are you?"

"Seventeen."

"Naughty, naughty girl!" He waved an admonishing finger at me. "Take off all your clothes and I'll be back with my instruments."

I wasn't sure why I needed to take everything off, but I also didn't think it was a good idea to ask questions. There was no hospital gown for me to put on, so I lay bare on the sticky plastic of the table, heels in stirrups and knees pressed firmly together. Hamid was probably back at home in Irvine right now, having a nice dinner with his family.

Bob erupted back into the room, trailing a device on wheels that I couldn't properly see. After craning my neck, I thought maybe it looked like one of those hair dryers my mom used at the salon, with the silver helmet that blew hot air evenly all over her head.

"I've got some good news and some bad news for you, naughty girl." Bob adjusted a lamp nearby, and suddenly I could feel heat against my legs. "The good news is that this is a state-of-the-art machine that's sort of like a vacuum, and it does the job really quickly. The bad news is that you might feel a little cramp. Can you handle a little cramp?"

"Sure."

"Okay, open wide." He slid a hand between my knees and I opened my legs.

Suddenly I felt his gloved hand inside me, covered in a cold slime. He grunted, withdrew, and pushed in the speculum. I could hear and feel its metal paddles clicking as he cranked me open until I thought I would rip. I focused my eyes on the ceiling, covered in white tiles, and tried to decide whether they were fissured or perforated. Then I heard rattling and what I thought was the low hum of a motor. Without warning, my abdomen wrenched with pain worse than anything I could have imagined.

I clenched my teeth and fists and stared at a place in the ceiling where a water leak had left a cloudy brown stain behind. I wondered if it was normal to feel like a giant lamprey was chewing and digesting my guts.

"Almost done." Bob sounded distracted. "It's not so bad, right? Some women love it. One of my patients had an orgasm when she was giving birth." He paused, as if pondering. "Maybe one day you will too, when you find the right boy."

Everything hurt so much that his words were just sounds that meant time was passing. Soon it would be over.

When he withdrew, it felt like I was giving birth to a machine. All the mechanical parts slimed out, and I was nothing but scraped tissue and diminishing anguish. I could feel warm liquid oozing out of me, like when I got my period.

"You'll be spotting for a few days, but if it starts to bleed a lot go to the emergency room right away." Bob scooted his chair around the table so I could see his face. For the first time, he sounded like a normal doctor. "Also, no sex for a couple of weeks. That's it. Feel free to go when you're ready."

He wadded up his gloves and threw them in a silver trash can, the kind that pops open like a mouth when you step on its foot. Then he jangled out of the room, trailing the vacuum cleaner. I sat up slowly and another warm lump dribbled out of me onto the plastic table, creating a heart-shaped puddle of lubricant and blood. I couldn't see any tissues or cloths for cleaning up, and finally hobbled to the sink to grab some rough paper towels. I washed up as best I could, and jammed some fresh paper towels into the crotch of my underwear just in case.

When I stumbled out of Bob's office, I suddenly needed to throw up. The only place to do it was in the receptionist's trash can, so he wound up with two samples of my bodily fluid that day. I didn't mind leaving the smell there for him to find.

Lizzy and Jenny jumped up as soon as I came back to the waiting room. They put their arms around me and we walked out together like that, squashing through the doorframe three abreast. It was awkward and warm and safe. I felt shaky when we got into the car, but my bleeding had slowed to a mild seep. I really was going to be all right.

The radio blipped to life as Jenny started the car, and that shitty Don Henley song "All She Wants to Do Is Dance" came on. I thought I was going to scream, but instead I started talking, my words coming faster than outrage.

"I *hate* this song. Because everybody thinks it's about a woman who is carefree and beautiful, but it's actually about how Don Henley goes to some war-torn country and meets this woman who is in the middle of the most horrible situation ever, and all he notices about her is that she's dancing. That's the *only* thing he sees. She's living in this dystopia where the government is bugging discos and mobsters are selling weapons to the military, and he actually thinks that all she cares about is goddamn *dancing!*"

My voice was a little too loud. Nobody said anything for a second, then Lizzy laughed. "I hate this song too."

Jenny smiled. "I realize that I am totally uncool because I like Don Henley. I like the Eagles, too." Then she shot me a serious look. "But yeah, let's listen to something else. Do you approve of Tracy Chapman?"

It was mom music, but I still liked it. We sang along to "Fast Car" and sailed down the freeway back to Irvine.

Hamid called me two nights later. I answered on the downstairs phone next to the kitchen, where my mom was washing the dishes after dinner and listening to everything I said. That was fine, because I didn't want to say much.

"Hey, it's Hamid. How's it going?"

"I'm good. How are you?" I twisted the curly cord around my fingers.

"Pretty good. What are you up to this weekend?" He didn't offer any explanation for why he'd waited so long to call.

"I have plans with Heather and those guys."

"All weekend? You don't even have time to watch a very special video history of the Mouseketeers?" His voice hovered between needy and sad. It reminded me of when we'd talked on the beach, where he'd pulled me into his melancholy and left an alien robot baby behind.

"Yeah, sorry. I'm just super busy."

"Well, what about next weekend?"

"I have a ton of SAT prep so . . ."

"So you're busy."

"Yeah."

I could practically hear him getting the hint. When he spoke again, there was no emotion in his voice. "Okay cool . . . well, anyway, maybe I'll see you around before I leave for UCLA. Or maybe not. Whatever."

"Okay cool. Bye." I hung up and tried not to feel anything.

My mom put down the dish towel and looked at me. "Was that a boy?"

"Yes."

"You were very nice. I thought you did a good job politely turning him down."

I had one of those split-second fantasies where I smashed every single dish my mom had painstakingly dried. The room was covered in powdery shards, and then it wasn't.

"I think I'm going out with Lizzy tonight, okay?"

I ran upstairs before she could finish saying yes.

Irvine Meadows was having a summer weeknight concert with

four indie bands, including Million Eyes, and we'd been planning to see it for a few days. Soojin and Heather were already in the station wagon when Lizzy picked me up.

"So what the hell happened with you and Hamid?" Heather turned all the way around in the front passenger seat, kneeling on the pleather to face me. "He said something about how you are going to be busy for the rest of the summer?"

After what happened with Scott, I figured Heather could keep a secret. So I told her and Soojin the whole story. By the time I got to the part where I'd puked in the trash can, we were parked in Irvine Meadows' most distant and secluded parking lot.

"Please don't tell Hamid, okay?" I looked at Heather.

She nodded slowly and then let out one of her crazy cackles. "Yeah, I can see why you might be busy all summer."

"It's not that Hamid is a bad person. Actually, he's really nice. I'm just not . . . I know it sounds weird, but I'm not in the mood to talk to him."

"That totally makes sense. I mean, he's my cousin, so I feel bad for him. But also he's kind of a dumbass." Heather stuffed some weed in a pipe and took a long hit. "You want some?"

"I want some! I'm done driving now, hello!" Lizzy reached for the pipe, still trailing smoke.

We passed the pipe around for a while, and then headed toward our seats. After the first opening act, I heard a familiar voice behind us.

"Hey, guys. Great show, right?"

It felt like the hair was walking off the back of my neck. I turned around to see our social studies teacher, Mr. Rasmann, smoking a cigarette and looking very non-teachery in a leather jacket. He'd graduated from college only a couple of years ago, and a lot of girls at school had crushes on him.

"Hey, Mr. Rasmann." Soojin smiled at him. "I didn't know you liked punk rock."

"Yeah, I miss going to shows in L.A. But this lineup is great. Have you guys heard Million Eyes before?"

I knew I wasn't going to be interested in whatever he said next. My guess was that he only asked as an excuse to barf out some giant explanation of a band I definitely understood better than he did.

But for some reason Soojin fell into his conversation trap. "I love them, but I've never seen them live."

And, as I predicted, he took her reply as pretext to launch into a long commentary about Million Eyes that he'd ripped off practically verbatim from an article in *LA Weekly*. Lizzy pulled out a cigarette to share, and Mr. Rasmann leaned forward to light it for us. It felt cool to have a teacher do that, but it also reminded me of Bob, with his "we're not standing on ceremony" routine.

Lizzy grabbed my elbow. "Let's take a little stroll before the next band."

We wandered through the loge section and Lizzy glanced back over her shoulder. "That teacher is so gross. He's always hitting on girls in my class."

"Really? Ugh."

Soojin raced up to us, almost crashing into the railing where we leaned. "Why did you guys leave me with that pervert?"

I waggled my eyebrows. "Why did you leave Heather with that pervert?"

"Heather went to the bathroom."

"What did he do?"

"Well, at first I thought he was being nice. He was like asking me to call him Tom and talking about cool music. But then he was like, hey you have skin like a china doll, and do you want to party after the show, and it was super gross."

"That asshole has been molesting girls at our school all year." Lizzy had a furious expression on her face that I'd only seen once before, on the night we never talked about.

"He's definitely got a molester vibe."

"We should teach him a lesson." Lizzy's mouth hardened into a smile. Soojin grinned back.

I thought that would be the end of it. But Mr. Rasmann was still there when we got back to our seats, and Soojin wore a fake flirtatious smirk she only used to fuck with people.

"Hey, ladies!" He was trying to riff on a Beastie Boys lyric, and it came out sounding awful.

"Hi, um, Tom." Soojin shot Lizzy a look as she spoke. "So where do you want to go party after the show?"

He bared his teeth. "You should come to my place. I have some good bourbon I got from my dad."

"Can my friends come?"

Mr. Rasmann raked his eyes over us. "Sure. What the hell. It's summer vacation, right?"

We followed his directions to an apartment complex in Tustin. It was one of dozens of suburban developments built during the 1970s to look woodsy and natural. As we wandered between amorphously shaped plots of grass and stucco walls masked by trees, I hung back for a moment to light a cigarette that Lizzy had stuffed in my pocket earlier.

"I'll catch up, you guys! I'm going to smoke for a minute."

"See you there!"

They climbed rustic wooden stairs and I leaned against a lamp post, blowing misshapen smoke rings and wondering what the hell we were doing. I kept thinking about Hamid, and how I wished he'd said he was sorry about not calling. I was raging, irrationally, that he hadn't apologized for that evening he knew nothing about, when I lay naked on a table with a pain machine inside me. Smoke and anguish pricked my eyes, making everything blurry.

Suddenly, a woman rounded the corner, walking straight toward me, her trench coat flaring open to reveal knickerbockers and a high-collared blouse that would have been fashionable during the 1980s Gunne Sax craze. Her brown hair was pulled back into a long, thick ponytail.

She stopped directly in front of me and spoke. "I need to talk to you about Lizzy."

"What?" I was too surprised to ask how she knew me and Lizzy. She looked oddly familiar, but I couldn't place where I'd seen her before.

"I want you to know that you don't have to do something you'll regret. You can stop now. Tonight." She tilted her head. "Do you understand? You can go home right now and forget about all this. Don't let Lizzy suck you into it."

Now I was seriously weirded out. "What the hell? Who are you?"

"I'm . . . well, there's no good way to say this."

Lizzy opened the door to Mr. Rasmann's place and called my name. In that moment, his apartment felt safer than whatever was happening here, with this familiar-yet-unfamiliar woman.

"I gotta go." I raced up the stairs and left her behind, mouth open to say something I couldn't hear.

We checked out Mr. Rasmann's living room while he rattled around in the kitchen. He had some worn sofas and easy chairs and an admittedly excellent stereo setup. There was a framed poster of Sid Vicious over the turntable, and some concert flyers tacked up next to it: Black Flag, Dead Kennedys, Bad Religion. Pretty good taste.

Soojin picked up one of those fat, clothbound books full of plastic pockets for photos and opened it to a random page. She held it up to show us. It was full of Polaroids of girls, some completely naked. I was pretty sure that one of them was in my fifth-period government class.

Lizzy gaped. "Why would he leave that out?"

Mr. Rasmann made a cheerful noise in the kitchen. "Found the glasses, girls! I'm washing them just for you, because this is such a special occasion."

Soojin put the book down slowly, in the exact place she'd found it. My entire chest felt like a vector graphic from that Disney movie *The Black Hole*: a flat, glowing grid with an abstract throat punched into it. I was nothing but a sketchy representation of gravitational forces.

But Soojin wasn't. As soon as Mr. Rasmann returned, she pointed at the book. "What the fuck is that?"

Improbably, he was unruffled. He arranged some tumblers around the bourbon bottle, then smiled at us. "That's my look book. I'm a photographer when I'm not being a high school teacher."

Heather narrowed her eyes. "What kind of photographer takes naked pictures of girls?"

"Those are art. A celebration of the female form. Beautiful women like you should understand that."

The astrophysical phenomenon in my chest suddenly exploded into life, filling my ears with radioactive particles, and I heard myself yelling from far away. "This isn't art! You're a fucking pervert!"

Soojin shot me a nasty grin and snatched up the bourbon bottle. "Want to know what we like to put in our look book?"

I was gratified to see the grin evaporate from his face. "What . . . what do you . . . are you photographers too?"

"I guess you're about to find out, motherfucker." Lizzy was practically growling. She'd added a streak of red to her mohawk, and it gleamed like fresh blood. Then she grabbed the bottle out of Soojin's hand and shattered it against Mr. Rasmann's face. He made a squeaking noise and collapsed. Soojin kicked his ribs with her boots. "Call me fucking china doll, you piece of shit? I'm Korean! And I'm *not a doll*!"

I started to laugh, then felt a throb of rage working its way up from someplace deep in my intestines. My body moved before my brain could catch up, and that's how I found myself on top of Mr. Rasmann, looking into the blood and bourbon that streaked his slack face. He had a faint haze of stubble and a few scabby pimples on his forehead. I pushed one knee into his chest, holding him down even though he was passed out and definitely not going anywhere. My abdomen cramped like it had in Bob's office, and then Bob's voice was in my head, telling me that my pain wasn't so bad. His words became a refrain, a maniacal repetition: *Some women love it. Some women love it. Some women love it.*

Mr. Rasmann opened his eyes and tried to talk. "What . . . what the fuck . . . you crazy bitches . . ."

I leaned down close to his face and put my hands loosely around his neck. "What do you think those girls were feeling when you took those pictures? Do you think they loved it? *Do you?*" Heather, Soojin, and Lizzy had come close, standing above me on the floor, witnessing.

"Answer her, you dick!" Soojin kicked him in the ribs again.

He started to whimper and struggle under my knee. "They . . . they wanted to!"

My arms felt loose and strong. "They didn't want it!" I was howling again, and my fingers were moving up his face, across the slime and roughness of his cheeks, until I was touching the soft skin of his eyelids. I could hear Lizzy and Soojin and Heather above me, taunting him and urging me on.

I thought about Bob putting his fingers and machines inside me, and Hamid's plaintive voice on the phone, and all the girls in that look book who couldn't tell us what they wanted. And then my thumbs were in the soft, warm place that Mr. Rasmann used to look through his camera. They curled in deeper. I bet he'd never realized that eyeballs were actually holes in his face. And every hole can be penetrated. I laughed again, as I jammed my fingers in as deep as they would go, maybe touching his brain, listening to his tongue slither around his mouth and deliver a final hiss of realization.

Then there were more sounds, and Lizzy was grabbing my shoulders and Heather was hyperventilating and I'm pretty sure I had shredded eyeball on my thumbs. I finally tuned in to hear Lizzy giving orders. ". . . take that bottleneck with us and get a towel to wipe our prints off anything you touched."

I moved in a daze through the apartment, trying not to touch anything, allowing Soojin to hold my hands under hot water.

It was only when we returned to the car that I remembered the woman I'd seen outside, the one who knew me and Lizzy. Was she a possible witness, somebody who could identify us to the police? For some reason, I felt certain she was not.

ELEVEN

TESS

In May, the Expo opened to rainy weather and thin crowds, but the Midway was packed. The entire length of the promenade was illuminated with electric lights, a futuristic novelty in 1893. You'd think that would draw gawkers, but the people of Chicago were far more interested in the bazaars, shops, and theaters that stayed open late for the after-work crowds. The Ferris wheel was still far from complete, so the guys running the ostrich farm next to the Algerian Village sold rides above the Midway in a giant, hydrogen-filled balloon. Floating above us, tourists saw the full glory of our artificial Islamic world: the Tunisian and Algerian Villages where I worked stood across the road from the vast, walled chaos of Cairo Street and the garish entrance to the Persian Palace. Every few feet, kiosks hawked beer. The air smelled like grilled lamb, burned sugar, and camel dung from the children's animal rides. Still, the crowds' biggest lure night after night was Lady Asenath's reputation, which shone like a fiery new constellation in the firmament.

The ruckus at the press club had naturally made all the papers. Everyone wanted to know about this mysterious woman from afar who had caused a riot with her dancing. The "afar" part was of course never identified as Arizona, where Aseel had actually grown up. Lady Asenath was "from the exotic Orient," or "from darkest Africa," or from an even more racist moniker for some distant geographical location. Her dance was described as the "*danse du ventre*" at best, and "the wriggling of a deranged tart" at worst. Soph had vowed to correct the lies and was furiously writing her article about the true spiritual meaning of North African dances. Aseel, meanwhile, was enjoying her status as manager and star of the most popular show on the Midway.

To the outside world, of course, Sol Bloom ran the show. But now when he visited the theater, he didn't bother pretending to be in charge. He puffed a cigar in the back and beamed like a guy who was making enough money to retire at the age of twenty-five. That's where I found him one evening in late May, watching the musicians banging out the tune he'd improvised at the press club. When our eyes met, Sol gestured for me to follow him outside the theater. We pushed through a rowdy group of men who smelled like the slaughterhouse, and ducked into the theater office behind a market stall piled with fezzes and carpets. It was a cozy room dominated by a heavy wooden desk, and Sol settled lightly into one of the ridiculously ornate upholstered chairs that passed as ordinary furniture in the late nineteenth century.

"Sit down. You want a scotch?" Sol jumped up again and withdrew a bottle from a locked drawer.

"I'll have a little."

Sol poured a few fingers of brown fluid into cloudy-looking tumblers stamped with the logo for the Columbian Exposition. "Aseel says you're a whiz with costumes. You happy with this job? You going to stick around?" I braced for him to say something sleazy or harassing. But he simply paused, waiting for me to reply.

"Sure. I like this job."

He cocked his head. "You a *landsman*?" It was a Yiddish word my father had used, but mostly in the middle of jokes. I'd never heard anyone use it as earnestly as Sol did. When I was working with the anarchists in New York, everyone assiduously avoided talking about how we were all Jewish. The revolution was going to eradicate every religion, including ours.

"I am, but not in a very serious way," I said.

"You might not be serious about it, but they are." He gestured vaguely at the window, indicating the throngs of visitors. "They're murdering our people every day in Russia."

This was not the conversation I'd been expecting to have. "I . . . yes, I know about the pogroms."

He took another sip. "I know what people say about me. I'm a greedy Jew businessman. I'm pimping girls for Satan or whatever imbecilic thing the *goyim* believe about us this week."

"It's definitely imbecilic."

"I want Americans to learn about other cultures. They pay two bits to see a pretty girl, but they learn a little about the world. Maybe they eat something spicy. Maybe they find out that Jews don't have horns. It's not just show business, see? It's politics."

I stared at him mutely and nodded. For an instant, I wondered whether he was a traveler too.

"I know you're one of those New Women. You want to wear pants. You want a lady president. Well, that's fine with me. But don't spread the rumor that this is some kind of crazy show for Spiritualists and radicals. I had to say this to Aseel, too. People love us. Families are on the Midway. We're making money here. Got it?"

"Okay. But . . . I thought you cared about politics?"

Sol raised a thick black eyebrow at me and tapped his temple with a finger. "You change a man's mind by showing him a good time."

I couldn't argue with that, even if I'd wanted to. He was my boss, after all, and this job put me in a perfect position to make my edit. So I nodded again and followed him back to the theater, where one of the dancers had ripped her gown during the sword dance.

When I wasn't doing mending, I kept an eye on the audience. It was only a matter of time before the Comstockers showed up again, and I wanted to be ready. Salina stepped onstage and I melted into a wall covered in thick rugs and curtains. The whole theater was hung with bolts of fabric to give the illusion that we were inside a giant tent, enjoying a show in the desert with our caravan. Though the audience was mostly men, there were always ladies in attendance, defiantly alone or clutching the arms of their escorts. Did I recognize any of the men from other missions? I strained to focus my eyes in the dim light, trying to pick out familiar features beneath voluminous moustaches and beards.

I could see Aseel working her way toward me almost a minute before she whispered in my ear. "You have to come to the Persian Palace. Right now." She was seething.

Fearing another showdown like we'd had at the press club, I raced across the street with her. Unlike the Algerian Village, the Persian Palace made no pretense of being what Sol would call "cultural." A barker stood outside on a wooden chair, his hat cocked jauntily. "Arabia makes the most beautiful dark-eyed dancing girls!" he yelled. "Looking to see some Oriental jewels, fellas?" He gave a broad wink to a pack of college students milling eagerly outside, waiting for the late-night show. We plunked down fifty cents each and pushed our way through, despite the ticket taker's half-hearted attempt to block our way. As soon as we got inside, I could see why they'd tried to stop us. There were no women in the audience at the Persian Palace. The place was decorated in feathers, glitter, and mirrors, like a standard burlesque theater.

Still, as we jostled for seats, I saw nothing around me but the usual crowd of mostly drunk men looking for something they could fantasize about later. There were no fights or speeches about vice.

"Why are we here?" I looked at Aseel.

"Wait and see." She looked like she was ready to kill someone.

Stage lights flared and the show began. A white woman minced out onstage, wearing the flowing skirts of an Algerian dancer and the lacy corset of an American showgirl. Her blond curls flowed around a scarf that had been knotted awkwardly over her mouth and nose: a poor imitation of the already ridiculous veils we'd made for our show. Then the music started. It was the tune Sol had written, but somebody had added supposedly funny dancehall lyrics:

> There's a place in France
> Where the women go to dance
> And the dance they do
> Was written by a Jew
> But the Jew couldn't dance
> So they kicked him in the pants

I felt sick. As I guessed back at the press club, I had been witness to the birth of a meme, and this was one of the first variants on it. The dancer did some high kicks and tore off her veil, revealing a Caucasian face slashed with rouge. She moved her hips back and forth in an awful imitation of Aseel's act. Cheers hammered us. The men stamped their feet on the sticky floor.

Aseel dragged me back outside, her nails digging into my arm, until we were leaning on the wall beneath fake Egyptian pyramids.

"They stole our show! They stole our song! People will think that stupid cunt is Lady Asenath!"

"Nobody who saw our show would mix it up with that garbage."

"Everybody will!"

As she spoke, I glanced back at the door to the Persian Palace and saw a man standing outside, ignoring the barker. He took a notebook out of his pocket, wrote something down, and turned with almost military precision to look at the Algerian and Tunisian Villages. He took more notes, frowning. I nudged Aseel and pointed at him. This was step one of our plan: Identify and investigate possible soldiers in the edit war. If all went well, Aseel and Soph would help me get to the next step. And hopefully the Daughters would know nothing about it, because they would all be living in the future of another timeline.

We followed the guy with the notebook, who stopped one more time in front of the Moorish Theater, appearing to study the ads for exotic dancing girls. Then he made a beeline for a group of Pinkertons who'd been hired to prevent visitors from falling into the half-finished Ferris wheel steam pipe trenches late at night. I could only hear snatches of their conversation from our vantage point, behind a shuttered Pabst booth.

". . . make a citizen's arrest! This is obscene!" That was our man, yelling at the bored Pinkertons, who didn't seem to give him the answers he wanted.

"Can't leave our post, sir . . ."

One jabbed him lightly on the arm. They seemed to be urging him to move on. But the more they demurred, the more wound up he got. We heard "citizen's arrest" a few more times, which pegged him as a Comstocker.

One of the strategies that Comstock pioneered in the Society for the Suppression of Vice was the citizen's arrest for obscenity. He would spy on sex workers or suspected pornographers, figure out where they lived, and surprise them with handcuffs when they least expected it. Then he would declare a citizen's arrest and drag them to the police, demanding justice. It was a technique he taught at YMCA meetings, inspiring hundreds of eager men to do the same. The Comstockers spent a lot of time discussing exactly the right handcuffs to use, and how to snatch a girl up so that she couldn't struggle. To find their targets, they pored over fat booklets of pornography and crates of rubber dildos they'd ordered through the mail under assumed names.

Over time, Comstock amassed a huge collection of dildos and erotic postcards. These he brought with him in a steamer trunk to a congressional hearing, thus cementing his reputation as a righteous man, passionately ferreting out moral crimes of the modern age. Indeed, his campaign was so successful that the federal post office granted Comstock "special agent" status, basically giving him and his goons permission to open everybody's mail and arrest anyone who violated obscenity laws. Under Comstock's reign, "obscenity" included information about birth control, abortion, and sexual health. His followers were eyes on the street, and his office gave him eyes on the mail. Some offenders were jailed for years, or financially ruined. Others, as Soph had told us in her parlors, killed themselves rather than face imprisonment.

I wondered what kind of crazy bullshit this lone Comstocker had planned, if he could get the police on his side. Would he throw the whole Midway in jail for indecency? Send the women of the Algerian and Tunisian Villages back to Africa? Luckily, he was getting nowhere with his increasingly loud complaints. Pinkertons were thugs for hire. They didn't mind smashing the skulls of strikers, but they weren't big on arresting pretty ladies. Especially when there was no money in it for them.

The Comstocker marched away in a huff, and we tailed him down the Midway. It was getting late, and only a few clots of stragglers were left beneath the warm reddish glow of carbon filament bulbs. Outside the west entrance, he met up with another man and started yelling again. These guys were not exactly masters of spycraft. Standing nearby and pretending to admire the lights, we could hear everything they said.

"We can't let this go on, Elliot! These dances are more lewd than anything I've ever seen in New York City!"

"I thought you were doing a citizen's arrest?"

"The police are all a bunch of Chads. They won't help. We've got to bring Comstock here, in person."

My breath quickened. He was using anachronistic slang right out of the Celibate4Life forums in my time, where "Chads" were men who had fallen for women's wiles and refused to join the fight. No way was this guy from the 1890s. Or if he was, he'd been spending time with C4L travelers. Which still made him an agent in the edit war.

Aseel and I exchanged looks and made a big show of oohh-ing and aahh-ing over the new subway entrance. She leaned over and spoke in a low voice. "I think that's one of the fellows from the press club."

I glanced over quickly, and sure enough, it was the creep who'd been handing out zines at the Grape Ape show. Now I had a name for him: Elliot. He scratched his muttonchops and grunted as the C4L guy continued to rant about how he was going to send a telegram to New York right now and teach everyone a lesson about virtue.

At last, Elliot cut him off. "I have a better idea."

"What are you going to do?"

"I think we should take this to the Lady Managers Board."

"The what?"

"You know the Woman's Building on the other end of the Midway? It's run by a group of upstanding women, and a lot of them are Prohibitionists. Good, faithful wives. If they get one look inside one of these places, they'll bring the wrath of God."

I could hear the C4L guy practically hyperventilating. "And then Comstock will have to come! He'll have to!"

"He'll arrest every one of those foul bitches."

"Meet at the usual place tomorrow night, and we'll figure it out with Ephraim."

"Yes, sir."

They broke apart and Elliot headed for the subway entrance. We turned our back on him and linked arms, walking at a leisurely pace like two ladies out for a stroll. When I glanced over my shoulder, Elliot had disappeared.

"We've got to do something to stop them."

"Perhaps we'll write our own song lyrics for that tune and start selling it, so those Persian Palace bints can't claim they're me."

I couldn't believe she was still obsessing about the Persian Palace. "Didn't you hear what those men said? They're going to bring the Lady Managers to the theater! They're the most politically powerful women in the city, and they have Comstock's ear."

Aseel was angry. "Look, I know you're on this traveler mission to stop Comstock, and I'm with you. But I can't go back to some fancy future like you can, okay? I have to think about what's happening right now. I can't imagine those bumpkins coming up with a fool-proof plan to stroke their own cocks. They're idiots! I'm less worried about the Lady Managers shutting us down than I am about losing business if everybody is copying my dance."

"But we have the jump on those guys. If we can get to the Lady Managers first, maybe they'll ally with us and we can fight the Comstockers together."

"You aren't hearing me, Tess." Aseel whirled to face me. "Didn't you understand what you saw at the Persian Palace? Not all women are your allies. You know that, right? We have to protect the village."

It was like we were defending a little town in the Maghreb against the Alexandrian army. I wondered, not for the first time, whether I'd been traveling too long. Times bleed together in my mind. But maybe that's because there are always villages being ground to a pulp by somebody else's war.

I hung my head. "Okay, I'm sorry. You're right. You should write some lyrics. Sol could sell them for a nickel outside the theater."

"He'll love that."

"But I still might visit the Woman's Building tomorrow. If nothing else, maybe I can get them to meet with us."

Aseel shrugged. "No harm in it."

"What are you going to write the song about?"

"I think it should be about those two sad little Comstockers. They'll never enjoy anything. They'll never see the hoochie coochie." She wiggled her hips, imitating the Persian Palace dancer imitating her.

"What the hell is the hoochie coochie?"

"You haven't heard? That's what they're calling the *danse du ventre*. Soph is really peeved about it, but I don't mind. Hoochie coochie! It sounds like being tickled."

I laughed. "It also sounds a little naughty."

"I'd be disappointed if it didn't."

The next morning, I stood in the long hall of the Woman's Building, its soaring walls punctuated by a comically large number of arched doorways and pillars. When I climbed a lacy iron spiral staircase to the second level, the place took on the appearance of a blimp hangar whose curving roof was improbably made of glass.

Sunlight poured into the building, playing over a timeline mural that unspooled the history of U.S. womanhood as I walked toward the Lady Managers Board office. Painted beneath 1700 were white women in pioneer outfits, cooking and cleaning. In 1840, they joined hands with black and brown women, marching for abolition and universal suffrage. At least twenty feet were dedicated to the year 1870, with women dancing beneath the text of the Fifteenth Amendment: "The right of citizens of the United States to vote shall not be denied or abridged by the United States or by any State on account of sex, race, color, marital status, or previous condition of servitude."

There was the election of Senator Harriet Tubman, under 1880, the only prominent brown face on the wall. A collage atop a waving American flag showed women voting, running their own stores, teaching children, working as nurses, and smashing liquor bottles in a Temperance march. Eighteen ninety was entirely devoted to the construction of the Woman's Building, of course, with women looking at blueprints and picking out some of the bizarrely mismatched interior details for the hall's décor. Beside the office door was a final panel devoted to the far-off year of 1950, where women were looking through telescopes and operating giant dynamos. A white woman's face, capped by a bulbous, "futuristic" hat, hovered over the words "Lady President." I stared at the political prediction, still a fantasy in my time, and could imagine Anita adding it to her ever-expanding list of "Great Moments in White Feminism."

I remembered Soph telling us that the Lady Managers were running an anti-abolition candidate for some office, but they were also devoted to promoting women's rights. There had to be some sympathetic members of the group, and maybe they would see our point of view.

A short, harried-looking woman with a pile of unruly black hair tangled into an updo answered my knock on the Lady Managers' office door.

"I'm here from the Algerian Village. Is there somebody I could talk to about hosting a meeting between the women in the village and the Lady Managers?"

She looked dubious. "You're Algerian?"

"I work there. We're on the Midway."

"Oh, you're one of those."

"There are a lot of women working on the Midway, but especially in the theaters, and I thought maybe the Lady Managers Board might like to meet with us. For the sake of female solidarity?"

She put one arm akimbo and stared at me like I was an idiot. I had to put this in terms she would understand. I needed something that would lead them gently away from that Great Moments in White Feminism playbook. If they met Aseel and Salina and the others, they might find it harder to team up with Comstock to destroy their sisters on the Midway. What would appeal to these women? There had to be an idea so innocuous that they couldn't say no.

"There are a lot of women in the villages who could benefit from a . . . cultural exchange," I said hesitantly. "They could talk to you about how women live in their countries, and the Lady Managers could teach them about American womanhood. Maybe we could have a . . . woman's cultural tea?"

Clearly one of those words was a magical key because suddenly she was smiling and nodding and showing me into the plush, oddly decorated interior of the office. Pink, fluffy curtains hung next to African prints, and Moorish tiles shared wall space with racist caricatures of indigenous Americans carved from corn cobs.

"Sorry about the mess. All this stuff was donated and we have no idea where to put it. I'm Sarah, by the way. This is Augusta." Sarah indicated another woman at a desk, busy writing something in shorthand.

"I'm Tess."

"So you're really not from Algeria?"

"I'm from California."

"I suppose that's almost as savage, really. Tell Augusta about your idea for a woman's cultural tea."

Fifteen minutes later, Augusta had two pages full of shorthand, and Sarah was already planning how many kinds of biscuits they'd need. None of the other exhibits had done any cross-cultural events yet, and they wanted the Woman's Building to be the first.

"The Woman's Building has a hard time selling tickets to our exhibits, but surely people would pay to watch a civilized meal with women in their bizarre costumes from all across the world." Sarah looked pensive. "Plus, don't you think it would be the perfect opportunity to teach these wild women some manners?"

The more she talked, the more I felt like I had eaten a spoonful of salt. It sounded like she wanted to turn our tea into a freak show. "I don't want to sell tickets," I said. "I thought we'd have more of a private meal, to get to know each other."

Augusta looked up from her notes, perplexed. "Whatever would we do at a private meal? A lot of those women on the Midway can't even speak! They use grunts and hand gestures." She grimaced and mimed grabbing something. "But wouldn't that be a fun show? Primitives with tea and biscuits?"

I stood up, my face filling with blood. I thought of a million things I could say, cruel and wrathful and right. I thought about how easy it would be to pierce these women's hearts with the letter opener on Augusta's desk and blame it on a man. But I did none of that. I cleared my throat carefully and said nothing. When I left, I didn't slam the door. Aseel had been right. Not all women were our allies.

I bought a hot dog for lunch and took a brief detour around the artificial lagoon next to the Woman's Building. It was full of paddle boats that bore visitors to an artificial island, planted with invitingly shady trees and dotted with park benches. The avenues here in the White City were wide and clean, and it seemed like every exhibit was devoted to mechanical devices and inventions that would make us richer. It couldn't have been more unlike the thronged, polyglot alleys of the Midway, where the villages sold trinkets and cheap entertainment. If the White City was the world that Americans imagined for themselves, perhaps the Midway was the reality they couldn't accept.

Aseel had almost finished her song. The lyrics were set to the complete tune Sol had improvised, going beyond the awful Persian Palace ditty. She belted out the first verse and chorus for a small afternoon audience as Salina danced and the musicians played drums and piano. The result was a cheerful cacophony:

> I will sing you a song
> While the ladies dance along
> 'Bout a very moral man
> Who swore he did no wrong
> Sad for him no girl was pretty
> He was not long in the city
> All alone oh what a pity
> Poor little lad
> He never saw the streets of Cairo

> On the Midway he was never glad
> He never saw the hoochie coochie
> Poor little country lad

I applauded until my hands hurt, and Soph let out a delighted squeal. She had finished her article about the *danse du ventre* and brought a copy of it for Aseel and me to read. *New York World* wanted to publish it, and she was excited that her byline would appear in the same pages that featured the reporting of Nellie Bly.

Aseel joined us in the dressing room a few minutes later, exuberant about her own creation.

"What did you think?"

"I love it but . . ." Soph looked anxious. "Well, do you have to say hoochie coochie? That isn't the proper name."

"Neither is *danse du ventre*, love. That's simply French for belly dance."

I interrupted. "In case you care about my opinion, I thought it was perfect."

Aseel laughed and Soph threw her hands into the air. "Fine, fine. Call it whatever you want." Then her face lit up again. "You guys are coming to the invocation tonight, right? You have to be there by half past eleven at the latest, because she comes at midnight."

"What? Who?" I remembered Soph mentioning a Spiritualist meeting tonight, but this sounded like something more elaborate.

"We're invoking the goddess!" Soph said.

Aseel grinned and winked at me. "You know . . . the *goddess*?"

I didn't know, but I sure as hell wasn't going to miss it.

When I arrived at Soph's chambers later that evening, a woman I'd never met before answered the door and shushed me as we came into the parlor. I could hear Soph speaking indistinctly and the murmur of other voices coming from her sitting room. The woman from the door handed me an ivory linen dressing gown. "Change into this," she whispered. "You'll need it to meet the goddess." I could see now that the parlor was lined in neat piles of ladies' clothing, each gown and skeletal corset balanced atop a pair of slippers. There must have been quite a crowd in there—I counted thirteen bundles, including my own.

The room smelled of sweat and incense when I slid between the pocket doors. Soph sat in the lotus position at the center of the room, surrounded by women lying back on pillows. Some rested heads on other women's bellies, while others stayed at the periphery, their backs against the wall. All of them had their legs spread, hands pressed lightly against the fabric draped over their pelvic bones. It looked disappointingly like a New Age-y tantra situation. Then Soph spoke and I knew it was something else.

"Today we're going to learn about a gift given to us by angels, because its sole purpose is to bring joy. It's called the clitoris."

"Praise be!" one woman cried. Then everyone giggled, including me.

I'd wondered whether Soph's rituals had an erotic component to them, but I had no idea it would be this overt. She was basically throwing a masturbation party, like something out of the 2000s sex positivity movement. After traveling through millennia, I'd seen a lot of sex parties. I wasn't completely taken by surprise. Still, none were quite like this.

Soph spoke again, a laugh lingering in her voice. "Let's begin by calling the directions. I call the Goddess of the East, who teaches us the mysteries of yoga and the importance of contemplation. I humbly ask the East to allow us the use of her teachings, and have patience if we bungle them. We seek her guidance, but sometimes we get it wrong. I ask her to grant us peace, despite trying encounters with annoying bosses and rogues and moll buzzers." There were a few titters at that.

"Now who wants to call the North?"

A woman I recognized from the Algerian Village volunteered, then a pink-cheeked lady with an expensive hairdo called the West. Each invocation was an alloy of irony and sanctity. As I settled into a pile of pillows next to Aseel, I saw a few more faces from the villages alongside the rich wives who made up most of Soph's paying clientele.

Soph completed the opening ritual on a more earnest note. "Now I call the Plural Goddesses, who encompass all lands and times, who bring new hope and new beginnings. They bring us pleasure and delight without shame, and they remind us that we find sanctity through the fusion of friendship. They love all bodies because they have been every shape and size. The goddesses are now with us, to bless us and give us permission to quicken the plush where life begins.

"And now, we witness the miracle of angels. Everyone take a deep breath."

The room filled with sighs. Some of the women began to hum quietly to themselves. I got the feeling that most of them had done this before, especially the ones who reached under their gowns and looked expectantly at Soph.

"Cup one hand over your *mons Venus*, ladies, and slowly move your fingers in a circle. Keep breathing."

A few of the women had pulled their gowns up, but most seemed more comfortable with the modesty of exploring themselves under the cover of soft cloth. There were a few muted "ohhs" and hums as Soph continued to issue gentle instructions on where to move next, and what kinds of motions to try. The longer I listened, the less it felt like a sex party and more like one of those consciousness-raising groups from the 1970s where women used mirrors to see their vaginas for the first time. Soph's goal was simply to teach these women where to find the clitoris, and how to use it. As the breathing slowly blurred into moans, she quietly checked in with each woman, guiding her if she needed it, making sure everyone's fingers found a spot that gave them pleasure.

Soph spoke again, her voice low. "Now I want you to think about something that makes you feel good. It could be a flower, or a nice breeze. It could be a man . . ." She was interrupted by a few breathless giggles. "Or a goddess, or a songbird. It could be how warm water feels on your feet, or silk against your neck. It could be the taste of sweets on your lips."

And then she was next to me, the pressure of her hips on the pillows causing me to roll slightly toward her. "Everything okay?"

I nodded and she winked before turning to Aseel, whose back was arched and breaths shallow. "Remember to take it slow. Draw it out for as long as possible." She rubbed Aseel's belly sensuously, which didn't exactly seem like it would make it easier for her to hold out. "Breathe, breathe."

Then, her voice raised, Soph switched tactics and urged us to take it faster. "The goddess is coming. I feel her. Do you feel her?"

There were sighs and moans and a few scattered cries of "Yes!" All around me were women with their heads thrown back, eyes closed, their bodies thrumming with desire. I felt it too. More than I'd realized. Cursing the lack of commercial vibrators in this period, I followed Soph's instructions as she guided us closer and closer to the palace of angels. "The goddesses want you to come meet them. Have no fear. Give yourself to them. Come to them."

One woman cried out, and then another. "I feel them! Yes!"

"Praise her!"

Aseel turned toward me, her eyelids heavy in the dim light and her lips parted. I watched a shiver possess her. As her breath caught, I felt an answering throb in my own body. My voice joined the others as muscles beneath my fingers took over, contracting and releasing, a flush washing across the surface of my skin.

I gave my faith to science long ago, but I'll take cosmic female power when it's offered. If any spiritual force could help us defeat Comstock, I'm pretty sure this would be it.

Quiet breathing settled over the group, and Soph told us to sit up when we were ready. There were spurts of laughter, and four women arranged themselves into a backrub chain as others handed out cups of fragrant tea. Someone lit candles and the room brightened. I felt damp and warm and unself-conscious. I was so used to keeping my sexuality under guard that it was like the relief of a constant pain I'd forgotten was there. Soon enough I'd be back on the streets of a hostile timeline, fighting a war that nobody would remember. But tonight I would tarry in a better world for a little while longer.

"Thanks for inviting me to this, Soph."

"You are welcome, Tess. We have always been on this path together."

I lay back on the cushions and watched our shadows merge on the ceiling, thirteen bodies wavering in and out of becoming one. There were more of us beyond this room, all along the timeline. Some were organized subversives, and others were only half-aware that something was wrong in the world. We were fighting for liberation, or revenge, or maybe for a simple night of pleasure without shame. We were fighting to save each other, though we didn't know each other. I thought about everyone else out there, walking this path with us, and wondered what they were doing right now.

T W E L V E

E N I D

**Excerpted from the memoir of Enid Song,
placed in the Subalterns' Archive Cave,
Raqmu (2029 C.E.)**

They stole my memories of the woman I loved, leaving behind an absence with no originating presence. It was hell. For weeks I'd been overwhelmed by the feeling that I'd lost something. I kept searching for my phone, thinking I'd misplaced it. Then I was sure I'd deleted a database before backing it up. A part of me was missing, but I couldn't identify it. And that's why I wasn't surprised when Tess told me about Berenice at the last Daughters meeting. It hurt less to know, but it also hurt more. Immediately, I wanted to do everything in my power to revert that edit and remember Berenice.

The problem is that geoscientists aren't trained to rescue people from certain death at the hands of late-twentieth-century queer-bashing assholes. Luckily I knew someone who could help. I texted her after the meeting, and she agreed to meet me for coffee.

Delilah and I had known each other since undergrad at Duke, where we met in a cultural geology class and did a presentation to-gether about a poorly understood travel ailment called "nostalgia for the present." I had continued my studies in grad school, while Delilah went into industry. Thanks to her background in the geosciences, she became one of the most valuable agents at Pacific Life. She'd saved the company millions of dollars by traveling to prevent accidental deaths. The more people she rescued, the less the company had to pay out. I knew she'd have some good advice.

Sweeping into the café in designer loungewear, a brightly printed shirt, and Nike slip-ons, Delilah had far more Hollywood lesbian chic than your typical insurance agent. We hugged and sipped our gibraltars for a while before I told her about Berenice. My gut wrenched with longing for a woman I'd never known. And I had no idea how to bring her back.

Delilah hit her Juul and surreptitiously blew vapor down one sleeve. "So she was killed outside a gay bar? I've done a few hate crime reversions—they're easy to prevent because they're usually random. Bigger problem if it's premeditated. Then you might prevent the death at one time only to have it crop up earlier or later."

"We think it was premeditated. Someone wanted to edit her out of the timeline."

"This is getting more interesting." Delilah raised one delicate eyebrow and started taking notes on her phone. "Why was she a target?"

I knew I could trust Delilah, but I still didn't want to tell her about the Daughters. "Cone of silence, okay?"

She nodded, intrigued.

"I'm part of a . . . working group. We're trying to edit the timeline, to get more rights for women and nonbinary people. Unfortunately, we've caught the attention of some men who are reverting our edits. We think one of their goals is to edit trans women out of history."

"They killed her because she's trans?"

"Not just that. She *is* trans, but she was also documenting trans history and . . ."

"No, Enid. You had me at killing trans people. I'll take this one pro bono. Let's make those fuckers pay." Her eyes had a nasty gleam as she packed up her purse. "Well? Are you coming?"

"What are we doing?"

Delilah typed into her phone with her gel nails and talked at the same time. "I booked us at Flin Flon. Guy who does travel for Pacific Life totally loves me. I told him it was urgent. Are you burned out of the week leading up to the murder? That's all we need."

I checked my online calendar against the date of Berenice's death according to the AP article we'd found. I'd burned through most of 1992 on research trips already. "I could do the two days leading up to it, which means realistically I'd arrive day of, if you factor in the flight time from Flin Flon."

"I'll go ahead of you then. I can make contact with the client . . . I mean, the victim." Delilah sounded embarrassed. "It's good for me to do this kind of thing once in a while, you know? Otherwise I forget why I went into this business in the first place."

We hugged again, and agreed to meet at Flex Nightclub in Raleigh, North Carolina, approximately thirty years ago.

I had never seen Berenice before, or at least this version of me hadn't. I wondered how we met before the edit, and what it was like when we fell in love. All I had to go on when I arrived for Karaoke Night was her blurry picture from the AP. Flashing my ID, I walked into a large, dimly lit bar painted black with the occasional scarlet highlight. At one end of the long room was a stage flanked by the KJ booth and a screen flashing lyrics. A man with a perfectly coiffed beard and flannel shirt was belting out a show tune with the cute-butchy fervor of a deeply dedicated bear. The place was already packed with every permutation of queer, from high femme to gym queen, plus all the party kids who defied categorization.

It was the night of Berenice's murder. And there, at the center of everything, was Delilah. I smiled with relief. Her ability to slide into any social situation with panache was practically a superpower. I joined the small circle of women around her and said hi.

"This is Enid, my friend from L.A."

Everybody introduced themselves, and I promptly forgot all their names except Berenice's. She called herself Flame. Either she wasn't going by Berenice yet, or she had a preferred nickname at this time in her life. Her curly hair was bright red, like her lipstick. There was a glow about her that I recognized from other friends who had recently transitioned. Berenice was happy in her own skin—maybe for the first time—and it was infectious. When somebody started singing a Madonna song, she shimmied along with it, bouncing against us and twirling. "Do you think it's weird to dance to karaoke?" she asked me with a flirty smirk. "I'm bad at listening without moving."

My heart ached. She was so beautiful. I couldn't believe that one day she would be planning to move in with me.

Delilah's voice snapped me out of it. "Honey, you should always dance. You look amazing." Delilah moved her hips to the beat, then caught my eye. "Come with me for a smoke, Enid?"

Outside, she wasted no time getting to the point. "I think I've got our man. He's a straight guy named Fred who comes here to pick up trans ladies, and a few people have already warned me about him. I guess his dates sometimes disappear." She frowned. "You know what I mean?"

I felt a chill that had nothing to do with the night air. "Have you seen him?"

"Not yet. But I'm sticking close to Berenice. The problem, like I said, is that this sounds premeditated. I might need to render him."

"Render? What? You mean . . ."

Delilah flicked her hair back and winked at a woman in a Boy Scouts shirt. "You said he was part of some conspiracy to edit trans women out of the timeline. What the hell do you care if he's deleted? I'm helping you out here."

I swallowed hard. My research trips involved going to public hearings and lobbying policymakers. Assassination was never an option.

But Delilah was right: the Comstockers had already killed Berenice. If we left Fred to his own devices, he might slaughter more. It wasn't like the cops were bending over backward to catch the dude responsible for killing so-called "men in dresses." I scowled at the memory of those words.

"Sweetie, this isn't my first rodeo," Delilah continued. "Sometimes it's cheaper to render someone. Especially when there's a multimillion-dollar policy on the line. I can handle it."

We went back inside. Berenice was deep in conversation with a young guy at the bar whose blond hair brushed the collar of his polo shirt. Edging closer to them, I noticed his skin was preternaturally clear, as if he'd never had a pimple in his life. He smelled like baby powder.

"Who's your friend?" Delilah asked, gesturing for the bartender at the same time.

Berenice opened her mouth to speak, but the man talked over her. "I'm Fred. And who are you?"

"I'm Delilah. Can I get you a drink, Fred?"

He held up a glass with brown liquor in it. "I'm good."

"Oh good. Come here often, Fred?"

Berenice was getting restless. Our eyes met and it was almost too much. I tried to imagine what she'd look like in thirty years, when we would be figuring out how to consolidate our couches and what colors to paint the walls. Then she smiled and I threw off all the weight of a future I'd lost. It was time to make a new future.

"Hey, Flame . . . let's dance! I love this song!"

Two women onstage were singing the hell out of En Vogue. Berenice jumped up with me instantly, and we wiggled around the floor with a few other people, singing along:

> MAYBE NEXT TIME
> YOU'LL GIVE YOUR WOMAN A LITTLE RESPECT
> THEN YOU WON'T BE HEARING HER SAY "NO WAY"

I kept Delilah and Fred in my line of sight. She'd lured him in completely; he couldn't seem to take his eyes off her. The lights strobed, and Delilah snuck something into his drink. I needed to keep Berenice away from the bar. "Why don't you sing something? I bet you have a favorite karaoke song."

She gave me a mischievous look. "Maaaaybe."

"What is it?" I played along.

"I'll do it if you promise to dance."

I nodded enthusiastically and Berenice flipped through the thick song book to find her number. Meanwhile, across the club, Fred was stumbling against Delilah like he was blackout drunk. Motioning to Berenice that I'd be right back, I made a beeline for them.

"Oh look, it's my friend Enid! Remember Enid, Fred?"

"Sh-sh-good to meeyou . . ." Fred put his arm around me. "Lesgo honey."

"Let's go? Yeah, that's a good idea, Fred." Delilah looped his other arm around her shoulder and we practically dragged him into the street. We tried to prop him against the side wall of the club, but he kept sliding down. I caught a glimpse of his mark as his shirt rode up. 2365 C.E.

"Holy shit." I pointed at it and Delilah's eyes widened.

"Oh, Fred. You've come a long way to meet girls, haven't you?"

Fred regarded us blearily. "Sno girls . . . jus mew-mewtalated men." He grabbed my shirt in a desperate attempt to stay standing. "You know? Do you know? Iss wrong. Sad. Men sh-should have pride. Women serve. Snatural."

I tried not to recoil in disgust. "What did you give him?"

"A lot of GHB. Mix it with booze and people will melt." Delilah gave me a hard smile.

"I think you're right that this is our guy."

"Great. Can you hold him a sec?" Delilah was rooting around in her purse. "Oh, perfect." She pulled out something that looked like a scrap of paper, which she folded in half. Now a tiny needle stuck out of the fold, and she quickly jabbed it into Fred's neck. "You can let go now. Let's have a drink."

I heard Fred thump to the ground behind us.

"What was that?"

"Don't worry about it. Let's just say I know a guy in Virginia who is great at causing heart attacks."

We got back in time to see Berenice take the stage. Her earrings winked stars as she threw her head back and belted out an old Runaways song that sounded new again.

I'M YOUR CH-CH-CH-CHERRY BOMB

She had a great growling voice, and suddenly all I wanted to do was dance. With each pulse of the disco lights, another memory of Berenice bloomed. We met at a Daughters meeting in 2020; we shared mojitos afterward; she always laughed at my obscure critical theory jokes with genuine appreciation. We kissed for the first time in Powell Library, on the wide sunlit stairway with its worn Spanish tiles. At an applied cultural geology conference in Phnom Penh, we skipped out early to get sugary cakes at Brown Coffee; we played footsie under the table and I looked into her face and knew at that moment that I loved her. We watched a particularly terrible episode of *The Geologists* on her beaten-up old sofa and decided it made sense to move in together and share my new couch. I jumped up and down, hands in the air, making sure Berenice saw me cheering for her with crazy, intoxicated joy. I couldn't wait to get back to 2022 and tell her all about it.

THIRTEEN

BETH

Now we were murderers for sure. What happened with our teacher Mr. Rasmann wasn't like with Scott. We hadn't been surprised or attacked. We'd killed him to get revenge for something he hadn't even done to us. I don't think any of us could forget the way we left his body on the floor, ripped up and battered like an old sleeping bag after a summer at Girl Scout camp.

Four days after that night at Mr. Rasmann's apartment, we met at Lizzy's house to listen to records. That was the pretext, anyway. All we could talk about was what we'd done.

"I mean, the guy *did* deserve it. You saw those pictures in his shitty, fucked-up look book—he was molesting girls at our school." Lizzy was plucking invisible things out of the shag rug on her bedroom floor as she talked. Soojin, Heather, and I drank peach wine coolers we'd stolen from the fridge. Lizzy's parents were on a trip to Jordan again—some kind of academic conference. Lizzy's mom had given me an extra-long hug when they left earlier in the evening, and made both of us promise to clean up any "riot grrl ragers" in the works. I couldn't decide whether it was more embarrassing that she knew the term "riot grrl," or that she'd used the word "rager" non-ironically.

"I guess, but . . ." I kept thinking of that strange woman, telling me I didn't have to do something I'd regret. Then I thought about Mr. Rasmann's eyeballs and wanted to barf.

Soojin broke in hotly. "He was raping a ton of girls. We had to do something."

"It's not like he *wasn't* going to do something creepy to us. He probably put Valiums in that booze." Heather screwed up her face as she contemplated it. "Plus, think of all the other girls we saved. Maybe we even saved their lives. Guys like that start with rape but they become serial killers." Heather had been obsessed with serial killers ever since the Night Stalker murdered some people in Orange County when we were kids.

"What if we get caught?" I asked. "I don't think we can say it was self-defense." I looked expectantly at Lizzy, our decider.

"We've got to get our stories straight. We can say he tried to get us drunk and told us to take off our clothes. Which, basically, that was going to happen."

"But then why didn't we run away and call the police?" I was dubious.

"I dunno . . . maybe we reacted in the moment? Or, like, he grabbed one of us?"

"I think maybe . . . he grabbed me and you guys jumped him to protect me?" Soojin extemporized as she played with one of her bar-rettes, opening and closing it with a click. I felt like I'd stumbled into an awful after-school improv theater class project. Just a bunch of girls, doing an enrichment exercise, using our creativity to invent an alibi for why we killed our teacher.

"I still think that . . . technically . . . this was murder. It wasn't like with Scott." As I said it, I glanced at Heather, who knew better than any of us what it was like with Scott.

She looked back and shrugged. "Do you want to go to jail for life because we killed a guy who was going to kill us, or kill some other girls in the future? For all we know, he's killed girls before."

"Look, I'm not saying he wasn't heinous and evil and obviously . . . I'm the one . . ." I trailed off. I wasn't actually sure who among us had delivered the killing blow. It was a blur of glass shards and globby viscera in my memory. But I was the one jamming thumbs into his eye sockets. I was the one holding him down.

"So just in case . . ." Lizzy's tone held a burr of annoyance. "Let's settle on a story. Setting aside all this other stuff. Because I think we all agree that we shouldn't go to jail over some fucking assface molester."

"Okay."

"The story is that he invited us to his house, tried to get us drunk, and said we had to take off our clothes. Then he grabbed Soojin, and we attacked him without thinking."

"And we didn't go to the police because we were so scared."

"We didn't realize he was dead when we left."

"Oh yeah, that's good. We thought we'd only beaten him up."

"Are you okay with that, Beth?" Everybody looked at me.

"Sure." I nodded vigorously, but some unnamable feeling compressed my chest so hard that black dots fizzed at the edges of my vision.

Our homicidal improv exercise turned out to be overkill in the end. A week later, the story hit the papers everywhere. It wasn't a snippet in *The Orange County Register* like when Scott died. The cops claimed they'd discovered the mastermind of a child porn ring, right at Irvine High School. They suspected that Mr. Rasmann had been murdered by some of his co-conspirators. We all got letters on official Irvine High letterhead, explaining that nobody had reported any wrongdoing at the school, but they were doing a "thorough investigation" anyway. They helpfully included a list of churches we could call for counseling.

Also, apparently, Soojin hadn't been entirely wrong about the serial killer thing. Police were reopening the unsolved murder case of a girl who went to an L.A. high school where Mr. Rasmann had been a student teacher. Several of the evening news shows ran pictures of her and said the police had evidence that she was one of his victims. One of the girls in his look book, perhaps? I should have felt better, but instead it made me feel worse.

I couldn't sleep, but I couldn't open my eyes either. My mom knocked loudly on my door at noon on a Friday. "Lizzy's on the phone! Do you want me to tell her to call back whenever you decide to get out of bed?"

Waking up was like swimming through reeking hydrocarbons. "I'll get it. I'll be down in a sec."

Bleary and exhausted, I went downstairs and picked up the phone. "Meet at the usual place?" Lizzy sounded breezy. "Soojin and Heather are coming out too."

"Sure. Can you pick me up?"

Lizzy and I met up with Soojin and Heather at the mall cookie shop across the street from UC Irvine. We shared sugar and cigarettes in our favorite spot at the top of an unnecessarily elaborate bridge leading to the quad where a scene from one of the *Planet of the Apes* movies was filmed in the '70s.

Heather kept high-fiving us. "Heroes! We are goddamn heroes!"

Lizzy grinned and blew a smoke ring.

I still thought we should have done it differently. But I couldn't say that out loud. It was getting hard for me to keep track of all the things I couldn't talk about: the sex, the abortion, the murders, and my worry that we'd done something really, really wrong. Nothing felt real. The physical world was a blob of light at the end of a long, elastic tunnel that kept squeezing shut.

"Who's our next target?" Heather rubbed her hands together and cackled.

I knew she was joking, but suddenly I couldn't deal. "Hey, so . . . I promised my dad that I would get all my chores done this afternoon," I said. "I think I'm gonna take off."

"Are you sure? Do you need a ride?" Lizzy sounded genuinely concerned.

"Naw, I'll take the bus."

As I walked away, I heard Heather ask Lizzy if I was doing okay.

"Obviously she's dealing with a lot of shit . . . ," Lizzy replied.

And then I was out of earshot. I really did need to do my chores, but first I wanted to sit in the middle of all the huge eucalyptus trees at the center of the UCI campus. The place was pretty deserted in summer, except for a few wandering college students who ignored me. If I concentrated hard enough, I could pretend I was one of the trees, eating light and sucking energy from soil.

"I thought I'd find you here."

I almost jumped up and ran. It was the woman from the night of the murder, sitting on the other end of the bench. What was she doing here? Suddenly, I couldn't stop feeling Mr. Rasmann's eyeballs under my thumbs. My hands shook and ice clotted under my skin, but I couldn't move. The woman wasn't in that Gunne Sax outfit anymore. Now she looked relatively normal in jeans and a baggy sweatshirt. In the light, I could see her long hair was streaked with gray, and her tiny wireframe glasses looked like something out of a Merchant Ivory movie.

"It's you again." I was too freaked out to say anything else.

"We really need to talk."

"Yeah, I think we do."

She looked relieved. "Oh good. That wasn't what I thought you'd say."

"Who the fuck are you, and how do you know Lizzy and me?" It came out harsher than I intended, but I was too strung out to translate my feelings into words a grownup could handle.

"Beth, this is going to sound really strange, but bear with me." The woman took a deep breath and resettled her glasses on her nose. When she spoke again, there was a tremor in her voice. "I'm you. From the future."

My brain was doing the thing that happens when a PC crashes and the screen turns a blank, menacing blue. I couldn't fully process anything. Finally I found my voice. "Isn't that against the law?"

"Well, it's not technically against the law unless I tell you something that would limit your agency or give you an unfair advantage? But yeah, it's a gray area. I could get in a lot of trouble."

I scrutinized her face, looking for traces of myself, but all I saw was a middle-aged stranger. Our conversation had gone from unnerving to seriously dangerous, and I considered the possibility that every fucked-up thing in my life had finally driven me insane. Given that, I might as well find out what this possibly imaginary person had to say. "So . . . what are you . . . am I . . . doing here?"

"I'm here to tell you to get away from Lizzy. She's going to keep killing people and it's . . . you know it's wrong. Plus, she's a toxic friend. She's not good for you."

Those were words I had not allowed myself to think and I desperately wanted to change the subject. "You're a traveler? I thought we were going to study real geology . . ."

"A lot changed after you . . . after the murders. I can't tell you much, but it was really awful. I wanted a totally different life. I changed our name, too. I go by Tess now."

"Are you serious? I hate that name."

"Remember how we used to hate dark chocolate in elementary school? Now it's the best ever, right? Things change."

"I guess." I shook my head, trying to imagine a future where I traveled through time and called myself Tess. "I read that you can die or go insane if you meet yourself when you travel."

"Yeah, I was worried about that. There is almost nothing in the geoscience journals about it. That's because of legal issues, obviously. But there could be other problems, like an edit merging conflict where two versions of history overlap. That could cause ... extremely negative cognitive effects. I'm taking a risk."

As I listened, I realized that Tess's eyes were the exact same color as mine. Of course they were. And her right ear was triple-pierced; I could remember getting that done last summer at the mall. For the first time, I considered that this was actually happening. This was real. I was having a conversation with my future self and I was murdering people ... or maybe I was being fucked with on a grand scale. If this woman was not a hallucination, maybe she was some kind of con artist.

"How do I know you're really me and not a scammer?"

"I know you had an abortion. Because of what happened with Hamid. I also know you only told Lizzy, Soojin, and Heather. And Lizzy's mom."

"You could have found that out from the doctor, or from any of my friends, or who knows what."

"Your ... our father. We never told anyone what happened that one night."

I dug my fingers into the park bench so I could feel the splinters go in. Tess was right. I had never told anyone. Hearing someone talk about my secret—even if she was technically me—had an almost physical effect. A stagnant pool of feeling was evaporating out of my chest. Tess had confirmed that my memories of that night were real.

"Now do you believe me? Can we talk about Lizzy?"

"Is something bad going to happen to us? Are we going to get caught?"

Tess shook her head. "I've already said enough. I'm not going to tell you anything else about the future. Let's focus on the present."

I couldn't reply. There was too much happening. I kept grinding my hands harder into the bench and thinking about how every time my father touched me it felt like drowning. I stared at Tess—at myself—and wondered what pronouns to use for her. It sounded weird to call her "me," but scientifically inaccurate to say "her" or "you." Still, if I really was me, I was an unknown me, or possibly a potential me. We were altering the timeline right now. I decided to go with "she" and "her" as pronouns, at least for the moment.

It didn't seem like Tess was having the same lexical vertigo. "Lizzy has a lot of problems and she's sucking you into them. Do you know what I mean?"

"I have problems too. I'm the one who killed Mr. Rasmann. I'm the one whose dad . . ." I stopped myself. There was no easy word, like murder, for what my father had done.

"Yeah, but Lizzy caused that. I mean, she caused the murder." She shot me a nervous frown, and for the first time something looked vaguely familiar about her. Trying to find my features in her face was the inverse of hunting through my mother's baby book, packed with snapshots of a tiny, puffy-faced stranger. I couldn't believe either of them was me, separated only by years of cell division.

"Okay, so what do you want me to do about Lizzy?"

"Do about . . . ? No, there's nothing you can do. You have to get the hell away from her."

"She's my best friend. Our best friend! I can't do that. Plus, what about Heather and Soojin? I can't stop talking to them, too."

Tess seemed pensive, as if she hadn't really considered any of that. "You don't have to stop talking to them. But you have to get away from Lizzy. If she tries to pull you into this murder thing again, you have to say no. You have to leave, no matter where you are. Do you understand?"

THE FUTURE OF ANOTHER TIMELINE 143

"Why aren't you talking to Lizzy instead of me? Shouldn't you be telling her to stop murdering people too?"

She sighed. "No. It's about more than the murders. Lizzy is a bad person. At least, she is right now. She's out of control. She gets people to do things and then doesn't take responsibility for it. Do you understand what I mean?"

I thought about how Lizzy was always the decider. Then I remembered how she'd hugged me when I was scared. How she and her mom had rescued me from the worst possible thing I could imagine. I shook my head. "I don't think Lizzy is like that. I mean, she's not perfect, but . . . she wants to protect us."

"She didn't have to murder Scott to protect you. She didn't have to murder Mr. Rasmann. And now all of you are implicated."

"I mean, she's angry sometimes . . . and I know we shouldn't have killed anybody. I know that. But it's not going to happen again."

"It will."

"But maybe we've already changed the timeline, right? Maybe I can stop Lizzy next time and then there won't be more murders."

"Travel can cause a lot of random effects, so I suppose that's remotely possible. But typically edits of that magnitude are a lot more difficult than you might think." She sounded like a professor, which I guess she was. At least she'd gone into geoscience like I planned.

Tess regarded me with her uncanny face, half-self, half-other. I knew she was right that we'd done something very wrong, and we had to stop. But I didn't want to be on her side about dumping Lizzy, especially when she used her teacher voice. I stood up. "You don't know for sure! I might be about to change the future right now!"

"You're not. And besides, you don't need to change the future. You need to deal with what's happening today. This situation with Lizzy is going to get really dangerous. These murders have consequences."

"You said before we're not going to get caught. Do you think anyone believes that we could kill a serial killer? Or a rapist? No! They blame it on drifters and criminals! They say men did it!" My voice was jagged with rage, and I was saying everything that came into my head. "I don't care if you are me—you aren't me! I would never stop being friends with Lizzy! She's a good person! So whatever fucked-up shit you did to become you, I'm not going to do it!"

I walked away fast, before Tess could reply. When finally I glanced back, she was hunched over, hands covering her face.

My mom was on the phone when I got home. She ignored me as I pulled the vacuum cleaner out of the hall closet and dragged it upstairs. My father's shoe obsession had evolved into a more generalized obsession with preserving the cleansed state of the rug. I vacuumed upstairs twice a week, making sure to get every corner. Sometimes dirt and fluff would hide between the edge of the furniture and the wall. The worst was the hair, though. My mother and I both had long hair, and removing it from the rug was a key part of this chore ritual.

I began in my room, using the hose attachment with its bristly mouth to get beneath the narrow bed and around my dresser. I shook out the comforter covered in horses I'd gotten for Hanukkah seven years ago. Then I dusted my desk and bookshelves, all part of a fancy wooden wall unit my father had installed with maniacal precision, deploying rulers and specialized screwdrivers and a level full of golden liquid that caught the light as he worked. My books covered up the indentation where he'd punched the wall when one of the screws didn't quite fit. I could still hear his voice from that day, rising to a high, birdlike pitch as he reached the peak of his rage. "You know why this doesn't work? Because the people who put this kit together are goddamn lazy! There's no reason why they can't give you good materials! No reason other than . . . deliberately cutting corners!" And then the blur of his arm connecting with the wall as his words crashed together to make one, furious sound.

I moved into the hallway, around the nook where we kept the Mac SE on a tiny table, its only companion a tidy plastic box of floppies. As the roar of the vacuum cleaner sank into me, it became a soothing overlay on everything that had happened this afternoon. I wondered if I should have stayed to talk with Tess for longer. Maybe she could have told me more about what was going on. Or maybe she would have kept insisting that I dump Lizzy as a friend. Which—it's not like I hadn't considered that on my own. But I loved Lizzy, and we'd been best friends since we were little. I couldn't imagine my life without her. I wasn't going to stop being friends with her just because some asshole from my future said so.

I was so deep in thought that I almost jumped when my father's hand wrapped around my shoulder from behind. Thankfully I remained outwardly calm and switched off the motor. In the years since that night—the one Tess confirmed was real—I'd learned to make no sudden moves.

"Thanks for doing the vaccuming, Beth." His pale blue eyes revealed nothing. I couldn't tell what his mood might be, which meant the best tactic was to play along. Pretend I'd done the cleaning to be nice, rather than to avoid punishment.

"No problem." I smiled brightly. Were we friends today?

He smiled back and I didn't relax at all. "Let's see how it looks." He walked into my room and swept his fingers through the rug, leaving a jagged claw mark behind. One long hair was snarled between his fingers. "Huh." He sounded perplexed, as if he couldn't understand how the strand had gotten there. Then he looked meaningfully at me.

"I'm not really done yet. Almost, though!" I smiled again, his friendly daughter, having a perfectly normal conversation with her perfectly normal father.

He walked back downstairs without saying a word. I wasn't in trouble, but I'd been warned.

A few hours later, the rug was clean enough that it was safe to

call Lizzy. The answering machine was on, and I had to yell after
the beep. "Hey, Lizzy! It's Beth! Pick up, pick up, pick up! Are you
there?"

A series of bumps and clicks. "Hey, Beth! Can you go out tonight?
I found out about this awesome backyard party in L.A.! It's a total
lucky edit. Grape Ape is playing! It's going to be fucking amazing.
Can you come?"

I glanced over at my father, who was swirling a stir-fry together in
the wok. The kitchen smelled like garlic and ginger. "Can I go out to
the movies with Lizzy tonight?"

He smiled and nodded: I was in his good graces for now. I'd gotten pretty good at tiptoeing around his moods, but he could still be
unpredictable. This time I got away without a scratch.

Lizzy picked me up around eight, and we headed up the I-5 into L.A.,
inhaling the fossil fuel stench of street and air, blasting a Screamin'
Sirens song. We sang along, and talked about how ska was more
intersectional than punk, and then wondered what the modern
equivalent of a band like the Sex Pistols would be. Maybe Green
Day? Maybe Nirvana? We didn't like either of those bands: they were
definitely the slick, mainstream face of punk. As traffic thickened
around us, brake lights occasionally flaring red like an ephemeral
river of blood, I wondered whether there were any flecks of evidence
left in the back of Lizzy's station wagon. But I didn't ask. It was nice
to have a conversation that never once touched on the topics of men
or murder.

I hadn't been to a backyard party before, though I'd heard a lot
about them from people we knew in the scene. Lizzy had scored
a flyer from somebody at Peer Records. I touched its uneven edges
and took in the sketchy, Xeroxed graphics of headless mannequins
and skulls. Letters and words cut from magazines spelled out the
evening lineup: GRAPE APE x CHE MART x XICANISTAS x

BRAT PUNXXX. The address was on a narrow street off Whittier in East L.A. I glanced at the flyer again as we cruised for parking, and wondered if we'd need to show IDs to get in. I had a really shitty fake ID that I'd never used, tucked into the inner pocket of my craziest plaid pants. It was still warm outside, so we left our jackets in the trunk and did a final outfit check. Lizzy readjusted the skinny black suspenders over my Grape Ape T-shirt, the one with an aerial view of the Machine stamped with the word "STOLEN." I held up a mirror so she could darken the mascara rings around her eyes. She had on a ripped-up, glittery '60s dress and Docs.

"We look amazing. We are total babes," Lizzy said in her best Valley Girl accent. We giggled before joining the clot of kids waiting to pay the bouncer. The venue was on a nondescript row of single-story family homes, slightly faded and cracked around the edges. There was no way to know what kind of backyard lurked behind these facades, but I couldn't imagine it was very big. Two dollars and we were inside, walking down a long cement passageway that smelled faintly like beer, until we emerged into an enormous open space. Nobody in my neighborhood had a backyard like this, with a sound system on one end and a perfectly modified gazebo for selling booze on the other. A few little kids peeked out the windows of neighbors' houses and waved. If we'd been in Irvine, somebody would have definitely called the police by now. Here, the promoters had rigged up a huge bank of lights, their whirling beams visible from the street.

Some of the lights illuminated the stage, which was in a corner of the yard covered by a canvas shade structure. There was no formal bandstand; the musicians played on the same level as the audience, sometimes indistinguishable from it. Brat Punxxx thrashed and howled and shoved the hurtling bodies who swirled past in the mosh pit. That was the final shock for me, after the size of the yard and lack of cops. At Irvine Meadows, the mosh pit was a tiny spot near the front of the venue. Here, the mosh pit *was* the venue. There were chairs and spots to stand still around the edges of the action, but I could tell right away that nobody stayed there for long.

We went to the bar to get some beer, listening to the girls behind us move fluidly between Spanish and English, talking about how the Xicanistas had started their own zine. Finally I got up the nerve to say something.

"I'm so excited for the Xicanistas! I've never seen them."

One of the girls gave me a weird look. "Where you from?"

Suddenly, I could hear my suburban white girl accent clearly. I'd come to this backyard party in East L.A. from my middle-class Jewish family in our freshly painted neighborhood and I felt like an interloper.

Lizzy jumped in quickly with a vague answer. "Down south?"

"Where . . . like Santa Ana? Long Beach?"

I didn't see the point in lying. "Irvine."

Now all three of the girls were looking at us dubiously. "Irvine? You got punk rockers down there?"

"Some. Not much. We came because we love Grape Ape. I have all their EPs." I sounded so stupid. I thought about my dad scoffing at the *goyim* and wondered if I was like that to these girls, right now. Wasn't *gringo* another way of saying *goy*?

Then one of the girls cracked a smile. "My cousin lives in Irvine. He says it's totally dead down there." Her eyeliner was as thick as Lizzy's.

"It's the worst." I shook my head.

Another girl threaded thumbs through the belt loops on her jeans. "What did you think of 'See the Bitches'?" She was talking about the newest Grape Ape song, which was only available on a compilation from this tiny riot grrl label called Fuck Your Diet.

"I love that song." It was true. I had listened to it over and over again, rewinding the tape so much on my Walkman that I worried it would snap. "Also, the bass sounds really good now that they have

Patty G. playing with them. I'm glad she's doing something since Team Smash broke up."

The girl whose cousin lived in Irvine nodded vigorously. "I know, right? I'm Flaca, and this is Elba and Mitch."

"I like your dress." Lizzy gestured at Flaca's modified cocktail dress, as black as her eyeliner, covered in safety pins and patches. She'd added a bunch of studs to a cracked vinyl belt around her waist, and it did look objectively great. "I'm Lizzy, and this is Beth."

I was about to ask Mitch if she knew whether Fuck Your Diet had any new albums coming out when a familiar voice boomed over the cement yard.

"HOLA CHICAS! LET'S SEE THE CUNTS IN THE FRONT! I DON'T GIVE A FUCK WHAT THE BOYS ARE DOING!"

We put our beers down and raced toward the mosh pit carousel, bouncing between each other, smashing and laughing. Glorious Garcia ripped into her first song, swinging one foot up on the amplifiers. When her voice rose, her face contorted with ecstasy and rage. My scream almost shredded my throat because it was the new song, the one I had been yelling in my head and out loud for the past two weeks.

> WE'RE ROCKIN AT THE SHOW
> BUT HE CALLS ME A HO
> SO I SMASH HIS SHIT
> THAT FUCKING DICK
> HE TRIES TO HIT ME AGAIN
> HE'LL NEVER WIN
> WE'RE RISING UP WE'RE RISING UP
> AT THE SHOW AND AT THE POLLS
> THAT'S WHERE I LIKE TO SEE YOU OH YEAH
> I LIKE TO SEE THE TALL GIRLS
> I LIKE TO SEE THE SHORT GIRLS

I LIKE TO SEE THE FAT GIRLS

I LIKE TO SEE THE THIN GIRLS

I LIKE TO SEE THE TRANS GIRLS

I LIKE TO SEE THE CIS GIRLS

I LIKE TO SEE THE BROWN GIRLS

I LIKE TO SEE THE BLONDIES

I LIKE TO SEE THE SWEET GIRLS

I LIKE TO SEE THE BITCHES

THE BITCHES THE BITCHES I LIKE TO SEE THE BITCHES

We were all singing along, chasing each other in a thickening circle. It was like Glorious Garcia's voice turned my heart into a fist that could punch through my ribcage and smash everything wrong in the world. I ran toward the biggest guy I could see and rammed my shoulder into his chest. He pushed back, and I stumbled into Flaca, who shoved me into another guy. His arm was thick and bare and covered in tattoos; when he thumped it into my side, the pain shot like sunlight through my bones. I ran hard into two bodies of indeterminate gender, going blind with the chaos of our movement, each hit reminding me that I was alive. I could survive anything. The harder I charged, the more certain I was that I would not fall.

FOURTEEN

TESS

I slumped on the shady bench where Beth left me and tried to parse where I'd gone wrong. There was the immediate failure, of course. I hadn't been prepared to look into the face of an angry teenager and explain why she needed to do something painful to benefit herself in an ambiguously defined future. But then there was my bungling over a week ago, the first time I actually talked to Beth. I hadn't bothered to change my clothes after racing from the Machine at Flin Flon, through three airports, to that ugly subdivision where Mr. Rasmann died. Of course Beth had thought I was a crazy person and didn't listen to me.

So now she was a killer, and I knew all too well how that felt. How it was going to feel for the rest of our lives.

I looked up at the towering eucalyptus trees that dominated this part of the UCI campus and took a long, shaky breath. The tangy scent of crushed leaves permeated the air, and a cloud elongated overhead, its body torn apart by air currents. There was an uncanny quiet here, in the nature zone. The Irvine Company had fabricated a plot of wilderness at the core of an academic habitat that was indistinguishable from the malls that surrounded it. Two young women walked by, their hair streaked with blond highlights, upper thighs coyly revealed in the flow of silky shorts from the Express. Flirty, but not slutty. Tan, but not brown. Fuck. I hated this place, where we'd had to choose between artificiality or invisibility.

I never should have come back upstream from 1893. It was a ridiculous extravagance to make the long trip to Flin Flon, and now I was stuck here. This wasn't an episode of *The Geologists*, where everybody was always bouncing back and forth between times, despite the difficulty of reaching the Machines before we had airplanes. In real life, if I wanted to see Beth again, I had no choice but to stay in 1992. After that night at Mr. Rasmann's, I'd scrounged up a dorm room at UCI for visiting scholars. But I couldn't afford to stay here much longer. My covert visit was definitely in the historical record now, and extending my stay would raise questions in my home time. What the hell was I thinking?

I reached down between my feet, scooped up a stray acorn, and picked at its thick skin. It was useless to be angry with myself. After joining the ritual in Soph's parlors, I'd felt strong again. Purified. There was no way I was going to leave my past alone. True, I'd missed my chance to intervene after the Grape Ape concert. But there had to be a way to revise that night in Pasadena—the one when I stood on the bridge, looked over the edge, and saw the crumpled, broken body. I dreamed about it every night. I'd wake up in my Chicago boardinghouse, dizzy with nightmares about how I was getting old and might never have another chance to repair myself. Once I was finished with this edit in the nineteenth century, I wouldn't be in a position to go back to 1992 without raising a lot of questions. I had to change my life now.

Comstock was arriving at the Expo in August, and it would take me weeks to get to the Machine and back. If there were any delays, I might miss my chance to make the edit. But I went anyway. I told

Aseel and Soph that I had traveler business, and I told the Algerian Theater performers I had a family emergency in California. When I'd gotten off the CP Line, I'd found passage with a group of Cree trappers doing a run past Flin Flon. My only peaceful nights of sleep came then, in the bush, on the watery road to my past. Once I was at the Machine, it had been easy to convince Wax Moustache to tap me forward to 1992.

And now I was here, feeling almost as shitty as I used to when I was murdering people with my friends.

I stood up and looked at the greenbelt around me. I could invent some semi-legitimate excuse to stay at UCI for the summer quarter, deliver a few guest lectures, and try to talk to Beth again. Or I could get out of here, back to my mission. There was obviously a reason why so few travelers reported editing their own lives, and maybe it wasn't demon-induced madness or edit merging conflicts. Maybe it was failure.

A clot of students walked past, arguing about the upcoming presidential debates. My editorial efforts were nothing compared to what people did every day to change their own times with something as simple as an election. I needed to forget my conversation with Beth the same way I'd forgotten the night in Pasadena and most of high school. Whenever a memory emerged, I made myself think about something else. I focused on the blank anti-sensation of traveling through the wormhole. Inside its impossible mouth, history was obliterated.

Two days later, I got off the bus at the Flin Flon campus. But as I waited in line, I realized I couldn't face returning to the nineteenth century quite yet. Talking to Beth had shattered my sense of purpose. I needed to see my friends again. Luckily I had the budget for a flight to L.A. up in '22, so I told the tech to tap me there. She stuck a floppy disk into her PC tower and consulted an incomprehensibly huge spreadsheet. Everything was in order, and they had an open slot right now. I was going home, to my present.

I walked onto the smooth, damp rock of the interface and knelt, pressing my fingers to stone. I was surrounded by a ring of six tappers, connected to each other by wide, flat cables. A tech behind a row of humming CRT monitors typed a few commands, and the tapper closest to me started to pound out a pattern. Its felt-muffled mallets beat the ground like a bass drum, and then another tapper started, its rhythm complementing the first. A third joined with staccato bursts. Now I could feel the vibrations in my body, and the water rising up my arms and legs. But when the wormhole opened, nothing went the way it was supposed to.

I had a shocking, vivid sense of sliding down water-slick stone in the dark. Then I materialized in a dark, shallow cave, its mouth a perfect rectangle of sunlight. Where the hell was I? This wasn't Flin Flon, nor anywhere I recognized. Terrified, I stumbled toward the cave entrance, which sucked me back into the wormhole's familiar nothingness. When I emerged, I was cold and slimy and staring at a tech whose bendable tablet told me I'd reached the Flin Flon Time Travel Facility in 2022.

"You're the second one to do that this week." She looked startled.

"What are you talking about?"

"You're completely covered in . . . is that algae? Are you okay?"

I touched the gooey blobs on my shirt, shivering. Then I flashed back to the cave. "Was there anything else unusual when I came through?"

She checked her tablet for readings. "Nothing that jumps out here. "

"I think I . . . It seemed like I fell out of the wormhole on my way here. Into a cave. Is there a way for me to get today's sensor logs?"

"You can, yeah—the Machine sensors have a Slack channel where they output readings." The tech jotted some notes, then looked up and cracked a grin. "It's not totally unusual to see or feel strange things in the wormhole, but it's impossible to fall out."

"But this . . ." I gestured at a streak of bright green slime on my arm.

"Yeah, that's definitely strange, but we're seeing it once in a while. It doesn't mean you left the wormhole. I'm going to take some samples."

We scraped as much as we could into sterile vials, and then I desperately needed a shower. Good thing I'd left a change of clothes in a locker along with my mobile. That was months ago, but only a few hours had elapsed in local time.

I spent most of the flight back to L.A. distracted, staring out the window at wildfire plumes whose white fingers stretched across Saskatchewan and British Columbia. What had happened to me in the Machine? It was like I'd jumped in space as well as time. Could it be that the Machine was treating me differently because I'd changed the timeline? Geoscientists knew the Machines had some way to track the behavior of individual travelers, which is how they prevented us from going back to times we'd burned—or forward to futures we hadn't yet lived through. Was there some specific reason I'd been rerouted to that cave?

Maybe my edits had altered something fundamental. I bought thirty minutes of slow airline internet and poked around in UCLA's legal databases, looking for changes to the Comstock Laws. Nothing obvious. Abortion was still illegal, and doctors were barred from providing information about birth control in most states. I checked Nexis for 1990s news stories. Everybody who had been dead the last time I was in 2022 was still dead.

Was I suffering early effects of merging conflict dementia, caused by my meetings with Beth? A terrifying possibility. But then something more disturbing occurred to me. Maybe the Comstockers were making progress in their efforts to disable the Machines. My visit to the cave might have been a cosmic bug, the result of their sabotage. I needed to talk to the Daughters right away.

Wandering through the Space Age glory of LAX, I texted Anita. *Want to grab a drink? I'm here for a few days then it's back to the nineteenth century.*

Hell yes. Hipster gin bar tonight?

Neither of us could remember the actual name of the gin bar, partly because we'd insisted on calling it "hipster gin bar," and partly because it was in one of those old buildings with preserved historic signs that advertised defunct newspapers. The place was quiet on weeknights, and we met up at a cozy table in the corner whose fake Victorian chairs were far more comfortable than the real thing. The gin was better too.

I drank a shot and enjoyed the brief hot tingle in my fingers and nose. "I think those Comstockers are affecting the behavior of the Machine."

Anita raised her eyebrows. "What happened?"

I told her about the cave and the algae.

She looked puzzled. "I've definitely had some strange visions in transit, but usually they're sort of abstract colors or smells or sensations."

"Sure—I have too. But never anything that left a physical trace, like the algae. We need to get more data from the Machine facilities, to see if it's a widespread phenomenon."

"Yeah, we should call a meeting."

A flurry of texts, and we were set to meet tomorrow in one of the more battered conference rooms in the geology building. By then I'd have some preliminary results on the algae question, too.

Anita and I spent the rest of the evening catching up on news about the latest horrible memes on Instagram. It turned out some billionaire had paid hundreds of operatives to run a conspiracy campaign proving that women who'd had abortions were now giving birth to fish because "they had ruined the bodies God gave them."

Gory, doctored pictures of naked women surrounded by dead fish were spreading fast. Some flak at Instagram said it was impossible for their algorithm to eradicate it, but the company was working on "making social media safe for everybody again." Venting about politics with Anita was making me feel normal. Things were terrible, but at least I was trying to do something about it.

The algae turned out to be cyanobacteria, one of the oldest life forms on the planet, and also one of the most common. It would have filled the oceans at the time the Canadian shield was forming, over half a billion years ago. The techs in Slack had a preliminary hypothesis about it. Given that the five known Machines were all built into shield rock that formed beneath the primordial seas, they thought it made sense that the Machine might sometimes spit up cyano along with water. At this point, they said, six other travelers had emerged from the wormhole covered in ancient ocean microorganisms, all in the past week.

I turned this over in my mind, wondering whether people up and down the timeline were experiencing similar anomalies.

We'd called this Daughters meeting to talk about my news, but that went out the window when Enid told us what she remembered. Berenice had been deleted from the timeline, but Enid reverted it. She held Berenice's hand tightly as she described the would-be killer, a man with a mark that put his home time hundreds of years in the future. I noticed Enid carefully avoided explaining how exactly she'd saved her future girlfriend. In my bloodthirsty frame of mind, it was easy to fill in the gaps.

"Tess, you were the only one who remembered Berenice." Enid reached out to squeeze my arm tearfully.

I shook my head, wondering at the lost memory, a spray of neurochemicals from an undone time. This was how historical revision worked; only travelers present at the time of the edit would remember the previous version. Now I recalled nothing but the timeline with Enid's revert. Still, something about the scenario seemed off. I had to say something.

"Berenice was killed around the same time I saw those Comstockers at the Grape Ape show. Otherwise I couldn't have remembered her." I was thinking out loud, and Berenice nodded for me to continue, red hair flopping in her eyes. "That doesn't seem like a coincidence anymore. We may be dealing with travelers from the twenty-fourth century, doing coordinated edits in 1893 and 1992."

"Makes sense to me," Berenice said. "Those were transitional phases, heavily revised. The spooky part is that I can't find any records of these guys coming through the Machines in '92. It's possible they had a cover story, though. Or they came through in the past and reached '92 by living in real time."

"I bet they were in real time," Shweta replied.

"Or they made up a legit reason to be here, the same way we would if we were doing edits."

We debated for a few minutes, and then C.L. broke in. "I know we have a lot to discuss, but I wanted to say that I'm so glad you're here, Berenice. I can't imagine the Daughters without you."

"It's true." Anita's voice was rough with emotion.

"You are the best, Berenice." Enid embraced her partner fiercely.

C.L. brought out some cupcakes they'd made with representations of atoms printed on the icing and we took a moment to celebrate a world with our friend in it.

At last I got around to describing my experience falling out of the wormhole, and C.L.'s eyes widened with excitement. They unsuccessfully tried to wipe a streak of blue buttercream off their cheek before jumping in. "Okay, this is going to sound weird, but it almost sounds like you were in an archive cave."

All of us stared at them. They were referring to the as-yet-unexplained phenomenon that drew geoscientists from all over the world to Raqmu in Jordan. There were hundreds of these caves, dug into the soft sandstone of the city's canyon walls. Somehow, they could prevent written documents from changing with the timeline. Raqmu was home to records of all the times we'd forgotten throughout history—some cut into stone and hide, others in densely printed books and digital storage. Now that I thought about it, C.L. was right that the place I visited looked a lot like some of the smaller archive caves, especially the ones devoted to minority history.

C.L. continued to muse. "What if the Comstockers really are sabotaging the Machines and this is the first sign?"

I nodded eagerly—this confirmed what I'd been thinking.

C.L. met my eyes and spoke again. "Maybe the Machine took you briefly to Raqmu? As you know, I've been studying the Machine at Raqmu, and I've found—"

Abruptly, the door to our conference room banged open. A woman stood there, her short black hair mashed up on one side like she'd been sleeping on it. Her skin was dark brown, and her eyes bright blue; she wore a vibrant Hawaiian shirt over a gray technical jumper. Before she spoke, I knew she was a traveler.

She settled heavily into the last remaining chair, looking at each of us in turn. "Daughters of Harriet. I'm Morehshin." Her accent was unfamiliar but easily understood. "I have come from the future. I will give anything, even my life, to help you." She withdrew something small from her sleeve and set it on the table. It was almost impossible to look at, but with great effort I perceived what seemed to be a spherical globe of water throbbing and rolling slowly on the fake wood grain. Had she brought this thing with her from the future, despite all the limitations we thought we understood about how the mechanism worked?

We all started asking questions at once.

"Where is your mark?"

"What is that thing? Is that a weapon?"

"When are you from?"

"What past do you remember?"

She drummed a military rhythm on the table with her fingers, and the jumper parted over her traveler's tattoo. "As you can see, I'm from exactly 512 years in your future. I came because my . . . colleagues and I believe that this era is the last common ancestor of our timeline and one that is strongly divergent."

"What do you mean, 'strongly divergent'?" I asked. I had never met a traveler who made these kinds of claims. Usually we talked about editing, not diverging.

"I didn't come to change a few laws in the United States, or study the price of meat. This is something bigger. I had to come a long way back to make it happen."

Our conversation about Raqmu and the archive caves was completely forgotten. I'd met future travelers when they gave lectures sponsored by the geoscience department, of course. But none had ever come to find the Daughters of Harriet specifically. If what Morehshin said was true, people still knew about our working group half a millennium from now. A hot, unfamiliar sensation of optimism spread through my ribcage. We had made a difference. Things would get better. Wading through the garbage can of history had actually been worth it.

Morehshin spoke again. "Obviously I'm not going to tell you about the past that I remember. It's irrelevant anyway, since nothing I remember has happened yet."

"What's that?" Shweta pointed at the unidentifiable blob on the table, roving slowly.

"Evidence that I am serious. One thing I will tell you is that there's a lot you don't understand yet about the Machines. We can pull certain objects through with us—more than garb. And people. We can travel together, up to five at a time."

C.L. was excited. "I thought that was one of the hard limits on the interfaces—no simultaneous travel. To stop people from bringing an army through, or maybe to prevent mass temporal abandonment when things get tough."

Morehshin shrugged. "Your ignorance is not my problem. I'm here because of the edit war. The one you first described in your writing, Anita. In the subalterns' cave."

We all looked at Anita, whose face was morphing from disgruntlement to shock. "What . . . no. I haven't left anything in a cave."

"Somebody named Anita from the Daughters of Harriet left a detailed history of the edit war, starting with the Comstockers. Is that you?"

"No . . . it's not me. At least, it's not me now."

Morehshin sucked in her breath at Anita's implication. Exposing the future was a major violation, and apparently the taboo still held in this traveler's present. Nobody was sure what to say next.

I broke the silence. "I've been tracking the Comstockers. What can you tell us about this divergence?"

"Nothing. Obviously. I've already been foolish with my words. But . . . we need to kill Anthony Comstock." She pointed at the blob on the table. So it *was* some kind of weapon.

"You're about a century too late for that." I folded my arms.

Next to me, Anita looked like she'd eaten hot coals. Her voice came out in the clipped phonemes she used for arguing with old, tenured white men at academic conferences. "In addition, evidence suggests that killing and saving individual lives doesn't affect the timeline. The Great Man theory has been disproven. Only social movements and collective action can change history."

Now Morehshin looked frustrated. When she spoke, her unidentifiable accent thickened. "You take your sterile pleasure in hell, don't you?" I got the feeling that she'd translated directly from some nasty future curse. "You know nothing about travel. You haven't cracked layer one of the Machine interfaces. We have centuries of data demonstrating that we can change the timeline by targeting key individuals."

Anita glanced at Berenice, and I knew what she was thinking. This traveler could be lying or wrong. Or she could be right. It was true that that we barely understood how history worked. Theories of timeline change went in and out of style; every geoscience student read about the many hypotheses that had been adopted and discarded, only to be adopted again with seemingly more nuance. Clearly the geoscientists of Morehshin's time were in a Great Man phase. At least her sophisticated Machine techs hadn't managed to deposit her in the right period. We still had a chance to stop her from killing anyone, and possibly making things worse when a more profoundly devious bastard rose up to take Comstock's place.

"We have centuries of data too." C.L. tapped their ancient laptop with a finger, as if all of history lived on its sad little hard drive.

I piled on. "Your data can't be that great, if you overshot your target by over a century."

Shweta made a wiping gesture with her hands. "Let's stop arguing about theory. Can you tell us why you want to kill Comstock? That might help us understand your mission."

"We believe that he's the reason for the divergence. He started the process . . ." She searched for words. "He started misogyny? Does that make sense?"

Now I was really confused. "There was misogyny before Comstock. Can you be more specific?"

"No. I cannot." Then her face softened. "But I will say that in my time it is worse. Much worse. We are dying out."

I watched panic and mistrust distort everyone's faces. Maybe the Daughters weren't going to fix the timeline after all.

"Humanity is dying out? Like a species extinction?" C.L. sounded intrigued.

"Not humanity. Women. Queen type women who are . . . on our side."

"Queen type?" Anita twirled a pen between her fingers. "You mean women with power?"

Morehshin shook her head. "More than power, but also less. You know I am saying too much already. I hope you will help me. This is our only chance."

I thought about my disastrous conversation with Beth at UCI, and wondered if I'd sounded as crazy to her as Morehshin sounded to me now. Recalling Beth's rejection, I felt a rush of sympathy for this traveler with her strange curses and stranger story.

"I know how to find Comstock, if you'll promise not to kill him. I have a better plan. Maybe you can help."

Morehshin pocketed the thing on the table. "We are all sisters." She said it like a formal invocation. "Let us act as one."

"Does that mean you won't kill him?"

"I won't kill him. Unless your plan is bad."

"So what *is* your plan, Tess?" Anita sounded dubious.

"I told you I've been organizing with women in 1893. It's collective action. For Comstock, there are things worse than death. We're going to destroy his reputation."

Morehshin's snarl became a grin. "His individual reputation?"

"I guess you could say that."

"I'm harmonized."

I wondered how Morehshin had studied twenty-first-century English. Probably from flawed historical documents, or incomplete media files left in the archive caves. Sometimes she spoke in perfect idioms, and sometimes she sounded like bad translation software.

I looked at Anita. "I'm going to take her back to 1893 with me. It can't hurt."

"What the fuck, Tess. Of course it can hurt. Plus, you can't take anyone with you anyway."

"Well, Morehshin says she can take more than one person back. If she's wrong, then we know she's a fraud. If she's right, then we've got a valuable ally in this edit war."

Shweta took a deep breath. "I can't believe I'm saying this, but I think Tess is right. Berenice was dead, and she's probably not the only one. We need to do everything we can to stop the edit war and prevent these Comstockers from destroying the Machines."

Morehshin nodded. "We need to follow this thread back to its beginning. It's the only way to survive."

Several other Daughters were nodding too.

We called a vote and it was unanimous. Morehshin would come with me to fight the Comstockers, without using violence. Whether we faced a strong divergence, a plot to destroy the Machines, or simply a melee in the edit war, we were on the same side. Unless Morehshin decided to go all Great Man assassin on me. I glanced at her, registering that her irises had no imperfections in them at all. It was as if she'd been engineered. I looked down at my hands, the knuckles slightly swollen, skin creased. Would I be able to stop her, if Morehshin decided murder was the only way? Then, guiltily, I wondered if I'd actually want to.

We arrived in Flin Flon two days later. I still had official permission to continue research on the Columbian Exposition, and I wrote Morehshin into the meager budget as a research assistant. After the usual flight delays, followed by scheduling difficulties at the Machine, we were in position. Rumor spread quickly that a traveler from the future would be demonstrating new functionality, and several off-duty techs showed up to watch. This was a lot more unusual than a traveler covered in cyanobacteria. Many people didn't believe group travel would ever be possible. I braced myself for a disappointing plan B, where the wormhole didn't open and I had to go through alone.

Around us, the tappers thrummed to life, four joining in to beat a light rhythm on the rock. Morehshin put her left arm around my waist and scratched the air overhead with her free hand. A black square materialized beneath her fingers, like she'd revealed a circuit breaker box hidden in the fabric of reality. Instead of switches and buttons, the square glowed with thin strands of rippling fluid. I could hear a few gasps in the room, and I realized that my own mouth was hanging open. Abruptly, Morehshin mashed her hand into the square, and her fingers took on a faint luminescence. I thought of all the rules I'd memorized in school about how the Machine worked. One of the best-known limits was that it never sent multiple contemporaries to the same place at the same time. Trying to send several people sequentially to the same time didn't work either—it had been tried repeatedly, with occasionally disastrous results.

Morehshin's arm tightened around me, the floor rushed with silty water, and the air exploded into wormhole nothingness. Then we stood, still touching, in a dark, smoky cabin. We'd made it back to 1893. Together.

FIFTEEN

BETH

A week before school started, my father called a family meeting to discuss what he called "our agreement." Ever since fourth grade, when teachers started giving letter grades instead of stars and sad faces, I'd been under contractual obligation to get straight As. If I failed to keep my end of the bargain, I would be placed on restriction until the next report card came. I can remember my mother's earnest face as she explained it to me when I was eight, quoting from a book she was reading about how to maintain student discipline. I'm pretty sure my parents still had the paper I'd signed back then, consenting to their terms.

The contract had led to a lot of lonely months in my room during elementary school, imprisoned for a B-minus in penmanship and a C in language arts. Eventually I'd learned all the tricks to getting As, almost none of which had to do with being smart. Which was why my father had to detain me for new reasons all the time. But not today, apparently.

"You've stuck to our plan to get straight As in school, Beth, so we're going to extend weekend curfew to 1 A.M. As long as you keep your grades up, and start working on your college applications when school starts."

My mother looked up sharply from a pile of open binders on the table, made an indistinct noise of affirmation, then returned to color-coding her semester calendar.

My father was looking expectantly at me, and after years of dodging bullets I knew what he wanted to hear.

"Wow, thanks! I already started working on my college applications." Then I gave him the nice daughter smile and he nodded.

Apparently, I was in their good graces. But I knew from years of experience that these promises of freedom were often quickly followed by new infractions of as-yet-unknown laws. Possibly it would turn out that we'd always worn shoes in the house, and I was supposed to be cleaning the windows every week. Or I'd get home at 1 A.M., only to discover that I should have known the rule only went into effect after I'd put those college applications in the mail. I watched my father eating, totally absorbed by the curried shrimp he'd made, his hands covered in scuffs and scars from decades of working on cars.

When we were in friend mode, my father would tell me how much he hated his job. He'd never had a chance to do what he really wanted because his parents didn't have the money to pay for college. Plus, when Grandpa went to jail, somebody had to run the shop. So he'd been stuck fixing cars while my mom got her B.A. and teaching credential, all paid for by her middle-class parents. Now that the repair shop was thriving, he was trapped there for life. He'd never get to be a writer or a chef or a musician. When I was younger, I used to wish that one day he could go back to college. Then he would be happy. And maybe I wouldn't feel every muscle in my body bunch up when he walked by. Lately, though, I'd started to think that nothing would ever make him happy.

Suddenly he stopped eating and narrowed his eyes at me, as if I'd already done something wrong. A familiar nausea crept up my throat until it felt like I was being strangled from the inside. I had to get away, so I used the least controversial excuse. "I'm going to go upstairs and read." I put my dishes in the washer and raced up the stairs, freshly vacuumed carpet squeezing between my toes.

As I fled, I could hear my mother's dubious commentary. "Do you think she'll actually do her applications without you pushing her? You know how bad senioritis can be. I see it in my students all the time."

"Let's give her a chance. She's not always lazy, even if she's done the minimum required to get those grades."

I closed the door quietly, wondering what it would feel like to slam it so hard that the knob came off in my hand along with a splintered collar of wood.

Fall semester was like one of those poorly preserved movies from the 1920s, where missing scenes have been reconstructed with still photographs from the production. I sutured the sound of my father's voice, raised in anger or something worse, into hazy, scratched scenes. I tunneled through homework, applications, and classes I barely remembered a day after they happened. At least I didn't lose my 1 A.M. privileges. Lizzy, Soojin, Heather, and I kept going to the backyard parties for punk rockers. Those moments were like brief glimpses of a fully restored print, the grays rich against deeply textured blacks. In the mosh pits, I earned every scuff on my boots and every tear in my combat jacket. But I wasn't so sure I earned that early admission to UCLA, especially after my parents rewrote the admissions essay five times.

When I showed them the acceptance letter, my mother gave me a rare smile. "I loved going to UCLA. It's a great school."

My father gave us both a measured stare. "It's not as good as getting into Berkeley. But at least you'll have a chance to do better for grad school."

I had a vivid memory of Tess, older than my father was now. She'd confirmed what he was capable of doing. Knowing that, remembering the recognition in her eyes, I said something I should have swallowed. "I thought you said that if you'd gone to UCLA your life would be way better."

Bewildered rage gathered in his face, and for once my mother noticed. She made a quick cutting gesture in the air. "Go to your room, Beth. That was a nasty thing to say."

The silence I left behind, I knew, was more dangerous than a scream. But something was different. My father didn't come to my room with a list of new restrictions, nor did he spend the next hour breaking things and yelling about me downstairs. Maybe it was that admission to UCLA. No matter what happened, I would be gone at this time next year. My father could no longer claim to be my eternal watchman, ever vigilant. His tour of duty was almost over.

When the phone rang, my mother tapped on my door and said Lizzy was on the line. It was like nothing had happened. I grabbed the upstairs extension next to the computer, crumpling the curly cord in my hand so hard that it left little half-moon shapes in my palm. One thing hadn't changed, at least: a clicking sound meant that my father was listening to our conversation from the downstairs phone. He only did that when he was looking for reasons to say I was breaking the rules.

We had to be on our guard, so I spoke first. "Hey, Lizzy! Did you still want to get together to finish our presentation for class?"

She got my drift immediately. "Yeah, that's why I was calling. I figured if we finished it tonight we could actually have some free time this weekend."

"I have to ask. Can you hold on?" I made a big show of putting down the phone and walking loudly downstairs so my father would have time to hang up. If I caught him, I'd have to listen to his lecture about why he was justified because I couldn't be trusted. I found him at the table, morosely reading a novel by V.S. Naipaul. He barely looked up as he gave me permission to leave the house.

When Lizzy picked me up, she was jumpy with excitement. "What are you doing over winter break?" The school called it Christmas Vacation, but the kids who weren't Christian usually came up with other names for it.

I thought bleakly about spending two weeks with my family. "I have no idea."

"Heather and I want to go to this private show in Beverly Hills. I heard about it from one of the older guys at that backyard party on Saturday."

"What's the show?"

"I guess somebody from Matador Records is in town and there's a rich record exec throwing a 1993 preview party for new indie bands?"

"That sounds . . . potentially interesting." I used my bemused scientist voice, which was our code for "holy shit yes."

We turned onto the cul-de-sac where Heather's chocolate-colored house was exactly like all its neighbors. Lizzy killed the engine. "Want to get stoned before we go in?" She gave me her best naughty pirate smile. For the first time since that day with Tess, I felt a rush of unambivalent love for her. This was my best friend, who understood geology and never judged me and was a disobedient badass like Glorious Garcia. I was right that we weren't going to murder anyone else. That was a seriously fucked-up thing that had happened, but maybe it wasn't the most fucked-up thing I'd survived.

I took a hit off the wood-and-plastic tobacco pipe we'd bought improbably at a drugstore. "I am so glad we are getting the hell out of here in . . ." I counted on my fingers. "Six months? Do you think we could move up to L.A. in the summer?"

Lizzy blew smoke over her shoulder, into the murky wayback. "I don't think we can get into the dorms until fall. But maybe there's a way?"

We passed the pipe a few more times, and I felt the last remaining toxins from my father's gaze draining out of me. Beyond the foggy windows, Irvine was evaporating, its endlessly repeating contours replaced by UCLA's Spanish colonial architecture and the ragged, strobe-lit concrete of East L.A.'s hidden backyards.

When Heather let us in, I could see the remains of a large family gathering in the dining room behind her, full of aunts and uncles and cousins. Hamid was there too, clearing up dishes. His hair was longer, and when he looked over at me I felt a jolt that wasn't an alien seizing control of my cardiovascular system. It was only my heart, beating faster. He grinned and I realized that I had forgotten to keep walking down the hall to Heather's room with Lizzy.

"Hey, Beth." He walked to the foyer and leaned awkwardly against the wall where everybody hung their coats.

Though his family was in the next room, and my friends were waiting pointedly in front of the X-Ray Spex poster on Heather's door, it felt like we were completely alone. Nobody could hear us.

"Hey . . . are you back for winter break?"

"For a couple weeks, yeah." He glanced at Heather and Lizzy. "Can I talk to you for a sec?"

My head buzzed with more than a few hits of pot. "Um . . . sure."

"Let's take a walk."

I left Heather and Lizzy listening to records and promised to be back in a few minutes.

Outside the air was sharp with a damp chill, and I shoved my hands deep into my jacket pockets. We walked for a few seconds silently, our shadows rotating around us as we moved from one pool of lamplight to the next.

"I've been thinking a lot about last summer," Hamid said, his words coming out in a rush. "I guess I just wanted to know what happened? I thought we liked each other and then you stopped talking to me. I was talking to one of my friends in the dorm about it—I mean, part of it, I wasn't breaking our privacy—and she said that I was a jerk. Was I a jerk? Were you mad?"

I balled my hands into fists and thought about how there were certain kinds of pain that Hamid could never feel because he literally did not possess the biological parts for it. Still, there were many kinds of pain that we had in common.

"I don't really think you were a jerk."

"Then what happened?"

I wasn't going to tell him, and then suddenly I was. "Something . . . I mean, there was nothing you could do. But I got pregnant. And it's all over and taken care of, but . . . I didn't want to talk about it."

"Holy fuck, Beth. What the fuck. Oh my god." Then he paused, as if everything I'd said was sinking in. "What do you mean that it's over?"

We turned onto another cul-de-sac where the houses hadn't been built yet. Clean gray sidewalks led to square plots of gravel where one day there would be condos whose backyards could hold nothing larger than tables bisected by folding umbrellas. I stopped to stare into the invisible places where people like us might live one day. Or not.

"I got an abortion."

"Why didn't you tell me? I could have . . ."

"What? What would you have done? Become a traveler and edited time?" I snarled the words before I could stop myself. I wondered if this was what happened to my dad—if he felt one way inside, but it always came out as rage.

Hamid scuffed his foot on the ground. "How did you . . . ? I mean, I thought that was illegal."

"It is." I folded my arms and glared at him. "This is another reason I didn't really want to talk to you about it."

Hamid didn't say anything for a long time. When he spoke again, it was almost a whisper. "I think I can see why you didn't tell me."

"It's nothing against you. There was nothing you could do." I wasn't furious anymore, just talking.

"I know, but . . . I'm so sorry. It was my fault."

"It was my fault too. It's not like I grew up in a world without condoms. It was . . . an unlucky edit."

He laughed and shook his head. "I know, but . . . I want you to know that you are a true friend for taking care of that . . ." He broke off, his voice woolly with emotion. "I haven't had very many friends in my life who would do something like that for me."

"I didn't do it for you."

I turned away and took a shortcut to Heather's house through the shrubbery. I thought maybe he would try to catch up to me, but he didn't.

SIXTEEN

TESS

Flin Flon, Manitoba-Saskatchewan border (1893 C.E.)

The Flin Flon camp was waking up. Smoke rose from a fire pit at the center of a small plaza created by half a dozen cabins arranged in a loose horseshoe pattern outside the Machine shack. Two carefully smoothed logs served as benches on either side of the hearth.

Moreshin took in the scene, hands in the pockets of her coveralls. "Smells like coffee."

I peered more closely at the fire, and indeed there was a sooty, bell-shaped kettle dangling over the low flames.

"You again. The singer with rational clothing." It was Seacake, speaking behind us. He ambled to the fire, looked into the kettle, and then glanced back at us. "Well, do you want some?" He was still wearing his Levi's, now fully faded into grainy hipster contours.

Moreshin looked at me in horror. "I can't . . . it isn't . . ."

"Sure you can. I have two extra cups." Seacake sat on one log, and gestured at the other. I noticed that his sarcasm lost its edge when he spoke to Moreshin. "You a traveler too?"

She nodded mutely, sitting down with me and reaching out to warm her hands over the glowing coals.

"You're not from her time, though. Further upstream, eh?" He handed Morehshin a cup, half-filled with brown liquid and steam. Then he handed me one, and his tone regained its usual ironic distance. "You probably want a ride down to Winnipeg again, don't you?"

Morehshin shuddered visibly and put her cup down on the dusty ground between her feet. "This drink isn't for me."

Seacake looked startled. "Who doesn't like coffee in the morning?"

I scooped up Morehshin's cup and dumped its contents back into the kettle. "More for everybody else." She shot me a grateful look, and I wondered about her highly divergent timeline. Was there some taboo against coffee drinking?

I turned back to Seacake. "You got me. What do you say to another trip down to Winnipeg? Did you get the money I left for you at the general store when I came up a few weeks ago?" In the bush, the best way to pay somebody was usually to start an account at the general store. Seacake would convert my deposit into supplies and food.

He nodded acknowledgment, and gestured at Morehshin. "She can cook too?"

"Cook? You mean make food? That's built in!" I thought Morehshin had used another one of her oddly translated idioms until she pulled the invisible blob thing from the sleeve of her jumper. She squeezed it over her lap, like wringing out a transparent sponge. A bento box rained into existence on her knees, as if it were being 3-D printed from an ultra-fast nozzle. Each compartment contained colorful shapes and lightly browned cubes. I leaned over to look closely, caught the scent, and realized it was some kind of tofu-like protein, sliced vegetables, and a bit of cooked grain.

"What *is* that thing?" I pointed at the blob, still in her hand.

"A multi-tool."

Not a bad translation, probably. Seacake nodded approvingly. "Okay, good. That will make cooking very easy."

"That's amazing . . . I mean, people in my present have speculated that we could alter matter like that, but that is . . ." I paused, trepidatious. "Can you make anything with it?"

Now both Morehshin and Seacake were looking at me like I was an idiot. "No." Morehshin pocketed it again.

"Obviously." Seacake rolled his eyes at Morehshin, and she laughed for the first time since I'd met her. Then he hooked a thumb at me. "Her people can only travel into the past."

Morehshin's eyebrows jumped. "You can travel to the future?"

He sighed. "I am not having this conversation again. Let's pack up." He poured himself another cup of coffee, pulled the kettle off the fire, and walked toward the river.

We were about halfway down to Winnipeg when Seacake told us to stay in camp for a day while he checked traps he'd left deep in the woods. There was nothing for us to do but wait and fish for dinner. Morehshin could make vegetarian food, but I'd grown up with meat. Nothing could replace the taste of roast fish, especially combined with fresh herbs provided by the multi-tool.

I had a trout turning on the spit when Morehshin squatted down beside me. She'd wrung basil, chile, and olive oil from the multi-tool into one of our pans, and was crushing it up with a spoon before swishing it around gently.

"Is everyone in your time a vegetarian?"

"No. But some food is not for me."

"Do you mean like the coffee?"

She nodded. "Yes. Meat and coffee are queen food."

I thought about the ancient and medieval civilizations where I'd traveled. Sometimes elites ate very different food than ordinary people. Kings who gorged on corn and deer with every meal ruled over settlements where everyone else ate squirrel and cabbage with humble grains.

"Well, I hope you don't mind eating fish."

Morehshin made a gesture with her finger like she was drawing a question mark in the air. "I'm getting used to it."

Now that she was talking, maybe I could get some answers about the divergent timeline. "Who are the queens? Are they rulers?"

"It's not like your idea of a queen in a castle. They aren't in charge."

"Why do you call them queens, then?"

"I shouldn't tell you more, but I'm never going back there anyway." Her body straightened, as if she'd put down a heavy sack. "It comes from the idea of a queen bee. Do you see what I mean?"

I felt a chill. Queen bees were a reproductive class, often heavily guarded and unable to move. C4L crazies talked in their forums about creating a queen class among human women, locked into camps. The rest of us would be sterile workers, unable to produce offspring with inappropriate ideas.

Was that what had happened in Morehshin's time? I couldn't believe it. "Do you mean women who can reproduce?"

She nodded and swished the olive oil around again.

"So reproductive women are dying out?"

"Not all of them. Only the ones like me."

"Like you in what way?"

"Genetically related. But also . . . on our side. In the edit war."

No matter how much I pushed, she wouldn't tell me anything more. I was left imagining a world of bioengineered sisters, their mothers trapped in baby-making prisons by Comstocker drones. When I served Morehshin the fish, she didn't flinch. "Thank you, Tess. I believe we are going to win. There will be no more queens. We will be people again."

I hunkered down next to her to eat. "I hope you are right."

SEVENTEEN

BETH

Beverly Hills, Alta California (1993 C.E.)

On New Year's Eve, Lizzy drove the four of us to Beverly Hills for the Matador Records preview party. We'd gotten dressed up in our fanciest vintage dresses and Soojin had swapped her plastic barrettes for metal ones crusted with rhinestones. I had cheap silver rings on every finger, ranging from chunky 1930s-style dinner rings to a coiled snake.

I probably should have known this party was going to be a shit-show as soon as we arrived. When we got to the gate, Lizzy told the bouncers we'd been invited by Richard—the guy from the backyard party who had told her about it. Their hard faces melted into juicy winks as they patted us down, joking about how it was an "ass check." As we walked into the front yard, one made sure to say loudly that Richard's girls were always the hottest.

"What the fuck kind of party is this, Lizzy?" Soojin paused half-way up the winding driveway. Her index finger picked out an illumi-nated tent ahead of us on the vast lawn, where a bunch of white guys were playing what sounded like warmed-over Nirvana.

"It's a party with free alcohol?" Lizzy adjusted her studded belts to fit perfectly over her vinyl skirt. Then she shrugged and stuck out her tongue. "You can treat it like a scientific expedition into the heart of commercial rock music."

I have a hard time resisting the idea of a scientific expedition, and Lizzy knew that would make me smile. "Onward!" I cried. I raised a fist as if I were hoisting a flag.

Beyond the awful music tent was an enormous peach-colored mansion built to look like a box nestled inside an artful explosion of Tinkertoys. Triangles and cylinders stuck out of the walls at odd angles, painted in wavy yellow-and-black lines. Plaster rectangles hovered over the massive brushed-steel front doors, hanging from two skeletal towers made with crazily angled struts painted in various neon colors. It reminded me of mall architecture in Irvine, full of roofless pseudo-gazebos that suggested places to sit but contained no benches and cast no shade.

The door banged open, and a guy in a tiny pink sweater stumbled outside to throw up under one of the towers. Soojin and I exchanged glances. Clearly there was alcohol.

"Let's do this, kids." Lizzy marched ahead of us into the house. I'd never been around so many adults who were obviously wasted. Most of the backyard parties in East L.A. were full of high school kids, and the few people older than us were easy to avoid. Here, it seemed like we were the youngest girls in a one-mile radius. The house itself was weirdly un-house-like. The bottom floor was a giant party room edged by a full bar and DJ rig. At the center of the room was a massive, transparent spiral staircase that rose up through a shadowy hole in the roof. Somebody had strung a thick chain between the banisters at the bottom and hooked a DO NOT ENTER sign to it. Which was probably a good idea, because the place was packed.

We could barely move through the dancing, drinking, and yelling bodies. A guy grabbed my ass and laughed. It felt a thousand times more deadly than a mosh pit. As we squashed our way toward the bar, another guy offered us a bump of coke that he'd cleverly scooped into the indented filter of his cigarette. I shook my head and grabbed Lizzy's hand so I wouldn't lose her in the crowd. Soojin grabbed mine, and Heather took hold of one of Lizzy's belts.

We got beers and stood in a corner. "I think there's another band back there!" Lizzy pointed at a hallway to our left. "Want to check it out?"

Nothing could be worse than where we were, so I nodded.

We found ourselves in a less crowded room with a slightly elevated stage. It was darker in here, and a band was setting up. It really looked like Million Eyes, but they couldn't possibly be here, could they?

"Is that—"

"Holy fuck it's Million Eyes!" Heather started jumping up and down. We were five feet away from them, and could practically have walked onstage and hugged them if we'd wanted to. Which I kind of did.

Kathleen Hanna grabbed the mic. "Hey, everybody, we're trying to make our instruments work." Her hair was in a half-wrecked ponytail and she was wearing gym shorts. After a few more shrieks of feedback, she let out a whoop. "This is a song about the seedy underbelly of the carnival! The part that only the kids know about. This is a song about sixteen-year-old girls giving carnies head for free rides and hits of pot. I wanna go . . . I WANNA GO TO THE CAR-NIVAL!" The guitars screamed and we screamed too, and slammed into each other, and forgot that we were at a shitty party in a bizarro rich guy's house. Finally, we had a reason to be here.

That's when Richard showed up behind Lizzy. He wore a Kill Rock Stars T-shirt under his expensive blazer with padded shoulders. Spotless Converse sneakers poked out from his pegged pants, and a six-o'clock shadow stood out like a layer of ash on his pale cheeks. I guessed he was in his late twenties, and I tried to remember where Lizzy had met him. "Hey, girls! Wanna see the rest of the place? The upstairs is rad."

"Sure." Lizzy gestured frantically for us to follow.

Million Eyes continued to march around the tiny stage, cursing the patriarchy. I looked back yearningly in their direction as we pushed under the DO NOT ENTER sign and I felt the heavy chain cables pass across my stooped back.

"This is the VIP area." He gestured at the world we saw after passing through the ceiling portal. It looked like a regular apartment, with a kitchen and dining room and a long hallway lined with closed doors. A few other people were sitting around on couches, and VH-1 was playing on a TV the size of a refrigerator.

"Okay cool, well, let's go back to watch Million Eyes." My voice sounded more whiny than I intended.

"What? You girls just got here. Let's go to the music room and do some coke." Richard put his arms around Lizzy and Heather, practically dragging them down the hall. Soojin and I followed. When Lizzy looked back at us over her shoulder, she had a look on her face that I'd hoped never to see again. That's when I noticed the leather garter buckled around her upper thigh, peeking out from her skirt. It had a knife sheath built into it.

"Oh no." I breathed it in Soojin's ear. "No no no."

She managed a shaky laugh. "Don't worry. Nothing is going to happen."

Something definitely was. Had they planned this behind my back? Was everyone in on it except me?

The "music room" was actually a spacious bedroom with a turntable on the dresser beneath a framed poster from a 1979 Cheap Trick concert. Candles burned in niches on the wall, and Richard gestured grandly at the bed. "Have a seat, darlings. We're going to have a feast." He started to chop lines on a mirror built into the bedside table.

When all of us turned him down, Richard shrugged and rolled a ten-dollar bill into a tight tube. "More for me." He snorted two of the eight lines he'd prepped, then seemed to change his mind and snorted a third. "Hell yeah! Let's do something awesome!" He pulled off his jacket and yanked the T-shirt over his head violently. "What are we doing?" He bounced on the bed several times, then repeated himself. "What are we *doing*? Music? Music?" He raced to the turntable and put on whatever record was next to it.

It turned out to be a Def Leppard album. This was getting terrible in ways I couldn't even quantify. Richard launched himself onto the bed, nearly body slamming Lizzy, who was leaning calmly against the pillows, her Docs digging into the comforter. Heather and Soojin watched with the same expression I'd seen on their faces during the beheading scene in *Re-Animator*.

"God, you are so fucking hot." Richard grabbed Lizzy by the hips, dragged her toward him, and bit her right breast through her camisole. Then he looked up at the rest of us. "You are *all* hot. Don't be jealous. Let's do something!"

Lizzy made her left hand into a claw in his moussed hair and gave us all a blank look. "Take off your pants, Richard. Let's see you do something."

She let him go and he jumped over to snort another line before wriggling out of his pants and tightie whities with hyperactive intensity. "Now you're talking! *Yes!*" He sat down at the edge of the mattress, spread his legs, and hooked Lizzy around the waist, practically scooping her into his lap face-first. She knelt between his legs and he lay back, closing his eyes but not his mouth. "Suck it, you slutty bitch. God, you love it, don't you?"

Lizzy moved so deliberately that she reminded me of a monitor lizard I'd seen at the zoo, its body operating in some ambiguous space between mechanical and organic. When she went for the sheath, I slid off the bed, trying to get as far as possible from whatever was going to happen next. Lizzy had the knife positioned over his artery, in the soft place where his leg connected to the rest of his body.

"You love really shitty music, don't you, Richard?"

He opened his eyes in confusion. "What?"

And then Lizzy made the cut. That knife must have been incredibly sharp because she opened two holes, quickly—one on each thigh. Unfortunately, the coke had made Richard's reflexes preternaturally fast. He sat up instantly and grabbed Lizzy around her neck. As Lizzy struggled, Heather rocketed forward and snatched the knife. Richard gurgled as Heather stabbed him in the back and blood sprayed intermittently out of his crotch like an X-rated Cronenberg flick.

I wanted to reach in and stop what was happening, but a more powerful force was pulling me toward the door. I stumbled backward, trying to look and not look at the figures on the bed, jerking in time to "Rock of Ages." I crashed into the door, my arm on fire with pain, and then I was in the hallway running. It wasn't some supernatural power propelling me after all. It was Soojin, her nails digging into my arm so hard that for a blissful moment I felt nothing but physical pain.

"Let's go now! Fuck that guy. Fuck everything!" She was crying and so was I, and nobody on the sofas in the other room seemed to think that was strange at all. Was it normal for girls to come screaming and sobbing out of a room where Richard was listening to music? Maybe it was.

"Bye, ladies!"

I heard the lazy voice behind us as we spun down the spiral staircase, under the chain, out the door, and into the cold air that still carried the sounds of bad grunge from the tent. It had only been about half an hour since we'd arrived.

The guys at the gate saw our smeared makeup and became oddly subdued and chivalrous as they called a cab. One patted me on the head. "Hope you had a good time tonight."

I looked into his face and wanted to kill him.

Soojin and I hugged without talking for most of the ride home. She promised her sister June would pay for the cab—they had some kind of mutually assured destruction deal that involved rescuing each other from the surveillance apparatus of their parents. I buried my face in the good smell of Soojin's neck, inhaling unidentifiable perfume and clove cigarettes. It was strangely comforting to realize that Tess had been right. I'd told myself so. I couldn't be Lizzy's friend anymore.

EIGHTEEN

TESS

Chicago, Illinois (1893 C.E.)

Morehshin and I reached Chicago in early August, our clothes stiff from three weeks on Seacake's boat, and rumpled from another few days on the train. Back at the boardinghouse, I returned to my room down the hall from Soph's parlors and set up a cot for Morehshin. It was stuffy, and opening the windows did no good. The heat mixed with stench from the river, forming an almost visible fog in the air.

"Do cities smell like this in your time?" I was always trying to get details of the future from Morehshin by asking seemingly innocent questions.

"Every city is different."

"This one is particularly rancid, though. It's all the butchery."

"I don't mind."

I made a disgusted noise. But I had to admit that when we walked to the Algerian Village, it felt a little bit like I was coming home. In the two months since I'd been gone, the unionized construction crews had finished the Ferris wheel—getting their overtime pay for all those late nights—and the crowds had swollen considerably. Celebrities like Mark Twain were writing about the Midway theaters, luring tourists from as far as the coasts and Europe. Before, the place felt like a carnival. Now it was absolutely Disneyland. Families argued over sweets and rides, while crowds of men slurped beers and groups of young women shopped for keepsakes. The Expo was in full swing, and would continue to obsess the nation until it closed at the end of October.

Morehshin and I caught the tail end of morning prep at the theater. Aseel was overseeing the guys setting up chairs and tending to the stage lights. A few musicians were practicing their beats.

As soon as she saw us, Aseel made a squee noise and ran over to hug me. "I'm so glad you're back! I've had to fire three seamstresses because nobody knows how to sew the coins onto our vests properly." Then she turned to Morehshin. "Are you the . . . uh . . . cousin that Tess told us about?" Our cover story for my absence was that I'd had to rush back to California for family reasons. Aseel was improvising.

"Yes! Aseel, this is Morehshin."

The two women faced each other uncertainly. "Morehshin, Aseel has been working with me on our project."

"I am happy to meet you, sister."

Aseel tilted her head, bemused by Morehshin's formal greeting from the future. But she replied in kind. "Welcome to the village, sister." Now that I knew about the queens, I realized sisterhood wasn't strictly metaphorical for Morehshin. I tried to imagine a world where a small class of reproductive women produced thousands of sterile sister babies.

Aseel had more pragmatic topics on her mind. "Do you know how to sew as well as Tess does?"

Morehshin patted her pocket. "I have a multi-tool."

"That thing sews, too?" I asked.

"Sure."

"Really?" I was amused. "Does it also clean the house?"

Aseel clapped her hands at us. "I don't care what your sewing kit looks like! Fix those damn costumes! We're doing six performances every day now."

In the dressing room, Aseel sorted skirts and chemises into frothy piles. "These can be salvaged, but these . . . I'm not so sure."

Morehshin peered at a skirt with a long rip and ran the multi-tool over the fabric absently. When she saw us staring at her, she spoke. "I'm sampling. Now I can sew." And with one smooth gesture, she ran her index finger along the rip, aiming the uncanny gleam of the multi-tool. The fabric healed in its wake, reproducing a few small stains and flaws to match the surrounding cloth.

"You're not from Tess's time, are you?" Aseel raised an eyebrow.

"No."

I broke in. "Let's not talk about this here. Aseel, tell me what I missed."

"I got Sol to hire a song plugger, and she performed 'Country Lad' at one of the big theaters. Now the sheet music is selling like crazy—plus the show is booming." She gestured at the costumes and sighed. "Which is why there's so much more work."

"I don't think you're actually sad about it." I poked her.

"Do you know I'm the only woman managing a show in all of Chicago? Maybe in all of America." The pride in Aseel's voice was unmistakable.

Morehshin looked up from sampling a gold-embroidered vest. "You are one of the lucky ones who has broken the chains of her time."

Aseel nodded, thick black braids shifting slightly on her head. "I suppose that's true. You must have done the same."

"No. That is why I am here."

A somber mood settled over us and I picked through the ragged cloth listlessly.

"There is one thing you'll be very interested to know, Tess."

"Oh yeah?"

"One of the girls from the Irish Village told me that the Lady Managers are planning a visit to the Midway to investigate how we're corrupting public morals. And guess who is coming with them?" She paused dramatically. "Our favorite upstanding gentleman from New York: Anthony Comstock. He's already here in Chicago."

A thrill ripped through me. Despite my foolhardy trip to 1992, we'd arrived downstream in time to organize a collective response and make the edit. I'd even brought backup.

Morehshin narrowed her disturbingly crystalline eyes. "This could be the moment of divergence."

I folded my arms. "Transformation of that magnitude is never the result of a single event—"

She stood up, palming the multi-tool. It throbbed with white light. "Do you want women to die? Worse than die? Every event has the potential to split history."

I froze, trying to pull meaning from her odd syntax, wondering if Morehshin had already gone rogue.

Aseel ignored the tension. "All I know is that he got two unlicensed bars shut down in the city last week. He's trying to make a big splash."

"Let us defeat his splash with . . ." Morehshin paused, seemingly lost in thought.

"With a plan?" I asked cautiously.

"Yes. A good plan." She sat down and picked up her sewing again.

Aseel nodded. "Let's meet at Soph's parlors tonight."

Outside it was warm, sticky, and dark, but Soph's parlors were comfortable. I was glad to discover Morehshin had no taboo against drinking gin. Apparently alcohol was not a queen food.

I stubbed out my cigarette and started thinking aloud. "Comstock is riding high. Artists in New York are fighting his obscenity lawsuits, and the newspapers love to make fun of him. But he wants that. It's publicity. Shutting down the Midway theaters means he can expand his battleground." My voice faltered.

Soph nodded. "The first question is, who is on his side?"

"Obviously the Lady Managers." Aseel wrinkled her nose.

"And the courts, upholding the anti-obscenity laws he's helped create. Plus there's the Society for the Suppression of Vice, which we know includes travelers." I felt suddenly hopeless. I was in the right time and place, but we were still up against institutions whose longevity resisted editing. Could we really do this?

Morehshin drank two shots in one gulp. "You are thinking about this like drones. Comstock is not a collective. He is an individual who has convinced other individuals that he represents something more." She struggled to find words. "You realize he is unlike other people, don't you? His isolation has made him sick in a very specific way. We have to show the public how alone he is."

This emphasis on Comstock's uniqueness sounded like shades of the Great Man theory. But it was an interesting perspective. There were certainly other moralists like Comstock, but they weren't driven by the same obsessive desire to peep inside people's mail and hoard dildos. He gained power by breaking communities, not making them.

Soph pulled a pin from her hair and started playing with it. "It's true. We need the public to see Comstock as an individual loon who hates the great people of this city. People are already angry that he's shutting down their favorite bars."

"He's always blathering about protecting the morals of women," Aseel mused. "That's why he's teamed up with the Lady Managers. What if we could show the city that women love our show? Then there's nothing to protect. All he's doing is ruining our fun."

"We'd need an audience of women, packing the house. We can rally our friends, but will it be enough?" Soph scratched her head.

I felt a breeze coming in through the window, then realized it was from the air Morehshin displaced as she jumped up, fast and silent. "Keep talking," she mouthed.

I raised my voice. "Let's have more gin!"

Aseel, who was used to playing along with strange traveler behavior at this point, answered just as loudly. "Yeah, let's get drunk!"

Morehshin crept up next to the door, multi-tool suddenly in hand.

"I'll go to the cabinet and get a bottle." Soph made a big point of clattering around and making noise.

That's when Morehshin twisted the knob. A glittering cone of light shot from her fist into the dark hallway. In its fading glow, I could see Elliot collapsed on the floor, an ear horn rolling out of his hand. He'd been eavesdropping.

Before any of us could respond coherently, Morehshin dragged him inside and slammed the door.

We stood over his unconscious form. "This is convenient for you," mused Morehshin, nudging Elliot with her foot to wake him up. "I suspect this spy knows Comstock's plan—and a lot more."

"I won't tell you lascivious harlots anything!" Elliot's perfectly waxed moustaches had been crushed in the tussle, making his face look lopsided.

"I don't mind killing you now, mateless drone. You are worth less than your sperm, which itself is worthless." The venom in Morehshin's voice made her oddly chosen words terrifying. She pointed her index finger at Elliot's chest, the multi-tool strobing red beneath the curl of her thumb.

I grabbed her arm, aiming the multi-tool at the wall. "No killing. That's not what we do."

"He understands nothing but death."

"No, Morehshin!" Soph pushed in front of us, blocking Elliot. "We cannot do good with evil means."

On the floor, Elliot spat. "Every day, I treasure my memories of a timeline where you mindless bitches never got the vote. You never agree on anything! You haggle over the rules of war. Yap, yap, yap, like the little doggies you are! That's how you ruined America."

Aseel put a slippered foot on his neck and pressed down lightly. "Too bad you are in this timeline, then. Be quiet while we vote on what to do with you."

"Fine, no killing." Moreshin grunted, and knelt next to Elliot. Then she aimed the multi-tool at his chest before we could stop her.

"No—!" I cried.

But she was only sewing his sleeves to his shirt, and weaving the legs of his pants together. "Harder to run like that. Now, drone, tell us when your boss is coming to the village."

When Elliot refused to speak, I had an idea. "This guy's a traveler. Check his mark. I want to know when he's from."

Another flick of the multi-tool, and Elliot's shirt parted over his tattoo. Born in 2379. So he *was* a contemporary of Berenice's killer. I wondered if Elliot really did remember a timeline where women didn't get the vote. Was that part of the highly divergent branch Moreshin remembered? Or another horrific possibility known only to Comstockers trying to revert the edit?

"From the Esteele Era. That's good," Moreshin sneered. "That means you know what I can do with this." She yanked off one of his shoes and squeezed the multi-tool over his bare toes.

For the first time, Elliot looked scared. "You know that's not . . . it's not permitted for you."

She showed her teeth in the opposite of a smile. "I have eaten meat. Do you think I care what is permitted?"

The multi-tool rained a few drops of green light onto his pale ankle, and Elliot began to struggle.

"What are you doing?" I asked in a panic.

"Don't worry. He's not hurt."

The green specks of illumination moved up his ankle and beneath his pants; we caught glimpses of light shining through his shirt, and then the glow circled his neck slowly before disappearing.

"When is Comstock going to visit the village?"

"I . . . he's . . . no!" Elliot was trembling, but not with pain. It was something else.

"Tell me when."

"W-Wednesday night."

I spoke up. "Now tell us what you're doing with the Machines."

Elliot's struggles were weaker now, as if he knew spilling his guts was inevitable. Soph met my eyes, her expression troubled.

"Reverting the timeline. We're fighting for—for men's rights! The vote! Full access to reproduction! *The natural rights you whores stole from us!*"

"What about your plan to sabotage the Machines?"

A whistling breath came from Elliot's throat. His eyes wandered, unfocused. This time when he spoke, I wasn't sure Morehshin had told the truth about not hurting him.

"Soon we will have full control of the Machines, and restore the moral order." His face turned gray as green pinpricks throbbed below his skin. "You will no longer be able to repress our true history."

"How are you going to control the Machines?"

Elliot wheezed. "The sword . . . in the stone. You . . . you . . ." He looked at me with those perfect eyes. "You will never understand. It is the destiny of men." His tongue started to loll, like a man being strangled.

Soph rushed to his side, feeling for his pulse. "Stop now! Can you not see he is dying!"

"Fine." Morehshin made a dismissive gesture with the multitool. "You can sleep now." A bit of glimmering dust swirled out of Elliot's ears and he snored, ruddiness returning to his face. With a few more sweeps of her multi-tool, Morehshin restored his clothes to their original state. She didn't bother to look up at us until she'd put his shoe back on. Then she registered the horror on Soph's face and shrugged. "What? He won't remember anything."

"What the hell is that . . . thing?" I'd never seen Aseel search for words.

"It's my multi-tool. You called it a sewing kit."

"Did you torture him?" I was sweaty with anxiety, and something worse. Memories from my past that I wanted to forget.

"No. I made him tell the truth."

"What—like Wonder Woman?" Embarrassed, I realized I'd made a reference to the future.

Morehshin cocked her head at me. "Not like Wonder Woman. Like a queen."

"But I thought you said the queens have no power."

"Hearing the truth isn't power. Doing something about it . . . that's different. That's where the Daughters of Harriet come in. Now help me get this sack of potatoes out on the street."

We wrapped Elliot in an old blanket and dragged him downstairs, snoring loudly, then deposited him unceremoniously next to the gutter.

Morehshin surveyed our work. "He'll have a headache when he wakes up, plus short-term amnesia."

Soph spilled gin on him, then planted an empty bottle next to his slumped form. "That completes the picture, doesn't it?"

Back in Soph's chambers, none of us felt like drinking except Morehshin, who tossed back another shot and rubbed her hands together. "We know when Comstock is coming to the village, so let's invite all our sisters to join him."

I was still stuck on what Elliot had said about the Machine sabotage. "What do you think he meant by 'the sword in the stone'?"

Morehshin shrugged. "He used wordplay to tell the truth without revealing anything. We can't afford to worry about that now—we're in real time. The Machines are stronger than men know. Let us turn to the abolition of Comstock. How can we reach all the women?"

I frowned, but she was right. We had only five days to plan. "This is going to be a major outreach effort. It's not like we can contact women psychically like one of those scammer Spiritualists."

"Oh." Morehshin sounded abashed. "Right. No neuro-magnetics in this haplotype."

It was another one of those bad translations, or maybe a perfect translation of a concept for which we had no equivalent. Aseel gave Morehshin a dubious look. "I suppose we don't. Soph, you must have a pretty big mailing list from your newsletter subscribers."

She nodded. "I can send out cards that say the angels are gathering at the Algerian Village on Wednesday night. I bet a lot of them will be curious enough to come. Plus we can hand out copies of my article on the *danse du ventre* at the show!"

"Oh, did it finally come out in print?" I grinned, remembering how she told me about it on the day we first met.

Soph nodded, flushing with pleasure as she showed us copies of *New York World* with her byline.

Aseel grinned too. "That's a good idea. I can take invitations around to women at the other villages on the Midway. All we need are about fifty women to make a crowd."

I thought about Lucy Parsons and her fiery speech. Maybe she wasn't willing to speak up about race and gender, but she was still our ally. "I'll make a few signs and put them up at the union meeting halls," I said. "Plus, I can flyer women's dormitories at the university."

Morehshin filled in as show seamstress the next day while I posted leaflets at the University of Chicago campus. When it opened a couple of years ago, the regents of the school had taken the radical position that education should be coed. Today there were a lot of young women in bicycle outfits and split skirts wandering around, though school was out for the summer. I couldn't help but smile at one who had a thick geology textbook in the straw basket attached to her handlebars. Still, it was a bittersweet feeling. This was the first

generation of college-educated women in America. Our place in this
nation was so fragile; it was still far too easy to edit us out.

Wednesday night was humid. Sunset spread like a rash over the
water, and the reek of rotting pig guts in the river mingled with
smoke from roasting nuts. When I arrived for pre-show prep, there
was already a line forming outside the theater entrance. By the time
we opened the doors, the crowd was twice its usual size and packed
with people who were not men. They kept streaming in, filling the
seats, taking Soph's pamphlet about the spiritual meaning of the
dances. There were performers from the Midway, some still in their
stage costumes. There were Spiritualists looking high goth, and New
Women from the university, wearing athletic outfits and smoking
cigarettes. There was even a gang of young, Lucy Parsons–style anarchists looking fierce with their union sashes. I could see people
with dark brown skin and pale pink skin and every shade in between;
among them were immigrants and travelers. We made a spectacle of
ourselves and enjoyed it.

When there were at least a hundred people crowding the theater,
laughing or smirking, men in the audience started to look around
them with discomfort. Why were there so many ladies in the room?
They thought the point of this show was to stare *at* women, not to
stare *with* them.

At last Comstock appeared, unfashionable muttonchops framing
his round face like storm clouds. Trailing behind him were three
of the wealthiest Lady Managers, famous society wives of hoteliers
and industrialists. One of them had brought doilies to spread on the
wooden seats where each would be placing her petticoat-muffled
bum. A group of burly, cigar-chomping people in the front row ceded
their seats to the ladies, and Comstock glared until a gray-haired suffragette, decked out in her lacy whites from the '60s, offered him the

seat alongside them. Soph surrendered her chair to the suffragette, and smiled sweetly at the Lady Managers as she gave them copies of her pamphlet. The four observed twenty minutes of dances with what appeared to be polite attention. None of them made faces or fainted. I watched closely, hypervigilant; we needed to keep track of their position if our plan was going to work.

By the time Aseel came out on stage, the men had forgotten their self-consciousness and stomped along with us. "LA-DY AS-EN-ATH!" We chanted her name, clapping for each syllable. As Aseel captivated the room with her movements, the whole audience—men, women, everyone else—hailed her with coins. Comstock and the Lady Managers collected themselves, stone-faced, and attempted to find the exit through the rowdy crowd.

Soph and I stood in the back, discreetly motioning for our friends to follow. The plan was to waylay our special visitors as they paraded out past the ticket booths. But then Sol erupted from the theater office unexpectedly, making a beeline for Comstock. Of course he was here. He knew the moralist's reputation, but was always hopeful that showbiz professionalism could win the day.

The air had cooled down and a witchy-looking crescent moon rose alongside Venus in the sky. Boisterous crowds swirled past us on their way to the attractions of Cairo Street and the Ferris wheel.

"I hope you enjoyed the show!" Sol held out a hand for Comstock to shake. "I'm so proud of all these performers. They're the first to bring these beautiful foreign dances to America. It broadens minds and creates a more educated people. Don't you agree?"

Comstock refused to shake Sol's hand. "I do not, sir. This is vile filth."

As the men spoke, we formed a loose circle around them, as if this conversation were part of the evening's entertainment.

The smile melted off Sol's face. "How do you mean? This is a family theater."

"You are corrupting the morals of everyone who walks through those blasted doors!" Comstock was spluttering with rage.

"Perhaps these dances are unfamiliar, but I can assure you they are innocent. They are enjoyed by everyone in Africa and the Orient, the way we enjoy ballet."

"You must think I am a fool." Comstock's voice cracked as he hit a high note. "The entire Midway must be razed to the ground to stop this assault on womanhood. We'll proceed to the police directly!"

I felt a gentle pressure at my elbow and turned to see Soph beside me, looping my arm through hers. All around us, the New Women and Spiritualists and Midway dancers and anarchists were linking arms, forming a closed circle around Comstock and the Lady Managers. Sol had a look of horror on his face. This was the exact group of rabble-rousers he'd told Aseel and me to keep away from the theater. I wondered if we would have jobs tomorrow.

We stood silently, dozens of us from dozens of places.

Morehshin spoke up. "You are one. We are many. You cannot make us feel your shame."

Comstock was so livid I thought he was going to pass out. "Make way for us, sinners! The courts will not permit you to abuse God with your . . . your . . . hoochie coochie!"

Somehow, that caused me to giggle. I think it was the incongruity of hearing the word "hoochie coochie" coming out of this man's mouth, with his erect whiskers and florid face. Then other people started giggling, and Morehshin hooted a laugh. There was a sudden, uncoordinated rush of shouts, in many accents.

"You are all alone!"

"Go back to New York City!"

"No one loves you! No one stands with you!"

"Your time is over, you moralistic hypocrites!"

"We are many! You are one!"

"Shame on you!"

"Praise be to hoochie coochie!"

Somehow that one caught on, and all of us began to chant: "PRAISE BE TO HOOCHIE COOCHIE! PRAISE BE TO HOOCHIE COOCHIE!" A few drunk union men on the Midway took up the chant too. When I stole a look at Sol, I was surprised to see that he'd linked arms with two Bedouin dancers and joined our circle.

Comstock headed straight to Morehshin and tried to rip through the link between her and a thick person in a newsboy hat. The person grimaced, shoulders squared and jaw set. "You'll have to try harder than that, you weak little man."

"Stand aside, Satanists!"

Morehshin held tighter. "Your god does not control history. Only humans can do that. Do you understand me?" Her eyes blazed like multi-tools.

Comstock looked uncertain, and the color drained from his face. He must have realized he was among travelers. Then he plowed into another part of the circle, dramatically shoving two women apart with his bulk. The spell was broken, and we stood aside to let the Lady Managers pass through.

Sol shouted at Comstock's receding form. "You'll never get away with this! If you sue, I'll get an injunction! The city of Chicago doesn't care about your goddamn . . . bullshit . . . New York Vice Society or whatever the *fuck* it's called!"

Comstock and the Lady Managers did not look back.

The next morning, the *Tribune* had the story: COMSTOCK DRIVEN FROM MIDWAY BY ANGRY MOB. It was something that had not happened in the timeline I remembered. Our edit was starting to take.

NINETEEN

BETH

A baby mammoth cried for her father, who was sinking slowly into a bubbling pit of tar, trunk curled upward in a hopeless bellow for his child. Probably he would be killed by sabre-toothed cats before the tar suffocated him. The cats, too, would be trapped and die. This scene, immortalized in a life-sized outdoor display at the La Brea Tar Pits, is where I fell in love with science. At first I was gripped by the horror of this ancient moment. As a kid, I understood helplessness. Standing at the edge of the stinking pond, holding my father's hand, I told myself that I would never let this happen to us. I would watch for signs of the Earth melting. I would always be vigilant.

But as we returned over the years, I gravitated to the open excavation pits where visitors could see the piles of bones, stained a dark brown by the asphalt that destroyed and preserved them. I watched the tar extruding bubbles around the grisly clots of long mammoth femurs, camel ribs, and dire wolf skulls. As my nose tingled with the acrid smell, I imagined the peaceful transformation of bone into fossil. After thousands of years, the pain of that scene with the baby mammoth would evaporate along with some of the petroleum. All that remained would be bone, and the analysis of bone. I emptied the school library of its tiny collection of books about Earth science. Lizzy and I became best friends at the edge of the playground, trying to identify pebbles that had come unstuck from the ragged fringes of asphalt.

It's how my father and I became friends, too. He was happier when I was a kid, back when he was still trying to get his college degree in night school. When he discovered I was excited about rocks, he bought me thick, heavily illustrated adult books on paleontology, chemistry, and geology. I pored over the charts showing the ages of the Earth, unraveling the eons in my mind, watching the continents form and shatter and bleed lava.

I wished I could talk to that father again, instead of the person he'd become. It was a hot, windy day in April, and for the first time in years, he and I stood at the La Brea Tar Pits. I'd just finished the new student tour at UCLA, and my father decided we should take a break here before heading home. Now we faced the square bulk of the Page Museum together, its carved stone facade crawling with Pleistocene life.

We strolled through the unchanging dioramas in the museum, pausing at the kids' activity station. You could test your strength by yanking weights out of buckets of tar. Helpful signage explained that we were reenacting the struggles of ancient megafauna, trying to extract themselves from asphalt upwellings under the pond. Nobody else was playing with the display, and it felt like we had the whole museum to ourselves.

My father seemed happy. There was no boring job to weigh him down here, and no rug to obsess about. He turned to me, a smile still luminescent in his eyes. "Do you know why my father went to jail?"

I froze. It was something we never talked about. Was this a test? One of those questions where an honest answer ended with me screaming under the deluge of his wrath? I gripped the plastic handle sticking out of the tar, mashing my rings into my hands, pressing nerve into bone.

Of course I had wondered about Grandpa's time in jail. He died when I was little, but was never far from my father's mind as the reason for all his unhappiness. Looking into the black muck of the display, I tried not to move any muscles in my face. Maybe he would forget that he'd asked and we could go back to making fun of the dusty woolly mammoth display.

"He was smart, but he was lazy." Except for the pronoun, it was the exact thing my father always said about me. "He always got tired of whatever he was doing when it got hard. He went from job to job, you know? First he was selling birdcages, then musical instruments. And somehow he always had money to start a new business. Then one day the police showed up at our house. I was nine. It turned out he'd been burning his shops down for the insurance." My father paused, the lines in his face erased by a taut bitterness. I could see the little boy he'd been, innocent and outraged. "He was an arsonist, and it was . . . you know the term 'Jewish lightning'?"

I didn't.

"It's a myth, that Jews burn their shops down for the insurance money and blame a lightning strike. Like the myth that we have horns, or we killed Jesus. But there he was, an *actual kike firebug*." My father spat the words. "The judge thought he was going to save all the good Christians of Los Angeles from us. Nobody was hurt, but the cops charged my father with aggravated arson, which is normally only for situations where people were killed or injured. But my dad used a timer device to set the fire, and that technically made it 'aggravated.' So his sentence went from three years to ten. I didn't see him again until after I married your mom."

I was shocked. I barely remembered my grandparents. They were two old people with thick accents who died before I was old enough to hold a conversation with them. "But how did you get the auto shop?"

"One of his business partners covered for us, pretended he'd bought the whole thing from my father. He let your grandmother and me work there so your uncles could eat. And then he cut me in for half when I turned eighteen."

"I didn't know that." I met his eyes awkwardly.

"That's why we have to push you not to be lazy, Beth. I worry you want to get things the easy way. You spend so much time with your friends that it interferes with your studies."

It was his usual accusation, and it never failed to paralyze me with frustrated rage. But this time, in this context, it meant something different. He was trying to warn me somehow, or maybe warn his dad retroactively through me. *Don't light things on fire. Don't leave.*

"Let's look at something else." I pointed ahead of us, where a team of researchers cleaned fossils behind a floor-to-ceiling glass window.

"What are they doing with those piles of dirt?" My father seemed glad to focus on something else too. "Shouldn't they be looking at bones?"

"Actually that's not dirt—they're sorting microfossils." Excited to explain it to him, I gushed everything I knew. "A bunch of tiny stuff got trapped in the tar along with the mammoths. There are teeth, insects, plants, and shells, and those can all tell us a lot about the Ice Age ecosystem." I was warming to the topic when a woman next to us interrupted.

"Not that many people know about microfossils. Are you studying paleontology?"

"I'm going to study geoscience at UCLA next year."

"That's where I did my undergrad! I'm doing a Ph.D. in paleo now." The woman pulled her hair back into a scrunchie as she talked, and I realized she was only a few years older than me.

"Are you studying microfossils?" The world had dropped away, and all I cared about was learning more.

"Do you know what paleobotany is? I'm studying pollen and seeds from the Pleistocene." She glanced around conspiratorially. "Do you want to take a peek behind the glass? I can take you in."

I barely restrained myself from jumping up and down. "Yes! That would be awesome."

She turned to my father. "Are you her dad?"

"No. I'm . . . a friend." His eyes had gone opaque, and he backed away. He hated talking to strangers, and always came up with bizarrely obvious lies to prevent them from knowing anything about him.

She looked confused, but continued cheerily. "I'm Quan. Do you like fossils too? Want a backstage tour?"

My father backed up more, his face blank. Quan was freaking him out. He sometimes got like this in unexpected social situations, and I couldn't predict what he would do. It might be really bad.

"You know, we should probably get going. Thanks for the offer, though." I hoped Quan wouldn't be offended by our abrupt withdrawal. We left her standing next to the lab door I'd been hoping to enter, to see what remained of the Ice Age.

Somehow we wound up outside, next to the mammoth scene of anguish that had joined us in the past.

My father cocked his head, eyes cloudless again, and seemed to realize for the first time that he was witnessing a horrifying death. "I guess that's kind of scary for kids, now that I think about it."

"I always thought it was cool."

He continued to contemplate the mammoths, then hung his arm around my shoulders. "You are really smart, Beth." His skin was rough where it touched the back of my neck, and hard with muscle. He gave me a grin I hadn't seen in a long time. "But I hope you know it's more than that. You're talented. You're not going to be some boring high school science teacher. You're going to discover something amazing. I bet people will be visiting your museum in a hundred years."

I felt proud and sad and suddenly very old. Older than my father, like Tess. I put my arm around his waist and hugged back. "Thanks, Dad."

The baby mammoth was still screaming silently. Her father was still trapped. Nothing had changed except me. I no longer believed I could save my own father from whatever was sucking him under.

Soojin was getting really good at playing electric guitar. She screamed and howled on key, too, which meant she could do a reasonable facsimile of Grape Ape's repertoire. Her parents wouldn't let her practice at home, though, so we had a perfect excuse to spend lunch in the music room instead of with Lizzy and Heather. Admittedly, it wasn't as if they were desperate to hang out with us either. We'd all adopted a policy of extreme avoidance. Saying hi in the hallway was fine, but there were no conversations. We were no longer phone friends.

I'll never know how Lizzy cleaned up her homicidal mess at the world's shittiest rock party, but it must have been pretty spectacular. Richard's death made the L.A. *Times*, but only as a tiny notice. According to the paper, he'd produced a few albums for Epic, then died tragically after taking a ton of drugs and jumping off the roof of that house into an empty swimming pool. Soojin and I talked about the possibility that maybe the guy who owned the house had covered up the murder. Because how could Lizzy and Heather have dragged that guy up to the roof? And even then—how do you make stab wounds look like injuries from a fall?

"Rich white men get away with everything!" Soojin half sang, half spoke the words as she played a distorted chord. Then she paused, hanging both arms over the body of her instrument. "Seriously, though, I bet this shit happens all the time. Cops don't care."

"But when a rich white man dies, doesn't that kind of invalidate the whole equation? Shouldn't the cops try way too hard to solve his murder?" We'd discussed this a million times, and it had become a kind of ritual to mull it over again.

"Then it's about who is richer. Dude who owns the house is super rich. Dude who dies in his house is like . . . junior rich. My mom says that back in Korea, you could get out of anything if you paid the cops a big enough bribe. I bet it's the same here. Super rich defeats junior rich." She smacked a fist into her palm, like she was squashing a bug.

"Have you talked to Heather or Lizzy at all?"

"Nooooo." Soojin fiddled with the knobs on her Boss DS-1 effects pedal, stepped on it with her boot, and played an intensely fuzzed-out chunk of sound.

For a few weeks after the party, Lizzy called both of us almost every day. She was apologetic and weepy. She begged me to meet her and Heather at Bob's Big Boy and talk it over. Every time I found myself about to give in, I remembered the expression on Tess's face—*my* face—when she said Lizzy was a bad person. Tess had also said she wanted to save me from something worse than the murders. Which didn't make sense, because what could be worse than that? I kept coming up with increasingly repulsive answers to that question, and none of them made me want to talk to Lizzy.

I listened to Soojin practice snatches of a Bratmobile song and pulled out my AP Geology textbook. Normally I wanted to learn everything I could about plate tectonics, but today that meeting with Tess was itching at the back of my mind. Had I averted the disaster she'd warned me about by dumping Lizzy as a friend? Why had Tess come back to warn me, instead of stopping Lizzy directly? Maybe she didn't care about saving a bunch of skeevy guys? I hoped that wasn't why. I mean, those guys were definitely giant bags of dicks, but they didn't deserve to die.

How the hell had I gone from being a kid who liked rocks to a murderer who traveled through time?

Staring at my textbook, I tried to imagine what the history of my family would look like as a geological time scale illustration. Over on the far left of the page, there would be a colorful hail of arrows representing the geophysical forces that made my grandfather decide to light his store on fire. In the next panel, we would see how those forces affected an underwater volcanic province, an angry red blob beneath the surface the planet, oozing upward into my father's brain like spreading lava. Then there would be an explanation of the chemistry involved. Nasty-looking clouds of greenhouse gases from the eruption bubbled up from the deep water, changing the composition of our atmosphere, raising temperatures, causing drought. My father's eruption left the parched land prone to massive forest fires. And that's where I lived. The world around me was still burning because of crustal formation on the Atlantic seabed millions of years ago. Maybe Tess was the person I would become because of what my father had done to me, somewhere between the boiling waters and the soot forests.

"Wake up, weirdo." Soojin waved her hand in front of my eyes. The bell for fifth period was blatting from the loudspeakers.

I walked to AP Geology in a daze, wondering whether I'd ever see Tess again. Would I grow up into her, and have to come back in time to visit myself? From what I'd learned in our unit on time travel, that was fake movie pseudoscience. It was more like her visit had reshuffled the timeline, generating a new history and future in its wake. Only Tess would remember the timeline that existed before her edit.

I wished she would come back. I had so many questions.

TWENTY

TESS

Chicago, Illinois . . . Raqmu,
Ottoman-occupied territory (1893 C.E.)

Sol was right about getting an injunction. None of the theaters had to shut their doors. As soon as Comstock and the Lady Managers filed their complaint, Sol was at the courthouse getting an order to stop it. The Midway was making good money, drawing more tourists to Chicago than ever before in its history. After the newspaper coverage of our protest, there was no way that local judges were going to let some fusty New Yorker try to ruin the city's new status as an international attraction. Our edit was propagating outward, turning Comstock's campaign into fruitless foolishness rather than the moral crackdown and mass closures of the villages that I remembered from history books.

"It worked! We won!" Salina raised a glass of imported pomegranate juice in the dressing room, while Soph poured champagne for those of us who drank alcohol.

Morehshin sighed heavily. "We won this battle. But we've made Comstock angry. He's not going to let this go."

I took a swig of sour bubbles and looked at her uneasily. We'd made an edit, but that didn't mean we'd made a difference yet.

Aseel poured a little champagne into her juice. "At least he's back in New York."

That was hardly reassuring. Comstock had ways of turning New York into a monster whose tentacles reached everywhere in the nation. After all, he was a special agent with the U.S. Postal Service. As our friends celebrated, paranoia needled me. I wondered who else was listening at the door, or opening our mail.

After appearing in the pages of *New York World*, Soph achieved a new level of notoriety. The *danse du ventre* was becoming a national obsession, and her article was one of the only decent descriptions of it written in English. A local Chicago press printed up two hundred more copies, selling them as pamphlets with crisp covers. Her parlors were full of new acolytes seeking enlightenment.

One evening in late August, Soph told us proudly that artists and writers from across the world were corresponding with her about the pamphlet. Aseel, Morehshin, and I were in her parlors, having a smoke before bedtime. Troubled, I touched Soph's arm. "Aren't you worried about sending it through the mail?"

Her face fell into seriousness. "Of course. But isn't this what we wanted? Now people can decide for themselves whether the *danse du ventre* is obscene, instead of having Anthony decree it from his infernal throne."

Aseel was anxious. "That's true, but maybe you should stop using the mail to talk about it."

"Don't ever forget that Comstock wants you to die," Morehshin added.

Soph laughed defiantly. "I'm not going to be quiet anymore."

I shot a glance at her, thinking of how Comstock bragged that he'd driven abortionists to suicide. Soph's friend was one of them. She was putting up a brave front, but clearly she knew the risks.

Morehshin grunted and stubbed out her cigarette. "If he kills you, then you'll have no choice but to be quiet."

"May the goddess protect us."

"What do you really know about the goddess?" Morehshin sounded like she was asking a technical question, not a mystical one.

"I have devoted my life to study of the goddess in all her forms. I do not pretend to know her will, but I think I know her benevolence." Her pale cheeks flushed. "Do people in your time still study the ancient Nabataean inscriptions devoted to her?"

"Yes. At Raqmu." Morehshin nodded.

"I spent years there in the libraries and archives, learning ancient Nabataean, Greek, and Arabic. That's where I began my career."

I sat up, suddenly intrigued. "How did you come to do that?"

"My mother was a very devout woman, and she raised me by herself. We spent many nights with the Bible, and though I would not call her a compassionate woman—" Soph's voice cracked and she took a quick drink. "Though perhaps she was not kind, she was progressive in her own way. She taught me that God came from a time in the universe before gender and sex. Our pronouns could not encompass God. And so when I came of age, I left our home in Massachusetts and went in search of a different kind of God."

"You went all the way to Raqmu?" I couldn't keep the incredulity out of my voice. "How could you afford that?"

Aseel shot me a nasty look and Morehshin wore an offended expression. I felt terrible as soon as I realized how my question sounded.

Soph held her head high. "I read fortunes. I told men what they wanted to hear. I did what I had to do."

"I'm sorry, Soph. I didn't mean it that way. I was curious because you took an unusual path."

She touched my arm gently, and the tension was broken. "I accept your apology. I rarely met other women during my studies, so I know it is rare. I have been blessed."

Morehshin rubbed her chin and turned to me. "Another woman who does not follow the rules of her time. We are a good cluster."

"I'm glad you approve." Soph said it gravely, but with the hint of a smile.

Later that night, I awoke to the sound of shouting. I stepped into the hallway to find two police officers banging on Soph's doors. Morehshin shoved me out of the way and approached the men from behind, pinching her jumper closed with one hand. Her other hand was a glowing red fist.

"You're under arrest for obscenity, Sophronia Collins! Come out now or we will use force!"

As Morehshin reached them, Soph flung open her door. She was fully dressed in the bridal gown she sometimes wore when invoking the goddess. Her hair spilled in blond tangles down her shoulders, making her look wild and dangerous. "There is no need for violence! I will come with you willingly because I have done nothing wrong."

Glimpsing Morehshin behind the police, Soph gave a minute shake of her head. The multi-tool stopped glowing, but I noticed that Morehshin did not put it away.

Despite her promise of cooperation, the police grabbed Soph roughly and put her in heavy iron handcuffs. "What's this getup, whore?"

"It pleases the goddess."

"Tell that to the judge." One of the men guffawed. "He'll see the slut under your white lace." They gripped her arms and practically lifted her aloft in their enthusiasm to drag her down the hallway. Then they noticed Morehshin. "Is this your pet monkey girl? Hey, monkey, monkey!" Morehshin ignored them and kept her eyes on Soph, who was mouthing something.

Frozen with rage and helplessness, I watched them march past. Soph smiled. "Tell Aseel. She knows what to do. Please don't worry, Tess."

"We'll get you out of this, Soph." I made my voice firm.

As soon as they were gone, anxiety fizzed in the pit of my stomach. Despite having warned Soph about this exact possibility, I hadn't been prepared to watch her seized and harassed. This wasn't part of our plan.

Morehshin padded back through our door, and hunkered down on the pile of rugs and pillows she used as a bed. "They are going to kill her."

"No, they aren't. No. No, that's not how it's done here. We'll get a lawyer tomorrow. That's what we'll do. First thing." My words came out in a quavering rush.

"A lawyer." She echoed the word like she didn't know what it meant; or maybe she did, and was exceptionally dubious.

At Aseel's request, Sol found us a young First Amendment zealot to take the case pro bono. Sitting in the gloom of his office, the lawyer told us exactly what I'd feared.

Comstock had men tracking all pamphlets coming to New York from Chicago. His men had seized several of Soph's newsletters, including one about how angels had given us rubbers because sex is more spiritually fulfilling when there is no fear of pregnancy. When information about birth control crossed state lines, it became a federal matter under Comstock's jurisdiction at the post office. The lawyer was excited about defeating censorship, but he didn't seem to care much about getting Soph out of jail. Meanwhile, Soph's friends in the press obligingly turned her story into shocking headlines:

COMSTOCK ARRESTS LOCAL WOMAN
OVER NASTY BOOKS!
WHY IS COMSTOCK PUTTING
THIS POOR WOMAN IN CHAINS?

Then the lawyer gave a few interviews, and the evening papers were all about him:

COMSTOCK CALLS IT FILTH, BUT THIS CHICAGO LAWYER CALLS IT FREE SPEECH! ATTORNEY PROMISES "FIGHT TO THE FINISH" AGAINST COMSTOCK!

We were back at his office the next morning, asking when Soph would be out on bail. He leaned back in his chair, slicked his hair down, and regarded us with an expression of extreme satisfaction. "Ladies, this case is going pretty well. Did you read the papers?" He gestured at one, with his name prominently featured. "But I won't lie to you. It isn't going to be easy for your friend. They've taken her to Cook County Asylum. Because she's hysterical, you know. A nymphomaniac."

I stared at Soph's lawyer, wondering why he'd taken this case if he believed that Victorian garbage about how women with an interest in sex were deranged. Cook County Asylum was a bug-infested hell south of the city in Dunning, notorious for abuse.

"We have to get her out of there."

"That would be ideal, but this diagnosis means she's totally inaccessible during the first few days of her treatment." The lawyer made a sweeping gesture. "I have other cases to attend to, so check back with me next week."

He put us off another week, and then another. Finally, Morehshin camped out in front of the lawyer's office until he got the idea that his client's well-being might be as important as constitutional law.

It took us over a month to get her out of the asylum.

The day Morehshin brought Soph back to the village, there was a particularly rancid smell hanging over the city. Slaughterhouse runoff was rotting in the sewer system, and it wouldn't wash out until the next big rain. Soph's usually sunny face was chalky, and her hands trembled when she reached out to embrace us in the tea house beside the Algerian Theater.

"My darling!" Aseel was stricken. "What did they do to you?"

Morehshin gave us a grim look. "You know what they do at that place."

"I believe I saw . . . true darkness." Soph spoke in a gravelly whisper, as if her throat was raw from screaming or sickness or worse.

I ordered drinks. The chairs were uncomfortable metal monstrosities, and the table was a piece of rickety carnival trash, but the mint tea was superb. Our waiter made a big show of pouring it from a great height into tiny, curved glasses, the steam making a soothing puff around our faces. We all sipped quietly for a minute.

"I can't go back there." Soph's voice was stronger now. "I know our fight goes beyond my puny life, and that there are women counting on us in the future." She grabbed Morehshin's hand. "But I would rather die than endure that . . . evil." Her eyes filled with tears and she shook her head over and over, repeating the twitchy motion until Aseel touched her cheek and murmured reassuringly.

"You're safe now. That lawyer says they can't put you back there unless you're convicted."

"Now I know why Penny took her life." Soph dipped a finger into her teacup and drew a pentagram on the table with the cooling liquid. "There are things worse than death. So . . . many . . . things."

I had seen Soph ecstatic and spellbinding and drunk and enraged. But I had never seen her like this. Terror distorted her posture, as if her whole being were focused on some amorphous danger. The problem was that nothing in the coming months was going to unburden her. The threat of further imprisonment was very real. As I watched her stumble through a conversation with Aseel and Morehshin, it occurred to me that the asylum had eroded her entire sense of self. She couldn't thrive on the cold ideological isolation that kept Emma Goldman sane in prison. Her strength came from rituals that exalted love and community. Soph was not going to survive this battle if we waged it here, on these terms.

I tasted bile in my mouth. This war—this long fucking arc of history—had destroyed too many good women and erased the evidence. Nobody would remember Penny or Berenice or Aseel or Soph, but Comstock's laws would last over a century. That self-satisfied lawyer who called Soph a nympho would have a civil liberties hagiography on Wikipedia. A memory invaded me, of watching a woman's body fall from a great height, crashing into death before she had a chance to live. It happened so fast I didn't have time to scream her name. All my heartbroken recklessness emanated from that moment, that person, that suicide I tried every day to forget. There were some things I couldn't set right, but there were some things I could.

"Soph, we need to get you away from here. You spent years at Raqmu studying the ancient Nabataean texts about women's spirituality, right?"

Looking up from the table, her eyes still red, Soph allowed herself a tiny smile of pride. "Of course."

"And exactly how many years were you there?"

"Almost six."

Flooded with relief, I looked at Morehshin. She was nodding slowly. Without intending to, Soph had already served her Long Four Years.

Soph continued. "I can speak a little Nabataean too, though I guess it's ridiculous to say that one speaks a dead tongue."

"It's not dead. Not where we're going. There's a safe harbor about two thousand years ago in the Nabataean Kingdom—it's a place where the Comstockers can't go."

Soph's eyes widened, and she burst into tears again. But this time, it wasn't a jagged, hopeless noise. It sounded like she was wringing demons out of her body. She warded off their return with the salt that ran through her fingers and down the fresh burn scars on her arms.

Aseel used her considerable powers of organization to get us the hell off the continent as covertly as possible. Sol had friends in shipping, and he was willing to do us one more favor—especially since Aseel had agreed to manage his sheet music business after the Midway shut down in late October. We would take the train to New York, travel by steamer to Lisbon, and from there catch another ship to Tel Aviv. There was a newly constructed train route that took us east from Tel Aviv into the Ottoman-occupied territories surrounding Raqmu, known in my present as Jordan.

Raqmu was a thriving city of scientists, travelers, operatives, and spies. Home to the first Machine discovered in recorded history, its towering stone monuments dated back at least four thousand years. Shadowed by mountains and surrounded by high, rocky cliffs the color of rose gold, the city was shielded from attack but open to countless nourishing streams of fresh mountain water.

Centuries of human engineering guided that water from a wild rush down foothills into an elaborate system of canals, waterfalls, and pools that fed the city's gardens and growing populace. Architecture here had evolved to suit the soft sandstone of valley walls, with buildings burrowed into the rock to form vast cave palaces. Building facades were grand edifices sculpted directly into the stone. Generations of workers had cut a second level of streets and sidewalks above the basin floor, reached by stairs that wound between jagged outcroppings. As a result, the city grid appeared to be filling the basin and sloshing up its sides.

There was only one way to enter this marvel of art and engineering, and that was through a narrow passage called al-Siq that wound between smooth, curving cliffs studded by sentry towers. No invading army had ever made it through.

We hired a porter at the train station to carry our tiny collection of bags into the city. As we passed through al-Siq, slices of sun illuminated the elaborately carved doorways, windows, and facades that marked the entrances to archive caves, old and new. Some were humble and neglected, while others were hung with flags and guarded by gunmen. These places were full of forbidden histories, official documents, state secrets, and untranslated assertions in languages no one remembered. Some held controversial memoirs from famous travelers, reporting highly divergent timelines whose dark arcs we'd narrowly escaped. Others were packed with ephemera like two-thousand-year-old receipts for grain and slaves, or board games from the seventeenth century.

Ancient manuscripts in Nabataean described how the city's first settlers dug shelters into the natural rock walls surrounding their hidden village—and discovered that any symbols recorded inside remained intact, no matter how much history changed.

Wind whistled past us, eroding al-Siq one microlayer at a time. Born from sediment swirling at the bottom of the Earth's oceans, these sandstone walls dated back to the Ordovician period. Raqmu's pink rock had first seen sunlight on the coast of a barren supercontinent drifting slowly across the South Pole. Though it was the first Machine discovered by humans, it was the youngest by far. It was also the only one that spawned archive caves. The four other Machines were millions of years older, embedded in rocks formed half a billion years ago during the Cambrian, when multicellular life first evolved. Raqmu's uniqueness raised unanswerable questions. Was it a more sophisticated version of the other Machines? Had we inherited the work of engineers whose technology could capture and program wormholes? Were the Machines built by one of those early life forms, long extinct? Extraterrestrials? Or were they completely natural phenomena that we'd need another two millennia of geoscience research to understand?

We found a pleasant room in the scholar's quarter at an inn popular with English-speaking students. From our tiny window, we had a view of the ancient temple al-Khaznah, its elaborate columns emerging out of the rough rock like an architectural apparition. Beyond its facade was the Machine—and the civil servants who supported it. We were decades away from the founding of the Chronology Academy, so travelers at Raqmu dealt with an imperial bureaucracy full of ministers, military officers, and priests.

After settling in, we distracted ourselves with a walk around the neighborhood to find dinner. It was early evening, and Raqmu's vertical streets teemed with people from all times and places. The high, embellished cliffs halved the sunset light, filling the canyon floor with purple dusk while minarets glowed orange over our heads. Students smoked and drank sweet, dark coffee at café tables dotting the sidewalks, while harried bureaucrats hopped on squealing cable cars that would take them to the suburbs. Temporal locals in their suits and robes moved through a crowd dressed in polychronological mashups of rayon, linen, hemp, and uncanny textiles that probably only a multi-tool could make. Without a doubt, Raqmu was the most chronopolitan place in the world, and it was one of the few cities where I felt at home. Here, no one ever pretended history was fixed. How could you, when the archive caves were everywhere, testifying to the existence of edits merged into and out of the timeline?

Over a meal of fragrant lamb and vegetables, Soph pressed me for more information about the archive caves. "Can we not simply figure out where this timeline went wrong by studying what other travelers have left there? We could discern the differences, and undo them."

"Maybe everything left in the caves is a lie." Morehshin grunted the words around a cigar. "Propaganda from another timeline." She'd taken up smoking and meat, but still wouldn't touch coffee.

I shot her a look. "I don't think it's as grim as that. Obviously what people say about their own timeline is biased. History is full of exaggeration and misrepresentation. But Soph, I never would have known to visit the Algerian Village without the caves. There is a lot of evidence that Comstock is at the center of heavy revision, especially after the Columbian Expo."

Moreshin tapped ash into the cobblestone street. "The archive caves are also how I found Tess. Comstockers appear in many timelines. So does Harriet Tubman."

"The Daughters of Harriet." Soph breathed the name as if invoking a supernatural power. Then she turned to Moreshin. "Do the Daughters exist in your present time, too?"

"No. That is why I came back to find them."

"But Harriet Tubman is part of your timeline?"

Moreshin was bemused. "We are all in the same timeline. There is only one."

"But you two are always talking about many timelines. And that Comstocker, Elliot—he said he remembered a world where women didn't get the vote. Where are all those other timelines?"

"They are . . . potentials. Discarded versions. Unseen by the narrative force." Moreshin's powers of translation were failing her.

I tried to explain. "In a way, there are many timelines. But only one exists in our universe. The others are possibilities. Every time we change history, it's as if we pull a segment from one of those other timelines into our own. The more we edit, the more our timeline becomes a patchwork. That's why travelers remember so many different timelines. Each of us recalls the timeline before we made our changes. Every traveler has a slightly different patchwork in our memories."

"Sometimes very different," Moreshin said.

"Rarely." I was firm. "Some people still believe the timeline can't be changed at all."

Soph widened her eyes. "But there's so much evidence . . . all your memories."

I thought about conferences where senior faculty denied the existence of a timeline where abortion was legal. It was our word against theirs, and they had tenure. "Soph, it's . . . very hard to prove scientifically that something happened in a previous edit of the timeline. Even if there's evidence in the archive caves. Like Morehshin said, it could all be lies. Some people believe that travelers like us invent fake memories to undermine the current version of history. That's why we have to believe each other."

Morehshin nodded. "What I read by Anita in the subalterns' cave was true."

Soph stared into the distance, where birds scooped scraps out of a fountain with awkward grace. "Have you ever wondered whether there might be multiple timelines that *are* real? Maybe each time you change history, you're diverging into a new timeline and leaving your sisters behind in the old one, where they have to . . . to fend for themselves. Alone." Her eyes flashed with anguish. "After all, a universe and a multiverse look the same from where we're standing."

I put my arm around her reassuringly. "There is only one timeline. Geoscientists have ways of expressing it mathematically, but another way of putting it is that the Machines are like . . . threads. They sew swatches together into a single quilt."

Morehshin said nothing. She was staring morosely at something in the cobblestones below her feet, and no matter how hard I tried, I couldn't figure out what it was.

TWENTY-ONE

BETH

I knew it was going to happen eventually. I came downstairs to dinner barefoot, and my father reached up from his chair to grab my arm so hard I gasped.

"Get back upstairs and put your shoes on! We always wear shoes downstairs!"

It was useless to protest. Still, I couldn't help looking over at my mother—I was always hoping that one day she'd notice that something seriously weird was going on. She was reading a book about intersectional education and completely ignored us. As my father glared, I wondered if anyone but me would ever question the blissful domesticity of this scene. I could smell something peppery cooking on the stove, and the table was set. Early evening sunlight tumbled through the orange tree in our backyard, and a cat walked furtively across the cinderblock fence that divided our property from our neighbors'. Everything was relentlessly normal, right down to the hum of the air conditioner.

Maybe I was crazy to think anything was wrong. But my arm stung and my dad was pretending that we had always worn shoes downstairs and I couldn't believe that my mom didn't know or care. I thought of saying something casual to her, like, "Remember how yesterday dad said our shoes would contaminate the rug?" Then I thought about screaming until every piece of glass in the kitchen was reduced to shards.

I stood for a few seconds longer, wishing she would at least look up and acknowledge me. Nothing. Either she was genuinely engrossed in her book, or she didn't want to deal. I wasn't sure which was worse.

"Well? Where are your goddamn shoes, Beth?" My father crossed his arms.

I walked to the foyer and grabbed my sandals. But then I didn't feel like stopping. Without thinking, I opened the door and left the house. I walked quickly out of our cul-de-sac, rounding a corner onto the path that led to the community pool several blocks away. I wanted to be long gone by the time my parents realized I'd left. It's not that I hadn't broken rules before, but usually I was secretive about it. I never openly left the house without their permission. Especially not when my father had just yelled at me.

It felt like I'd passed into another reality where rules no longer existed. My sandals slapped the sidewalk in a satisfying rhythm and I could hear distant splashes and shouts from the pool. A group of middle school kids yelped and shoved each other in the water. It was the same thing I would have done the summer I was twelve, waiting through the long weeks that divided my elementary school kid self from what I was certain would be my completely grown-up middle school self. I had been such a conformist back then. I filed my nails into perfect parabolas and wore tiny bathing suits, and squeezed lemon juice onto my head in the hot sun to bring out the blond streaks in my hair. I wore pearls with my preppy blouses and was absolutely convinced that if I could lose five pounds, I would finally be pretty. But then Lizzy and I discovered punk rock.

The girls in the pool were squealing and despite the distance I could see that they'd all used the same cherry red nail polish on their fingers and toes. I used to share nail polish with Lizzy too. My nostalgia sublimed into generalized melancholy as a train howled by outside the neighborhood boundary wall. It occurred to me that this might be the last time I'd have a chance to walk by the train tracks before I went to college and became an actual adult.

I turned my back on the pool and scaled the wall, curling my bare toes into the crumbling stucco footholds before launching myself over the top. I hit the dusty ground with a shock that traveled up my legs to my lungs. I could still see the diminishing train in the distance. It was one of those freighters full of endless rectangular cars that might contain anything: produce, animals, toxic chemicals, stowaways. There wouldn't be another train for a long time, so I crunched over the rock bed beneath the tracks and sat down on a thick, sun-warmed rail. Idly, I wondered where the rocks came from, and turned one over in my hands, studying reddish streaks on slate gray. Probably basalt, a volcanic rock packed with minerals that oxidized into a pinkish rust. I tossed it back among its rough-cut brethren. Some volcano spewed hot, gelatinous blobs millions of years ago, and humans eventually brought the results to this anonymous stretch of railroad track in Irvine, Alta California.

The clatter of footsteps brought me out of my reverie, and I looked up to see Lizzy walking on the tracks toward me. She stopped about twenty yards away, Walkman clutched in one hand and a lit cigarette in the other. Of course she was here. It was where we always went. She exhaled a long plume of smoke and waved tentatively.

My heart was vibrating so hard it was like I was standing next to an amp during a drum solo. Were my teeth chattering? I bit down hard and stood up. More than anything, I wanted to talk to Lizzy—the old Lizzy, before the murders, when we identified rocks and swapped mixtapes. It had been months since I'd seen her, and longer

since we'd said more than hi in the halls. I was about to leave Irvine forever. Maybe we could talk this one time. Maybe everything
could be normal again—not normal like in my dad's house, but truly
normal, like in a Judy Blume book about how it's really hard to go
through puberty but we survive it and then everything's fine.

I raised my hand and waved back. Lizzy pulled her headphones
down until they circled her neck and we walked awkwardly toward
each other over the solidified remains of a great eruption.

"Hey." She fiddled with the headphone jack, not meeting my
eyes.

"What's up?" I tried to sound casual.

"Taking a walk. Listening to Grape Ape." She snuck a glance
at me.

"That's cool."

We continued in this vein for a while, balancing on the rail, talking about summer vacation and college plans. We had both gotten
into the dorms at UCLA, but different ones. There was a chemistry
class that we both had to take first quarter, and we debated whether
it would be easy or hard.

At some point the conversation stopped feeling strange and
started to feel the way it used to. There was nobody else who wanted
to talk to me about science, and I missed it.

"You seem really good." Lizzy screwed up her face as she said it,
like she wasn't sure.

I thought about my parents, no doubt seething at home, planning
how they would punish me. "Yeah, I'm good. Is everything okay with
you?"

Lizzy looked down, hair falling into her face. "I mean, yeah. I
miss you. I wish we could hang out again. I know you're still mad
and stuff."

"I'm not mad. I'm like . . ." I tried to put it into words. "I feel like
we did something evil."

"What?" Lizzy let out a laugh. "Those *guys* were evil. We did the world a favor."

"You can't just kill people. It doesn't change anything. It's like how you can't go back in time and kill Hitler or whatever, because he's replaced by Bitler or Zitler. Another person takes his place and World War II happens anyway. Like we learned in geology about time travel."

"Well, when we killed those guys they went away permanently. They can't fucking molest other girls."

I didn't know what to say to that, because it was true.

Lizzy continued, her cheeks flushed. "I don't get why you are so upset. I mean, I was there when you had that abortion. Why should that be illegal? Guys like those shitty assholes we killed made it illegal. Because they want us to be helpless and scared of them."

"I can't believe you are making that comparison. Murder is wrong, Lizzy."

"Oh yeah? Is rape wrong? Is it wrong to take naked pictures of girls for a 'look book'? Who is stopping those guys? The cops don't care. We have to do it."

"No, we *don't!*" I yelled it right into her face, and felt my arms flailing in the air like random punctuation marks.

"Heather was raped right in front of you, Beth!" Lizzy's voice rose in fury. "How can you ignore reality and act like nothing is wrong?"

I remembered my father's hand on my arm and my mother's silence. This was too much. I whirled around and started back along the tracks. *"Fuck you!"* I yelled over my shoulder, meaning it and not meaning it at the same time.

"Beth! I'm sorry!" Lizzy ran up to me from behind, sobs jagged between her words. "I know I'm fucked up but I promise I'm not going to kill anyone else. I miss you so much. Can't we act like none of this shit ever happened and . . . I dunno . . . go to a show or something?"

I turned around and looked at her, my best friend since elementary school, her face torn up by something I felt too. Without thinking, I grabbed her hard in a hug. We sobbed on each other's shoulders and it felt sweet but also poisonous, like drinking blackberry liqueur to get wasted. But what the hell was I supposed to do? Go home to my parents? At least Lizzy wasn't pretending to be something she wasn't. Plus, it was true that she'd stopped killing people. I hoped.

"I'm so sorry, Beth. So sorry. Please don't be mad at me anymore." Lizzy was mumbling wetly into my shirt and I still couldn't say anything. Finally I let go of our hug because my nose was running and it was getting gross.

"I'm not mad. I really want to believe that you won't do it again, but I still don't totally trust you. Do you understand?" I untied the flannel shirt from around my waist and wiped my face with it.

She kicked the rubble listlessly. "Yeah, I get it. But do you get . . . my side of this? Do you understand how bad those men are?"

I put my damp hands on her skinny upper arms, now covered in goosebumps. "Yes. I really do. But we don't need to kill anyone."

She nodded, her mouth quirking into a wicked grin. "Maybe we could go smash the shit out of some dudes in the mosh pit."

I had to smile back. "That sounds like a plan."

"I have the car. Wanna go now?" She hooked her thumb vaguely in the direction of the place where the tracks crossed Culver Drive. I paused, considering. I didn't want to go home. We could go out tonight, and see how it went.

"Sure. Let's get a paper and see who's playing."

"Yes!" Lizzy jumped up and down and hugged me again. Then she turned serious as we started walking toward Culver, balancing on the rails. "You really are my best friend, Beth. I don't want to lose you."

"Yeah." Even as I said it, skepticism was sharp in my gut. Maybe she meant it, but Lizzy was also using her decider powers on me. She knew what I wanted to hear.

For the first time in my life, I wished I could use a Machine. I wanted to skip over everything in my life between this moment and the day I would become a real geologist, studying deep time. Of course that's not how the Machines work, but that didn't stop me from fantasizing about it.

TWENTY-TWO

C.L.

Excerpted from data logs compiled during the summer
2022 field season, retrieved from the Subalterns'
Archive Cave in 2024. A formal version of these logs
was included as appendix A in C.L. Khojaeva,
"Vacillations in Raqmu Time Machine Performance Are
Anthropogenic," *Nature*, vol. 624 (2023).

FORMAL RESEARCH PROPOSAL

In this research project, I'll be attempting to measure a possible perturbation in the Machines caused by human interference. Specifically, I'll investigate the connection between the rock interface and the wormhole.

There have been multiple reports, from Gilani, Berman, Callahan, Gupta, and others, of anomalous activity in the Machines, including travelers arriving wet, contaminated with cyanobacteria, diatoms, small invertebrates, and sediment dating back to the Ordovician period or possibly earlier. Lopez et al.'s survey of historical records shows similar but rare occurrences dating back to our earliest written sources five thousand years ago. My hypothesis is that the recent unusual activity may be linked to human-caused disruptions in the connection between the wormhole and interface.

Sumner and Zhang suggest that we can analyze the strength of the connection between the interface and the wormhole by measuring various kinds of exotic matter emissions. Here I'll be taking readings of photonic matter emitted at the instant of wormhole opening. Sumner and Zhang provide data on typical emissions levels from an open wormhole, and that will be my baseline. Photonic matter has the additional advantage of being easily detected by sensors in the instruments I'll have on my body.

By sampling photonic matter emissions over a 500 million–year period using the Raqmu Machine, I will determine whether there are weaker and stronger connections when the wormhole opens. I will also speculate about what causes these vacillations.

In terms of methods, I'm capturing one random sample during each 200,000-year segment.

FIELD NOTES

Brendan Chow is going to be my tech for most of this research, sending me back for each sample and handling readings at Raqmu. I've trained myself to tap out the standard return-to-present sequence as described in Hanniford and elsewhere.

. . .

We are starting from the present and are working our way backward. My first sample comes from 670. No unusual readings above or below standard levels.

. . .

I have had my first experience of unusual activity, 85 million years ago (mya). Exact dates noted in samples. I returned to the present wet, contaminated with diatoms from the early Ordovician period, 480 mya. That's right—these are organisms from roughly

400 million years earlier than my travel destination in the Creta-ceous. Photonic matter emissions fluctuated, dropping far below standard levels. I believe this is a sign of a weak connection, and possibly a dropped connection. On return, Chow and I ran a quick analysis. We found the fluctuations significantly similar to ones at Flin Flon during similar unusual activity.

. . .

I had my first look at the more complete interface, in the late Silurian, 420 mya on the megacontinent of Gondwana in the southern hemisphere. It's awe-inspiring to see the interface before it was eroded down to a flat rock surface. In this period, the still-unexplained rock ring is visible, its two curved halves floating over the exact perimeter of the wormhole's circular opening, almost like safety barriers. The fluid canopy is already eroded away. I expect to see more of the ring and canopy as I travel back farther.

. . .

Another strong fluctuation in photonic matter sampled in the early Hirnantian stage of the Ordovician, roughly 446 mya. Here the canopy is only slightly eroded; I can see streaks of sky through the rippling fluid dome that hovers above the ring. In this era, the ring is very robust, much thicker than in the Silurian. There are un-usual markings on the ring's surface, noted in digital images. I know of no other data from this period that show these markings. They appear to be scoring, or cut marks. Sampling reveals trace metals, possibly from whatever made the cut marks. They appear too regu-lar to be natural. Could it be that a traveler is trying to change the interface?

. . .

During the early Ordovician, 480 mya, the interface is com-pletely underwater. This is another awe-inspiring moment, to see an interface functioning in the ocean environment where it may have been forged or somehow come into being (see Ba et al. for a con-cise summary of the debate over forging vs. spontaneous emergence).

This Machine, and likely all the others, was originally located under the Earth's early seas.

Luckily, the coastal oceans here are shallow. When I emerged, I immediately popped to the surface and treaded water over the canopy, which feels like a warm, soft barrier about a meter above the ring. Here the ring is flat on top, like a console. There are still visible interface controls on it, glowing like buttons on a gamer's keyboard. The floor is also covered in illuminated "buttons." Their light reminds me of high-quality white LEDs, easily visible underwater. To return, I controlled the interface without tapping! It was very exciting. I pressed the pattern into the floor buttons with my fingers while holding my breath, which was extremely difficult.

Readings here were normal.

. . .

Data gathering is nearing completion, and we have a preliminary hypothesis to guide our analysis. We've observed the photonic matter emissions shifting dramatically when the wormhole connects, briefly, to an unprogrammed time. We speculate, based on the material and organisms coming through with travelers, that this time is likely during the early Ordovician, perhaps 480 or 470 mya. The Flin Flon Machine's wormhole also appears to have connected with Raqmu during the Ordovician. In addition, Varma has reported organisms of Ordovician provenance at Timbuktu (personal correspondence). I believe that when the connection between the wormhole and the interface weakens, the connection "drops," resetting to its earliest location. For Raqmu, that location would be the Ordovician ocean.

This is outside the scope of our research, but it is interesting to consider these findings in light of Anders's claim that Raqmu is some kind of master control device for the older Machines. Maybe Raqmu's interface can tap the other wormholes, or control them from afar.

. . .

This requires more research and analysis, and I will be applying for an extension on my field season to investigate further. Based on the cut marks I found, I believe travelers may be engaging in sabotage (wittingly or unwittingly) that is affecting Machine performance throughout the timeline. Also, if Anders is right that the Raqmu Machine is a control device, there may be mechanisms here that will affect the four other Machines, too.

Chow and I agree that I should travel back to the Hirnantian, the latest stage of the Ordovician, to investigate those fluctuations and scoring marks in more detail.

TWENTY-THREE

TESS

Our first morning in nineteenth-century Raqmu was full of warm light. Soph and I shared a bunk, curling together, and her hair had come loose to tickle my nose. I disengaged from her soft form gently, trying not to wake her. Today began our search for the right bureaucrats to get us a slot on the Machine.

Before anything else, however, I wanted news from America. The mail service at Raqmu was so reliable that we already had a stack of letters and telegrams waiting for us in the post office. I returned to our rooms with a thick envelope from Aseel that turned out to contain newspaper articles as well as pages of her tidy script. We read everything over a breakfast of hard-boiled eggs and sesame bread. Aseel wrote that Soph had been convicted of obscenity, a federal crime. Authorities were hunting for her, but only half-heartedly: Comstock insisted she had drowned herself rather than face imprisonment. He clearly wanted to add her to the list of other immoral women he'd driven to suicide. "It is not a question of sympathy, or lack of sympathy for this poor woman," he told the *Tribune*. "But it is a question of preventing the youth of this great country from being debauched in mind, body, and soul. I do not know of any obscene book that contains matters more dangerous to the young, than the matters this woman has published."

Soph let the papers slide from her fingers and stared into space. "I guess this is what the afterlife feels like."

"No." Morehshin smacked her hand on the table. "This is what it feels like to survive."

"Well, then I'm going to write Aseel and let her know that I haven't yet pierced the veil. I don't suppose there's a way for me to write once we arrive in the past." She looked hopefully at me.

"Not really. I mean, you could leave something in one of the archive caves, but frankly there's no guarantee it will stay there. There have been a lot of purges over the millennia."

"What about the subalterns' cave? The one Morehshin talked about?"

Morehshin shrugged. "I looked on the way in, but it's not here. Must have been dug later."

"All right, then." Soph sounded depressed as she rooted through her satchel for paper.

There were people I had to see about access to the Machine. So I left the two of them in the hostel, Soph writing sadly and Morehshin running her multi-tool over the walls, conducting an analysis that defied translation.

My destination was a nondescript two-story structure cut into the walls near an ancient theater, its facade bumpy with Victorian flourishes. AMERICAN GEOPHYSICAL UNION, read a large plaque mounted over the double doors. Over time, this archive for geoscientists had grown to become part professional association and part meeting-house. The AGU cave was also permanent home to a small council of underpaid academics who held positions in the Raqmu Machine bureaucracy.

A bell tinkled as I opened a wooden door set into the cave

entrance, as if this were a dry goods store. Beyond an unoccupied reception desk was the library, whose battered chairs and tables looked pretty much the same as they did in 2022—though they lacked a fleet of computer terminals. I was about to take some creaky stairs up to the council offices when somebody shouted my name.

It sounded like Anita, but that couldn't be right.

"Tess! You're here!" Definitely Anita. What the hell? Had something gone horribly wrong? I walked into the library, and found her sitting with C.L. and a few students, surrounded by piles of books. Despite the weirdness of seeing both her and C.L. in the wrong time, I suddenly felt like everything would be all right. My best friend was here. I practically knocked over the table next to her in the midst of our enthusiastic hug.

"Why are you both in 1893?"

C.L. cleared their throat. "We're . . . uh . . . researching . . . things?"

I was nonplussed. "What's going on? Has something happened with the Applied Cultural Geology Working Group?"

Anita and C.L. looked furtively at each other. "We need to talk to you about something."

"Tell me."

"It's . . . private."

The students made a big show of leafing through their books and tried to act like they weren't listening. Anita glared at them until they suddenly decided it was time to go out for brunch in Englishtown.

When the door slammed in a cacophony of bell noises, C.L. jumped up and started pacing. I noticed they had a new ocular implant, forming a faint crescent-shaped bulge over their right eye. "I've completed my field season, and anomalies are increasing at the Machines. A few more people came back covered in extinct single-celled organisms from the Ordovician. One told me off the record that he'd seen a glimpse of an archive cave, like you did. So I've been systematically going back to different periods in the Raqmu

Machine, trying to figure out if something in the mechanism has changed. I kept wondering whether the wormhole might be dipping into the past before linking to the correct time. It's kind of what you'd expect if the interface were . . . buggy, I guess."

"The Comstockers?" I felt cold.

"Well, it might be wear and tear. More people than ever are using the Machines, and we're using them in new ways. Morehshin showed us that there are parts of the interface that we didn't know existed, and we have to assume people are using those in the future all the time. But . . ." They looked uncertainly at Anita.

"But what?"

"The Comstockers may be getting somewhere. My guess is that they're destabilizing the wormholes. I went back to the Ordovician from here and found these cuts in the rock, with traces of metal alloy in them that could only come from humans . . ."

"Why would sabotage on the Raqmu Machine affect Flin Flon, though?"

"You know the hypothesis that the Raqmu Machine controls the others? If that turns out to be true, then all they have to do is destroy this one."

"And then we're completely fucked." Anita was grim. "We've got to stop these shitlords before that happens."

"I don't get why they would do this. If they lock the timeline, they can't make edits either. They might get stuck in a timeline where . . . I dunno, things are pretty much like this one. Universal suffrage."

Anita looked at me like I had eaten a library book.

"Don't you think it would be bad enough if we were fixed here in this timeline, where women can't get abortions and black kids are being murdered by cops? They don't need to take away our right to vote to make our lives hell."

She was right, as usual. "So . . . why did you come to find me?"

"We need Morehshin to take all of us back to 13 B.C.E. There's someone there I need to see."

"That's where we were headed anyway."

Anita nodded curtly. "Excellent. I've already booked us on the Machine."

"Okay, but I am still confused. How did you know that we would be here?"

Anita's expression was unreadable. "Ah. You don't know yet."

I blinked. "What do you remember?"

"A Spiritualist named Sophronia Collins committed suicide under very mysterious circumstances, after Anthony Comstock got her convicted for obscenity during the World's Fair. I wasn't sure, but I guessed that was your handiwork. Especially because you wrote that paper about secret travelers using suicide as a cover to escape their present. I figured you'd hidden her in the past, and that meant you'd come through here. I've been waiting for a couple of weeks."

"I came down a couple of days ago," C.L. added. "Anita said you'd be here."

"What about . . . is anything else different? The Comstock Laws?"

Anita shook her head. "Abortion is illegal."

The edit war was far from over, but I was intoxicated by the news that at least part of my edit had taken. I couldn't quite believe it. When I'd studied this period, there was no record of a person named Sophronia Collins fighting Comstock. I'd met her by chance at the Algerian Village. I allowed myself a moment of satisfaction. It was the first time I'd made an edit of any significance, and that meant I might be on the right track.

Early the next morning, Anita knocked on the door of our room at the inn. "We've got a slot at 9:30 A.M. Let's go."

Moreshin would be doing another demo of her collective travel technique for a small but admiring audience of scholars and techs. The Machine room at al-Khaznah was already full when we arrived, its sandstone walls carved with abstract designs and inscriptions in pre-Nabataean. Some of these explained the rudiments of the interface, which the ancients treated like rule-based magic. Now, there were two steam-driven tappers in place to pound out the pattern that would open a passage to our destination. We stood at the center of a shallow bowl worn into the smooth rock by thousands of travelers over thousands of years.

"You must all be touching me when we do this." Morehshin waved us in close. I wrapped my arm around Morehshin's waist, then positioned Soph's back against my chest, her arm curved around Anita. Anita tucked C.L. between the two of us. At last, we were all spooning each other and hugging Morehshin as tightly as we could. From above, we must have looked like we were doing a Busby Berkeley dance. But from eye level, we were merely a group of travelers, slightly sweaty and desperate. Morehshin reached out and clawed the air open overhead, revealing that square black interface controller I'd seen for the first time at Flin Flon. Inside it, attenuated light wavered like it was traveling through fluid. Then Morehshin drew a zigzag shape in the air, while palming the multi-tool. It strobed pink.

"Hold on!"

I had never gripped my sisters harder than I did in that moment. Fluid sloshed up from the floor, filling my nose and mouth with a swampy froth, and then we were in wormhole free fall until we landed hard in the middle of nowhere. There were no bureaucrats or techs. We stood on a bright, sandy cliff, sterile except for a few patches of lichen that looked like black stains. A shallow emerald ocean stretched below, thick with vegetation that broke the surface. The air smelled intensely of salt. And then, with a shock, I noticed the rock ring, its rough red surface encircling us. Overhead, the canopy looked like a parasol made of fluid, filtering the light through rippling waves.

A peculiar silence hung over everything, and I realized there were no birds calling to each other over the swells. I could hear only faint waves and wind scouring the seemingly infinite volume of empty yellow rock behind us.

"Where are we?" I muttered it into the skin of Morehshin's neck, and tightened my grip.

C.L. looked around wildly, their hair brushing my cheek. "Holy shit. I think we're . . . in the Ordovician." They started to pull away from our cluster, pointing at something huge and armored that swam through the waters below.

"Don't let go!" Morehshin was pounding a travel pattern into the ground with her feet and trying to torque something in the canopy overhead.

Abruptly a hot rain gushed from the crust beneath us and the air became void. We emerged on the floor of a smoky cave lit by torches. All of us were covered in a thick layer of dust that made me cough uncontrollably. Eight slaves sat in a semicircle around us, flanked by baskets of bones and lithics. These people, some with the dark complexions of Africans and others with varying shades of Mediterranean tan, were the tappers of classical antiquity. Property of the Raqmu Machine's priesthood, they pounded out rhythms that programmed the interface. A bored-looking man with oiled brown skin and gold bangles on his upper arms sat on a stone bench beside us, its contours softened by several layers of furs and rugs. He nodded, his clubbed beard protruding stiffly from his chin, and made a quick notation on a damp slab of clay.

"Welcome, travelers." He spoke Nabataean. As my eyes adjusted, I realized we had arrived at our destination. Barely.

"That was . . . not good." C.L. was shaken. "I haven't seen anything like that before."

Anita whirled on Morehshin. "What did you do to get us back?"

"Reset to last destination."

"There's a reset button?" C.L. perked up.

"It's complicated."

"Get out of the circle. You are blocking travel." The bureaucrat was irritated. "And show me your marks."

Soph addressed him in halting Nabataean. "We apologize. Thank you for your hospitality." Then she followed us awkwardly out of a thick red circle painted onto the floor. It marked the boundaries of the wormhole opening the same way the ring once had.

"So many of you," he marveled. "I did not know that was possible." He made another notation on the tablet, then checked our marks. When Soph shook her head, he frowned. "You cannot travel without a mark."

"She's my student, so she travels on my mark." Anita was brusque, as if this were done all the time.

"I'll need to inform the Order." He referred to the priesthood that controlled access to the Machine during this period. "Travelers without a mark are in violation of the law."

"Well, you've never seen five people come through, have you? We're part of a new experimental group in 2022 C.E.," I said. My grad school Nabataean was rusty, but he seemed to get the gist.

The bureaucrat frowned and stood up, blocking our exit. "You need to come back tomorrow and speak to the Order."

"I will." Anita drew herself up to full height, towering over him. People in the ancient world were usually at least a foot shorter than modern humans, and Anita was imposing even in our present. He bowed his head and stepped aside.

"See that you do."

"Let's go before he starts asking more questions," Anita whispered in English as she led us out of the travel chamber into the temple proper, an atrium with high, curved ceilings and red walls. Light spilled in through the doorway and windows, illuminating scholars studying tablets and scrolls at a wooden table. Incense curled into the air beside a few shrines. People came and went from various side rooms on traveler business, barely noticing us. They were used to people in anachronistic clothing wandering out of the Machine chamber in a daze.

"Are they going to send me back to my time?" Soph raced to keep up with Anita's pace.

"They would if we brought you back tomorrow, but we won't."

"Why not?"

"Because if all goes well," I said, "we're going to sacrifice you to the goddess al-Lat."

TWENTY-FOUR

BETH

After not speaking to Lizzy for so long, sitting in her car felt like returning to a childhood playground. It was familiar, but also somehow smaller and less colorful than I remembered. She drove up the I-5 while I pored over the *LA Weekly* listings, pausing to read a story about how geoscientists were reporting strange activity at the Machines. Unfortunately the bit about Ordovician algae was only two sentences long, lost in a boring discussion of whether the Chronology Academy was corrupt. I crumpled the paper under my seat and sighed.

It was too late to scrounge up an invite to a backyard party, and besides it was Tuesday. The legit venues were probably pretty dead too. We decided on an all-ages show at Starless, a café in Echo Park that was a regular hangout for some of the girls we'd met at backyard parties.

Sure enough, Flaca and Mitch were there when we arrived, sitting at one of the tiny circular tables that wobbled so much nobody used it to hold drinks. Tonight it served mostly as an ashtray pedestal.

"Hey, girlies!" Mitch waved us over excitedly, her heavy wallet chain clanging against a chair. A couple of other kids we didn't know were there, and Flaca introduced them in a blur of names. All the girls from East L.A. had perfect eyebrows. They were in the middle of dissecting the latest details about some bullshit where Tower Records wouldn't carry Fuck Your Diet albums.

"It's racism!" Flaca folded her arms.

"They said it's because they have fuck in their name." Mitch shrugged.

"But everybody says fuck in their band names now. They can put little stars over it or something." I scowled, but I was also relieved to be upset about something that wasn't murder or my dad.

"Oh shit, it's that dude from last week," Flaca hissed and pointed at a guy who had arrived with a couple of friends. He looked like a Billy Idol impersonator, with spiky bleached hair and a pasted-on snarl.

"That poseur? What did he do?" Lizzy checked him out in an extremely non-covert way.

Mitch lit a cigarette and picked up the story. "He came here last week and started hitting on a bunch of girls, telling them he likes Chicanas because they know their place and understand that men are men. Usual white boy line—sorry, Marcus." She nodded an apology to a ginger in the group and he shrugged. "But it got really fucking insane. What was that thing he said to you, Flaca?"

"He went off on how he'd treat me like a queen or some shit? He said he had a special room where I could have babies and never worry again. It was creepy as fuck. Like serial killer talk. The boy is crazy."

Flaca's mention of serial killers got everybody debating who was scarier—John Wayne Gacy or the Night Stalker? What about Jack the Ripper, who traveled through time to eat Victorian hookers? But Lizzy kept her eyes on the guy after the show started. In the mosh pit, she kept racing up to him then pulling back from a body slam with a little smile. He ate it up. Pretty soon he was chasing after her in the pit, delivering soft little swipes to her ass.

THE FUTURE OF ANOTHER TIMELINE   243

We were panting at the counter between acts when the serial killer decided to make his move. He leaned right up into our space and pulled the cigarette out of Lizzy's hand.

"You're a lot prettier when you're not smoking and trying to push men around in the mosh pit."

Ugh. Of course he was one of those guys who flirted with pseudo-insults.

Lizzy emitted a fake giggle and grabbed the cigarette back. "You think so? I bet that's what you tell all the girls."

His face became serious for a minute, and I realized his pale skin was impossibly smooth. Literally no pock marks or scabs anywhere, as if he were made of plastic. "I don't talk to girls. I talk to queens. You could be my queen." When he smiled, his teeth exhibited the same uncanny perfection.

"Wanna talk outside? Your queen requests an audience."

I should have known Lizzy was lying when we were at the rail-road tracks. This was exactly like that night at the horrible party with Richard. Was she still carrying a knife? There was an alley behind Starless where everybody went to do drugs and have sex. Etiquette dictated that nobody looked at anyone back there—you had your dark, private spot, and you let your neighbors have theirs. It was the perfect place to murder a scumbag.

The scumbag in question gave Lizzy an appraising look. "I'm Elliot." He grabbed her hand and lifted it to his mouth for a kiss. She reached her other hand around to her back pocket and adjusted something that had the unmistakable shape of her knife sheath. I had to intervene.

"Hi, Elliot. Wow, it's great to meet you. I bet you are a really fun guy, but my friend is unfortunately *super* busy right now. *Super* busy. Like until the end of time." I yanked as hard as I could on Lizzy's arm and unglued her from the counter.

She was so surprised that I had her halfway to the door before she protested. "What, Beth? What the hell?"

"We are leaving. *Now.*" I was so pumped with adrenaline that I thought maybe I was having one of those moments of super-strength where people lift cars to rescue trapped children. I dragged her to the alley where I was pretty sure she'd been planning to kill Elliot and pushed her against the graffiti-caked wall. "I thought you said you weren't doing that shit anymore. Remember how like three hours ago you said that?"

"I wasn't doing anything."

I glared.

"I was just going to scare him."

"No. I saw the knife in your pocket."

"Fine. Maybe I was going to fuck with him. But you heard what Flaca said. You heard how he talked to me. That guy is a shitstain of epic proportions."

The door to the café slammed and Elliot and his pals stumbled into the alley. One of them hooted drunkenly. "There's your little feminazi cocktease."

Elliot took a step in our direction then changed his mind. "Let's go to a bar with some real women."

"Yeah. I hate these cuck-making bitches."

They wandered away, their insults growing fainter as the street swallowed them.

"Did he say 'cock-making bitches'? Or . . . 'duck-making'? What is that? I need to know for my research into neologisms of the asshole class." Lizzy gave me a quizzical scientist look that used to crack me up. Now it made me tired.

"I can't be your friend anymore." Saying it out loud made it real at last. More real than months of pretend politeness. "I'm going to take the bus home."

"Beth, you can't take the bus. At least let me drive you."

"I don't ever want to get inside your car again."

I didn't care what she would say next. I didn't want to see the expression on her face. I walked into the street and aimed myself in the exact opposite direction from the one Elliot and his friends had taken.

I wasn't actually sure how I would take the bus home, but my mood was so big that I didn't feel pragmatic about my situation for about five blocks. I was in a residential neighborhood with no bus stops, and I was starting to see a lot more chain link fences. Probably not a great place to be walking alone at midnight. Maybe I could use the pay phone at Starless to call a cab. I had my mom's emergency credit card, and it's not like I could possibly get in more trouble tonight anyway.

"Beth!" The voice came from behind me. Great. Now I was going to have another argument with Lizzy.

But when I turned around, it was Tess, in the Gunne Sax outfit she wore when I first met her. It knocked the wind out of me. "What the hell! Where did you come from?"

Before I could splutter anything else, she crushed me in a hug. "Oh my god, Beth, it's you! You're alive! Oh my god." Her voice wavered and she pulled away awkwardly.

My stomach churned. Her face was so familiar, like her voice. As familiar as my own. But something had always been off.

"Why wouldn't I be alive? You're alive. I couldn't possibly be dead if you are alive." My voice sounded a lot more reasonable than I felt.

"Right, right." Tess looked down, hair falling across her cheek. "Yeah, right."

With a sense of dread, I realized that I already knew what was wrong. The times I'd met her before, it had been dark or I'd been so weirded out that I wasn't thinking straight. Now I could see her clearly.

"Tess. You're not me, are you?" I took in her skinny shoulders, and the way she flipped her hair to the side, briefly creating a mohawk-like shape over her forehead. "You're Lizzy."

When she met my eyes, it was the same expression she'd worn at the railroad tracks. Hours ago. Decades ago. I raised my hand to smack her but made a fist instead, bringing it down hard against my own thigh. "Why did you lie to me?"

"I'm sorry, Beth, I'm so sorry." When she started to half cry as she talked, I couldn't believe I'd ever mistaken her for anyone but Lizzy. She swallowed hard and composed herself. "I knew you wouldn't listen to me. I was a bad person. Maybe evil. You taught me that. I wanted to get you away from me, before . . . before . . ."

"*Before what?*" It was louder than I'd ever yelled.

She whipped her head around, looking at the darkened houses. "Let's talk somewhere private. I can drive you home."

"You just literally tried to drive me home and I said no."

Tess put a hand to her forehead and winced. "Yeah. I know. I mean, I am starting to remember. Fuck, it hurts. Please let me drive you."

Something about her tone was suddenly so unlike Lizzy's that I was jolted. She'd traveled through time to find me, more than once. This really might be more serious than murder. "Okay," I conceded. "Where's your car?"

When we slid into the seats, Tess gulped some aspirin and took a winding route to the freeway. She didn't say anything until we were on the I-5, heading south. I vacillated between rage and numbness, rewinding our previous conversations in my mind with different players in the roles. So it was Lizzy who had become the traveler, not me. I still didn't know what I would become. It was a relief to know my future was uncharted, and I didn't have to wonder anymore what would turn me into the kind of person who liked the name Tess.

Finally Tess glanced over, then back at the road. "I can't talk to you about your future, but there aren't any rules against telling people about their alternate present." She sighed. "Look—I came back here because I remember a timeline where you killed yourself, Beth. Right before we went to college. You jumped off that bridge in

Pasadena where we used to hang out. You know the Colorado Street bridge? We were standing there smoking and then you were gone. I couldn't stop you, and it . . . it destroyed me." She looked over again and I could see tears on her face. "I don't know if you can understand because you're not that person anymore. But I never killed anyone else after you . . . after that. My whole career has been about changing history without violence. It's been hard. I still have the same urges. You're one of the only people on Earth who knows what I'm struggling with."

I wasn't sure that was true, but it was my chance to ask something I'd been wanting to know for months. "Lizzy, why did you keep killing those guys? I mean, I understood when it was with Scott, but after that . . . what happened to you?"

I could see more tears making reflective tracks down her face, but she kept her eyes on the scatterplot of taillights ahead. "That first time was so easy. It felt—I don't know. Like we'd really fixed something. Made a difference. But also it felt good. Natural." She paused, thinking. "Remember that documentary we watched—jeez, I guess it was last summer for you. It was about how female lions hunt their prey, and we kept joking about how great our faces would look bathed in blood like that one lion who had fucking dipped her whole head inside an antelope's guts? It was like that. Magnificent and honorable. But also . . . natural? Because we were doing it to protect all the baby lions and the big fluffy male lions who just wanted to sit under trees and look pretty. I don't know if that makes sense."

I shook my head. "I remember the documentary, yeah. But we aren't lions, Lizzy. We're people. We don't need to eat rapists and creeps to survive."

She snorted a soft laugh, sounding exactly like the pre-murder Lizzy I had lost. "Beth, I'm so glad to talk to you again. I am so glad you are alive and in the world."

Lizzy's lion story had momentarily diverted my attention from that alternate self, the one who committed suicide. Had Lizzy and

I become best friends because we shared the urge to kill? Maybe we'd turned that urge in different directions, but it was still there, a fucked-up substrate to our love. Then the murders heightened everything. Each death took her closer to some kind of predatory ecstasy. But they took me deeper into the place my father wanted to lead me, where the solution to everything was a pure, self-destructive rage.

Still, my agony had eased after that day when Tess and I talked about what my dad had done when I was younger. That pulled me up short. How did she know that? Had my other self told Lizzy my secret?

"How did you know what happened with my dad? You said you knew what he did that one night."

"Beth, your dad was mentally ill. He did a million terrible things to you. I knew that." She touched my shoulder in the gentlest way possible and my eyes felt hot. "Yes, I was a shitty friend, but I wasn't shitty in that way. I care a lot about you. I knew you didn't want to talk about it, but I also knew it was . . . bad."

"So . . . you know the thing that happened?"

"Which thing are you talking about? The time he made you shower twice before dinner because he thought you were too sweaty to be inside the house? The time he freaked out because we had our shoes on? The time he put you on restriction for three months because you got an A-minus in typing class? All the times he pretended he wasn't your dad when he took us to the movies?"

My face hurt. "No. Not those times."

"Okay. I guess I don't know, then."

"Do you think you really changed the timeline forever? What if I kill myself next year?" I was fearful in a way I had never been before. It was mixed with self-consciousness and melancholy and something else I couldn't name.

Tess was silent for a long time. "It's true you could do that. I always thought that if you didn't have to see the murders . . ."

"I saw the murders."

"No. You saw some of them. Not the worst ones."

My body was thrumming with the uncanniness of everything. "You didn't have to lie to me, you know. You could have said who you are. I would have believed you. Why are you always lying?"

"That wasn't—I'm not. No. I had to say I was you because then you would know for sure you were going to survive. I wanted you to think suicide was not an option. I wanted to give you hope."

"You always thought lying was easier than telling the truth."

"No, I didn't."

"Now you're lying again."

I stared at her profile, illuminated by a chaos of freeway lights, and willed her to say something else. But she wouldn't. That's one way she'd changed. Lizzy would have argued with me for weeks about her innocence, and how she was totally not lying and never would lie to me. Tess knew when to shut up.

TWENTY-FIVE

T E S S

Raqmu, Nabataean Kingdom (13 B.C.E.) . . .
Raqmu, Ottoman-occupied territory (1893 C.E.)

I couldn't stay away from Beth, despite all my failures. After everyone settled down for bed in 13 B.C.E., I snuck out at midnight to bribe some tappers who could send me forward. With the Machine right here at Raqmu, and airline travel on the other side, I thought I could pull a move from *The Geologists*. I'd save Beth on the night of her suicide, then travel back to the Nabataean Kingdom for Soph's sacrifice. This might be my last chance to travel upstream to 1993 from a time with spotty record-keeping. Getting back down might be dicey, but I could talk my way into it. The techs in the early nineties knew me now.

I'd psyched myself up for failure, or something more ambiguous. But I had no way to prepare for the mental onslaught of a merging conflict. When I slithered back out of the wormhole into the chamber at ancient Raqmu, it felt like I'd been vomited up by an ancient ocean. The saline smell was horrible, and I had the crunchy remains of a graptolite colony in my soaking-wet hair. Which meant I'd been dragged through the Ordovician again—graptolites were common plankton in that period, known for nesting together in tiny chitinous tubes made from their own secretions.

"Welcome back." It was one of the slaves whom I'd bribed to send me through, a man with a deep voice and dark brown skin who spoke in Greek. It had been a week in travel time, but only a few minutes here. Bringing a hand to my face, I realized the catastrophic headache I'd had in 1993 was mostly gone. It was such a relief that I almost started crying again. Though my memory was blotchy, I could move without wincing. I stepped out of the circle and drifted into the shadowy atrium, wondering if I would ever reconcile the two histories vying for dominance in my mind.

Beth was dead. Beth was alive. I had finally changed my past.

On the street, I stared at the shuttered shops and tried to figure out who I was. I'd known exactly what I was doing right up until that moment when I hugged Beth and alien memories started to pour into me. It was like suddenly remembering a vivid dream, except it was an alternate version of my own life. Not completely alternate—I was still here, still on the same mission for the Daughters. I was a traveler, teaching at UCLA. But there was a violent sense of emotional dislocation. Especially when I tried to remember what had happened during my undergraduate years at college, when Beth was there and not there at the same time. Or maybe it was more like she wasn't there in two different ways. And the new way was so much more painful than the old one had been. How could her survival hurt more than her death?

I wove between stone houses, slowly finding my way to the rooms we'd rented at an inn. A sleepy goat crashed into my knees and I tripped on the offerings at a shrine outside somebody's family tomb. The moonlight was blinding.

When I slipped back into bed, I was shaking with exhaustion. I wedged myself into the cot next to Soph and fell asleep instantly.

———

"Wake up, Tess! It's almost midday." Anita stood over me, brandishing three scrolls and a small basket of grain. "I've got everything we need for tonight."

My anxiety latched on to a new target as I remembered our plans for Soph's sacrifice to al-Lat. "What is all that?"

"Some background material and an offering."

"Isn't Soph our offering?"

"I hope so, but I figured it wouldn't hurt to bring a little extra. Every goddess likes some grain, right?"

I had to laugh. "I don't know about goddesses, but I'm a huge fan of grain." The headache twisting in my sinuses had ebbed away completely. As long as I focused on my recent history, this mission, my mind was relatively clear. But I still felt unlike myself in a way I couldn't yet quantify.

During her studies at Raqmu, Soph had written about the goddess al-Lat. Here in the Nabataean Kingdom, she was a multipurpose deity associated with fertility and change. In other times and places, people worshipped her attributes under names like Mefitis, Isis, Venus, Kali, and Madonna. But Anita and I knew something about al-Lat that Soph didn't. Here in ancient Raqmu, her temple offered protection to the Timeless who were not men—people like Soph, refugees from a moment when they faced death or extreme persecution. In other temporal localities, Soph might have gone to a convent or a women's shelter. In this one, she had another choice.

Thanks to an unusual loophole in Nabataean law, religious orders could receive gold from the city-state for sacrifices. As long as a refugee claimed to be a "sacrifice," the Temple of al-Lat had coin to spend on their food and clothing. It helped that the city's rich women put huge annual donations into Raqmu's coffers to support this practice. Also, since the "sacrifice" was technically dead, she couldn't be arrested for traveling without a mark. It was the roundabout and slightly underhanded way that the city made itself a sanctuary.

That evening, Anita led Soph, C.L., Morehshin, and me to an older part of town reached by a long set of stairs curving up the canyon walls. We ascended to the second level of the city here, with houses and shops cut deep into the sandstone along a wide promenade. The Temple of al-Lat was set back from the walkway, behind a garden of fruit and nut trees fed from an elaborate network of cisterns, pools, and pipes.

"This is beautiful." Soph's face was radiant. She'd been reading the scrolls with Morehshin and memorizing the ceremony to join the ranks of al-Lat's protected Timeless. I looked at her sidelong, taking in the kohl-smeared eyes, braided hair, and pale linen robe Anita had dug up somewhere in the AGU quarters. When I first met Soph, I thought she was a sex radical using the language of Spiritualism to spread the cause. Now I knew she was a believer, too. Maybe not a conventional one, but close enough that the Temple of al-Lat meant something more than political asylum to her.

Soph smiled at me and I took her hand.

We entered the temple through an atrium with high windows that brought in sunlight across a brightly painted ceiling. Benches lined a central pool, and people crowded onto all of them, talking and gesturing and eating dinner and staring off into space. Anita introduced us to a dark-skinned woman named Esther, who wore a dress laced up over a loose white blouse that looked vaguely fifteenth century. Her fingertips were dyed with shimmering green ink and she tucked a wooden writing kit under her arm before gesturing us down a long, lamplit corridor. The air cooled as we got further into the rock.

After a minute of walking, we made a sharp left and emerged into a palatial room whose walls were covered in wooden shelves of scrolls, mechanical instruments, and jars. A fifty-foot statue of al-Lat rose from the floor to tower over the center of the room, her three faces seeing into every corner. Beyond her skirts, at the far end of the room, a dais was backed by several rows of semicircular stadium seats cut into the high walls. Fresh air came in through portals in the arched ceiling. Dusty beams of sunlight shot through them to a floor mosaic of astronomical charts.

"Welcome, women and new genders." Esther addressed us in modern English with an accent I didn't recognize. "The ceremony will take place in the amphitheater." She gestured at the dais, where a very bored-looking teenager was setting out some candles and our offering of grain.

"Should we go over there and wait?" I'd read a lot about the Temple of al-Lat, but had never actually visited. From my research, though, I had been anticipating something with a little more ritual to it. Everybody's nonchalance made it seem like Soph was getting a library card rather than temporal amnesty from a cosmic mother goddess.

Esther ignored my question and knocked on a polished wooden door. "Your sacrifice is here, ma'am!"

A woman whose black hair was wound into tightly coiled ringlets emerged from behind the door, wrapping a blue shawl over the deep brown of her shoulders. "I'm Hugayr. These are my students, but you can ignore them. They'll be observing." She spoke in crisp Nabataean, though she obviously understood English, too. Following her were three women with writing kits like Esther's, all wearing identical harried expressions. We trailed Hugayr to the amphitheater, where the teenager lit candles and joined a few other women on the benches. Everything smelled pleasantly of beeswax.

Hugayr pulled three carved stones from her robes and set them on the dais. Each had been cut to resemble a flower and emitted a blue glow, as if infinitesimal LEDs were embedded in its crystal matrices. "There will probably be a crowd of students here," she said. "I hope you don't mind. We only get a couple of sacrifices every year, so it's a great chance for them to get some experience."

When Hugayr invited Soph to lie down on the dais between the candles and stones, more women in the room wandered over to sit down, or left discreetly through the doors. At last there was enough of a crowd that it was starting to feel properly ceremonial.

"All right, everybody, let's get started." Hugayr said it with an unmistakably southern American accent from the twentieth century, then switched back into Nabataean. "Welcome, Soph. Your offerings and sacrifice are pleasing to al-Lat, who gives shelter to women and new genders who have been cast out of the time when their mothers birthed them."

"Praise be to al-Lat." Soph spoke in a clear, strong voice.

"This the most difficult part, so pay attention." Hugayr addressed the audience. A few had taken out scrolls and ink. I could hear the faint scratching of reed pens on papyrus. Palming two of the stone flowers she'd set out, Hugayr held her fists over Soph's chest and let out a prolonged cry. "DIE AND LIVE AGAIN!"

Blue fire enveloped Hugayr's arms and fell across Soph's body like lumps of lava. She sucked in her breath and let out an ecstatic scream. My muscles tensed. This looked too much like a real sacrifice, and not the metaphorical one I'd expected. But no one around me was panicking, so this was obviously part of the ritual. I peered more closely. Where had the fire come from? It burned everything, but consumed nothing. That's when I realized: the stones. They were raining illumination, like Morehshin's multi-tool. Somehow these ancient priestesses had access to technology from thousands of years in the future. I tried to relax. This was not going to end in carnage. Soph would be fine.

"CALL THE WATER IN THE ROCKS, SOPH! CALL IT!" Hugayr opened her hands and the stones blazed. Though at first I'd thought they were carved into flowers, perhaps those petals were flames.

Soph stood up, towering over us, cloaked in fire. "I CALL THE WATER!" The air instantly poured with rain and fog. I could smell the Ordovician again, and through the mist I saw embers dying.

"Is she going to be okay?" I couldn't help but whisper it.

C.L., grinning next to me, practically bounced with glee. "Yes! This place has its own mini-wormhole. You'll see."

Now Soph was floating upward, her hair free around her face. Smoke and steam plumed from the rocks below, where Hugayr gesticulated for her students to clean up spilled wax and water. Soph spun slowly toward the statue of al-Lat as she reached the height of the goddess's faces. She was fully thirty feet above the dais now. Electricity buzzed around her.

"GODDESS, DO YOU ACCEPT MY SACRIFICE?"

A ball of lightning cracked where Soph hung suspended. She winked out, then reappeared on the dais in a burst of seawater.

"LET DEATH AND LIFE JOIN IN THE BODY OF THE TIMELESS!" Hugayr raised her arms and the air was clear again. I could hear water dripping from Soph's robe onto the floor. The students were working frantically to soak everything up with sponges and cloth. C.L. applauded enthusiastically, and the rest of us joined in, some snapping fingers or stamping their feet.

"Nice job, everybody! Very controlled." Hugayr beamed and folded her arms. "You are now Timeless, Soph! Welcome!"

Soph grinned and wrung out her hair. I still felt a little shaky, but joined the others swarming her with hugs while students in the audience headed back to work.

Morehshin eyed the flower-fire stones that Hugayr was slipping back into her robe, then addressed her in a language I couldn't understand.

"Is that English?" Hugayr cocked her head, and spoke with her southern accent again. "I'm afraid I only speak Atomic Era."

"Where did you get those multi-tools?" Morehshin switched back to Nabataean.

Hugayr readjusted her shawl and glared at Morehshin. "This temple belongs to the Raqmu women and new genders of its time. Do you understand? We shelter the Timeless, but it is *our place.* You get no special privileges because you are from the future. If you want to learn our secrets, you must join us and never travel again."

Looking sheepish, Morehshin took out her own multi-tool and showed it to Hugayr. "Do you mind if I ask you some questions about this?" Immediately the tension evaporated and they got into a long, muttered discussion about its technical features.

Ignoring them, C.L. nudged Anita and pointed up to the spot where Soph had been eaten by lightning. "It's a Machine that only leads to its present. Isn't that cool? Probably a beta test that somebody forgot to turn off half a billion years ago."

"What makes you so sure it isn't magic?" Soph jumped off the dais, stripped off her wet robe, and took a fresh tunic and trousers from one of Hugayr's students.

"Because it always works the same way every time. It's repeatable." C.L. sounded extremely certain.

"Isn't that what a magic spell is?" Soph retorted.

Anita rolled her eyes.

Hugayr's student began piling the remaining cloths into a basket. "Sorry to interrupt, but I should show you to the dormitory." She glanced at us. "Timeless and priestesses only."

"Are you a priestess?" Soph asked.

"I will be one day. Hugayr is training me."

"Well, according to your training, would you say that what we experienced here was magic or science?"

The student shot a neurotic look over her shoulder at Hugayr. "I'm not sure what you mean by 'science.'" Soph had used two Nabataean words that translated more literally as "knowledge device."

"Do you know the word 'science'?" C.L. said the word in English.

The student shrugged and continued in Nabataean. "I haven't started English yet. But I speak Hebrew and Greek."

"What about Plato? Do you know him? We're talking about his idea of logical deduction." C.L.'s Nabataean was terrible, but the student understood them.

"Plato hates women. His work is useless to us."

"I don't mean him. I mean his method."

"Talking to other men to discover truth?"

I snickered. She had a point. C.L. frowned at me.

Anita broke in and tried to restate the question so it made more sense in Nabataean. "I think Soph was asking whether you think this is a spirit or a mechanical device." She pointed at the dais.

"Oh, I see." The student set down her basket. "We discuss this question often. It is one way to contemplate the three faces of al-Lat, who represents many kinds of power in one woman. She is an engineer, she is a mother, and she divines the answers to cosmic mysteries. So I guess . . . sometimes she is a mechanical device, and sometimes she is a spirit."

"That was very well said, Ahed." Hugayr had been eavesdropping.

Ahed bowed her head respectfully and fought to suppress a pleased smile. "Thank you, Priestess."

"And thank you, Ahed. I'm ready to see my new home." Soph scooped up the basket of wet fabric and linked arms with the student. "Should we drop this off at the laundry?"

"Yes, let's do that."

Hugayr nodded at us. "Well met, travelers. I believe we still have something to discuss."

We sat on cushions in her chambers and Anita presented our case. "We think there are men who are trying to destroy the Machines." She paused, searching Hugayr's impassive face. "I have heard . . . you might know something about this."

The priestess nodded. She withdrew a multi-tool from her robes and turned it over in her hands, pondering. I wondered if she'd gotten it from someone like Moreshin, fleeing a future of bioengineered patriarchy. At last she spoke, sounding weary. "It's happened before. We have records of it, from several times."

"How did people stop them before? Do you have any advice?"

Hugayr pocketed the multi-tool again and straightened her shoulders. "Kill them, obviously. Find the men and kill them."

A glass shard lodged itself in my gut. "We can't. Killing might make things worse. There must be some other way."

"Don't be stupid. There is no other way." Hugayr was losing patience. "Do you want to imprison us in a history that cannot be changed?"

"We aren't murderers." The words ached in my mouth. I wanted so much for them to be true.

"Killing for al-Lat is not the same as killing for yourself."

I started to say something else, but Anita pinched my arm. "Thank you, Priestess. You've given us a lot to think about."

As we left through the tunnel, none of us wanted to talk about what Hugayr had said. It was almost a relief when C.L. started griping about our conversation with Ahed after the sacrifice. "I thought al-Lat was some kind of fertility goddess. That's what Wikipedia said. She's not an engineer."

Anita gave C.L. some side-eye. "I think you'd better quit while you're ahead. Pretty sure you're starting to be offensive with all that explaining of things you know nothing about."

"Offensive, yes. I think Hugayr would be displeased." Morehshin took out her multi-tool and shook it like a kid turning a soda bottle into a spray weapon. "Look what she showed me." Ball lightning cracked five feet ahead of us, and every hair on my body stood on end.

"What the fuck, Morehshin!"

"What?" She shrugged. "It's harmless at that distance."

I decided not to say anything about the scorch marks she'd left on the walls.

A representative of the Order accepted Soph's sacrifice as legitimate, made some marks on a tablet, and gave us the next AGU slot on the Machine. After some debate, we decided to return to 1893 to deal with the Comstockers nonviolently. All of us except Morehshin instinctively recoiled from Hugayr's advice; there had to be a way to defeat them that didn't involve death.

Six slaves pounded with stone and bone on the floor to activate the interface, and two added a quick rhythm with small iron mallets. Morehshin used her multi-tool to send a bright finger of blue plasma into the control panel that hovered overhead.

Emerging from the wormhole with a jolt, it took a moment for me to realize there had been no unexpected trip to the Ordovician. Morehshin gave a triumphant whoop. "Much easier with those settings! Hugayr is a genius!" My neck ached. The memories of Beth felt closer here, harder to push aside. A muted clang of cable cars came through the windows and into the Machine chamber. The slaves had been replaced by steam-driven tappers, and the bureaucrat with his tablet and clubbed beard had morphed into a tidy row of four wooden tables staffed by people in a range of nineteenth-century fashions, from white robes to tweed suits.

We returned to our quarters in the scholars' neighborhood and had a late meal of goat cheese, lemon-scented chickpeas, flatbread, and dates soaked in wine. Then we washed it down with more wine. It started to rain, and someone cursed loudly outside as a cart splashed through manure-laced puddles. It reminded me of Chicago when I'd arrived in early spring.

"I think we should target the Expo," I said. "That's where Elliot and the other saboteurs are. Plus, I think we have a chance to get abortion legalized if we can do another big anti-Comstock protest."

Morehshin nodded eagerly. "Comstock must be stopped. His laws are at the root of the divergence. He's going to inspire similar men in Europe."

"I still don't understand why Comstock is so important to these travelers." Anita fiddled with a cube of cheese.

"He's some kind of inspiration to them—"

I had more to say, but Morehshin cut me off. "He put men in charge of reproduction. Do you understand? That is too much power for any one group."

Her point wasn't nuanced, but I knew what she was getting at. "Morehshin is right. Comstock is making it illegal for people to have agency over their futures. Over the future of the species, even." I thought back to Elliot's pamphlet about how women's inferiority was simply a matter of evolutionary biology. According to Morehshin's hints, her present was ruled by people using science to control reproduction in line with the Comstock Laws.

C.L. sipped wine and shook their head. "None of this will matter if the Comstockers destroy the machine at Raqmu. I think they're back there in the Ordovician, hacking on it."

At that moment a spray of water hit the window, and I felt a burst of excruciating double memories. Beth was dead, her suicide a needle in my gut; and she was alive, saying she never wanted to see me again. Calling me a liar. An unfamiliar feeling of shame burrowed into my chest. Was I really going to organize anti-Comstock protests while the Machines were in danger and the timeline froze?

I pondered our options. I understood edits and reversions, merging conflicts and orthogonal deletions. But I couldn't quite wrap my mind around how a Machine shutdown would propagate across the timeline. "Aren't we technically in a version of the timeline where they failed?" I asked. "I mean, C.L. saw the cuts and the Machine is still working."

"It's a good question, and all I have is a hypothesis right now." C.L. set down their wineglass. "What I saw is probably part of an extreme kind of merging conflict. My guess is that there are many divergences that split at some point before those cuts were made. We're in a version where they fail but we're getting closer and closer to one where they succeed. That's why we're seeing those interface bugs with increasing frequency. Essentially, those are signs that we're living in a timeline where the Machines are being damaged. Soon, we could be in one where the Machines don't work at all."

"How soon?" Anita was troubled.

"Based on my readings, I'd say six months to a year. There seems to be a regular progression to their edits. But they could accidentally hit the right button tomorrow. I suspect the mechanism is a lot more complicated than that, but you never know."

Anita put her chin on her fists. "We have to travel back to the moment right before they make those cuts and stop them. That way we revert back to a timeline where the Machines are undamaged."

C.L.'s face was grave. "Are we going to do what Hugayr told us?"

"No," I replied firmly. "We can stop them some other way."

Morehshin gave me side-eye. "What will we do? Talk them out of it?"

"I think we can agree that whatever we do, a mission like this could be a one-way trip for some of us," Anita said. "Or all of us."

As her words sank in, I realized this might be our last chance to stop Comstock. "We wouldn't need more than six months to do our edit here in 1893. Once we've done it, we can face whatever meets us in the Ordovician."

"None of that will matter if the Comstockers control the Machine." C.L. was getting angry.

"It *will* matter if we don't make it back from the Ordovician." Emotion had winnowed my voice down to a whisper. "I want to leave a better timeline behind. Not just an open timeline, but one where people who are not men can control the means of reproduction."

Morehshin grabbed my hand inside her fist and I felt a hardness in her palm. "I will go with you. Let us defeat Comstock before dealing with the men who are sabotaging Machines."

"It's risky." Anita exchanged glances with C.L.

"All of this is risky. Let's finish the edit that we began at the Expo." I was pleading now. "Maybe that will propagate forward and eliminate our Comstockers."

"That sounds like a Great Man view of history. Stopping Comstock doesn't mean you destroy the social movement that made him. We have to tap down to the Ordovician in six months." Anita sounded doubtful, but I could tell she was coming around.

C.L. was unconvinced. "I'm going to stay here to keep monitoring the Machine, and if the emissions reach dangerous levels I'm going back there to . . . to do something."

Anita cut them off. "I'll stay here with you, C.L. If it comes to that, I'll go with you. Let's use 1893 as our home time, so neither of us is too far ahead of Tess when we get back to 2022."

"Yes. When we get back to 2022," I affirmed. "That will be a lucky edit." As I mouthed the cliché, I realized I'd never thought about its actual meaning. A lucky edit was an event out of our control, the side effect of a fungible timeline, sometimes good and sometimes bad. But of course there was no such thing as luck. There were only deliberate revisions, hard-won changes, and their unintended consequences. A headache worked its way down my neck and beneath my shoulder blades. I needed sleep.

Everyone agreed it was time to turn in. Morehshin took the bedroom with C.L. and I rolled myself up in a thick rug next to Anita. We had a cubby next to the dining room to ourselves.

"Anita, I need to tell you something." I couldn't keep the anxiety out of my voice.

She propped herself up on one elbow. "Sounds serious."

"You know when I told you guys about seeing that Comstocker back at that concert in 1992? Well . . . I did something else while I was there."

"Did you make an edit?"

"No. I mean, yes . . . but that was later. My younger self was at the concert, and I felt fine after seeing her. So . . . then I snuck back upstream. From Flin Flon once, and then a couple nights ago from ancient Raqmu. I changed something in my past."

"Tess." I could tell she was biting back what she wanted to say.

"I know. It was stupid. But it seemed . . . I don't know. I thought it would be okay. But it wasn't. And now I feel really, really awful. I'm in a lot of pain."

"Oh fuck. You need to tell me everything."

I put my head in my hands. For my whole adult life, I'd striven to make significant edits. I'd dreamed of saving Beth. And now I realized that those goals had always been part of the same fantasy. I'd drawn Beth into terrible, fucked-up things when we were young. But there was one time I'd helped her, when she got that abortion. Maybe, all this time, I'd been trying to propagate my gift to Beth across populations and years. If our edit of Comstock took, there would never be another teenage girl driven to desperation by laws that turned her body into a destiny she could not change.

I looked at Anita, waiting for me to spill my guts, and decided to stop lying to myself. Beneath the modern political rhetoric and academic theories of history, I had an ancient hope that was indistinguishable from Spiritualism. If my edit took, maybe the good I'd done would outweigh the evil.

TWENTY-SIX

BETH

Irvine, Alta California . . .
Los Angeles, Alta California (1993 C.E.)

I stood in front of the double doors to my house, which were actually one door made to look like two because that gave the illusion that we lived in a castle instead of a condo. The moon was up and there were no lights on in the windows. I shivered. It was 2 A.M. and I couldn't stop thinking about Tess calling my dad "mentally ill." Not crazy or psycho or nuts. Her use of the more clinical term made it real. It also meant that Lizzy had seen what nobody else had. She knew my family wasn't normal.

As quietly as possible, I unlocked the door, took off my sandals, and crept upstairs in the dark. My parents' bedroom door was closed, and I made it to my room without any confrontations. I was suddenly so tired that I couldn't do anything other than climb under the covers in my clothes and fall asleep.

The next morning, there was the same eerie silence as the night before. I pulled on jeans and sneakers before going downstairs, my muscles tensed for a fight. But my father had gone to the shop and my mother was on the phone, talking about the Orange Unified

School District's leadership training. She glanced up once from a notepad full of her tidy handwriting, its extreme legibility optimized for filling chalkboards with instructions. I stood in her gaze, waiting for a reaction. But almost immediately, her eyes abandoned me for the notepad.

I poured a cup of coffee and made toast for breakfast, stepping into the familiar role of pretending everything was normal. The L.A. *Times* was tossed on the table, and I forced myself to read the comics before flipping anxiously to news. There was a slightly more in-depth story than the one in the *Weekly* about how the Machines were exhibiting new behavior, but it mostly dealt with how India might leave the Chronology Academy and form its own regulatory agency. Nobody in the story talked about actual science, and I had nothing left to distract me from worrying about last night. Had Lizzy followed that guy Elliot and murdered him after I left? What did it mean that Tess remembered a timeline where I'd killed myself?

"You're on restriction until you leave for UCLA," my mother said. She'd hung up the phone and was using the impersonal voice she favored when meting out punishments. "Your father and I will talk to you about your behavior tonight."

That was what I had expected, especially the part where my parents prearranged a yelling session for after work. I knew rationally that the whole situation was absurd because I was moving into the dorms next week. But I felt my eyes throbbing with tears anyway. This always happened when I was in trouble with my dad. It was a physical reaction I couldn't control, like throwing up. At least this time I was able to blink my eyes clear, dislodge the lump in my throat with a cough, and nod at my mom.

"Do you understand what that means? You do not leave this house until we get home. No talking on the phone, and no inviting friends over."

"Yeah, I get it."

As my mom backed her car out of the garage, I thought about

Tess. At least there was someone out there, somewhere in time, who knew how fucking shitty this was. Even if it was actually Lizzy, or some version of her. I still didn't quite understand how that worked. It was scary to think about that other timeline of my life. Based on what Tess said, I must have stayed friends with Lizzy, and killed more men. That might have been enough to make me want to die. Still, I wondered if something else had been different for the other Beth too—something Tess didn't know. Like maybe there was another horrendous shitshow along the way, some epiphenomenon that spun out of our friendship. Maybe jumping off the bridge was an emotional reflex like my tears, an uncontrollable reaction that took possession of my body. Maybe it was something I'd planned for weeks.

Probably I would never know. Whatever had changed, this version of me did not want to die. All I wanted was to get the hell out of my father's house and never come back. Monday was move-in day at Dykstra Hall. That meant five days of restriction, then I was gone.

Those thoughts sustained me several hours later, when the plates were cleared from dinner and it was time for our "talk." My father always started by telling me that he and my mother saw a pattern in my behavior that revealed my basic terribleness as a person. My disobedience was a symptom of how flawed I was. I was a sneak, a lazy cheat, and I was already on my way downhill despite my young age.

During these lectures, I coped by staring at one specific corner of the dining room. It was behind my father's head, so it looked like I was paying attention, but I was really thinking about the calcium in the white paint, the chalky drywall below it, and then the cellulose and minerals that made up the bones of the house. When that got old, I recalled the first time I saw Grape Ape at a backyard show and how Glorious Garcia sang, "RISE UP RISE UP." I thought about that painting from their EP *Our Time Was Stolen*, where the curved rock of the Machine sat undisturbed millions of years ago, long before humans learned to wreck each other's histories. If I focused hard enough, my father's face disappeared and so did his voice. It was me and the molecular structure of our house and songs about smashing the chrono-patriarchy.

"We are serious about this, Beth. If you can't get your act together, that's it. Say goodbye to the dorms. We won't pay for them. You'll live here and commute to L.A. with your dad. And if you can't handle that, we'll stop paying for your college, too." My mother folded her arms.

I thought about my puny bank account, fed by a weekly allowance and summer jobs. If my parents cut me off, I wouldn't have enough money to pay for a quarter in the dorms. I looked wordlessly at my mother, terrified. The prospect of going to college and getting away from them was the only thing keeping me sane. What if I had to stay here, with no escape hatch?

"You have to earn your right to go to college, Beth." My father spoke with slow intensity. "You need to show us that you are committed to it. If you disregard rules, it's clear you're not ready for this level of responsibility."

I couldn't zone out on this conversation anymore. If I didn't do what they said, my whole life would end. I was so panicked that I couldn't figure out what exactly they were threatening. Had they already decided to cut me off? Were they saying I couldn't go to college at all, or that I couldn't live in the dorms? Everything I'd depended on was being yanked away.

Putting on my good daughter face, I nodded vigorously. "I understand."

"I want to believe you, but you've let us down so many times." My father sounded sorrowful. "How are we supposed to trust you after the way you've acted?"

This was the problem with tuning in to what my parents said during one of these sessions. At a certain point, it was impossible to know what they were upset about. Obviously they wouldn't nuke my college education for not wearing shoes in the house. But I hadn't left the house without permission before, so I didn't understand the "so many times" part. Tess said my father was mentally ill, but that was hard to believe when he sat right in front of me with my mother agreeing with him. They both sounded so rational. I searched my mind for other crimes I might have committed, infractions so huge they added up to the punishment of taking college away. Was it possible they secretly knew about all the shows I went to with Lizzy over the past year? The abortion? Had I done something I didn't remember?

Tears burned down my cheeks before I could help myself. If I tried to speak my voice would tremble so much it would be an additional humiliation. So I sat silently as my father painstakingly explained how I was a nothing who deserved nothing. If I didn't pay attention, if I disappeared into the opening of the ancient Machine, I might incur further penalties. I had no choice but to take it all in. Every single word.

In the movies, going off to college is this tearful farewell with the parents forcing their kids to take bags of cookies and saying things like, "Don't forget to write!" My parents said nothing on the drive from Irvine to Los Angeles. My mother had prepared a list in her tidy handwriting, reiterating our new rules and agreements. I would call them every night from the dorm phone to prove that I wasn't going out; I would send them Xeroxed copies of all my syllabi so they could track my assignments; I had to earn straight As. Before I got out of the car, I had to sign the checklist. My mom had gotten this idea from one of her books about dealing with "problem students."

My father helped carry luggage up to the dorm room I'd be sharing with another girl. When we arrived, my new roommate was standing in the middle of the room, eyeing the bunk bed.

Immediately, she gave us a big smile. "Hi, roomie! I'm Rosa

Sanchez, from Salinas. Do you care whether you get top or bottom? Because I don't care." Her black hair was cut into a short wedge that flopped over the shaved back of her head. I liked her instantly.

"Hi! I'm Beth Cohen. From Irvine. I like the top."

"Done! This must be your dad?"

My father put some bags carefully on the floor. "No."

She glanced at me uneasily. "Okay, well, nice to meet you!"

My father ignored Rosa. "Beth, remember our agreement."

"I will."

He turned his back to leave without saying goodbye. I looked out the dirty window, straining to glimpse my parents driving away. But all I could see was a distant courtyard, surrounded by more residence halls.

"Was that your uncle or something?" Rosa was unpacking clothes and books on the lower bunk.

"It was my dad. He just doesn't like to say that for some reason."

"Parents are so weird."

"Yeah." I laughed, glad there was an easy way to frame that conversation as if it were a wacky moment from a teen comedy. "They really are. You never know what they're going to do next."

Rosa and at least a dozen other students on our floor were also in my chemistry class. Everyone said it was one of UCLA's most terrifying weeder classes, jammed with so much information that only a tiny handful of people got higher than a C-plus. And it was almost impossible to ask questions. Weeders were taught in auditoriums that held hundreds of students, and were seemingly intended entirely to dissuade the vast majority of us from majoring in science.

At least that made it easy to avoid Lizzy. I spotted her once across the room, but she was busy taking notes. I usually sat with Rosa and other people from the dorm. With so many of us crammed into the same classes, it was easy to study and socialize in packs. My days began to blur into a routine. Every night I stepped out of the student lounge, leaving my books under Rosa's care, to call my parents on the pay phone in the hallway. Depending on my father's mood, I was either on my way to scientific superstardom or on the precipice of doom. I tried to keep my voice steady and friendly, to obey all the rules. I kept picturing what would happen if they cut off my dorm payments. One day I'd find all my stuff in the hall and someone else in the top bunk.

But for now, I had a weeder class to deal with. The night before the chem midterm, it seemed like the whole fifth floor of Dykstra was freaking out and pulling an all-nighter with the help of coffee, NoDoz, sugary snacks, or meth. A woman snorting glittery powder off her physics textbook in the hallway shrugged at me. "What? It's only speed. You want coke, you gotta go to the fancy dorms."

Rosa and I stuck to cigarettes. After my nightly parent call, I grabbed a lighter and poked Rosa. "Let's take a smoke break." We took the elevator down to the butt-encrusted smoking area outside, trading questions about the differences between organic and inorganic acids. The midterm was in roughly fifteen hours, and it was definitely time to inhale some gas and particulates.

"Do you think you're ready for the test?" I exhaled and flicked some ash in the general direction of the bin.

"Yeah. I'm pretty good with tests. That's how I got into UCLA, you know?"

"What do you mean?"

"I got 1550 on my SATs."

My eyes bulged. "Wow—that's super good."

"Yeah. It's how I got my scholarship. But I still need to do work study to pay for everything." She blew a smoke ring.

"What's work study?"

"It's like a financial aid thing. I work part time in the library and it helps pay for tuition and dorms or whatever." She wouldn't look at me. "I guess your parents pay for college, huh?"

"Yeah. Right now they do." An idea was forming in my mind. "But they won't be soon."

Rosa glanced up. "It's expensive, right? I know lots of people who start work study in sophomore year. It's good if you can focus on school when you're a freshman taking all the weeder classes. Working is a pain."

I offered Rosa another cigarette and we kept talking about financial aid. Listening to her made it seem reasonable and real. Maybe I could do work study and support myself. I imagined a future without the nightly calls. Without the fear. It was a tiny vein of hope.

I went to the financial aid office the next day, after the chem midterm. An administrator with a cheesy UCLA tie walked me through some of the forms, and promised I could apply for winter quarter if I needed to.

"Get your parents to fill this out."

"I'm independent from my parents. I mean, I want to be classified as independent."

The admin paused. "How old are you?"

"Eighteen."

"So do you have legal documentation? You need to prove your parents aren't supporting you."

"What if I can't get documents from them? Like is there a way for me to declare myself independent?"

He shrugged. "I don't think so. But you should ask a lawyer about that. We have lawyers available for students—make an appointment down the hall."

Walking down the tiled hallway reminded me of leaving my parents' house without permission. I had no idea what to expect, or where I was going. I was breaking the rules.

Soon I sat on a cracked leather sofa facing a woman with a fluff of gray-brown hair and droopy stockings.

"I'm trying to find out how I can declare myself independent from my parents so I can get financial aid on my own."

"Well, that's something I don't hear every day." She perked up and jotted something down on a legal pad. "What's your reason?"

I thought of a million excuses, and then I remembered what Tess had said.

"My father . . . he's mentally ill. I need to be on my own." I could barely hear myself over the blood throttling my ears.

The lawyer nodded and I thought sympathy inhabited the lines of her face. "I see. Let me research this and get back to you? I think we can figure something out." Then she jotted down another note, as if everything was normal. I was flooded with relief. Her reaction didn't feel like the fake normal I knew from home. Maybe she was actually going to help me.

I had one more midterm left, and it was the worst. Cultural geology was my least favorite part of geoscience, and this class involved a lot of hypotheses about travel that couldn't be proven with repeatable results. Yet somehow Professor Biswas made it interesting. Besides, anything was better than weeder bullshit like chem. The problem was that Biswas had assigned a midterm essay about the Great Man vs. Collective Action theories of history. I was still struggling with those concepts, so distant from the molecular structure of acid or the decay of metals over time. Checking my watch, I decided I still had time to make it to her office hours.

The geology department was in a cluster of old brick buildings surrounded by plots of thick ivy and pine trees. Inside, the upper floors were a maze of narrow hallways lined with office doors. Some boasted a plain placard with the professor's name; others were covered in cartoons, GIS maps, cutaway views of sedimentary layers, and covers of scientific journals. I waited my turn to see Professor Biswas, sitting behind a few other students on the cool linoleum floor, staring at a two-hundred-year-old map of the Caribbean islands taped to her door. A few minutes later, Biswas motioned me inside. Her window looked out onto the dingy geoscience courtyard, mostly used as storage for particularly large rocks.

"Nice view, Professor Biswas." I immediately regretted my terrible attempt at a joke, but she smiled.

"Please call me Anita. My father is Professor Biswas. What can I do for you?" Sitting across from her, I realized Anita was pretty young for a professor—possibly in her early thirties.

"I don't understand the difference between the two theories of history. Isn't collective action still aimed at affecting a few great men? I mean, a protest is a form of collective action, but aren't they protesting because they want to change what powerful politicians do?"

Anita twirled a pen over her thumb and nodded. "That's a good question. The difference is that the Great Man approach assumes there are only a few people who can change the timeline at any given moment, and by the way they usually happen to be male." She snorted. "But the Collective Action approach assumes that change is a complex process that comes from many quarters, with many people participating. So the end result might look the same, but the process is quite different."

"But it still seems like you have to be a powerful person to change the timeline."

"Maybe. From my perspective as a traveler, I think the main advantage of the Collective Action hypothesis is that it accounts for context. Let me give you an example. In 1993, I can be a professor and order you to write a midterm essay and you'll do it. I'm kind of a great man, if you think of it that way. But when I'm back in the eighteenth-century Caribbean, where I do my research, most people assume I'm a slave. Sometimes I get classified as a free person of color because I'm half-Indian. My point is, there is no way for me to become a great man in that era, no matter how great I might be objectively. If I want to change anything, I need a community that recognizes my inherent awesomeness. That's where your collective action comes in. You can't become great without a community that recognizes you. But the Great Man theory suggests that certain special people are great regardless of context."

I thought about that for a while. "So does collective action mean a bunch of people have to band together to edit the timeline, or can they be . . . kind of disconnected people making a lot of different edits?"

"It's probably a mix of both, but the honest answer is that nobody knows for sure." She ran a hand over the close-cropped froth of her hair and I noticed she wore purple nail polish. "Are you interested in traveling one day?"

"I like your class a lot, but I'm more interested in the physical side. I want to study the origins of life in the Cambrian."

"Well, most of the Machines seem to originate in that same geological period, so maybe you'll wind up studying them a little bit too. There is some great work on wormholes happening here at UCLA."

I'd never thought about researching time machines, and I was suddenly intrigued. "Where do you think the Machines come from?"

Anita gave an elaborate shrug. "It's not really my area, but the jury is definitely out on that one. Some people say it's a natural consequence of crustal formation that we don't understand yet. But that doesn't explain the interface, and why it filters out weapons but not clothing. I've always been fond of the idea that it was aliens."

I was surprised. "Really? Do people think that?"

"Sure. Or that it was a primordial civilization on Earth. There's so little evidence that you can imagine a lot of things. Most geologists agree that the Machines were built, or at least the interface was. There's some kind of intelligence behind them. It's not a phenomenon created by plate tectonics or weathering or any other known geophysical process."

"But there *is* a physical process involved. The timeline itself—"

"Sure. The Machines seem to be exploiting a force that pulls potential timelines into our own. But there's a conundrum there, too.

Let's say there is a cosmic force that is engaged in a constant background shuffling of timelines in the universe. It's like gravity, or an unknown form of energy—it's causing historical change all the time. If that's true, maybe the Machine is simply a viewing booth that allows us to see the shuffling. So we think we're changing things, but that's an illusion. We're merely witnessing, or remembering, a change that would normally be imperceptible."

Now I was frustrated. "So nobody knows how historical change works culturally *or* physically? How can we . . . I mean, what are we even doing?"

Anita grinned. "You really should study time machines. We all start out with that same what-the-hell feeling. It's probably the main driver of scientific insight."

I wasn't any closer to knowing what I wanted to write in my essay, but I was intrigued by the idea of studying the Machines. As I wandered into the afternoon sun, I thought about all the possible timelines reshuffling in Tess's wake. Was it a natural process that Tess could see because she used the Machines? Was she a tiny part of an unfathomably complex collective action that caused the shuffle? I wandered south toward Westwood, barely noticing as the hangar-sized campus buildings gave way to city streets. I passed a few bars and a Tower Records before finding myself at Falafel King, where I realized that I was incredibly hungry.

Falafel King served up the best pita sandwich in L.A., topped with crispy disks of potato and at least five kinds of spicy salad. As I ordered, I wondered with a twinge if I'd be able to afford this place once I was on financial aid.

All the tables in the restaurant were jammed, so I hunkered down on the warm sidewalk outside, watching a line of students waiting to order stoner fuel from Stan's Donuts nearby. I was wiping some white sauce off my T-shirt when I heard a familiar voice.

"Hey, Beth?"

I looked up and immediately wished I wasn't holding a messy

sandwich that kept dripping tahini. "Hey, Hamid." I scrambled up and surreptitiously wiped my hands on my jeans.

"Fancy meeting you here." He had the same lopsided smile that made me want to kiss him, and I tried not to think about that as I twisted the edges of my sandwich wrapper.

"What are you up to?"

"Getting some donuts for my study group. Midterm madness."

"Oh yeah? What class?"

"History of film."

That was unexpected. "What happened to pre-med or business?"

"I keep forgetting to take classes in those." He leaned easily against the wall and I realized he wasn't exuding that melancholy neediness I remembered from high school. He seemed more stable. Happier.

"I'm getting ready for a midterm too. I have to write about collective action in history, but it turns out that nobody knows how history works."

We started talking about the timeline, and the montage technique in film, and whether chocolate donuts were better than glazed. After I finished my pita, I decided to get a donut at Stan's. Hamid said his study group was at the library, in the same general direction as the dorms, so it made sense to walk together back to campus.

"I'm glad I finally ran into you. I thought I would probably see you at some point." Hamid ducked his head and looked embarrassed. "Not that I was hunting around for you or anything."

"I'm glad we ran into each other too."

"Hey, do you have . . . an e-mail address?" Hamid said the word "e-mail" like he was describing something extremely obscure and fancy.

"Of course. I got one on my first day of classes."

"I just got one! I could send you my first e-mail!"

"Really? Your first e-mail? Didn't your family have AOL?"

"I mean, I guess my sister had AOL. I never used it, though. It seemed like it was mostly for people talking about boy bands."

I rolled my eyes. "Well, allow me to introduce you to the wonders of e-mail. I'm elizabethc@magma.ucla.edu."

"Easy to remember. I'll mail you some electrons!" He gave me a quick hug and raced off in the direction of the library.

I stood there for a moment thinking about the hug, and what I wanted it to mean. Then I took the long way back to the dorms, puzzling over my essay for Anita. By the time I got back to my room, I was still unsure what to write. I knew history could be changed, but none of the hypotheses fit my own experience. Why wasn't there a scientific theory that described how we change our own lives and the lives of our friends?

TWENTY-SEVEN

ANITA

**Excerpted from the memoir of Anita Biswas,
found in the Subalterns' Archive Cave,
Raqmu, Jordan (2030 C.E.)**

There are some memories I will never share with the Daughters
of Harriet, and this is one of them. I remember a nation without
women's suffrage. It's where I grew up. As a little girl in Los Angeles
in the 1970s, I was one of the lucky ones; Alta California gave us the
vote a few years before I was born in 1968, and the UC system had
been coed since the 1950s. When I was in middle school, my mother
and I watched a soap opera called *The Geologists* every week because
it had two African characters who traveled through the Machine at
Timbuktu. Exposed to liberal ideas, treated to a college education,
I had no doubt a woman like me could become a traveler. I landed
a good position at Flin Flon. Then I spent my Long Four Years at a
think tank called Past Engagements that provided evidence-based
historical analysis to policymakers in Washington, D.C.

The first time I traveled, it was to Mississippi in the late 1860s.
My assignment was simple: gather firsthand evidence for a lobbying

group trying to prove that women's suffrage movements are always doomed to fail.

My supervisor sent me to the period before the Fifteenth Amendment was ratified. This was during the bitter post–Civil War congressional debates over whether enfranchisement should extend to male former slaves, a subset of "educated" male former slaves, or both genders of all races. Conservatives were so angered by the process that they started defecting to the once-marginal Democratic Party, whose main platform was basically white nationalism. Lincoln's Republicans were fearful of losing ground to Democrats in the South, so they hatched a desperate plan to make universal suffrage attractive to their dubious GOP brethren.

First, a group of Republican abolitionists persuaded the war hero and beloved cultural icon Harriet Tubman to run for U.S. Senator in Mississippi. Of course she couldn't vote—and, therefore, couldn't technically run for office. What she could do, however, was bring out huge crowds of women and ex-slaves at rallies and events where they filled out "provisional registration" forms as Republicans. The abolitionist Republicans were betting that activists in the South could get thousands of these people to fill out their forms. Behold: so many untapped voters, eager to toe the party line! It might persuade conservative members of the GOP to support universal suffrage. More Republican voters was a good thing, no matter how questionably human those voters might be.

I was the only Black person among the travelers at Past Engagements, so my supervisor decided I would be the ideal observer of this unique historical moment. "You'll blend in. They'll trust you," he said. He didn't understand that a mixed-race girl from California might have as little in common with a recently freed slave in Mississippi as he did. I couldn't contradict him if I wanted this assignment, though, so I nodded and said nothing. Of course, I was right. During the six months I traveled, the activists kept asking me what I was. Sometimes the locals did too. Southerners were used to mixed-race people, because so many ex-slaves had white fathers, uncles, or grandfathers. But nobody had a father from India like I did.

I tagged along with a group of younger activists from New York, who treated me like their pet alien from the future. In late 1869 and early 1870, I took notes as they registered thousands of people in Mississippi, riding from town to town in a wagon with Harriet Tubman's face painted on the side. Sadly, I did not get to meet the senatorial candidate herself; she was always campaigning or managing the elder care home for ex-slaves she'd founded outside Jackson.

The campaign was a spectacular failure. Men achieved universal suffrage, and women were sacrificed for the sake of Republican unity. A freedman named Hiram Revels won the Mississippi senate seat. Harriet Tubman went broke, and was forced to beg Congress for the soldier's pension she hadn't been granted previously because she was a woman. I returned to 1991 full of rage. We were so close to winning! Maybe if I'd participated, committed one small edit, it would have changed the fate of over half the people in the United States. I felt the effects of our loss in my present, and in my bones. Women still couldn't vote in Mississippi, nor in most of the South and the Midwest.

My supervisor was extremely pleased with the data I brought back, and immediately turned it into a research paper for lobbyists about why women's suffrage had a long history of failure in the United States. I got fourth author credit, and he offered me another assignment right away—this time for a State Department committee evaluating whether to fund human rights organizations in Haiti. "You may have a career in witnessing key political failures," he mused. "What do you think about traveling to Haiti in the late 1790s, to record how the slave uprising was put down? You'll fit in there, too." I looked into his watery blue eyes and stopped believing that he was ignorant but meant well. He was fucking with me, and profiting from my research to boot. That's when I decided the point of travel was not to observe history, but to change it.

I have recorded my experiences during the Haitian Revolution in another document. Hopefully, if you are reading this, you are in a timeline where my edit has not been reverted. The uprising was a success, though I nearly lost an arm in the fighting. Transformation rippled down the timeline. Seventy years later, abolitionists and suffragettes rejoiced together when Harriet Tubman was elected to the Senate in the United States. When I returned to 1991, my supervisor treated me differently. He never once suggested I wouldn't be first author on our paper about what makes slave uprisings successful. There were also a few more brown faces in our lab. These small changes mattered.

I don't believe I was responsible for altering the timeline. I was merely one of many people authoring those edits across many generations. What I learned on that trip to Haiti is something I try to teach to my students, and to the Daughters of Harriet. Nothing is inevitable, and you always have to go back farther than you expect.

But like I said, I don't tell them everything about the timeline I remember. I don't want them to know how close we are to that other version of history. I want them to have hope.

TWENTY-EIGHT

TESS

We'd given ourselves six months to complete the Comstock edit, but Morehshin and I couldn't book passage on a ship back to Chicago for three weeks. It was an annoying delay, but it gave me a chance to spend more time with Anita, processing everything that had happened. To earn money while waiting for us, Anita took on some research duties with the American Geophysical Union and taught public classes at Raqmu Technical University. Meanwhile, C.L. traveled back and forth to do more analysis and possibly get some clues about what those cuts in the Machine interface might mean.

As long as I kept busy with research at the AGU library, I could put aside my emotional vertigo from what had happened with Beth. The local pharmacist got used to my requests for willow bark extract, which made my stomach burn but took the edge off my near-constant headache. After a couple of weeks it got so bad that I bought some opium to relieve the pain.

I tried to keep it to myself, but it was hard to fool Anita for long. We were sharing a small room. One night she came home early from the university and caught me with a dab of opium, blowing smoke out the window.

"Tess." She folded her arms. "You know that stuff is seriously addictive."

"Sorry. I don't do it very often. Sometimes it hurts too much to sleep."

"You're still getting those headaches? From the double memories?" Anita sat on the edge of our cubby while I stashed the remaining nugget of opium in a silver snuff box. I hadn't smoked very much, but my agony had dulled to a twinge. I was probably too high to have this conversation, but I knew she wouldn't let me off the hook.

"Correlation doesn't equal causation, so we can't be sure the pain is related to my memories." I was mumbling. "Besides, the memories aren't the difficult part. It's more . . . the feelings."

"What do you mean?"

"I used to feel certain about our mission. Like we are definitely making the timeline better. Now I feel . . . divided. What if we're making things worse?"

Anita sighed. "I've been feeling this way a lot since my mom died."

"Wait, what?" Some of my drug haze lifted. "Your mom died? Why didn't you tell me?"

"It was right after you left, and there's been so much going on . . . I guess I didn't want to deal with it."

I thought of Anita's mom, a fierce woman named Yvonne who had raised Anita by herself and worked the whole time as a nurse—then, when she had time to get more education, a doctor. When she visited L.A., I often went out to dinner with the two of them. I'd heard the story about how Yvonne hooked up with Anita's dad while carousing across the U.K. with hippie friends. Anita's parents had one of those baby boomer relationships I didn't really understand, half-traditional and half-liberated. They never married, but her father had taken care of Anita financially, given her his last name, and invited her on summer trips to London, Mumbai, and Singapore. He'd been in and out of Anita's life, but Yvonne was there every day. Anita called and texted her all the time. I couldn't believe we'd been talking about my stupid headaches when Anita was dealing with this.

"Anita, I'm so sorry. What happened?"

"You know . . . getting old. She died in her sleep. But somehow that makes it worse. It's like her time came, and it was peaceful and natural, but I wasn't ready at all. I feel like I'm in the wrong timeline, even though I know this was supposed to happen. Suddenly I can't figure out who the hell I'm supposed to be. She was the only person who remembered my childhood other than me, you know? I keep wanting to get her advice, and thinking that I see her . . ." Her voice cracked, but she didn't cry. Somehow that made her face look more raw and broken.

I hugged her and listened for a long time. We talked about how death feels like abandonment, especially when you lose your mother. "Mothers are a primordial force that links us to our history," Anita said through tears. "When they die, it's like some of history dies too." In the early hours of the morning, we kept whispering through our exhaustion. I wondered whether the timeline itself was an endlessly repeating cycle of loss that divided humanity from itself, and Anita nodded, her face wet on my shoulder. Wrapped in blankets together, holding hands, we finally started to drift off.

"Anita, don't ever do that again, okay?"

"What?"

"Don't not tell me when something huge happens to you. You are my best friend. I don't want to feel like we're in one of those crappy movies where the black girl has to fix all the white girl's problems and deal with her own shit too."

Anita snorted. "So you're saying I have to tell you my problems to alleviate your white guilt?"

Now she was sounding more like the Anita I loved. I laughed sleepily. "You know what I mean. I'm here for you. I know I can't be what your mom was to you, but you are my family."

"You are my family too, Tess."

"I'm sorry I was so caught up in my own bullshit that I didn't ask how you were doing sooner."

"I'm sorry I didn't tell you sooner, too." She gave me a hug that blotted out more pain than opium ever could.

Morehshin and I made it back to Chicago in December. It was almost 1894, the Expo was over, and Aseel had moved into Soph's old rooms now that the Algerian Village was gone. She made beds for Morehshin and me on the floor as we told her about Soph's sacrifice.

"I suppose she loved that. Calling on the goddess was always her specialty." Aseel looked down. "I miss her."

"She misses you, too. I'm sorry it had to be like this."

"We did the right thing. Plus, Soph's 'death' got people riled up about how terrible Anthony is. Have you seen the pictures of him doing the hoochie coochie?" She pulled out a copy of the *St. Louis Post-Dispatch* and spread it on the soft rug where we sat on cushions. Holding up a lamp so we could see clearly, Aseel pointed at a long article about Comstock's fight against the dancers at the Expo. Apparently he had tried to get another theater shut down in New York, and granted a press conference about his efforts. To describe the horror of the dance, he stood up and did some wobbly gyrations, much to the amusement of the audience. A political cartoonist had quickly drawn a sketch of the portly Comstock, buttons bursting on his waistcoat, face flushed, shaking his ass. That picture was more of a blow than the twenty inches of arch commentary in the article. It turned Comstock from a moral authority into an out-of-touch loon.

This was progress. But unfortunately, politicians didn't care what the newspapers said about Comstock. He still had powerful people on his side, including wealthy New Yorkers who dumped cash into Congress.

"We need to organize another anti-Comstock protest, but even bigger than the last one," I said.

Aseel made a face. "I don't think a protest will work."

"But the last one was great! I have some ideas—"

"We need to switch tactics. If we protest again, without the Expo, we look like crazy children. It's easy to ignore us."

That stung a little, especially when Morehshin grunted assent.

"All right then, Aseel—what's *your* plan?"

"I started thinking about this a few months ago, when the burlesque girls stole our moves and . . . our song." Aseel dropped her eyes for a moment, and I remembered her helpless rage that night at the Persian Palace. "Now that Sol and I are selling the sheet music at the shop, it's become incredibly popular. What if we had an event to celebrate the hoochie coochie? People really hate Comstock for going after hoochie coochie dancers. That's the biggest stumble he's made. We could do something in New York that was so spectacular that even those rich socialite Astors would come see it. Comstock would have to go after us, and it would make him terribly odious to everyone."

Morehshin nodded. "It would put him in a very bad position. He'd damage his reputation if he tried to stop it, and damage his reputation if he didn't."

I imagined a hoochie coochie protest and was filled with so much glee that it almost chased my headache away. "Yes!" I yelped, pumping my fist in the air like I was at a show.

Sol and Aseel named their new business the Independent Music Company, shortened on the sheet music to *Ind. Music Co.* Far north of our old haunt on the Midway, it was nestled among tall brick buildings in the riverfront district along Wabash Street. Cable cars clanged outside, and the theater next door had a massive billboard advertising "The Original Midway Dancers Here." In the mornings, when the street was redolent of bacon and fresh bread, the neighborhood had an air of respectability. But as the afternoon wore on, and the barkers hawked their ten-cent tickets, packs of young men with beer foam in their moustaches smoked cigars on the street. The stench of rotting meat drifted in from the water. That's when it was obvious that the Midway had found a permanent home in Chicago. Still, it hadn't been domesticated. Not yet.

The Independent Music Company storefront was crammed with carefully alphabetized offerings in wooden racks labeled with signs advertising COMIC SONGS and HITS. A modern cash register with brass fittings occupied most of the marble-top counter, and a glass-front display case held a hodgepodge of impulse items: piano strings, guitar picks, wood polish, Smith Brothers cough drops for singers. Cozy and well lit, the place attracted a steady stream of musicians and promoters. But it wasn't the heart of Aseel and Sol's operation. That lay behind a door in the back, which opened into an airy warehouse. The previous owners used it for storing barrels of liquor, and a few busted casks still huddled in a corner, smelling faintly of sherry. Now half the room was taken up with a printing press and paper, and the other half was a woodworking shop where a former drummer from the Algerian Theater made fiddles. A spiral staircase led to the manager's office, where Aseel worked from Sol's favorite chair at a large conference table.

This room became our informal planning headquarters. We met for the first time on an icy Tuesday, as Aseel was going over sheet music mockups for a new dance hall hit. The cover would be in two colors, and she used a red fountain pen to sketch out where she wanted the title to swirl upward, spewing flowers and curly lines. At last she looked up at Morehshin and me, gathered earnestly at the table. Here, at the center of a thriving music business, it was more obvious than ever that Aseel was one of the few turn-of-the-century women who had managed to unbind herself from the strictures of her time. Partly that was thanks to her strength and talent, but also to the lucky edit that brought her a male boss who recognized both and rewarded her for them.

I was certain she would bend history to make room for more women like her.

She motioned for us to sit down at the table, and we talked for a while about her idea for a New York event. "But how will we organize it?" I asked. "Comstock has eyes on the post. Given what happened to Soph, we have to assume he's still watching our correspondence. We can't mail anyone if he's spying on us."

There was a banging on the stairs, and one of the printers knocked on the door. "Miss Aseel? Do you know how many copies of 'Chicago Dancers Polka' we're going to need?"

"Make two dozen." She waved him off.

That gave me an idea. "What if we sent something through the mail that looked completely innocent? You could issue a special edition of the hoochie coochie song, but with a new name, something innocuous like . . . 'Country Lad.' We could include the description of our event in the sheet music booklet."

Aseel's eyes gleamed. "What if we made it a dance contest? Twenty-five bucks to the best interpretation of . . . 'Country Lad.'" She giggled. "I bet we could get some of the Four Hundred to shell out for prizes and a ballroom." She was referring to a fabled group of New York socialites, whose number supposedly never topped four hundred. Rumors swirled in the gossip pages that some of their secret parties included private dances from a Lady Asenath imitator.

"How are we going to do that?" Moreshin was zapping tiny holes in the table with her multi-tool, then repairing them. When Aseel glared, she made a protesting noise. "What? I'm practicing!"

I twirled a pencil around my thumb, lost in thought. "There must be some dumb, rich dudes in New York who want a bunch of hoochie coochie girls to perform for them."

"You know who is really dumb, and in thick with the Four Hundred? Archibald Fraser, the son of that guy who does animal shows." Aseel put the sheet music aside excitedly. "His dad owns performing seals and elephants and sells a million tickets. Sol knows Archy, and I bet he would introduce us. If we pull this off, it's good for the business."

Aseel and I debated where we could hold the event. The problem was that I hadn't been in New York since hanging out with Emma Goldman's crew over a decade ago. Aseel only knew about venues through Sol and the gossip pages.

Oddly, Morehshin turned out to have in-depth knowledge of Gilded Age New York. "Do you know Sherry's Ballroom?" she asked. "That's where the Four Hundred like to throw their parties." Then she told us about Louis Sherry, whose catering was so sought-after among the city's elite that he'd had to move his venue twice to accommodate bigger and bigger shindigs.

"Let's aim for that, or something like it," I said. Then, perplexed, I turned to Morehshin. "Why do you know so much about New York society in this period?"

"I learned Atomic Age English from historical romances. Nobody asks questions when a woman watches ancient love stories about heterosexuality."

Over the next two weeks, a flurry of letters passed between Aseel, Sol, Archy, and the booker at Sherry's. Archy was, as promised, a socialite playboy with way too much money to spend. When Aseel told him he could invite his bachelor friends to be "judges" at the contest, he was sold. She figured out the logistics around money, food, seating, and staging, while he sent telegrams with useless advice about ribbons and trophies. It was just like old times at the Algerian Theater.

We set the date for the contest in late April, five months from now, when the weather would be warming and the Four Hundred would be ready for debauchery after the staid "Lenten season" that followed their winter balls. That would also give us plenty of time to blanket the East Coast with Ind. Music Co.'s "special commemorative edition of the Midway Hit known as 'Country Lad.'" On the last page, we included a full-page ad for the dance contest to be held at Sherry's Ballroom, hosted by Archibald Fraser. All contestants were to line up at the servants' entrance and, if admitted, would be allowed one chaperone and one musician to accompany them.

We made no mention of the hoochie coochie or *danse du ventre*, so it would slide past Comstock's front line of censors. But any dancer familiar with the song would know exactly what we were talking about. If all went according to plan, Comstock wouldn't figure it out until we were already in New York, where he would be forced into a humiliating face-to-face showdown with us at Sherry's.

My headaches were getting worse, and I measured the days in willow bark and opium dabs. Moreshin and I worked in the music shop, and rented a bigger room above Soph's old parlors. There were bad nights and not-so-bad ones, but I never felt like myself except on days when I received a letter from Anita. She'd gotten a few nineteenth-century students interested in the idea of collective action, despite the fact that Great Men currently ruled geoscience departments. I wished we were back at UCLA together, and then I wished I were back at the Temple of al-Lat with Soph. Anywhere but here, where the mornings froze me in ice and memories polluted my brain like soot.

We started our heaviest promotion for the show in late March, sending out freshly printed releases and posters, and I fell upon the project with the shaky, starving energy of a bear out of hibernation. The press was calling it "Lady Asenath's Musical Revue," and the Four Hundred dubbed it "Archy's big bash." We kept selling out of "Country Lad" at the store. By the time we decamped for a suite of rooms in New York City, the sheet music had gone into its tenth printing.

Which was why Sol was footing the bill for our trip, and puffing delightedly on a cigar when we arrived at the venue.

Sherry's looked like something the peasants would have trashed during the French Revolution. In the ballroom, copper laced the edges of a high arched ceiling encrusted with molded plaster protrusions that dribbled chandeliers. The floor was a polished dark wood spread with thick carpets beneath upholstered chairs. Dinner would be spread across this vast room and spill into the more formal dining room beyond.

The Carpenters Union sent out an apple-cheeked rep barely out of apprenticeship to explain excitedly how they would build the stage on Saturday and have it ready in time for staff to decorate. Sherry's chef created a special twelve-course menu, including dozens of pheasants, hundreds of oysters, Jerusalem artichokes, carrot soup, and a bewildering array of after-dinner cakes and dessert cheeses. Of course, Archy had ordered two dozen barrels of liquor. Every time a new delicacy was added to our tab, the Sherry's event manager jotted it down with a polite nod. His nonchalance made me realize this was an ordinary party for him. Everyone who rented Sherry's expected cartloads of fancy meats and crates of imported champagne. Our show was an exotic dessert for the children of robber barons, and for a second I was revolted by what we were doing. Teaming up with these Gilded Age sleazeballs might not be collective action after all—maybe it was simply pandering.

Too late for second thoughts now. I needed to focus on why we were here. I was doing this for the women of the Midway, their daughters and mothers. Maybe some of them would be here this Saturday, showing off their hoochie coochie moves. I hoped so. I wanted to see all of them one more time before leaving this moment forever.

On Saturday, we dodged last-minute preparation disasters at Sherry's and puddles of freezing water in the filthy gutters along Broadway.

Cocktails began after sunset at 7 P.M., and that slid into dinner. People kept arriving and arriving; it seemed the entire Four Hundred had come with at least one or two friends, all wearing glittery ball gowns and plumes in their hair, or tuxes with rakish waistcoats.

Morehshin stood outside the servants' entrance to check in the dancers and their escorts, while I played liaison with the staff. I saw the dinner from the sidelines, catching snatches of conversation and vague impressions of white skin gone florid with conspicuous consumption. My trepidation from yesterday returned. These people were here to consume us, not to join our struggle against reproductive moralism.

Upstairs, the dancers were oblivious to the stakes—they were here for the fabulously lucrative $25 prizes, or maybe for fame. They crowded into a dining hall repurposed as a dressing room. Costume racks jostled against a wall of full-length mirrors. Musicians waited in the hall outside, smoking and drinking from a crate of champagne I'd asked the staff to bring upstairs.

Gradually the composition of the party underwent a metamorphosis. Elderly men filtered out, along with a few dozen ladies. The women who stayed for the show were younger and dressed in French fashions. They ate rosewater ices while the men stood up to mingle, drinking cognac and smoking. It was starting to feel like the hipster gin bar.

Staff cleared tables from the ballroom. As promised, the Carpenters Union had built a low, sturdy stage piled with rugs, drums, and some wooden camel tchotchkes. Sherry's also supplied us with a handy backdrop from storage with an "exotic orient" theme, including an oasis surrounded by veiled women and some pyramids looming in the distance. Apparently it was left over from a costume revue staged by a secret men's society. It set the tone for our evening, where the entertainment would wobble between appropriation and authenticity.

Six ornate thrones for the judges dominated the front row. I looked at them, full of dread. Would there be an execution or a revolution?

Upstairs, the dressing room was perfumed insanity. Women crushed against each other at the mirrors, coins and beads on their outfits jingling, applying makeup or veils or sparkles or elaborate headdresses. Some were like the white dancers from the Persian Palace, adding a few fake Bedouin touches to their burlesque flounces. Others had costumes that were very close to indigenous North African styles. Dancers practiced their moves, undulating and humming bars of Aseel's song. It was impossible to say who was inhabiting an identity they'd lived, and who was simulating a culture they'd never known. The many shades of brown skin revealed beneath bodices suggested these women might be from the Maghreb. Or India. Or Mexico. Or the Bronx. Maybe all of those places.

We handed out a number to each woman, noting their stage names so that Archy could introduce them. Many used monikers that were variations on Lady Asenath, which made sense given her international renown. I counted two Lady Asenaths, two Mademoiselle Asenaths, a Dusky Asenath, and one particularly saucy Asenath the Temptress. After witnessing Aseel's rage at the Persian Palace, it worried me. Were these acts ripping her off, or paying homage? Only she could decide.

I found Aseel across the room, helping a woman with her signup sheet. "A lot of these women are using your name. Do you want me to make a rule that they have to pick an original stage name?"

Aseel rolled her eyes and laughed. "I'm not surprised. I've heard through the grapevine that lots of people have been performing as Lady Asenath."

"Are you okay with it?"

"On another night, I'd likely say no. But tonight, I'll take it as a compliment."

I leaned over and whispered in her ear. "You will always be the best Lady Asenath."

She winked. "I know." Then she turned back to the line. "Okay, ladies, let's get started! Where is number one?"

Aseel deputized me as an escort, which meant my job was to bring acts downstairs and guide them to the stage. At first, I watched the crowd nervously. Archy sat on the biggest throne, with five other tuxedoed and mustachioed young men flanking him. They scored each dancer by holding up cards with carefully handwritten numbers on them. When I arrived with act number three in tow, none of the dancers had gotten higher than a 7. But that was about to change.

Act three gamboled around the stage, veils revealing nothing but blue eyes in a white face. Then she began to toss aside gossamer layers of fabric and a roar of appreciation hovered over the room like cigar smoke. When she dipped into a particularly vigorous shake, one of her breasts popped out of her top. I barely caught the sleight-of-hand move she'd made to release it; this was part of her act, and she was good at it. As she made a big show of fluttering her scarves and blushing, the judges held up their votes: 8, 8, 9, 10, 7, 8. And thus it became clear what was required to get a high score. This was what we'd wanted; this would draw out the Comstockers. But it didn't feel righteous like our protest at the Expo, where we'd linked arms and shouted the truth. What we were doing here might be more powerful, but it was more ambiguous, too.

By the time I arrived with dancer twelve, Mademoiselle Asenath, the ballroom had come undone like a man's tie after a night of bar hopping. People yelled and demanded lap dances. Staff cracked open another whiskey cask. Archy invited Mademoiselle Asenath to sit in his lap as part of the contest. "It's to be your weigh-in!" he yelped. "Like at the racetrack! You're a beautiful racehorse, honey, aren't you?" His friends roared with laughter.

I gripped the dancer's arm. She was one of the women in a mostly traditional costume, and the smooth, dark skin of her neck gleamed with necklaces. I spoke loudly enough for Archy to hear. "You don't have to do that. It's not in the rules."

The dancer was completely unruffled. "Oh no, it's okay, honey. These gentlemen are good tippers." Slightly taken aback, I let her go.

Archy loved that. "That's right! I pay top dollar for my fillies!" He bounced her on his knees and she pinched his cheek as if he were a naughty boy.

"You've never saddled one as wild as me, love."

Fingering one of her spangled sleeves, he stroked her arm and winked at the judge next to him. "Not a purebred, I think. But I'd ride her!" Though the dancer kept a smile carved into her face, I could tell she was no longer enjoying the banter. Archy and his friends speculated about her "breeding," and I felt something that I'd suppressed for a long time. I wondered where Sherry's kept its steak knives. Ever since Beth survived, it had gotten harder for me to banish those kind of thoughts.

These men were supposed to be our allies, but they treated us like animals. Was this really going to work? Had we made a terrible miscalculation? I surveyed the ballroom of glittering hypocrites, their eyes glued to the stage, delight on their faces. They didn't respect us, but they loved us. We'd ripped a giant transgressive hole in their expensive petticoats, and given them a chance to revel in a sweet, chaotic moment of freedom.

"It's time for the dance," I said, holding out my arm to Mademoiselle Asenath. She escaped Archy's lap and snatched a tip out of his fingers, perhaps a bit more violently than was strictly necessary. As the music started, her hips swayed and shivered, expressing a perfect hybrid of burlesque and hoochie coochie. Whirling in front of the thrones, skirts frothy with bells, she ripped off her modest bodice and scarves to reveal nothing but a lacy bra over her curved, naked belly. The room went wild.

"Take it off!"

"That's my doll!"

"Show us everything!"

"Yes, yes, yes!"

"That's a ten! A ten right there!"

Her stomach muscles rippled as she clashed finger cymbals and commanded the room to watch. It made me think of al-Lat's statue at Raqmu, or a Grape Ape concert. She was erotic and brilliant and something ineffable that none of these men would ever truly comprehend. I let out a laugh. Aseel really had created a show for the women of the Midway. Maybe the Four Hundred thought it was for them, but that was only because they assumed everything was for them and could comprehend no other possibility.

As the cacophony in the room reached a fever pitch, the noises moved from appreciation to anger. From my perch near the stage, I spotted a singular figure making his way from the back of the room, red face trembling with moral outrage and unfashionable facial hair. Our honeypot had lured in the drone to lead all drones. The revelers parted to reveal Anthony Comstock, flanked by Elliot and boys from the Society for the Suppression of Vice in their Puritanical plain suits. Two officers from the NYPD pushed members of the Four Hundred out of the way. Our moment had come.

Comstock stood on a chair. "THIS IMMORAL FILTH WILL STOP RIGHT NOW. YOU ARE INSTRUCTED TO LEAVE OR RISK ARREST."

Outrage came from every quarter, delivered in high-toned accents. Archy marched on Comstock and threatened to kick the chair out from under him until the man stepped down.

"What is the meaning of this? It's a private party! You can't barge in here . . ."

"But that's where you're wrong, sir. This is an obscene performance, and I have brought the police with me to enforce the law. No one, no matter how rich, is above the law."

"I beg to differ. Do you know who we are?" Archy made a large, drunken gesture at the room. It had gotten very quiet, and I had no idea what would happen next. I jumped onstage to bundle the dancer into a silk robe, hoping to lead her away unobtrusively.

But Elliot had his eyes on us. Raising his voice for everyone to hear, he declared, "HALT, MADAME. THIS WHORE IS VIO-LATING THE LAWS OF GOD AND NEW YORK CITY. SHE IS COMING WITH US."

Now Archy was pissed. He folded his arms and put on his best entitled-rich-guy expression. I had to admit it was pretty impressive. "No one is going with you, little man. The police commissioner had dinner with us last week. I believe he will have something to say about this ridiculous trespass on our private party!"

There were a few muffled noises of assent from the crowd. Some of the dancers crept down from the dressing room to watch. They hovered next to the stage, a glittering bonfire of bright fabric in the suddenly somber space. Comstock seemed to realize he was losing ground, but he stood firm.

"I have no beef with you, sir, as long as you clear off. But I must insist that you produce Lady Asenath, who authored this abominable performance. I have a warrant for her arrest!" Next to him, Elliot waved a piece of paper and sneered at me. I wondered how much he remembered of the night he eavesdropped on us. Comstock raised his voice again. "WHERE IS LADY ASENATH?"

My heart was pounding. What should we do?

That's when Aseel stepped forward. She'd changed into a ball gown of pale yellow silk with puffed sleeves and a wide sash. Her skin glowed a rich brown in the chandeliers' candlelight. "I AM LADY ASENATH."

What the hell was she doing? Sending Aseel to jail wasn't part of our plan. Then something unexpected happened. Mademoiselle Asenath broke away from me onstage to stand next to Aseel. "NO. I AM LADY ASENATH."

And then more came forward, all the various Lady Asenaths rais-ing their arms and yelling her name. "I AM LADY ASENATH! I AM!"

Suddenly, a society lady in the audience jumped on her chair and joined in. "I AM LADY ASENATH! ARREST ME!" Another lurched tipsily onto her chair, aided by a gentleman friend. "I AM LADY ASENATH!"

That's when I noticed Sol at the edge of the room, smoking his cigar, looking straight at me. He winked and tapped his temple with a finger, reminding me of what he'd said last year during the Expo: *You change a man's mind by showing him a good time.* Maybe he'd hit upon an odd, unknown corollary to the Collective Action hypothesis. The people in this room had come here looking for fun or for titillation or for justice, and maybe it was all right that we didn't see the same truth when we looked at the stage. So what if these soused men on their thrones didn't notice the connection between hoochie coochie dancers and women's reproductive freedom? It didn't matter. Because we all agreed on one thing. We were in this together.

"I AM LADY ASENATH!" I yelled from the stage. A reckless, strange solidarity gripped the ballroom, and more voices spoke her name. One of the judges scrambled up next to me and howled in a practiced falsetto, "I AM LADY ASENATH AND I'M A PERFECT TEN!"

Archy couldn't have been more thrilled. This would be all over the gossip pages tomorrow. Like a twenty-first-century reality TV star, he thirsted for the fame and party invites that came with his scandalous reputation. "I guess you'll have to arrest all of us, then," he said loudly. "I'm sure the police commissioner will be happy to hear about that."

Comstock looked at Elliot, and then at the police officers. "This isn't over. I'm going to bring charges."

"I welcome your charges." Archy glowered. "I can't wait to bankrupt you in court."

My headache was gone and I felt intoxicated in every part of my body. Archy was doing far more than we'd ever hoped he would—and so were his glitter trash uptown friends. For a triumphant second, I allowed myself to imagine history emerging from this moment in a perfect, uncomplicated arc. The Four Hundred's appetite for sexy entertainment would challenge the obscenity laws that bore Comstock's name. As he lost his grip on the mail, information about birth control and abortion would circulate freely again. The hoochie coochie dancers' edit was what we'd needed all along.

I looked at Morehshin, who was grinning fiercely. Maybe, centuries from now, her queens were becoming people.

Sunday morning's society pages were full of salacious drawings and exaggerated accounts of the evening. Archy's "bash" was duly condemned as racy and decadent, but Comstock emerged as the evening's biggest gossip target. The papers satirized everything about him, from his threadbare suit to his accent. His morals were absurd; they belonged to an era before the invention of electricity. George Bernard Shaw, a snarky British theater critic, made oblique reference to the scandal in a widely republished essay about how "Comstockery" was ruining American culture. Morehshin was excited to see the true slaughter of Comstock's reputation was under way. Sol and Archy gave everybody big tips, including to the dancers who hadn't won the prize.

In the light of day, I still felt sure we'd reached a transition point. This wasn't an "angry mob" protesting Comstock's moral cleansing campaign. It was New York's best and richest, simply trying to have a good time. We'd driven a wedge between the Four Hundred and the moralist who depended on them.

Of course, I might never know if I was right about the eventual outcome of last night's blowup. That would require me to get back to 2022. And I couldn't do that until Morehshin and I tapped back millions of years to deal with the men who were still trying to rob us of our history.

I realized this might be the last time we would see Aseel, and I was sorry to say goodbye. Hungover but happy, we met in the hotel dining room for a late breakfast of eggs, rolls, and various gelatinous meats beloved in this era. Morehshin poured a small amount of coffee into her cup from the carafe on our table and stared at it.

"You going to drink that?" Aseel was amused.

I tried to explain. "People don't drink coffee in her time."

"Some people do." Morehshin frowned. Then sipped. "Ugh, this is bad. Maybe some rules don't need breaking."

We laughed and I noticed that Aseel didn't seem as angry as she used to. Running a shop suited her, and she was publishing a lot of music that came from traditions outside the usual European oompa crap. "What are your plans for the Independent Music Company?" I asked.

"Sol and I talked last night, after everybody left. We're making a tidy profit with our sheet music, and he wants me to start organizing more events like this one back in Chicago." She got a faraway look on her face. "We could bring back some of the Midway dancers, like Salina, and put on shows in the dance hall next door. A bunch of venues are opening up on Wabash."

"That sounds fantastic! The Algerian Village lives on!"

She nodded. "I got a big raise, too. I can buy a house."

Morehshin talked around the bacon in her mouth. "That's good. A house is important. My sisters have a saying: *If you have property, you can't be property.*"

Aseel gave us both a quizzical look. "I'm not sure that's true, but I definitely feel more secure."

We talked about where she might move, and how Sol was going to let her take charge of hiring, and then finally it was time for us to go. Aseel took the train back to Chicago while we headed to the pier. We had a long trip ahead.

When we arrived at Raqmu, the news was waiting for us in tidy piles at the inn in the scholars' neighborhood. Literati and society types had taken up the "Comstockery" meme with zeal. It came to mean anything unfashionable, addle-brained, or dull. Comstock's raid had also cost him some very rich patrons, who quietly distanced themselves from his crusade. When he was harassing abortionists, smutty postcard peddlers, and low-class theaters, they considered it their duty to support him. But not when he tried to smear the reputations of Archy and the other lads, who were only having a bit of fun. Comstock's operation had always been on a shoestring budget, and now he had fewer resources than ever. If he wanted to continue his legal battles over obscene materials, he couldn't afford to sustain his regular busts in the street.

One of Soph's friends wrote to say that Comstock's boys from the Society for the Suppression of Vice had stopped harassing abortionists right after the party. For now, the women of New York and Chicago had precarious access to birth control—as long as they ordered the right euphemisms from the right catalogues, or called on a sympathetic midwife.

Comstock, who once boasted of driving sex educators to suicide and had attracted followers from across the timeline, was losing his grip on America's britches. His "special agent" position with the Postal Service was only as powerful as the elites allowed it to be. Without help from the Four Hundred and their politicians, he would be relegated to the status of a religious nuisance shouting in the halls outside Congress.

I imagined what Beth's life would be like if the Comstock Laws really were crumbling. What if getting an abortion was an unremarkable aspect of healthcare for anyone with a uterus? What if she didn't have to risk arrest for wanting a normal teenage life without the burden of early motherhood? Maybe she wouldn't need me to help her, but neither would all those other girls who hadn't been born to a mother like mine.

Of course, the reality would be more complicated than that golden arc I'd imagined last night when we invoked Lady Asenath's name. Clever moralists of the future might come up with new legal tricks to invade people's private lives and control reproduction. As long as we had Machines, no edit was permanent. We would have to stay one step ahead, adding loopholes and footnotes and exemptions to their power.

TWENTY-NINE

BETH

Los Angeles, Alta California (1994 C.E.)

I logged into my account from the dorm internet kiosk and opened Pine to read my e-mail. There were two messages: one from the campus lawyer, and one from Hamid. Looking around to make sure nobody could see the terminal, I opened Hamid's right away:

> Hi Beth. First e-mail!!! I'm trying to decide whether to
> see Short Cuts or Cyborg Cop this weekend. If you
> come along, you can cast the deciding vote! What do
> you think?—Hamid

My heart surged like a regular organ instead of an alien invader. I replied:

> Hi Hamid. Good job flinging electrons. I vote for
> Cyborg Cop.—Beth

Then I read the e-mail from the lawyer, who said she'd done some research and I could make an appointment any time to discuss it. I tried to focus on my midterm for Anita's class, but managed little more than a few paragraphs before falling asleep in a tight ball on my bunk.

I saw the lawyer the next day after class.

She patted a folder of papers on her desk. "This is a pretty unusual situation, but we do have something called a dependency override that allows a student under twenty-four to become eligible for financial aid without parental information."

I nodded. "That sounds good."

"I'm not going to soft-pedal this, Beth. It's a difficult process, and it's reserved for pretty dire circumstances. But I got the feeling, based on our previous conversation, that you are . . . estranged from your parents?"

It felt like somebody had punched me in the throat. "I don't . . . I mean, I don't know what that means."

"Are your parents paying for your college now?"

"Yes, but I want them to stop."

The lawyer gave me a hard look. "I need you to be honest with me, Beth. You told me before that your father is mentally ill. Your words. Is there some reason your parents can't take care of you?"

I didn't know what to say and I stared at my hands, digging into the wooden chair.

"Is your father abusing you?"

My ears burned as I thought about how my father acted at the La Brea Tar Pits. And then his rage over the shoes. Was it really abuse? The word sounded so extreme, like something that would leave scars all over my body.

The lawyer tried again, more gently. "Has he hit you? Or molested you?"

Feeling nauseated, I remembered that night—the one that Tess didn't actually know about. Maybe it hadn't been real. I shifted in my seat and watched an ant walk across the floor. My voice sounded very far away when I spoke again. "I don't know."

She pushed the folder toward me. "If your father is abusing you, I think we can make a case for dependency override. Especially if you get a job and show you are already working to support yourself. Why don't you look over some of this paperwork and think about it, okay?" I hazarded a glance at her and she leaned forward. "I don't know what your home situation is, but if you need help, I'll do what I can. Don't be afraid to stick up for yourself."

"Okay, I'll look at this and e-mail you." I jammed the folder into my backpack and walked out into the impossibly beautiful afternoon, where wind attenuated clouds in the sky and eroded the surface of the planet the same way it had for millions of years.

Cyborg Cop was a good choice. It was terrible by any number of measures, and we had plenty of joke material afterward. We sat on a bench near the library and watched students strolling through cones of light from the streetlamps. I lit a cigarette and tried to count the number of times the movie ripped off RoboCop and Terminator.

"Also it's set in the Caribbean, but there are no black people? Did they turn all the black people into white cyborgs?" I shook my head and Hamid laughed.

But then he turned somber. "I really thought you didn't ever want to talk to me again after what happened last year."

I exhaled a long stream of smoke and tried to put words together that I'd imagined saying to him for months. "I know. I shouldn't have blown you off like that. I mean—you didn't do anything bad." Stubbing out my cigarette, I looked up at the moon rather than face him. "But you were about to go off to college, and I barely knew you, and I thought it made sense for us to make a clean break, you know?"

"You didn't barely know me! We were . . . we're friends. You said you liked me."

"I do like you. A lot. That's why we're here, right?" I nudged his shoulder with mine. "But back then, I was doing a lot of really stupid things. I needed to figure shit out."

"Like what? What kind of shit? You totally stopped speaking to me. Heather said you wanted to pretend I was dead or something."

It's true that I'd said something like that, in the weeks after we killed Mr. Rasmann. "I'm really sorry about that. I was . . ."

"Dealing with shit. Yeah." Hamid was mumbling, and I realized that at some point his urgency had simmered down into defeat.

"I'm not going to do that again, okay? I've made a resolution to . . . to try to change the timeline for the better. Even though nobody knows how history works." I put my hands on his shoulders and looked at him. "Can I kiss you?"

He nodded and waited for me to lean forward and find his lips. Only then did he put his arms around me. We walked back to my dorm hand in hand, not saying anything.

I kept thinking about the day he drove me to the abortion clinic, right after he got back from Disney World. Looking back on it now was strange, as if my memories were being reassembled from broken pieces. As I recalled the colors and sounds of that time, they seemed to suture closed over a different set of events. With a shudder, I wondered if this feeling was related to the suicide I didn't remember.

We'd had to walk a gauntlet of Operation Rescue assholes lined up along the sidewalk outside Planned Parenthood. A woman in a "Jesus Saves" T-shirt held a canvas sack full of baby doll parts splattered with red paint. She threw severed plastic arms at me and the whole group chanted, "Murder! Murder! Murder!" I stared at the sidewalk, imagining the provenance of the clay and chalk that formed it. Then, without missing a beat, Hamid grabbed a bloody hand out of the air and pretended to chomp on it. "Tastes like chicken!"

I smothered a grin and opened the tinted glass door. He'd evoked a spirited rendition of "Amazing Grace" from the protesters, and suddenly I was seized with the spirit of punk rock. "ABORTION

IS LEGAL, YOU KNOW!" I yelled. "YOU'RE STUCK IN THE 1950s!" It wasn't a terribly cutting insult, but Hamid laughed. Then I slammed the door and walked to the waiting room, where a receptionist with a purple streak in her hair signed me in. The abortion itself was a haze of concerned, kindly faces, questions about whether I was comfortable, and mercifully effective painkillers. When I returned to the waiting room woozy, Hamid helped me to the car and drove me around until I felt good enough to go home.

Hamid was right: I *did* know him back then, and I'd definitely liked him. But I couldn't bring myself to get together again after that day. My mind was too crowded with the gory weirdness of what was happening with Lizzy and my father's ongoing threats. I wasn't ready for another layer of emotions, especially not after we'd had to deal with the abortion together. Things had gotten too intense too fast. The more I thought about who I was back then, the less I could imagine a place for Hamid in my past.

But there was a place for him now. I stopped suddenly and kissed Hamid on the cheek. He grinned. "What was that for?"

"I was thinking that it would be perfect if we could have met now, instead of back then. Can we pretend that's what happened? Like I ran into you at Stan's Donuts and we decided that our destiny was to see *Cyborg Cop* together?"

Hamid gave me his serious look. "I think we can do that. As long as we see *Short Cuts* next week."

"Does it have supersoldiers in it?"

"Probably. Or dinosaurs. Robert Altman is really into dinosaurs." And he kissed me again, in a way that felt familiar and yet completely unlike anything else in the history of the planet.

I'd left my midterm essay until the last possible minute on Sunday night. No big deal. I'd stay up, turn it in first thing in the morning, then crash for the rest of the day. Most midterms were already over, and the dorm hallways were unusually quiet. Rosa was out, so I put on the new Xicanistas CD to fill the room with something more inspiring than the sound of my keyboard clacking.

I still felt a lingering frustration with the idea that nobody knows for sure how history works. This feeling, more than caffeine and cigarettes, buoyed me through the night and into the early morning. I realized that my perspective had changed since talking to Anita in office hours. It wasn't that I didn't believe in great men anymore. But now I could see that every great man was actually a tiny piece of something much larger: a movement, an institution, or possibly a set of loosely interconnected people. Maybe the only real difference between the Great Man perspective and the Collective Action one was that great men had followers instead of communities.

Back when I was in high school, they taught us that changing history involves massive battles and heads of state. But by 7:30 A.M., I knew that was wrong. I reread the last line of my laser-printed midterm before I deposited it in the box outside Anita's office:

> Collective action means that when someone does something small or personal, their actions can change history too. Even if the only thing that person ever does is study ancient rocks, or listen to a friend.

Two weeks later, Hamid and I were cuddling in my bunk while Rosa studied in the lounge. We'd been spending a lot of time together, and I was starting to think that maybe he was my boyfriend. Were we supposed to have "the conversation" right around now? I looked at him and wondered how I would ask about our status without sounding like a cliché.

"Beth, I want to ask you something kind of intense, okay?"

Maybe I wasn't going to have to figure out how to have "the conversation" after all. I kissed his chin and nodded. "Sure—what's up?"

"Remember how you said you were going through some shit and that's why you stopped talking to me last year?"

My shoulders tensed. "Yeah."

"What happened to you? I know you and Heather stopped being friends too. You don't have to tell me if it's super personal, but . . . I really want to know about you. It affects me, too."

I took a breath and started to say something ironic about my friends being serial killers. Then I started to say something dismissive about how parents are the worst. Finally, I found myself telling a story I'd only ever narrated inside my head.

"I was feeling, I guess, anti-social? Mostly because my dad was . . . well, he's really strict. Both my parents are. Like we have a lot of rules in my house about how to act. Certain things I can't say, and—I dunno, weird stuff like how I clean my room or where I set my cup down on the counter. And if I broke a rule, they would ground me for a really long time. Usually a couple of months. I mean, I could go out for school, but other than that I had to stay in my room.

"Actually, I guess they made those rules because of something that happened a long time ago, when I was in sixth grade. I got kind of rebellious, you know? My mom was in the hospital for a few days because she had this condition—and anyway, my dad got mad because I didn't wash the dishes enough before putting them in the dishwasher. He said I was grounded for the next month. Because it was part of a pattern of me being disobedient or something. And I—I got really mad. I told him he was being unfair and crazy and I don't know what. I remember I was screaming, and he—he grabbed my face really hard. Then he pulled my pants off and started spanking me with his belt, and—it was really bad. Like I was bleeding.

"And then he freaked out and started crying and saying he was sorry and he made me get in the shower with him to clean up. It was really fucked up and scary . . . I mean we were in the shower naked and he was rubbing me with soap which really stung and he kept putting his fingers inside . . . inside me . . . and saying he loved me more than he loved my mother . . ."

Hamid was hugging me really hard and I realized my voice was shaking.

"I know it doesn't sound like that big of a deal. Parents are weird, right? It was a long time ago, and he never did that again. But he always acted like he was right about to do it, and he was definitely acting like that a lot last year. So I just couldn't deal with anything. He kept making these threats . . ."

Hamid nodded, his expression unreadable. Suddenly I needed desperately to know something.

"Does that seem normal to you? I mean, kids get spanked all the time, and he only did it once . . . and lots of parents are strict . . ."

"No." He whispered it into my hair, wrapping me tightly in his arms. My cheeks were wet. "It's not normal, Beth. That is *not* normal. I am so sorry that was happening to you and I didn't know."

I mashed my face into his shirt, flooded with relief that someone did know. Someone knew all along. And she saved my life.

I visited the campus lawyer the next day.

She smiled when I sat down in the wooden chair across from her. "I'm glad to see you again. How's it going?"

"I've thought about it and I want to get a dependency override. My father has been abusing me for a long time, and I need to get away from him."

"You're going to have to make a sworn statement to that effect. Are you ready for that?"

I swallowed hard. "Yes. I'm ready."

THIRTY

TESS

I was relieved to be back in Raqmu after a month at sea and on trains. There were more established commercial routes to Raqmu than there were to Flin Flon, but nineteenth-century travel was always exhausting. Morehshin and I settled into the rooms Anita had kept in the scholars' quarter during our absence, and I made some muddy, rich coffee for Anita and me while Morehshin rained a small lunch out of her multi-tool. Suddenly, C.L. burst through the door. "I'm glad you're back because I've done another analysis, and we are in deep shit."

C.L. had dyed their hair bright green, to match their nails. They looked older.

Anita was surprised. "How long have you been working on this?"

They scratched behind an ear. "I got an extension on my field season work, so I guess about a year in travel time, give or take. Mostly in the past. But I am about a month ahead of you in the present. I had to go back once in a while to use the computer cluster in the geology lab. Sorry about that."

That wasn't too bad; it meant we had to avoid them for our first month back, to prevent merging conflicts.

"What did you find?" Morehshin asked.

"They are very close to wrecking the mechanism that keeps the wormholes open on both ends. I have the data right here." C.L. patted their chest.

"You memorized it?"

"No, of course not. That's insane. I uploaded it to my shirt."

Now Morehshin was excited. "You figured out an interface hack!"

C.L. beamed. "That's right. There's no way to bring tools or computers through the time machine, right? The interface only permits clothing and implants. That's how Morehshin brought the multi-tool—she can absorb it into her body. At least, that's my hypothesis."

"You're right." Morehshin opened her hand and the multi-tool emerged from it, growing like a bubble in tar before taking on solid form. I had no idea she could do that.

C.L. continued their infodump. "So I have a friend who got me this prototype of a smart shirt that Alphabet is making—basically there are wires woven into the fabric, connecting the CPU and sensors and memory, so it's part of my clothing. All I have to do is output to a mobile device, which is why I got this implant." C.L. tapped their eyebrow. "I can save all my data and read it locally using ultra-wideband. The cool part is that it's great for fieldwork anywhere, not just during time travel, right? I'm going to use it for this project I'm doing with carbon dioxide in Antarctic meltwater because my shirt runs Fuchsia OS, and one of my labmates wrote a great API for gas chromatographs. Hey, did you guys know I finally got a National Science Foundation grant for that? It's going to be—"

Anita waved her hands. "Okay, okay, C.L.—we can talk about your funding later. Get to the point."

"Right. I've been taking photonic matter levels on the Machine at several critical points in the timeline. Each change is registered instantly on the other Machines, as far as I've been able to determine.

So that hypothesis about how Raqmu affects the other Machines—
my data suggests it's correct. There's a very real possibility that destroying the machine at Raqmu will destroy time travel completely."

"Oh shit."

"Also I figured out what the Comstockers are trying to do. I
traveled closer to the divergence and found a campsite with a stone
forge. They're making steel blades to re-create a part of the old
interface controls, from when the Machines had a console with
buttons. That's why they're randomly cutting into it—to activate a
trigger. Basically, there's a setting that decouples the interface from
the wormhole. Probably for maintenance or something. Anyway,
the result is you've got a wormhole and an interface, but they don't
connect."

"And where does the smelting come in?" My head was exploding
from all this news on top of my migraine, but thankfully C.L. liked
to explain everything.

"You need a metal alloy to unlock it. After I saw Morehshin use
her multi-tool on the canopy, I realized we'd been using the wrong
tools. I mean, not simply the wrong tools, but also in the wrong
places. The interface isn't gone; it's more like the user-friendly part
of it eroded away. Like when you wear the letters and numbers off
an old keyboard. You can still type, but finding the right button is
a crapshoot. Except this isn't a keyboard—it's an incredibly complicated mechanism that controls physical properties of the universe
that we don't yet have names for. I was thinking that maybe the
Machines aren't really for time travel—"

Morehshin cut them off. "Obviously they haven't found a decoupling switch yet. Neither have we, in my time. But they are getting
somewhere. That time when we landed in the Ordovician—the re-
boot fixed it then, but I don't think that will keep working much
longer."

"It won't," C.L. confirmed. "Photonic matter emissions are
through the floor."

"Why do these anti-travelers have to go back at all?" I wondered. "Can't they destroy the interface from their present?"

C.L. sighed in exasperation. "Tess, he has to go back to a period when the interface was still visible, but not underwater, so he can mess around without drowning. So basically that's the Hirnantian. You know—right before the gamma ray burst that scoured the Earth's surface, causing a rapid-onset ice age that killed millions of species in the ocean?"

Anita was nodding as if that explained everything. "It makes sense."

"So what do we do when we tap back?" I looked from Morehshin and C.L. to Anita. "We don't know how many of them there are."

"I have an idea." Morehshin had a smug tone.

"What's that?"

"Go back and kill him. Like Hugayr told us."

"First of all, no, we aren't killing anyone." My voice wobbled as I tried to convince myself. "And second, who is 'him'?"

"They don't know how to send multiple people through at once," C.L. broke in. "It's probably only one going back. Maybe two at most."

"Couldn't we overpower him and drag him back up to 2022?" I was getting desperate. "Sabotaging the Machine is illegal, and C.L. has digital evidence of what he's done."

Anita was dubious. "Do you really think the Academy would buy it? I think at most they'd send him back up to his time."

"I could take him back to his time," Morehshin said reluctantly. "What he's doing is still a crime in the Esteele Era. It was one of the last American democracies before the hives."

C.L. perked up. "Would you do that? I could leave evidence for you in the subalterns' cave."

"How can we be sure you won't kill him?" I asked.

"You can't. But you *can* be sure he will kill us and our daughters if we do nothing."

"All right." I nodded. "We'll go back and make a . . . citizen's arrest. We can knock him out or immobilize him, and tap you guys back up."

"Are you still prepared for this to be a one-way trip?" Morehshin was grim.

I thought about Beth and Soph, both alive; and I imagined Aseel, using the music business to make the world safe for women's bodies. My neck was a burning knot of pain. There was nothing left for me here, but there were billions of other people who needed the Machines to keep our histories open to revision. I nodded at Morehshin. "We've already talked about the risks."

C.L. and Anita nodded too.

We walked to the AGU together. Luckily one of Anita's students was scheduling slots on the Machine, putting in her Long Four Years, and she got us in quickly. As we left, she bowed slightly and whispered, "Safe travels, Daughters."

When we got into the chamber, one of the techs was mopping the floor. "I must warn you that the Machine seems to be covering people in mud and snails."

C.L. nodded curtly. "Like I said. Situation is getting worse."

We arranged ourselves around Morehshin, the floor still wet beneath our shoes. The tech positioned three small tappers around us, cotton-padded hammers poised to bang out a pattern in the rock. When our knees were covered with warm water, Morehshin used her multi-tool to access another part of the interface I'd never seen before. It looked like a jar of mud and darting lights, hovering in the air roughly where the ring once was. She reached into the jar, hand completely disappearing into the mud, and I could see blue flashes between her fingers.

Rain swarmed around us, full of fat hot drops and freezing bullets of hail, and we held each other in the void that meant history was still mutable. I concentrated on my friends, and how their breathing felt next to mine. We seemed to spin slowly, like a drifting asteroid or a diatom in the ocean's water column.

And then we emerged on the knife-edge of a continent, encircled by two enormous, floating parentheses of heavily oxidized rock the color of rust. The salty air was dry and thin, but breathable. Over our heads hung a translucent dome made from pearlescent oil and water, their colors oozing into and around each other in psychedelic patterns. It was shocking and beautiful and unnamable. Had someone actually built such a thing? Would we ever understand it?

Morehshin was unimpressed. "That's where I think the decoupling settings are." She gestured at a segment of the ring. "But they're hard to find because mechanisms tend to move around inside."

C.L. knocked on the floating rock and whistled appreciatively. "It feels so solid."

I touched one with my fingertips. It felt like a warm igneous rock, slightly powdery with rust. I ran my hands underneath it, and felt nothing but a bumpy, wind-smoothed surface. The structure was levitating because of something that I couldn't perceive. Abruptly, a light purple stain appeared in the air at eye level.

"Don't touch that!" C.L. and Morehshin yelled simultaneously.

"What the hell?" C.L. peered at it more closely and gently prodded one shimmering edge with their finger.

Morehshin joined them. "Looks like part of the system for choosing a direction. Whatever. For now, we need to . . . fast-forward. Have you done that before?"

Nobody had. We returned to the group hug position.

"Ready?" Morehshin twiddled her fingers in the oily water overhead and the patterns swirled into a throbbing spiral. The purple stain flashed pink. "Stay together!" Outside, the landscape changed fluidly, shadows lengthening and shortening as algae blooms turned the water emerald, then red, then a luminescent yellow only visible in the long nights of winter. We were traveling rapidly into the future, watching the continent erode and sprout rough scabs of lichen around us.

"I didn't know we could do this!" C.L. was wriggling to get a better view.

"Keep an eye out for the Comstocker so we know when to stop."

"Now!" Anita yelled. Everything solidified and I could see the remains of a crude rock forge several feet away. We filed out carefully, Morehshin palming her multi-tool, and took in the scene. There were deep, precise cuts in the floating rock, and footprints everywhere on the sandy ground.

In the distance I could barely make out the blue-gray bulk of a glacier creeping up the barren continent from the South Pole. We were in a slightly later phase of that ice age C.L. mentioned, when sea levels sank and the Machine stood on dry land, subject to the weathering that eventually erased the visible parts of its interface.

On the beach below, the Comstocker's entire operation was in plain view. Curtains of seaweed were spread out to dry next to a shadowy cave entrance, and farther away was a garbage pile of shells and armor plates from Ordovician fish, clams, and squid. A man emerged from the mouth of the cave, completely naked, dragging a large net bag. From our perch, his features were a blur.

"Everybody get down so he can't see us." Morehshin lay on her stomach and peered over the edge. Then she poked C.L. "Can you use that implant to see distance?"

C.L. nodded and tapped on their shirtsleeve. "He doesn't look good."

Even from this far away, I could see that his pale skin was blistered and his hair was patchy. "Looks like he has no protection from the sun, and he's been here awhile."

The man waded into the ocean and wandered away from shore, the waves lapping no higher than his shoulder. Ducking into the water, he scooped up something fist-sized and stuck it into the bag.

"What's he doing?"

"Looks like . . . hunting." C.L. made a twisting motion with their arm, activating some mechanism in the shirt. "He's got some . . . snails and trilobites? They love these shallow oceans, and we know from the fossil record that there were hundreds of species. He must be eating them."

Sure enough, he returned to land and started a small fire with the seaweed in a pit outside the cave. He went inside and returned with a clay pot, filled it with ocean water and a few snails and trilobite legs, then set it in the glowing coals. He wandered in and out of the cave, finally emerging with a loose gray tunic covering most of his body and something that glittered in his hand.

"It's a knife," C.L. breathed. "Must be one of the tools he smelted."

Hunkering down next to the fire, he pulled another trilobite from the bag, worked its legs off with the knife, and slurped tiny bits of meat into his mouth. Trilobites are distantly related to arachnids, but they looked like stubby green lobsters.

"Wonder if it tastes like lobster or spider?"

"Shut up, Tess," Anita hissed.

"We can take him. Let's hide up here and wait." Morehshin bared her teeth in a feral smile, palming her multi-tool.

That's when a woman emerged from the cave, also in a tunic, carrying an infant in her arms.

"Oh, what the fuck."

"Goddamn it."

Nobody knew what else to say for a minute.

"How did she get there?"

"Morehshin?" C.L.'s eyes were trained on the woman. "She looks exactly like you. But her hands . . ."

Morehshin made a strangled noise that was somewhere between a sob and a growl. "He must have . . . taken a queen."

"She has no hands." C.L. looked blankly at us.

"Is that your sister?" I was astonished.

"Yes. There are many in my line. They must have sent her back to meet him. For breeding . . . to make workers." Morehshin's expression shaded from horror into abjection, and she scrabbled away from the view. Standing up, she stumbled against the floating rocks, leaned over, and threw up profusely into the Machine. Then she gasped like she'd been punched.

Anita and I ran to her, while C.L. kept watch on the beach.

"Look! It's another layer to the interface!" Morehshin pointed overhead, her disgust forgotten. A hole was opening in the canopy over Morehshin's soggy offering. A shaft of bright light shot out, and abruptly the Machine's rocky floor absorbed her vomit, chunks and all.

"Another layer?" C.L. practically careened into us and waved their left hand. "I'm recording. Can somebody else keep watch on the Comstockery?"

"I will." Anita went back to the ledge.

Morehshin poked a finger into the shaft of light and it emitted a noise like a distant wind chime.

"Oh yeah!" C.L. kept waving their hand. "Light sensor?"

The chiming continued as Morehshin swirled her finger in a tiny clockwise circle.

C.L. could not stop the running commentary. "Must have been traces of DNA in the vomit. Or some kind of amino acid? What do you think, Morehshin? I can't wait to write a paper with 'barf-activated interface' in the title." They emitted a weird giggle. "Everybody will call it BAI."

"No." Morehshin said it distractedly, half to C.L. and half to herself. "This is some kind of safety menu." She plunged her hand all the way in, and the light prismed into rainbows. A tiny green bolt of lightning forked up Morehshin's arm, following the contours of her elbow, reminding me of the way she'd interrogated Elliot. She sucked in her breath. "Oh . . . this explains a few things."

"What did you do?" C.L. cocked their head. "I registered a bunch of high-energy particles. It's like . . . you let in a bunch of cosmic radiation."

Morehshin made a distracted noise and the light shut off. Her hand glowed yellow where it had touched the safety menu. "Those are the controls that prevent weapons from traveling in the Machine. They also filter—"

Before she could finish, Anita interrupted. "The Comstocker is climbing up here and he has a broadsword."

By the time the man heaved himself over the lip of the cliff, we were ready. But when Morehshin hit him with green light from the multi-tool, he laughed.

"It's you bitches again, is it?" Under the ragged hair and blisters, I recognized Elliot, at least fifteen years older than when we'd last seen him at Sherry's. Morehshin threw a ball of lightning out of the multi-tool and it fizzled on contact with his chest. "Can't fool me twice. I'm immune now."

There were Neolithic ways to knock him out too. We circled Elliot warily, and C.L. picked up a flat rock from the ground. Anita tried to grab his arms from behind, but he drew the sword, whirling it dangerously close to her head. His aim was terrible and shaky. Still, at close range, he was dangerous. Broadswords are glorified clubs, and he was angling to break bones or smash skulls.

"You're outnumbered, Elliot. We've destroyed Comstock's political career and . . . we know how to repair the Machine." I hoped he believed me. "If you come with us, nobody has to get hurt."

"You are on the wrong side of history." Elliot lunged forward with the sword and would have brought it down on my shoulder if Morehshin hadn't yanked me out of the way. But that left a break in our circle, and he ran through it toward the interface.

Morehshin tackled him as he reached the levitated rocks, and they fell in a furious tangle of limbs on the Machine floor. Elliot wriggled away and levered himself upright by gripping the damaged stone, jamming his sword into one of the grooves. The sword in the stone. A black sphere materialized in the air beneath the canopy, and C.L. let out a howl. They charged head-first with the rock, knocking him and the sword away from the interface. Moving faster than a starving, sunstroked person had any right to, Elliot swept his legs under C.L., bringing them down hard. He scrambled up and planted a knee on their chest, holding the sword point-down over their face.

All of us froze. And then, behind me, a baby started to scream.

I turned to see the woman with no hands, the queen, elbows locked around her baby. She wore Morehshin's face and snarled a rapid stream of words I couldn't understand.

"No!" Morehshin held out a hand and stepped forward.

Elliot's face was slack with shock, and his hands trembled on the sword. The woman positioned the baby's neck near her mouth and bared her teeth as if she were going to bite through an artery. Then she screamed more words.

Morehshin answered in the same language. I caught a word that sounded like "sister," but with the vowels shifted slightly. The woman narrowed her eyes and started to sink her teeth into the sobbing baby's neck.

Elliot stood up, releasing C.L. but keeping the sword clutched tightly in both hands like a baseball bat. C.L. crawled away from him, panting.

"You have no idea how to use the interface," he hissed. "When my brothers complete their edit, I'm going to shut it down for good. Comstock will stop your pathetic slut shows and the queens will rise." He turned to the woman and said something in her language using an equally condescending tone.

Her face twisted in spite. She yelled something that was unmistakably a curse and threw the baby at his chest. It had to be one of the oldest tricks in the book, but it took all of us by surprise—especially

Elliot. He dropped his sword to catch the infant, and in that moment my two histories resolved themselves into one. I was no longer holding myself back to honor the memory of a lost friend. I was nothing but a bloodthirsty animal. And I knew how to kill. I sprinted forward, grabbed Elliot's weapon where it had fallen, and drove it into his spine. As the blade scraped against bone, there was a crunching noise. A bloody metal tongue stuck out of his belly. The man fell to his knees and a grin cut across my face as I watched him dying. C.L. snatched the baby out of his arms before he slumped over.

Elliot spoke to me through teeth covered in blood. "Doesn't matter if you kill me. More will come. I've set up a colony here, with workers—"

I kicked him in the jaw. "Fuck off, drone." It was a curse Morehshin used, and I liked the way it felt in my mouth. Elliot's blood oozed into a preternaturally circular puddle under the curving stones of the interface.

The baby was hiccupping and gasping in C.L.'s arms, Morehshin and her twin were embracing, and I couldn't stop looking at Elliot's impaled body. I hadn't killed anyone in a long time, but my feelings were different now. This wasn't a chaotic spree murder, rash and wrong. I wasn't trying to burn down Irvine, or get revenge on men and the stolen authority that sustained them. This time, it truly was defense. I had made a calculation: him or all of us. Queens or people. Maybe, sometimes, death *was* the only answer.

Anita came to stand beside me, looking silently at Elliot's body. Now his blood was dribbling upward into the stone. It reminded me of what happened with Morehshin's vomit. Were bodily fluids the secret key to operating higher levels of the interface?

"Thank you for saving my life." C.L. held the infant out to Morehshin's sister, who crossed her arms and shook her head. "Don't you want your baby?"

Morehshin cut her eyes at C.L. "That man forced her to bear his worker. She's done with that job."

Disturbed, C.L. cuddled the baby close to their chest, buttoning the mewling bundle inside their data shirt.

After conferring with Morehshin, the woman led us to the beach down a twisting path cut through sandstone that glowed like cheap blush wine. In hundreds of millions of years, these rocks would form the valley walls at Raqmu. I wondered where the archive caves were in this era. "This is Kitty," Morehshin said over her shoulder. "I can translate for her."

"What does she know about the Comstockers' mission?" Anita asked.

Morehshin and Kitty had an exchange in their shared language. "Kitty thinks Elliot has been here for several years, but she's been here only eighteen months. She was sent from my present to grow workers born in this time, so they couldn't escape into the future. This is the only one so far." Morehshin gestured at the baby C.L. was cradling. "She knew Elliot would never let her kill the child, because his job was to set up a colony. After there were enough workers, she was going to be queen for a group of men who could turn the Machine on and off to preserve their rights."

"Can you ask Kitty what he was doing, making those cuts in the stone?" C.L. asked.

Morehshin and Kitty got into a long conversation, and Morehshin didn't bother to translate until we'd reached the dying embers of the cooking fire on the sand. "It's what C.L. suspected. He had a theory that those rocks were the remains of a much larger structure, and he was trying to re-create part of it. Some kind of metal lever or button?"

Morehshin had translated merely a fraction of what Kitty said. But at that moment, my body still jangling with adrenaline and emotional turmoil, I was too jacked up to ask more questions. Suddenly I was extremely hungry. Boiled snail sounded better than the feast we'd had at Sherry's.

Kitty gestured for us to sit down around the fire, and the general consensus was that we should have a meal before deciding on our next move. As we ate, Morehshin used the multi-tool to build hands for Kitty. Gently wringing particles out of the glowing device, she assembled a translucent scaffold of bone, fibrous tendons, and finally a layer of green muscle beneath deep brown skin. Kitty reached out her forearms, and Morehshin pressed the right hand into place. The seam between artificial hand and biological arm emitted a red glow as they knit together. The look on Kitty's face reminded me of Morehshin's back in Manitoba, when I suggested she drink some coffee.

"Queens are not supposed to have hands. They get in the way of breeding." Morehshin tinkered with Kitty's new fingers, and said something to her in the language I suspected English would become. Nodding, Kitty gently plucked a sliver of pale trilobite meat out of a cracked leg and ate it. Morehshin nodded. "I think that's working," she said. Kitty attached the left hand herself.

The sun touched ocean, and Anita sighed. "Let's get a good night's sleep, and make a final assessment in the morning before we go back."

Morehshin translated for Kitty, who agreed. She showed us into the cave, where she and Elliot had created beds with thick mats of seagrass. At last, she accepted the baby from C.L. for nursing. Everything reeked of the Ordovician ocean, a mixture of salt and seaweed, but I had gotten used to it. I stared out the mouth of the cave at the unfamiliar positions of the stars in the sky, and fell asleep without realizing it.

In the morning, Kitty and the baby were gone.

After we'd searched the beach, calling and calling, we gave up and climbed up to the Machine. I ran a finger over the semicircles of red rock, hovering beneath a nacreous blister of fluid. "Could she have used it to get away?" Anita asked.

"She could, but not the baby. A child born now couldn't travel to the future with her." C.L. fiddled with the settings on their shirt.

"Maybe she knew how to change that filter on the interface?"

"Maybe." C.L. looked grimmer than I'd ever seen them. "Or maybe she exposed her baby. Left it in the ocean for the squids."

Morehshin said nothing, and I wondered what she knew. Ultimately it didn't matter. We had work to do, gathering as much data as possible before going back to give the Daughters of Harriet our report. The official report, from the Applied Cultural Geology Working Group, would come later. We had to decide what information to keep to ourselves.

I tossed Elliot's body over the cliff's edge before we left, still penetrated by his own sword. Let the next great man find him, and witness what we had done.

THIRTY-ONE

BETH

Los Angeles, Alta California (1994 C.E.)

I hadn't spoken to my parents for two weeks. The loss of their voices over the phone was like those thirty minutes after a concert when I got out to the street and realized everything was muted, my eardrums thrumming with a missing, enormous sound.

On the fifteenth day, a Friday, Rosa said my father knocked on our door when I was in class, asking vaguely about his "friend" who lived in our room. "I said, 'You mean Beth, your daughter?' and he got really weird and said you needed to call home right away."

There was no need to call, because he showed up again that night. We were in the lounge. Hamid was writing an essay for film studies, and Rosa and I were working with our study group on yet another nightmarish chem lab assignment. My father walked right in and said my name. He was using his "we're friends" voice, his posture casual, a realistic smile on his face.

I shot a look at Hamid and walked with my dad into the hallway.

"Let's go to your room and get your stuff together. We're leaving right now." My father had dropped the pretense and his voice was gravelly with menace.

"I'm not going." I looked into his face and told myself not to cry.

"Your mother and I know about your little stunt. We got a notice from the tax board. I don't know what kind of lies you have been telling, but this is obviously an excuse to avoid facing what you've done. The laziness, the lack of discipline . . ."

I realized I didn't have to listen to those accusations anymore. I had an emergency loan from the university to tide me over until next quarter, when the financial aid officer assured me my big loan would come through. Suddenly, my father's familiar litany sounded bizarre.

"I am going to pay for college myself."

"No, you're not. We're in touch with the financial aid office. They will give you nothing unless we permit it."

I stopped feeling the urge to cry. I couldn't believe he would lie in such an overt way. Had he always lied to me like that? "They've already approved my loans."

He narrowed his eyes. "You've been lying and sneaking behind our backs. You know you'll wind up dropping out if you don't have us there every step of the way. You've never completed anything on your own."

I felt the scream coming from far away, like it had started in Irvine, or maybe six years ago, before reaching my chest and smashing against my ribcage to get out. But I held it in. It charged around my heart with a hatchet; it crammed a knife into my guts. I took a sliver of its rage into my mouth, rolled it around on my tongue, and spoke as quietly as I could.

"Get away from me."

"I'm not done here."

"Yes. You are." I crossed my arms and leaned against the dorm bulletin board, flyers wrinkling under my back. A couple of students walked by, and I could hear Rosa's high-pitched laugh as she made a terrible pun about covalent bonds. This was normal: people hanging out, doing work, helping each other. I tried to absorb all the safe feelings of normal around me as I stood my ground.

My father cocked his head the way he did when he was about to issue a punishment. And then he looked down, shuffling his feet, making a final stab. "You are delusional. I think you know that. We were wrong to trust you with all this independence, living away from home." He gestured vaguely at the lounge. "I hope you never expect to get anything else from us."

I kept silent because I was pretty sure that I had nothing left in me but that scream. My father turned around and left without another word. For an instant, I saw a massive fireball ignite behind him to fill the throat of the hallway with melting flesh and screams. And then he was gone, leaving a faint ringing in my ears.

Back in the lounge, I couldn't think. "Rosa, can I bum a cigarette?"

"Sure. I think it's time for a break anyway. I'll go down with you."

We worked on our smoke ring techniques and watched a raccoon raid one of the campus trash cans.

"Is everything okay with your dad?"

My eyes prickled and I took a long drag. "Just dealing with financial aid stuff."

Rosa put a warm hand on my shoulder. "That's always super stressful."

"We worked it out, though."

"That's really good."

Then we went back to talking about molecules, and class, and whether our midterm would be weighted the same as the final. Fleetingly, I thought about how I'd be graduating with almost fifty thousand dollars of debt. But that was so far away, and I didn't have to start repaying it for at least a year after that. More immediate was my sense of relief, which was so intense that it was like being stoned. It filled me with a crazy rush of love for everything: the raccoon, covalent bonds, adulthood, UCLA, and all the humans who populated this place.

"Thanks for being an awesome study-buddy and nefarious cigarette smoker, Rosa. You are the best."

She laughed in surprise. "You aren't so bad yourself, Beth. Maybe you'll come close to beating my score on the final. Maaaaaybe." And she flicked the last ember of her cigarette in a perfect arc toward the sidewalk, where it winked out harmlessly.

"Let's go finish that stupid lab."

I took Anita's advice and signed up for a class about time machines in the winter quarter. Hamid took an upper-division class in film theory, and we amused each other by coming up with imaginary names for new schools of thought. There were "The Great Man Gaze Theory" and "Subaltern Wormholes" and "Historical Amnesia for Beginners." Nobody else understood our jokes, and we liked it that way. I still missed Lizzy sometimes, but I had new friends who didn't think murder was awesome. I hoped that Tess had finally succeeded in her mission, whatever it was. Sometimes I thought about her out there, living with the memories of a different timeline where I'd killed myself. Was she the same person as the Lizzy I avoided in second-quarter chem? Probably not. The more I learned about how the timeline worked, the more convinced I was that Tess wouldn't exist in my future. And nobody knew where she would be.

THIRTY-TWO

TESS

The headache clamped down on my sinuses, drilled into my skull, and shot metal rods into my spine. And that was the easy part. When I stumbled out of the Machine at Raqmu in 2022 with Anita and Morehshin, I knew I wouldn't be staying for long. The light blinded me and my memories split apart again, making it hard to figure out what I was doing from minute to minute. My past was like a wadded-up piece of paper, and it looked different every time I smoothed it out.

Somehow, with the help of a lot of painkillers, Anita got me to the little airport that would take us to Tel Aviv, then back to Los Angeles. We checked our mobiles to see whether anything was different. Morehshin borrowed a tablet from Anita, poked it for a while, then made a mewing sound. When she looked up, I could barely recognize her underneath the weepy smile. "The Comstock Laws . . . they were overturned in the 1960s."

I swiped a search query into my mobile, flooded with disbelief and hope. I checked and rechecked what I found, to be sure I wasn't misunderstanding what I read. Then I practically shouted, "Abortion is legal in almost every state!" For a few minutes my pain was gone and we hugged each other, laughing and making squee noises.

It didn't last. I felt the throb of Beth's life in my memories again, along with something else—the agony of her rejection that night at the show, worse than the pain of losing her to suicide. After too many ibuprofen, I was able to lie back on the plane and think about it. I'd turned my life around after Beth died, choosing nonviolence, swearing to make it up to her under my new name. In a way, I'd tried to become Beth. But now the clean burn of that motivation was engulfed in smoke. There was no sudden moment of realization, no wake-up call. Beth was still around to look accusingly at me in chem class during freshman year. Instead of setting out on a crusade, I'd wandered through a series of murky decisions that brought me here.

But as I'd told Anita before, my pain didn't seem to come from holding those two histories in my mind. It was from holding two sets of feelings. The Tess whose best friend committed suicide knew who she was. She had a purpose. The Tess whose best friend lived felt . . . ambivalent about herself. Not all the time. She was happy, but always also sad about something. She'd built a new identity around an almost unbearable ambiguity, and the gradual realization that she would never be perfectly good or principled. This Tess would always know she had done bad things, and suffered the consequences. *That* was the awful new feeling scraping the inside of my skull: my best friend, whom I loved more than anyone at the time, had rejected me personally rather than rejecting life itself.

"Hey, Tess. We're here. Do you want me to drive you home? You look like shit." Anita shook me gently and I woke up at the Los Angeles airport to find the pain had not gone away at all.

"Yeah." I popped another few ibuprofen. "The feeling I told you about before . . . it's worse here."

Anita guided me to her car, and we said goodbye to Morehshin. The geology department would put her in travelers' housing. We promised to meet at the Daughters of Harriet meeting next week, when C.L. was reachable—we'd arrived in our present, during the timespan when they came back to research the machine data. Our present C.L. would be back in a few days, seconds after our past C.L. left.

I groaned as we got into Anita's old Prius.

"It seems like it's worse the closer you are to our present." She was thinking aloud. "Did it hurt this much in 1894?"

"No. It was uncomfortable, but not like this." I stumbled after her through the parking lot. Sunlight was painful, and everything I looked at left a neon stain on my vision.

"Did it hurt in Raqmu when we went back to the fourth century B.C.E.?"

"No. I mean, a very tiny bit, once in a while. But not really. And nothing in the Ordovician."

Anita raised an eyebrow. "That's interesting."

I was barely able to manage the seat belt fastener. "I really hope I don't have to go live in the Ordovician."

Back at my apartment, everything was maddeningly the same as when I left. I'd only been gone about four days in real time. Flopping on the couch, all I wanted to do was drown in the comfort of musical nostalgia. Squinting at my phone, I poked my streamer app and hunted for Grape Ape's rare EP, the one with "See the Bitches" on it. That was weird. It wasn't listed in my collection. Nor were any Grape Ape albums. I wondered if there'd been some annoying dispute with the streaming service that meant I'd have to get some other app if I wanted to listen to Grape Ape online. I didn't have the energy to investigate, so I knelt down next to the cabinet with my record collection. I'd gotten a new turntable and this was an excellent chance to try it out.

None of my Grape Ape albums were there.

Had somebody broken in and stolen them? I suppose they were worth a little money—I had a few collector's items, but only for that small subset of people who cared about feminist punk of the early 1990s. I rocked back on my heels, wondering if I'd stashed all my Grape Ape albums somewhere else during a fit of cleaning that might have been years ago in travel time. But then a terrible feeling started to grow in my gut.

I searched for Grape Ape online and found only references to a cartoon from the 1970s about a giant purple ape and his tiny dog friend. No matter what search terms I used, nothing came up. No Glorious Garcia, either.

Somehow, an orthogonal deletion had eliminated Grape Ape from the timeline.

I didn't care if the neighbors heard me screaming.

A week later, the Daughters met at Anita's house. We didn't bother with preliminaries, and instead gave the floor to C.L., who made a full report on how we'd saved the Machine. It was their first time presenting a formal edit, and they had overprepared in the best possible way, giving us a nicely formatted dataset with a clear explanation of how to extract and analyze any slice you might want. To be fair, the news was so good for our project that they could have dumped a malformed smear of numbers with no metadata and we probably would have cheered.

And then I said the words I'd dreamed about for so long. "I remember a timeline where abortion was illegal."

"So do I," Anita said.

"Me too," C.L. added.

"Holy shit." Enid stared at us. "All of you remember a timeline where abortion was illegal in 2022?"

"It's still technically not legal at the federal level. States have their own laws," Shweta grumbled.

"But there's no real enforcement," Berenice noted. "And it's only a couple of states."

I spoke firmly. "It was illegal everywhere. All over the U.S."

Morehshin broke in. "Women were dying. Men genetically engineered them to become breeders or workers. There was a whole biotech industry devoted to female containment and maintenance, and they had recently invented a way to replace a queen's head with a—" She stopped abruptly when she noticed C.L.'s look of horror. "Sorry. I shouldn't bring that up. That is not our timeline anymore. It is merely what I remember."

Everyone fell into an awkward silence.

Anita popped open a bottle of sparkling pomegranate juice. "We won the edit war!"

"A toast to Harriet Tubman!"

"Long live her daughters!"

"And her mothers!"

"And her nonbinary kin!"

I stood up to raise a glass, felt a wrenching agony in my sinuses, and everything buzzed into dark static.

"Tess, I am taking you back to the Temple at Raqmu. I think Hugayr might know what to do."

I was lying on Anita's inflatable guest bed in her study. The lights were off, and I could see the last shreds of sunset through the window facing her garden. As long as I didn't move a single muscle, the pain eased. But when I had to shift a little or stretch my neck to see something, it would all come roaring back. There was no point in arguing with Anita. I would do anything to stop feeling this way.

"Somebody will have to take over my lab. And finish teaching my class for this quarter."

"Don't worry about that yet. With any luck, we'll be back in a few days."

I slept most of the way to Raqmu, trying to outrun the agony with cannabis tinctures. We had to go through the Machine separately, and the only unburned time when we could arrive within minutes of each other was three years after we'd left Soph at the Temple.

It was my first trip since we'd shut down Elliot's operation, and it was smooth. When I knelt to feel the water rise, there was a burst of humid air and the unmistakable smell of soil that had been chemically altered by plants and animals for millions of years. It was the planet I knew—the one with angiosperms and tetrapods and pterygota. The one where both land and water sustained life. I wondered how many times C.L. and their colleagues had gone back to repair the damage in the Ordovician, and if they'd learned more about the interface. I might never know.

When I emerged in 13 B.C.E., my entire body sang with relief. As an administrator from the Order noted my name and mark, I stretched my neck and arms to enjoy the tingle of motion without agony. I felt like myself again. Or maybe it was more accurate to say that my new self—whoever she turned out to be—didn't hurt as much.

The temple was just as I remembered it, surrounded by a lush garden and artificial pools. A young adept brought Soph to meet me in the entrance hall, two scrolls and a writing box tucked under her arm.

"You caught me in the middle of afternoon study." She smiled. Her hair was pinned up in the style of the late nineteenth century, and she wore the simple linen tunic preferred by most women who lived here. "Have you come to visit?"

"I'm meeting Anita. We need to talk to Hugayr about something that I've done to the timeline."

Soph's eyes widened but she said nothing. "I can take you to Hugayr's office, but I have to warn you. She's not in a good mood."

I recalled how she ordered her students around and shrugged. "I've dealt with tenure committees, so I think I'm prepared."

It had been three years for Soph, and only a few weeks for me, so we had a lot of asymmetric catching up to do. Now fluent in spoken Nabataean, Soph had made herself indispensable to the temple. She started by translating a few manuscripts, but quickly moved on to writing interpretive treatises about how the goddess should be honored in everyday life. Visiting scholars had copied her work to take back to their own libraries across the Mediterranean.

"It's similar to what I wrote back in my present, but here they take it a lot more seriously." She had a note of pride in her voice. "And it doesn't get you sent to jail, which is nice."

"I'm so glad we got you out of that shithole, Soph."

She sighed. "I miss it, though. I miss Aseel and my other friends. I miss my parlors. I miss gin. I even miss the smell of the river!"

I put my arm around her and squeezed. "Aseel is doing great—she's running Sol's sheet music business. I've never seen her so happy. And busy!" Then I told her about the dance contest that changed the Comstock Laws, and Morehshin's sister from the future, and how C.L. had data so good they were sure to get published in *Nature Geoscience*, or maybe *Nature* proper. It was a big breakthrough for understanding the origins of the interface. "We changed the timeline, you know. We won the edit war."

Soph stopped me on the threshold of the chamber with the three-faced goddess statue. "One thing I've learned while studying here, Tess. There is no end to the edit war, and we can never claim victory. The timeline is always changing. So are we. I think perhaps . . . all we can hope for are small mercies. One life spared. One good deed. Do you understand?"

I searched the pale blue of her eyes, wondering if she knew more than she let on. "Anita always says that small things change, and big things don't."

"She's right."

When we knocked on Hugayr's office door, one of her students opened it right away. Over her shoulder, I could see that Anita was already there, deep in conversation.

"Oh hello, come in!" Hugayr gestured us to some cushions around a small table made from bronze and wood. Then she glared at the student. "You—bring us some beer, and then get back to work on your manuscript. It's showing some promise."

The student hurtled out of the room, a tiny smile of accomplishment on their face, and returned with ceramic mugs of a foamy drink that smelled like barley and pepper. I sipped experimentally. Didn't taste exactly like beer from my present, but close enough.

Hugayr put her mug down. "Tess, I have already told Anita. You can't go home. It will kill you."

I panicked, overwhelmed. "There's nothing we can do?"

"We have other Timeless here who have experienced the same thing. When you edit your own life, it can be very painful. Not for everyone. Some people—they do an edit, get their loved one back, and live happily ever after. Some people feel only a little discomfort and then it goes away. But you are one of those unfortunate people who is completely fucked."

"Why me? All I did was bring a loved one back, like you said."

Hugayr wore a dubious expression. "Anita told me what you did. You created a highly divergent timeline. You edited your entire adult life all at once. Of course it made you sick. Didn't you think about that before you did it?"

"Well, yeah . . . but it seemed like it was going okay until . . ."

"Until the edit actually took?"

I picked at a sliver of wood on the table leg. "I don't get it. That was supposed to be a small change. But we made a huge change to women's rights and abortion law, and nobody else is sick. Shouldn't that have changed all our lives profoundly?"

"What is abortion?" Hugayr glanced at Soph for clarification.

"Ending a pregnancy."

"I see. You changed some laws made by men. Yes. Did you change any women's lives?"

"I guess . . . I changed Beth's life."

Anita scratched her head. "We changed Kitty's life, I think."

"Did either of those women's lives change specifically because of what you did to men's law?"

"They were two of the *millions* of women whose lives were changed. Reproductive rights improve our choices, give us freedom, allow us to follow new paths . . . it was a profound alteration of history." I trailed off when Hugayr gave me the frown she usually reserved for students.

"Think. Why would you feel a big change less than a small one?"

I thought about all those people linking arms to protest Comstock at the Expo, the dancers at Sherry's, Sol's strategic carnival wisdom, and the Four Hundred on their thrones. "It was collective action. So many of us worked to change the laws that the effects are spread out and attenuated. I guess all of us feel it a tiny bit. But with Beth . . . that was something small I changed for myself alone."

"When we say small things change, we do not mean that they are insignificant."

I took a long swig of beer to drown the lump in my throat. "I guess I'm staying here, then." The realization was bittersweet: I would miss the twenty-first century, but I felt at home here in ways I couldn't entirely explain.

"My chambers are comfortable." Soph touched my shoulder, and my heart skipped a beat. "You can stay with me for a while if you want."

"You can be our next sacrifice!" Hugayr made it sound completely decided. She pulled out a scroll and flattened it in her lap. "Let's figure out a job you could do as a member of the Timeless. How about . . . scribe? Gardener? Engineer? Assassin?"

"Wait, what? You have assassins?"

Hugayr looked concerned and showed Soph the scroll, written in Nabataean. "Did I translate that right?"

Soph squinted and made a seesaw wiggle with her hand. "You could perhaps say 'killer' or 'defender'? But I think 'assassin' is probably the best word."

I could still feel the weight of Elliot's sword in my hands, and the way I'd known exactly how to sever his spine. Maybe that was why I belonged in the first century B.C.E. In Nabataean, there was a word for what I did best. There was actually a job that combined my skills as an academic and a murderer.

"I think I'd like to be an assassin."

Hugayr smiled. "Great! We've really been needing one. Let's schedule your sacrifice."

HISTORICAL SOURCES:

A GUIDE

As you may have noticed, this book is an alternate history. But many of the events and people in it are based on ones that existed in our timeline. Here is a comprehensive list of facts and sources for anyone who wants to see how deep the wormhole goes.

The Ordovician period—which witnessed the biggest diversification of life on our planet—did end with a disaster that killed over 75 percent of all life on Earth. Two ice ages hit the planet in rapid succession (at least in geological time), turning those lush coastal ecosystems to ice. Nobody knows for sure how it happened, but physicist Adrian Melott and his colleagues have suggested a gamma ray burst (https://www .nature.com/news/2003/030922/full/news030922-7.html).

Before the United States took control of California, the state was part of the Las Californias province, divided into **Alta California** to the north and Baja California to the south. First it was owned by Spain, then by Mexico. After the Mexican-American War ended in 1848, Alta California was claimed by the United States and became a state in the union in 1850. Baja California was claimed by Mexico.

Flin Flon is an actual city on the border between Manitoba and Saskatchewan. After discovering copper there, a prospector named the city after a character in a pulp sci-fi novel he was reading, *The Sunless City* by J.E. Preston Muddock.

Harriet Tubman was a Civil War hero, leader of the underground railroad, activist, and escaped slave who almost certainly would have been elected to the Senate had women been given the vote at the same time freed slaves were. But in our timeline, she had to petition the government to receive the same pension granted to any man who fought in the Civil War as she had. After the Civil War, she lived in New York, where she ran one of the nation's first elder care homes for African Americans. You can learn more about her extraordinary life in historian Catherine Clinton's biography, *Harriet Tubman: The Road to Freedom*.

The **abolitionist and women's suffrage movements**—connected before the Civil War—were driven apart when women were not given the vote at the same time freedmen were. During Reconstruction, the Democratic Party emerged as a white nationalist alternative to Lincoln's anti-slavery Republican Party. Republicans deliberately ran black candidates for office in the South to capture the votes of recently enfranchised freedmen. Eventually, the South went Democratic, and stayed that way until the mid-twentieth century. You can read more about the Democratic Party's origin story in Bruce Bartlett's *Wrong on Race: The Democratic Party's Buried Past*.

During the **Haitian Revolution,** a highly successful slave rebellion overthrew the French colonial government and left freed slaves and free people of color in charge of the nation. The French government insisted that Haiti pay steep reparations for "stealing" its slaves and plantations, thus destabilizing the burgeoning nation's economy for decades to come. For more about this revolution, along with historical documents from the period, see Laurent Dubois and John D. Garrigus, *Slave Revolution in the Caribbean, 1789–1804*. Dubois has also written a popular history of the revolution called *Haiti: The Aftershocks of History*.

Anthony Comstock was appointed a "special agent" with the U.S. Postal Service, where his job was to open mail and hunt for obscene materials. He cemented his power by bringing a trunk full of nude postcards, novelty items, and rubber dildos that he had ordered through the mails to a congressional hearing, where he demonstrated how widespread the moral menace of obscenity was. His activism with the YMCA and citizen's arrests of abortionists and sex educators made changes to U.S. obscenity laws that lasted almost a century. As a result of his work, any information about contraception and abortion was defined by the courts as obscene, and therefore illegal. He bragged in public speeches that his work had driven many women to suicide, and he was right. I learned a lot about Comstock's life and legal battles from Amy Werbel's incredible book *Lust on Trial: Censorship and the Rise of American Obscenity in the Age of Anthony Comstock*. I also took some of Comstock's dialogue from his writing collected in Robert Bremner's edition of Comstock's 1883 book *Traps for the Young*.

Comstock's persecution (and prosecution) led Spiritualist and women's health advocate **Ida Craddock** to commit suicide in 1902. The character of **Sophronia (Soph)** is an homage to Ida, who was arrested after publishing a book about having very explicit sex with an angel named Soph. Though First Amendment lawyers (including Clarence Darrow) worked pro bono to argue Ida's case, she was convicted of obscenity and sentenced to a lengthy jail term. Rather than go to prison, she killed herself. Ida also published an impassioned essay defending the sanctity of the *danse du ventre* on the Midway, which is how her work first came to Comstock's attention. You can read Craddock's work, including her essay on the *danse du ventre*, in Vere Chappell's collection of her writing, *Sexual Outlaw, Erotic Mystic: The Essential Ida Craddock*.

Comstock, with **the Lady Managers,** did visit the Midway dance attractions and convinced the general-director of the fair to get a court order to shut down the Persian Palace. A court immediately granted representatives of the Persian Palace an injunction and none of the dance attractions on the Midway were shut down. You can read more about this in *Popular Culture and the Enduring Myth of Chicago, 1871–1968*, by Lisa Krissoff Boehm.

All of the **Midway** attractions and World's Fair locations in the novel are real, based on maps of the Expo drawn at the time.

A lot of seemingly insignificant **details of 1893–94 Chicago life** are based on truths about our own timeline, gleaned from historical documents available online. Seamstresses were in fact paid about $1.50 per day, and there was a successful strike led by steelworkers at the Expo to get overtime pay on weekends and after hours. Sheet music companies popped up on Wabash Street after the Midway closed, along with theaters advertising dancers from the Midway. Many commentators of the time complained that the entire city smelled like rotting meat because of runoff from the slaughterhouses in the river and sewer system. The problem continued until engineers working with the city's newly formed Chicago Sanitary District reversed the flow of the Chicago River in 1900.

Raqmu, heart of the Nabataean Kingdom, is what I imagine Petra, Jordan, might still be called today if ancient Greeks and Romans had not colonized the city over two thousand years ago. Petra is the Greek name for a city that once called itself Raqmu.

Lucy Parsons was one of Chicago's most respected anarchist leaders, and a founder of the IWW. Though she claimed to be indigenous or Spanish, scholars today believe she was an African American born into slavery. This is thanks entirely to new research by historian Jacqueline Jones for her book *Goddess of Anarchy: The Life and Times of Lucy Parsons, American Radical* (which is what Tess had read, and referenced when she talked to Aseel and Soph). Lucy and **Emma Goldman** did in fact get into a very public fight over sexual liberation, equal to today's biggest Twitter train wrecks. And yes, Emma did have **a boyfriend named Sasha (Alexander Berkman)**, who failed spectacularly to assassinate Henry Frick. Emma continued to date him after he got out of prison. She was jailed by Comstock more than once for her writings and speeches about sexuality.

Aseel's alter-ego **Lady Asenath** pays homage to an elusive figure called Little Egypt, who was rumored to be the greatest belly dancer on the Midway. After the Expo ended, many different performers called themselves Little Egypt, particularly white women who appropriated dances from nomadic groups in North Africa for their burlesque performances. Aseel is extremely loosely based on many of the dancers described by Donna Carlton in her excellent history of belly dancing, *Looking for Little Egypt*. One, Fahreda Mahzar Spyropoulos, supposedly came to the Midway from Arizona and later settled down in Chicago to run her husband's restaurant. But Carlton can find no evidence that anyone calling themselves Little Egypt ever performed on the Midway. The name seems to have become popular afterward among burlesque and vaudeville dancers. It was used most famously by a dancer named Ashea Wabe. In 1896, Wabe was hired by two grandsons of P.T. Barnum—members of **the Four Hundred**—to perform the *danse du ventre* for their bachelor party at Sherry's. After she was arrested on charges of stripping, the event became an enormous scandal, dubbed by the press "the awful Seeley dinner." Wabe went on to become a notorious performer and very wealthy self-made woman. She died of gas asphyxiation in 1908. It was likely a suicide.

Grumpy theater critic **George Bernard Shaw** did indeed coin the term "**Comstockery**" to mean prudery or over-the-top moralism— though he did it about ten years after the events described in this novel. You can read his first use of the term in a letter to *The New York Times* in 1905 (https://timesmachine.nytimes.com/timesmachine /1905/09/26/117951415.pdf). It became a popular term in the early twentieth century to mock people who wanted to censor art, or who were culturally ignorant.

Sol Bloom, remarkably, was a real person. In his early twenties, he was a music promoter who brought the dance troupe for the Algerian Village over to the United States from France, and wound up landing a job managing all the attractions on the Midway. Famously, he didn't want the job and demanded a salary higher than the U.S. president. To his surprise, the city of Chicago met his salary request. After a very successful stint in the music business, he became a U.S. senator who advocated for immigrant rights until the day he died. He published a book about his life, called simply *The Autobiography of Sol Bloom*.

The song Aseel writes is a variation on the one attributed to Sol Bloom in our timeline. You can listen to Bloom's song here: https:// www.youtube.com/watch?v=6A5yJ5Z2Ezw. I prefer Aseel's version, partly because it actually makes sense. Sol always regretted that he didn't act fast enough to sell the song as sheet music, thus securing the exclusive rights to it. The song was appropriated so quickly by other dance acts that it became basically a folk song, impossible to copyright. You've probably heard the tune, if you grew up in an English-speaking Western country, where it is synonymous with cheesy stripper music and Orientalist tropes. One of the common variants on the lyrics does include the line (presumably about Sol Bloom) about how the dance the ladies do "was written by a Jew." And yes, the tune is also in a delightful Ke$ha song called "Take It Off."

The **American Geophysical Union (AGU)** is a real-life international organization whose members include scientists, industry researchers, and public servants who study Earth, our atmosphere, and space. They have advocated tirelessly for government and industry to recognize the reality of climate change. If we ever do find time machines in the Earth's crust, AGU members will be all over that.

Most of the locations that Lizzy and Beth visit in **Irvine** and **Los Angeles** are based on places I knew as a teen in the late twentieth century. No, I never killed anyone, though I will confess that I might have thought about it a few thousand times. As we said back then: Irvine sucks. Some of **Beth's family backstory** is based loosely on things I experienced. My great-grandfather was jailed for arson in the early twentieth century, and my grandfather owned an auto repair shop in Los Angeles until the 1980s. My father committed suicide many years ago, after struggling for a long time with depression. He and my mother went to college together at UCLA, and took me to the La Brea Tar Pits a lot.

I remember a world where abortion was legal in my country. I hope you do too.

ACKNOWLEDGMENTS

This book was a work of collective action, and thanks are due to the many people who talked to me about it, read early drafts, and generally listened to me stressing out about it for two years.

First, thanks to the many scientists, researchers, and friends who gave me ideas. Physicist Adam Becker talked to me about the impossibility of time travel, and cosmologist Sean Carroll agreed that time travel was impossible, but kindly suggested I think about wormholes and a "narrative force" that creates a timeline. Geology researcher Josh Zimmt speculated about what people could eat during the Ordovician and what it would smell like. Ethnomusicologist K. Goldschmitt told me about the nineteenth-century music industry and appropriation. Archaeologist Sarah Wenner talked to me about the Nabataean Kingdom in the first century C.E. Historian Karen Ordahl Kupperman let me interrogate her about social change over centuries, and pop history chronicler Lynn Peril gave me tons of sources about rational clothing and New Women. Adrienne Crew, creator of the incredible Louche Angeles Instagram, told me about being a Black girl in the L.A. punk scene during the 1980s. Science history aficionado Esther Inglis-Arkell suggested that the villain of this novel should be Anthony Comstock. Author Jess Zimmerman talked to me about witchcraft. Critic Lynn Rapoport and filmmaker Fivestar spent many late nights talking to me about indie music, indie porn, and all the good things in between. L. A. Kauffman inspired me with her writing and political actions more times than I can count.

I also got tons of feedback from extremely kind, patient early readers. A zillion thanks to Tempest Bradford and Jaymee Goh for sensitivity reads, and to Claire Light, Charlie Jane Anders, Meg Elison, Chris Palmer, Maggie Tokuda-Hall, and Katya Lopez for feedback during revision.

I owe pretty much everything to my amazing editor, Lindsey Hall, who read three separate drafts and improved the book immeasurably. Also thanks to Liz Gorinsky for first believing in the book, and to Devi Pillai for making it happen. And of course, thank you to my astounding agent provocateur, Laurie Fox.

A very special thank-you to Mike Burns for Flin Flon advice, and to Peter Burns for his stories about getting there (and beyond) by boat.

For helping me to survive my teens and twenties, thank you to Kathleen Hanna and Bikini Kill (and Le Tigre and Julie Ruin), Pauline Black and The Selecter, Alice Bag and The Bags, L7, Poly Styrene, Queen Latifah, and every other woman who yelled so loudly in my young ears that she drowned out my fear.

As always, I couldn't have written this without the timeless love and support of Jesse Burns, Chris Palmer, and Charlie Jane Anders.

extras

www.orbitbooks.net

about the author

Annalee Newitz is an American journalist, editor and author of both fiction and non-fiction. She is the recipient of a Knight Science Journalism Fellowship from MIT, and has written for *Popular Science*, *Wired* and the *San Francisco Bay Guardian*. She co-founded the science fiction website io9 and served as editor-in-chief from 2008–15, and subsequently edited Gizmodo. As of 2016, she is tech culture editor at the technology site Ars Technica.

Find out more about Annalee Newitz and other Orbit authors by registering for the free monthly newsletter at www.orbitbooks.net.

if you enjoyed
THE FUTURE OF ANOTHER TIMELINE

look out for

THE RAVEN TOWER

by

Ann Leckie

*A usurper has claimed the throne. Invaders amass
at the borders. And they have made their alliances
with enemy gods . . .*

*For centuries, the kingdom of Iraden has been protected
by a god known as the Raven. But in their hour of need, the
Raven speaks nothing to its people. It is into this unrest that
the warrior Eolo – aide to the true heir to the throne – arrives.
In seeking to help his master reclaim his city, Eolo discovers that
the Raven's tower holds a secret. Its foundations conceal a dark
history that has been waiting to reveal itself . . . and to set in
motion a chain of events that could destroy Iraden for ever.*

I first saw you when you rode out of the forest, past the cluster of tall, bulge-eyed offering stakes that mark the edges of the forest, your horse at a walk. You rode beside Mawat, himself a familiar sight to me: tall, broad-shouldered, long hair in dozens of braids pulled back in a broad ring, feathers worked in repoussé on gold, his dark gray cloak lined with blue silk. More gold weighted his forearms. He was smiling vaguely, saying something to you, but his eyes were on the fortress of Vastai on its small peninsula, still some twelve miles off: some two- and three-story buildings surrounded by a pale yellow limestone wall, the ends of which met at a round tower at the edge of the sea. On the landward side of the wall sat a town's worth of buildings interrupted by a bank and ditch. Gulls coasted over the few bare-masted ships in the harbor beside the fortress, and over the gray water beyond, flecked white with the wind, and here and there a sail. The white stone buildings and more numerous ships of the city of Ard Vusktia were just visible on the far side of the strait.

Mawat—and Vastai—I knew, but I had not seen you before, and so I looked closely. Slight, and shorter than Mawat—it would be a wonder if you were not, the residents of the fortress in Vastai eat so much better, and so much more regularly than the peasant farmers who were your likely origins. You had cut your hair close to your scalp, a single arm ring and the haft of the knife at your side the only gold on you, your trousers, shirt, boots, and cloak solid and sturdy, all dull greens and browns. The hilt of your sword was wood wrapped with leather, undecorated. You sat stiff in the saddle, even at a walk. Possibly because you'd woken early to a summons and then ridden for three days with only what rest the horses required, and likely before you became a soldier you'd had very little experience riding.

Mawat said, "We've made good time, it seems, and the Instrument is still with us, or there'd be black flags on the tower, and lots of movement in the tower yard. And even if there were, we don't have to rush now. It would be easier for you—and the horses for that matter—if we went the rest of the way at a walk, I think." And then, at the expression on your face, "What is it?"

"It's just…" You took a breath. It's clear that you trust him, more than you trust a lot of other people in the world, or I suspect you wouldn't have been there, riding beside him. And you must have concluded that he trusts you. Though perhaps his is a more confident trust, he has so much power over you, and you none over him. "My lord, people usually don't just... talk about that." People generally don't, even in Vastai. The Raven's Lease himself does, and his heir, and his close family.

And their servants, of course. People so often forget the servants.

"I haven't said anything secret," said Mawat, "or anything I'm not allowed to say."

Was it strange to hear him talk of his father's impending death so blithely? For the death of the Raven's Lease of Iraden would be the necessary consequence of the Instrument's death. And as heir, Mawat would step into his father's place, commit himself to dying when the next Raven's Instrument died.

Mawat's father's rule as Raven's Lease had fallen less harshly on the common people of Iraden than it might have. Which wasn't to say he'd been particularly generous, or the peasantry noticeably happy during his tenure, but he could have been worse, and a new Lease was an unknown quantity. Accordingly, the people of Iraden generally spoke of Mawat's father only to wish him long life. You're young enough for that to have been as long as you've been alive.

You both rode for a while in silence, sheep-dotted fields to either side of the road, two ravens high above, swooping and soaring, black shapes in the blue of the sky. Mawat frowning as you rode, until finally he said, "Eolo."

You looked at him, your expression wary. "My lord."

"I know I promised I wouldn't pry. But when I'm Lease, I'll be able to ask for things. I mean, anyone can, but there's always a question of whether or not the Raven will listen, and there's always a price. The Raven will at least hear me out, and my price is already paid. Or it will be. I can ask for some extra favors. The Raven is a powerful god. He could...he could make it so you could..." He gestured vaguely. "So you could be who you are."

"I already am who I am," you snapped. "My lord." And after a few moments of silence, "That's not why I'm here."

"No, it's not," replied Mawat, affronted, and then recollecting himself. "You're here because that's not why you're here." He gave an apologetic smile. "And also because I ordered you out of your bed and into the saddle. And you've ridden three days without complaining, even though you're not much of a rider and I know you must be sore by now."

After a while you said, "I don't know if that's something I want."

"No?" asked Mawat, with surprise. "But why wouldn't you? It would be more convenient for you, if nothing else. You wouldn't have to trouble yourself with bindings, or hiding anything." And when you didn't answer, "Ah, now I *am* prying."

"Yes, my lord," you said, voice tense despite the mildness of your tone.

Mawat laughed. "I'll stop, then. But if you decide... Well."

"Yes, my lord," you replied again. Still tense. You rode the rest of the way to Vastai in silence.

Vastai is small compared to cities like Kybal, source of the silk in Mawat's cloak. Or far-off Therete, that possibly no one in Iraden has even heard of. Or Xulah for that matter, that wide-conquering city in the warm and arid south. Compared to these cities—compared, even, to Ard Vusktia across the strait—Vastai is no more than a town.

You rode behind Mawat through the narrow, stone-paved streets of Vastai. People in homespun dull greens and browns, and even one or two in brighter, finer clothing cleared out of your way, pressed themselves against the yellow limestone walls without a word, looking down at their feet. You would have no cause to realize this, but the streets of the town were far more empty than they ought to have been, given the unseasonably warm, sunny day, given boats in the harbor.

Mawat didn't seem to notice. I think he had been tense and uneasy since before you both rode out of the forest, though he concealed it. Now I thought his mood sharpened, his thoughts bent inexorably to his double-edged purpose in coming here: to see his father die, to step into his father's place. He did not stop or slow, or turn to see if you followed him, but rode, still at a walk, down the main, widest street of the town, through the broad, stone-paved square before the broad fortress gates, and, unchallenged, through those gates and into the tower yard. It was paved with the same yellow stone used throughout Vastai. Several buildings—the hall, long and low, with its kitchen behind it; stables and storerooms; two-story buildings that held offices and apartments. In the middle of the yard was a wide stone basin with a ledge around it—the fortress's well. And, of course, the round, high mass of the tower. All in that yellow limestone.

You started as a raven swooped down to land on the pommel of your saddle.

"Don't worry," said Mawat. "It's not him."

The raven made a churring sound. "Hello," it said. "Hello."

As you stared at the bird, Mawat dismounted. Servants ran forward to take his horse. He looked up at you and gestured you down, so that other servants could take yours. "Glad to be out of the saddle?" he asked as you dismounted, his voice good-humored, a smile on his face, but an edge to it.

"Yes, my lord," you said, with a small frown. The raven sat placid as the servants led your horse away. I thought you were going to ask some question, but then a flurry of green and red silk caught your eye, and you turned your head to watch a tall woman stride by with a basket of carded wool on her head, the gold and glass beads braided into her hair swinging and clicking against each other, shining against the brown of her skin.

"Oho," said Mawat, watching you watch her go by, her skirts swirling with the briskness of her walk. "Someone caught your eye?"

"Who is the lady?" you asked. And then, perhaps covering your discomfiture, "She seems very…" You failed to complete the sentence.

"She *is* very," Mawat replied. "That's Tikaz. She's Radihaw's daughter."

You knew that name, likely it had been in Mawat's mouth more than once since you'd met him and besides, it's likely nearly everyone in Iraden has heard of the lord Radihaw, the senior member of the Council of the Directions, the highest-ranking of all the advisers to the Raven's Lease. One of the most powerful men in all of Iraden. "Oh," you replied.

Mawat made a short, amused noise. "We've been

friends more or less since we were children. Her father has never given up hope that I might marry her, or at least get her pregnant so he can have a chance at a grandson on the Lease's bench. I'll be honest, I wouldn't mind. But Tikaz…" He gestured, perhaps waving away some thought. "Tikaz will do as she pleases. Let's go to the hall and see if we can…"

He was brought up short by a servant in the loose black overshirt of a tower attendant. "Lord Mawat, if you please," said the servant, bowing. "The Lease desires your presence."

"Of course," Mawat replied, with slightly forced geniality. You frowned, and then, likely realizing that here in Vastai you would need to watch every word, every twitch of expression, you put on a look of bland inoffensiveness. "Come with me," Mawat said to you, shortly. Not a question, not a request. He did not wait for your response but turned and strode across the pale yellow stones of the tower yard. And of course you followed him.

The Raven Tower is a tower only in comparison with any other nearby building. It stands on the farthest point of the tiny peninsula on which the fortress of Vastai is built, three broad, circular stories of yellowish stone, its roof surrounded by a parapet. A single broad entrance on the windowless ground floor, through which you followed Mawat. The guards flanking the door did not look at him, didn't move as you both strode in. The ground floor was paved with yet more yellow stone strewn with mats of woven rushes, a single guard standing at the foot of the stairs that ran up the curving wall to the next floor. He raised a hand to halt you both, but Mawat ignored him and strode up the stairs, face forward, shoulders square, stepping determinedly but not hurriedly. You trailed behind, glancing back at the hapless guard, with some fellow feeling perhaps for his dilemma, but you turned to face Mawat again after only a moment. As you ascended, your frown occasionally showed through your carefully blank expression. You didn't grow up surrounded by the sort of maneuvering that's so common in Vastai, you clearly hadn't had much practice at it, though I'd say you were doing a creditable job, all things considered.

There is a sound in the tower, a constant, low, barely audible vibration. Not everyone hears it. I thought maybe you did—you looked down at your worn boots, then toward the wall to your right, tilted your head just the slightest bit as though trying to catch some faint noise. Then the stairs reached a landing, and you came up into the wide, round chamber on the next level, and Mawat took three steps into the room and then abruptly stopped.

Here was a dais. A wooden bench carved with a jumble of figures, stylized reliefs of leaves and wings. Beside the bench knelt a man in a gray silk tunic embroidered with red. On the other side of the bench stood a woman in dark blue robes, her thick, gray hair cut short. A man sat on the bench between them, wearing all white—white shirt, white leggings, white cloak, the sort and amount of perfect, unstained white that can be achieved only by a god's intervention, or else the labor of dozens of servants with no other work than bleaching and laundering.

No doubt you assumed that the man on the bench was the Raven's Lease himself, Mawat's father. No one else would have dared sit in that seat, not and survived the attempt. Every Iradeni knows that sitting on that bench—and living—is the last, final proof of the Raven's acceptance of a new Lease. You had never seen it before, but you surely recognized it the moment you set eyes on it.

Likely you knew who the kneeling man was by the angular lines of his face, having seen his daughter just minutes before, but even if that didn't tell you, I'm sure you realized that this was the lord Radihaw of the Council of the Directions. Who else would be so close to the Lease? And the woman, then, would be Zezume, of the Silent. Away from Vastai, meetings of the Silent are little more than an occasion for gossip and feasting by the old women of the area, but it began as a secret religious association. Those village sessions of the Silent still include rites meant to feed and propitiate gods long absent from Iraden. In Vastai, though, the Silent have an essential role to play in the affairs of the Raven's Lease.

Before the dais, facing the Lease, stood three Xulahn visitors, bare legged, in short cloaks and tunics and open-toed boots. A fourth person, dressed more sensibly in jacket and trousers, was speaking to the Lease. "Only to cross the strait, good and generous one. It is only these three Xulahns and their servants, who have come from the far south on their way to the north."

"That is a long journey," observed the lord Radihaw. "And there is nothing in the north but ice and stone."

"They wish to see places they have never seen," said the person in jacket and trousers. "When they have seen enough, if they do not die first, they will return home and write down an account of their travels, for which they expect to receive the esteem of their fellow Xulahns."

You were watching this, staring by turns at the white-clad Lease and at the party of half-dressed Xulahns. You'd surely already heard of Xulah. Every now and then goods from Xulah will make their way over the mountains into the hands of the Tel, one of the peoples who live south of Iradeni territory. Or those goods find their way onto a ship. Any sizable ship sailing between the Shoulder Sea and the Northern Ocean must pass through the strait, and must perforce pay a fee to the rulers of Iraden and Ard Vusktia. So the Lease, and the Council of the Directions, and the prominent members of the Silent, wear silk, drink wine, and even, on occasion, eat figs preserved in jars of honey.

Mawat also stared. Not at the Xulahns, but fixedly at the Lease himself, and then blinking, disbelieving, at Radihaw and, frowning, at Zezume, and back again to the Lease.

"Mawat," said the Raven's Lease. "Welcome home." Mawat did not move or speak.

Finally you noticed Mawat's state, his stunned stare, as though, having thought himself safe in secure and familiar territory, he had suddenly taken a blade between his ribs. He seemed paralyzed, unable even to breathe.

"This is my heir," said the white-clad man on the bench, into Mawat's silence, the gaze of the Xulahns, variously appraising or mildly interested. "Come, Mawat, stand with me." He gestured behind him. Radihaw and Zezume were still as statues on either side of him.

Mawat did not move. After a moment, the Lease turned his attention to the Xulahn visitors again and said, "I will consider your request. Come back tomorrow."

This seemed to discomfit one of the Xulahns, and then the others when it was translated. Two of them frowned at their interpreter, then at each other. Looked to the third, who turned to the Lease and said, in strangely accented Iradeni, "We thank you for your consideration, great king." The Lease is not a king, and the word the Xulahn used is from Tel, a language that is familiar in the south of Iraden.

I daresay you speak it yourself. All the Xulahns bowed low, then, and departed.

"What," said Mawat when they were gone, his voice toneless. "What am I seeing."

A moment of silence, but for that ever-present grinding, barely audible, more a sensation felt through the soles of your boots than a sound.

"Where is my father?" asked Mawat, when no answer was forthcoming. "And what are you doing in that seat?"

Ah, that surprised you! You had assumed that the person before you was none other than Mawat's father, the man who had been Raven's Lease for all of your life. There would be no way for you to know it was not.

"My lord Mawat," began Radihaw. "In all respect, recall to whom you are speaking."

"I am speaking to my Uncle Hibal," replied Mawat, still in that tight, flat voice. "Who is inexplicably sitting alive in the Lease's seat, when no one should sit there but my father. Unless the Raven has died and the Lease followed him in death, in which case this tower should be hung with black, and everyone in the fortress and the town should be in mourning." He turned his head to stare at blue-robed Zezume. "And this bench should be empty until I step up to fill it."

"There was a complication," said Zezume. "The Instrument died just hours after the messenger left for you. Much sooner than anyone expected."

"I am still at a loss, Mother Zezume," said Mawat.

"A complication, yes," said Radihaw, still kneeling at white-clad Hibal's side. "You could call it a complication, that would be a suitable term."

"Mawat," said Hibal, his voice disconcertingly like Mawat's. "I know this must be distressing. Please understand we would never have done this if we had any other choice. When the Instrument died, the attendant sent immediately for your father, but..." Hibal hesitated. "He couldn't be found."

"Couldn't be found," repeated Mawat.

"My lord Mawat," said Radihaw, "no other conclusion could be reached but that your father had fled rather than pay the lease."

"No," said Mawat. "No, my father never fled."

"He could not be found," said Zezume. "Mawat, I know this is upsetting. None of us could believe it."

"You will take those words back," said Mawat. Voice still tight and even. "My father never fled."

"Your father could not be found," said Radihaw. "Not in the tower, not in the fortress, not in the town. We asked the Raven where your father was—despite the complications involved in talking to the god when it does not have a body to answer with—we asked the Raven what had happened. But the answer was equivocal."

"What was that answer?" Mawat asked.

"The reply was, *This is unacceptable. There will be a reckoning*," said Radihaw.

"You were still three days' ride away, Mawat," said Zezume. "Urgent matters required the presence of the Lease."

"What," asked Mawat, now incredulous and visibly angry, "a ragged party of shivering Xulahns required the personal attention of the Raven's Lease of Iraden?"

"You have been away from Vastai too long, Nephew," said white-clad Hibal. "It is to our advantage to have access to goods from Xulah, to have the good opinion of Xulahn traders. More comes from Xulah than wine or silk. They also have weapons, and disciplined soldiers who might be lent or hired to help us against the Tel who press us from the southwest, as you well know."

"Oh, and mighty Xulah will lend us an army and then go back over the mountains again, because we ask nicely, out of their goodness and generosity," said Mawat.

"Sarcasm does not become the heir to the Lease," said Hibal.

"No pledges are pledged," said Radihaw. "No deals are struck, no terms even suggested. This is merely caution and good sense. It behooves the Lease to look to the future."

"Indeed," acknowledged Hibal. "And given the last few days, I think you should stay here and become acquainted with such matters, rather than return to your frontier post. Clearly you should have a better understanding of the issues we face here in Vastai. We have warriors enough to guard our borders from the ravaging Tel; I have only one heir."

"My father never fled," said Mawat again, flatly. "And you are sitting in my seat. I want to ask the Raven now why you are sitting in my seat. I have that right."

Mawat would not trust you as he does, would not have brought you with him, if you were not shrewd enough to guess what was happening here. Mawat had known one purpose for all of his life: to step up to that bench when his father died, to rule Iraden, and to die in his turn in order to bolster the power of the Raven, for the good of Iraden.

The office of Raven's Lease offered many privileges and a share (along with the Council of the Directions) in the rule of Iraden, as well as the rule of Ard Vusktia across the strait. But there was a price: two days after the death of the Raven's Instrument—the bird embodying the god that called itself the Raven—the person occupying the Lease's office must die, a voluntary sacrifice for the god. Shortly thereafter, while the next Instrument of the Raven lay in its egg, the next Lease would be secured and pledged. This was a process that took several days. A raven's egg, even one inhabited by a god (or at least this god), takes nearly a month to hatch, but matters are nearly always arranged so that there is still plenty of time to be sure things happen as they ought, to be sure the Lease dies as he promised, and to be sure there is a new Lease ready to take his place before the next Instrument hatches.

To be the Lease was a tremendous honor, though not, you can perhaps understand, one that was much fought for. The ambitious generally aimed at the Council of Directions, or Motherhood in the Silent, positions that would grant one a good deal of power and influence without such a limited life span. Leases' Heirs were generally born and raised to it—as Mawat was—and despite their privilege and ostensible power, had very few options should they refuse to step up to the bench.

"If it were not my seat," replied Hibal, evenly, "I would not be speaking to you now. I would have died the moment I tried to seat myself here if the Raven did not accept me. I took that risk, for the sake of Iraden. There is no need to question the god again. You've just arrived after a long and tiring journey. And a shock at the end of it. I only wanted to be sure you immediately heard how things stood. Go, nephew and heir of mine, and rest and eat. We'll talk more soon."

"Take a moment and think, Mawat," urged Zezume. "Please understand. We could not have done anything else, and you are still the Lease's Heir. You haven't lost anything by this."

"Except my father," said Mawat. And again, "My father never fled."

Had you seen him like this before? Ordinarily he is all easy smiles. Up till now his path in life had been set, and he had been assured of respect and every luxury Iraden afforded. But sometimes he seizes on a matter, takes it between his teeth, and will not let it go, and when that mood takes him he is grim and implacable. He has been that way since he was small.

If you hadn't seen it before, you saw it then. It startled you, I think, or frightened you, because with your eyes still on Mawat you stepped back, and half turned and put your hand on the wall, out of the need for support, or else the fear that you would lose your balance so close to the top of the stairs. And you turned fully to stare at your hand against the wall, and then down at your feet, feeling that constant, faint, grinding vibration traveling through the yellowish stones.

Could you hear me, Eolo? Can you hear me now?

I'm talking to you.

Stories can be risky for someone like me. What I say must be true, or it will be made true, and if it cannot be made true—if I don't have the power, or if what I have said is an impossibility—then I will pay the price. I might more or less safely say, "Once there was a man who rode home to attend his father's funeral and claim his inheritance, but matters were not as he expected them to be." I do not doubt such a thing has happened more than once in all the time there have been fathers to die and sons to succeed them. But to go any further, I must supply more details— the specific actions of specific people, and their specific consequences—and there I might blunder, all unknowing, into untruth. It's safer for me to speak of what I know. Or to speak only in the safest of generalities. Or else to say plainly at the beginning, "Here is a story I have heard," placing the burden of truth or not on the teller whose words I am merely accurately reporting.

But what is the story that I am telling? Here is another story I have heard: Once there were two brothers, and one of them wanted what the other had. Bent all his will to obtain what the other had, no matter the cost.

Here is another story: Once there was a prisoner in a tower.

And another: Once someone risked their life out of duty and loyalty to a friend.

Ah, there's a story that I might tell, and truthfully.

When I look back, the first memory I can find is of water. Water above, water all around, a great weight of it pressing down. The regular alternation of dark and dim wavering light. Feathery creatures, like flowers, anchored to the ocean floor, waving in the current, straining the water for the tiny lives that drifted past. Fish with heavy, bony-armored heads and sucking mouths. Scuttling sea scorpions and trilobites, coil-shelled ammonites. I had no names for these things, did not know that the light, when there was light, came from a sun, or that there was anything above the ever-present, all-surrounding water. I merely experienced, without urgency, without judgment.

There *was* something above the water, of course. Air and land, bare stone except where mosses grew, and tiny, leafless plants. Later there were trees and ferns and a host of scuttling exoskeletoned creatures, scorpions and spiders and centipedes and even, eventually, fish whose ancestors had dragged themselves out of the sea. I felt no similar impulse to move or explore. I had no questions.

I think it likely that I existed a long while before these earliest memories. But I cannot say for certain.

At length the trilobites disappeared—this after an earthquake that stirred the seafloor I rested on and the calm waters around me, and then a long period of cold darkness. The bone-armored fish dwindled to nothing, leaving fish with jaws and scales to rule the waters. And a long time after that—I don't know how long, I never even thought of measuring it, but judging by things I've learned since, it was a very, very long time—the water grew shallower, and shallower still, until finally I found myself, without having moved, on dry land.

It was now, finally, that I began to have some hint, some faint suggestion, that I was not entirely unique and alone in the universe, that other beings something like myself existed.

This new and (for me) drier, land-bound age teemed with crawling beasts: amphibians of all sizes; squat, beaked reptiles that grazed on the many ferns and horse-tails; huge, long-snouted, long-toothed predators; smaller two-legged hunters that might have reminded one of birds, if birds existed yet. And smaller, hairy, almost dog-like things—but there were no dogs, not yet.

I was not like any of these things, as I had not been like the fish, or the trilobites. And when the first other gods I ever saw came storming across the hills where I lay, I did not recognize them. I felt the earth shake, the air grow dry and cold and then suddenly hot and humid by turns. Trees swayed, heaved, and were cast down. One hillside in my view broke apart and collapsed into the valley. A river miles away burst its banks and surged improbably into the hills, washing away the insects and the small birdlike reptiles that prowled around me. I was too large for the flood to move, but I felt the bedrock crack beneath me.

I had lain watching long enough to know what was ordinary. I had seen storms, even violent ones. I had felt the distant tremors of faraway earthquakes or volcanoes. This was different. For the first time I can remember, I felt fear.

At length the battle—for it was a battle—moved on. But it had been so suddenly different from anything I had ever seen or experienced that I could not but wonder what it had been, or if it would happen again.

This, then, was my first sight of gods—not counting myself of course—though I did not know it. It had been so frightening, so abrupt and surprising, that for the first time I began to look around me with purpose, to try to understand what had just happened.

In later eras there would have been humans to tell me what I was, who might have recognized me as soon as they encountered me, as indeed the first humans I encountered did. But there were no humans yet.

Does that surprise you? I know that among people who think about such things it is commonly assumed that gods could not possibly have existed before humans did. After all, gods live on the prayers and offerings of humans. What god could live without that basic food, that essential source of power?

I cannot tell you what I lived on. I can tell you only that I lived. In fact, I still don't quite understand how those other, battling gods I saw could do what they did—how they moved at all, let alone acted with such devastating, destructive power. But they did—and so did many others, though I didn't learn about them for a very long time. Not, in fact, until many of them were gone.

Quite a few gods today still have a superstitious dread of those Ancient Ones. Rumor says some live yet, that they are immensely, implacably powerful, and difficult to kill. That even dead they may return.

But I knew nothing of this. I lay and watched and thought, as the beasts around me gave way to yet other sorts of animals, as the plants and trees changed around me. Slowly mosses gave way to grass, and flowers appeared.

And birds, though I did not know then how birds would complicate my life in the future.

I suppose I could have moved. Could have roamed over the earth, as those other gods did. But somehow I never wished to, never felt the impulse to do it. I wished only to sit under the sun—I could see the sun, these days, and I liked it a good deal, enjoyed its warmth, its daily coming and going, its steady arc across the blue sky from month to month. Enjoyed the stars wheeling thick and bright in the night sky, the occasional comet, the sparking trail of meteors. I wanted to know what those other gods were, but I did not want to do what they did.

I was still profoundly alone. And I remained alone, watching the stars—did you know, aside from their regular nightly and yearly cycles there is another, longer movement? So, so much slower, and I was watching this, and admiring it, alone, until someone arrived to break my solitude.

By then ice had overtaken me. Ice had overtaken everything, for as far as I could see, for so long that I began to wonder if the world would only ever be ice henceforth. But eventually the ice had begun to withdraw. My old hillside, and the shattered hill across the valley, had been pressed and ground flat by the immense weight of the ice, but as it retreated it left behind new hills; mounds of gravel, boulders, and silt.

I found myself atop one of these. And I began to wonder why that was. I ought to have been pressed flat as everything else had been, trapped under the glacier or buried under the debris that had accumulated on its surface over so very long. But I had not. I had stayed above the ice, and now I sat on this new, rounded hill surrounded by rolling, treeless, grass-covered plain.

I had not wanted to be buried in ice, and so I had not been. Thinking back, I had not wanted to be buried in the seafloor, covered over with layer after layer of drifting sediment, and so I had not been. I had willed, and I had acted, so very subtly that I myself had not realized I was doing it.

One night, while I pondered this, a ball of fire streaked across the sky, brighter than any star I'd seen in the night, or any comet. It disappeared somewhere to the west, and then, not long after, I felt the rumble of an impact.

After a while gravel, dirt, water, and dust rained down and there was a smell of burning. For the next several days smoke and fog obscured the sun, and the sky was hazy for weeks after.

This was, of course, a particularly notable event, but I did not realize its true significance to me until years later, when I first saw humans.

They wore deerskins sewn with beads of bone and stone and shell. They carried spears of wood and bone, with tiny blades of chert embedded in the points. These they used to hunt reindeer and moose, which they followed across the grasslands. What I thought were wolves ran alongside them, but of course I would later learn that they were not wolves, though their ancestors had been.

They camped at the foot of my hill, built fires, and emptied pouches of mushrooms and berries and other things they'd foraged along the day's walk. They settled down to cook or watch the fire, or set out to see if anything interesting might be found by the swampy banks of the small river that wandered lazily through the plain.

One of them climbed the hill and addressed me. This did not surprise me in the least, because I barely noticed it was happening. Animals wandered over to me all the time and did the sorts of things that animals do. These animals were fairly novel, but not so much that I was paying them any sort of close attention. Until the person poured milk at my foot.

I understand now why I noticed that, why I found myself suddenly intrigued by the milk, and by the actions of this person who continued to address me. At the time, though, I did not. But rather than tiresomely detailing my experience from moment to ignorant moment, I'll just explain.

The person was a priest of her people. She had been taught by her predecessor, and her predecessor by her own predecessor, and so on for generations, to look for the presence of gods. Any unusual animal (an all-white reindeer, a particularly large eagle, a by then rarely spotted mammoth) or particularly striking natural feature might be the sign of a god's presence. Once a priest had noticed or heard tell of such a thing, they would confront the animal or object, if possible, and speak a series of predetermined words paired with specific actions, and make a series of set offerings. They would repeat this over a series of years, or even generations, passing the details of the procedure down to their successor, until eventually the god responded, or the priest's regular travels stopped bringing them into the vicinity of the possible divine presence. This priest knew to be patient. She knew from experience, hers and her predecessors', that it could take a very long time to teach language to a god.

Because that is what she and her successors were doing. It took quite a while for me to catch on—or not long at all for me, relatively speaking, but several generations of priests. Human brains are remarkably effective at recognizing and learning language, and as a rule human infants will respond to it quite soon after birth, and for the most part will eventually understand and speak a language merely from hearing the people around them speak. But I was not a human infant, and even the possibility of language had not yet occurred to me.

You may find the idea of a god without language impossible or ridiculous. After all, if there is anything people know about gods, it's that they exercise their power through speech. A god's words are inescapably true, and gods make things happen by speaking them—so long as a god has sufficient power, of course. To say something beyond one's power to enforce can wound a god badly, can take decades or centuries or even millennia to recover from. To speak an utter impossibility—there are such, I assure you—is to drain one's own power endlessly, to no purpose. But with sufficient power, with carefully chosen words, a god can do anything it is possible to do. How can a god be a god with no language?

And if language is a thing humans had to teach to gods—my experience suggests this was the case—how did those other gods I saw so long ago do anything?

I do not know. I can only assure you that my account of my history is true.

Enter the monthly
Orbit sweepstakes at

www.orbitloot.com

With a different prize every month,
from advance copies of books by
your favourite authors to exclusive
merchandise packs,
**we think you'll find something
you love.**